Pamela Evans was born and brought up in Hanwell in the Borough of Ealing, London, the youngest of six children. She is married with two sons and now lives in Wales.

Her previous London sagas have been warmly praised:

'A good traditional romance, and its author has a feeling for the atmosphere of postwar London' *Sunday Express*

'Well peopled with warm personalities' *Liverpool Post*

'Very readable' *Bella*

'The leading characters are finely drawn . . . crisp prose . . . a superb and heartwarming read'
                                        Irish Independent

Near And Dear

Pamela Evans

HEADLINE

Copyright © 1997 Pamela Evans

The right of Pamela Evans to be identified as the Author of
the Work has been asserted by her in accordance with
the Copyright, Designs and Patents Act 1988.

First published in 1997 by
HEADLINE BOOK PUBLISHING

First published in paperback in 1997 by
HEADLINE BOOK PUBLISHING

10 9 8 7 6 5 4

ISBN 0 7472 5601 2

Typeset by Avon Dataset Ltd, Bidford-on-Avon, Warks

Printed in England by
Clays Ltd, St Ives plc, Bungay, Suffolk

HEADLINE BOOK PUBLISHING
A division of Hodder Headline PLC
338 Euston Road
London NW1 3BH

To Alma and Harry,
for all they have done.

Chapter One

Because Mick Parker thought material success was the key to admiration and respect, it was with a great deal of satisfaction that he drew up on his driveway in a brand new Jaguar and parked beside the small car he provided for his wife.

Singing along with the Beatles to 'We Can Work It Out' on the radio, he lingered awhile before getting out, running his fingers over the soft leather upholstery and relishing the status value of his latest acquisition.

Standing on the drive in the rain, he continued to admire the fruits of his labours gleaming in the street lights, too deeply absorbed in the sight to care about getting wet. His and hers, side by side, he thought. Symbolic of their life together.

His happiness mounted at the sight of his young son and daughter waving to him at the window. Coming home from work was the highlight of Mick's day, which wasn't surprising since he had a devoted wife, two lovely children and a beautiful home on a modern executive development.

It was a murky March evening in 1966. Darkness had already fallen and the smart detached dwellings of Maple Avenue were bathed in an amber neon glow, mist floating patchily above the dripping pavements, trees and grass verges.

This tranquil scene on the outskirts of Twickenham was a world away from the council flats where Mick and his wife had grown up. When he thought of the quality of life he had achieved for them, he was proud to the point of physical pleasure – and he hadn't finished, not by a long chalk. At twenty-nine, the future held endless possibilities for him.

Excited childish voices interrupted his thoughts as the front door opened and Jane and the children stood in the porch to greet him, the children dressed in pyjamas and bright red dressing gowns.

'Cor, is that car yours, Daddy?' asked Davey as Mick walked up the path with his usual swaggering gait, trendy black leather jacket worn over a business suit, dark hair shining in the porch light.

'That's right, son,' he replied proudly. 'Nice, innit?'

'It's lovely,' said the soon-to-be four year old, breathless with admiration because he was mad about cars and had lots of toy ones. 'Will you take us for a ride in it?'

'Sure . . . we'll go for a run at the weekend.'

'I wanna go now.'

'Oh, no, son, I don't think Mummy will want you to go out in the rain.'

'We wanna go now, Daddy . . . please,' chanted three-year-old Pip, short for Philippa.

'But you can't go out in your pi-jams, Princess,' said Mick with a smile.

But they all went anyway, anoraks and wellies excitedly donned over the kiddies' nightclothes, all four of them enjoying the latest family possession as they cruised through the wet suburban streets.

'Well, your father certainly does things in style, kids,' said Jane, a petite woman of twenty-eight with caramel-coloured hair and huge hazel eyes. This was the first she'd heard of a new car. Not that she'd expect to be consulted about such a purchase because anything outside the domestic side of their family life was strictly Mick's domain.

'Can I have a car like this one to put in my toy garage?' asked Davey excitedly.

'Yeah, I should think we can manage that, son,' agreed Mick amiably.

Indulging his children was part and parcel of being well-off and Mick revelled in it. Pip was promised a treat, too, then both children became overexcited and noisy and were threatened with the cancellation of their trip to the toyshop if they didn't quieten down.

At home it was hot milk and a story for the children before they were put to bed, after which Jane and Mick had a peaceful supper of grilled pork chops.

'So how was your day then, babe?' enquired Mick as his wife served them with a mouth-watering dessert of home-made apple sponge and custard.

'Smashing,' said Jane, who enjoyed being a full-time housewife.

'Did you do anything nice?' he asked, just to show an interest.

'Nothing special,' she replied casually. 'Had coffee and a chat with a woman whose children go to the nursery school. Pottered about here ... did some shopping. I know it sounds really boring but I enjoy it.'

'It suits us both then, doesn't it? 'Cause I'd hate it if you had to go out to work,' he said. 'I'd never let that happen.'

She observed him with affection, eyes shining with warmth, cheeks flushed from the wine they had become accustomed to having with their evening meal since they'd become so comfortably off. Being slim and small-featured, Jane had remained youthful, her hair in a short bouffant style. She wore a mini skirt which she'd teamed with a black polo-necked sweater.

'I'm quite happy to stay at home and leave the exciting things like buying posh new cars to you,' she said.

The smile he gave her was devastating. Even though she'd known him all her life and been married to him for eight years, it still made her breath catch in her throat.

'The Jag will do wonders for our image, eh, babe?' he said.

'Yeah, I suppose so.'

'No doubt about it,' Mick said forcefully. 'Having one of those on the drive means instant prestige.'

'You won't be putting it away in the garage then?' she teased.

3

'Not likely! Not until it's been well and truly noticed anyway.'

Status symbols meant so much to Mick, Jane often wondered if he derived more pleasure from the statement they made than from the possessions themselves. He didn't seem able to enjoy life for its own sake, as she did. Some deep-rooted sense of inferiority had created in him a profound need to be noticed. Happiness for Mick meant victory in competition.

Her husband's success mattered to her only because it was so important to him. Over the years they had become as one in their aims and opinions. On the rare occasions that she was even aware of his domination of her, Jane didn't object. Loving him so deeply, she was happily in thrall to him.

'We'll go out for a long run at the weekend, shall we?' suggested Mick.

'Sure.'

'We could go to the coast for the day on Sunday, if you like?'

'That'd be lovely.'

'It's time we booked a holiday too, if we want to go abroad,' he said. 'We've left it late as it is.'

'Mmm, I suppose we have, now you come to mention it.' Jane paused, remembering a conversation she'd had with their neighbour. 'The people next-door are going somewhere in the Canary Islands this year.'

'Are they now?' said Mick, frowning. 'Don't they usually go to Majorca?'

'Yes, that's right,' she said, not sounding terribly concerned. 'Perhaps they think that's a bit ordinary now that so many people are going there?'

'Oh, really?' he said, suddenly pugnacious. 'In that case, we'll go one better.'

'We're not in competition with them, Mick,' his wife pointed out.

'Ooh, not much,' he said with a cynical grin. 'We'll soon show them who can afford the best holiday around here!'

'But why bother?'

'Because I'm not having anyone lording it over us, that's why,' said Mick dogmatically.

'I don't see that it matters where people go for their . . .'

'Well, it does,' he cut in firmly. 'So you'd better go to the travel agent's tomorrow and pick up some holiday brochures.'

'Okay.'

'It'll give us something to talk about on Saturday night over dinner as well,' he said, because he'd invited a business contact and his wife for the evening. Mick would much rather take his leisure at the pub but considered a spot of home entertaining to be appropriate now that they had moved into a different class.

'Holidays are always useful as a back-up if the conversation starts to flag,' Jane agreed, adding lightly, 'I must give some thought to the meal on Saturday, too.'

'They'll be impressed whatever you make,' he said, for cooking was her forte.

'I'll certainly be aiming to please,' she said, welcoming the opportunity to stretch her culinary skills.

'Wherever they say they're going on holiday, we'll say we're going somewhere more exotic, even if we still haven't decided,' Mick declared, sounding intense.

'But that's so silly,' she replied in mild rebuke. 'It's supposed to be a social occasion, not an excuse for one-upmanship.'

'Wake up, Jane,' he said dismissively. 'The whole purpose of having people to dinner is to make sure they know you're worth a few bob.'

'But trying to go one better is so pointless,' she argued.

'Everybody does it.'

'Not *everybody*.'

'Most people.'

'Well, I think it's a complete waste of time. Because no matter how high you rise there will always be someone further up the ladder.'

5

'But I intend to make sure that someone *is* me,' said Mick, his mood lightening again.

'Oh, I give up!' But Jane was smiling too for she rarely criticised Mick in any serious way.

She didn't query the cost of their expensive lifestyle because Mick had always been in sole charge of their finances and didn't welcome any interest from her. The facts that he'd recently moved his wholesale business into larger premises, and that brand new Jaguars didn't come cheap, indicated that he was doing well, but she deemed it wisest not to enquire.

Being provider, protector and decision-maker was almost an obsession with Mick, so Jane concentrated on her role as wife and mother and left him to it. Even the fact that she didn't have access to a bank account and had to ask him for every penny she needed didn't bother her, partly because she'd known nothing else and also because he never kept her short of cash. Having her independence wasn't a thing Jane gave much thought to, though she knew it was a burning issue with many modern women.

Mick had been her first and only boyfriend. He'd lived in the next street to hers on the Berrywood Council Estate on the Chiswick-Hammersmith borders. She'd known him by sight all her life and had become better acquainted with him through his sister Marie, who'd been her best friend at secondary school.

Jane had been fifteen when she and Mick had gone out on their first date and there had been no one else for either of them since. Even now she couldn't understand what a charismatic man like him saw in someone as ordinary as her. But he loved her, of that she was certain. Safe in this knowledge, she never felt threatened by infidelity, especially as all Mick's time and energy outside the home went into making his fortune.

When they had finished their meal, Jane washed the dishes in their luxury kitchen while Mick relaxed with a cigarette in front of the television set in their elegant lounge. She didn't expect him to help in the home. She considered that to be solely her job, in the same way as providing for her and the children was his.

Her chores done, she made some coffee and joined him on the sofa where they sat snuggled up together watching I Love Lucy, utterly content in each other's company.

'Oh, no,' said Mick suddenly.

'What's the matter?'

'I've left something in the office that I meant to bring home.'

'Can't you get it in the morning?'

'I'd rather get it now,' he said, standing up with a purposeful air. 'It's the catalogue for the sale of bankrupt stock that I'm going to first thing tomorrow. I want to have a look through it so that I know what I'm aiming for when I get there.'

'Any excuse to go out and drive that Jag,' she said playfully. Trusting him so completely, she wasn't in the least possessive.

'I won't deny it,' he grinned, teeth white against his dark complexion. 'But I really do need that catalogue.'

'Will you call in and show your mum and dad the new car while you're out?' she asked. 'Or did you show them on the way home?'

'No, I wouldn't show it to anyone before you'd seen it.'

'That's nice.'

He looked down at her, his expression becoming serious, dark eyes soft with love, hair falling boyishly over his brow. He'd changed out of his business clothes and was wearing a brushed cotton checked shirt with denim jeans. Square-jawed and rugged, he was a rough diamond for all his pretensions but his common touch was the essence of his appeal.

'You're everything to me, Jane . . . you and the kids,' he said.

'I know that, love.'

A certain look passed between them and they both chuckled.

'I could go to the warehouse a bit later on,' he said meaningfully.

'When you get back,' she said, eyes meeting his expressively. 'I'll be waiting. So go and do what you have to do.'

'In that case, I'll get back as soon as I can,' he laughed.

'If you have time, could you pop in and see my dad?' she said, because her father and Mick's parents still lived on the Berrywood Estate, though they had all moved to smaller flats now that the children had left home. 'Just to make sure he's okay.'

'Will he be in?'

'When is he not in?' she said, her expression darkening. Since her mother's death two years ago, her father had become something of a recluse outside working hours. 'The only time he goes out is to work and to visit us of a Sunday. He wouldn't come here if I didn't absolutely insist on it. Tell him one of us will pick him up about midday on Sunday – and I won't take no for an answer.'

'Will do.'

'See you soon, then.'

'Just as soon as I can,' said Mick, kissing her on the lips.

Then, slipping into a casual jacket, he left the house singing 'We Can Work It Out'.

Listening to him go, Jane was smiling. He was terrific and she was crazy about him.

Mick drove through the grey streets of his childhood and pulled up outside a block of flats. It had stopped raining and a chilly breeze had sprung up, blowing the litter around his feet as he hurried towards the building. Making his way up to the first floor, his footsteps echoed on the concrete steps.

'How are you, Mum?' he asked, pecking her on the cheek on the way in. Stale echoes of his parents' evening meal lingered inside the flat.

'Mustn't grumble, son,' said Rita Parker with a smile.

8

A docile, good-hearted woman, she had grey hair, gentle blue eyes and a permanent look of defeat about her. 'I wasn't expecting to see you tonight.'

'I didn't intend to come over but as I had to go out to the warehouse anyway, I thought I might as well call in.' He peered into the empty living room. 'Where's Dad?'

'Three guesses.'

'The King's Arms?'

She nodded.

'I might have known.'

'Cuppa tea?'

'Not for me, thanks.' Mick sat down on the sofa in the garishly furnished living room with its glaring orange suite, multicoloured carpet and abundance of cheap ornaments, the whole ambience reflecting the personality of his father rather than his mother. 'I think I'll pop into the pub on my way past and buy the old man a drink, though.'

'Okay.'

Settling herself in an armchair, Rita asked after Jane and the family and he entertained her with some amusing anecdotes about her grandchildren.

'You'll have to come over for the day one Sunday soon.'

'I'd like that but you know your dad won't go visiting.'

'Why not come on your own then, Mum?' suggested Mick. 'That'll shake him. I'll come over in the car and pick you up. I usually come to collect Jane's dad on a Sunday anyway.'

'And leave your father to get his own Sunday dinner!' exclaimed Rita. 'Can you imagine how he'd react to that?'

'He'd go spare.'

'It might be easier to organise if you didn't live so far away.'

'Come off it, Mum,' he said, grinning. 'Twickenham isn't far.'

'It's off your dad's patch, which amounts to the same thing.'

'I'll buy you a little place near us one o' these days,' Mick promised lightly.

'Your dad wouldn't move away from here if you paid him.'

'But he could still work around here if you moved to somewhere nicer. He'd keep the greengrocery round.'

'Wilf still wouldn't go,' said his mother. 'All his mates live around here. He's the cock of the walk.'

'He'd be that anywhere . . . he's that type.'

'I know. But he wouldn't leave this place if you bought him a mansion to live in.'

'Seems daft.'

'Not really. We're both settled here . . . I'm used to it too.'

'There is that.'

Rita cast an approving glance over her son: a fine figure of a man, dark and swarthy like his father with the same coal-black eyes and winning smile, but taller and bigger altogether. Both father and son had the gift of the gab, but Mick had been shrewd enough to use his outgoing personality to make something of himself. For all his happy-go-lucky ways, he must have a sharp brain to have done so well, she thought. But with all his success, he still hero-worshipped his father, a man who lived from day to day selling fruit and veg from a van around the streets.

'Business still doing well?' she asked.

'Great.'

'It's wonderful what you've done, son. I'm proud of you.'

'Thanks, Mum,' he said, adding triumphantly, 'I bought a new Jaguar today.'

'Blimey, Mick, you really must be raking in the dough!' Rita threw him a sharp look. 'New business premises *and* a posh new motor? Are you sure you're not over-stretching yourself?'

'No, not me.'

'Well, you know the old saying about the higher they fly . . .'

'Don't worry, I know what I'm doing.'

'I hope you do,' she said, but sounded reassured. 'Anyway... what are we sitting here for when you've just bought yourself a Jaguar? Come on, let's go and have a look.'

She followed him down the stairs to the street in her carpet slippers and duly admired the car which he'd parked under the street light.

'It wouldn't stay in that condition for long if you lived around here,' she remarked. 'The vandals would have a field day.'

'If I still lived around here, I wouldn't be able to afford a car like this.'

'True.'

She shivered and hugged herself. 'Ooh, that wind has really blown up! I'm going back indoors before I catch a cold.'

On the way up the dimly lit stairs that smelled faintly of urine and had obscenities scribbled all over the walls, Mick said he ought to be going. At the front door, he took his wallet from his pocket and handed her some notes.

'I can't take this,' protested Rita. 'You've more than enough to do with your money, with a wife and two kids to support.'

'If I can't give my mum a few quid now and then, I don't deserve to have the money,' Mick told her, swelling with pride at his own generosity. 'Enjoy it. Treat yourself.'

'I don't know how much longer you're gonna stay in the money the way you flash it about.' She smiled and kissed him on the cheek. 'But thanks, Mick. I really do appreciate it.'

'I know.'

'Tell your dad not to stay out drinking till closing time.'

'I'll tell him but it won't make a scrap of difference,' said Mick. 'You know he won't come home until he's ready.'

'Tell him there's wrestling on the telly. That'll shift him.'

'Okay.'

'And, Mick?'

'Yeah?'

'I meant what I said about being proud of you,' she said.

'I know you did, Mum. Thanks.'

As Rita closed the door behind him, her smile turned to a frown. She knew that *her* pride in him wasn't what Mick really wanted.

On the short drive to the pub, his mother's words lingered in Mick's mind. Humility not being a strong point with him, he had no difficulty in agreeing with her. She was right, he had done very well *and* stayed on the right side of the law to do it, too. Plenty of other lads from the estate had become small-time villains. Some had tried to tempt him into crime over the years but Mick's refusal had had more to do with self-preservation than integrity. He didn't fancy the idea of rotting away in some prison!

Looking back on his meteoric rise to success, he couldn't help being proud . . .

He'd left school without qualifications but with plenty of ambition. After a spell in a factory, he'd worked on the markets for a man trading in cheap clothing and household linens. Mick's business acumen had soon been spotted and he'd been given responsibility for the stall while his employer concentrated on other interests. An insight into buying had attracted Mick to the lucrative wholesale side of commerce at a time of new national affluence following the period of post-war austerity.

Thanks to his flat feet, he'd been spared two years' National Service and been able to concentrate on his business plans uninterrupted. Running the stall by day, he'd worked evenings as a bouncer at a club in the West End to get enough money to buy a secondhand van and some stock.

Trading in anything from working boots to bedsheets, he'd kept his eye on trade publications for bankruptcy sales and auctions of government surplus stock. He'd touted for business among traders in the London markets and further afield, storing his wares in a rented lock-up garage until he could afford his first warehouse, where customers could either visit or order goods for delivery.

Nowadays he dealt in anything he judged to be a mover, from household goods to working men's overalls and cheap clothes for both sexes. Small shopkeepers now bought from him as well as market traders. He also had door-to-door salesmen on his books.

In retrospect, those early years hadn't been conducive to a happy love life, with him working all hours and ploughing back every penny he earned into the business. But Jane had given him her full support and now they were both reaping the rewards of his hard work and her patience.

Life was good. His business was thriving and he was able to keep up the payments on the house, the furniture, the cars, and all the other luxury items that made their life so comfortable. Thank God for credit – a convenient short cut to stylish living.

Turning into the car park of the King's Arms, Mick felt a sickly feeling of nervous apprehension in his stomach. He turned off the engine and lit a cigarette, inhaling deeply, his hand trembling slightly. For all his swank, there was one person who could destroy his confidence in an instant – his father!

The pub was smoky, crowded and noisy as there was a darts game in progress. Mick couldn't see his father but knew he was there; the roars of raucous male laughter told him that.

A group of middle-aged men stood at the far end of the bar and Wilf Parker was among them. His magnetic personality ensured that he was always the life and soul of any party. He was often crude and downright ill-mannered but still drew an audience, albeit exclusively male. He made an absolute point of being the centre of attention.

'Watcha, Dad,' said Mick, nudging his way through the crowd.

'Mick – what are you doing round here?' asked Wilf, sounding none too pleased to see his son. 'Doing some slumming?'

'Don't be daft,' he said defensively. 'I come from round here, remember?'

'I'm not the one who needs reminding o' that,' said his father meaningfully.

'What are you all having?' asked Mick, ignoring the jibe and turning to his father's cronies. 'I'm in the chair.'

'I'll have a double scotch as you're paying and I'm not driving,' said Wilf, laughing heartily. His mates thought anything he said was hilarious and this had them splitting their sides. 'Have whatever you fancy, lads, my boy's paying . . . that'll teach him to flash his money around!'

Wilf Parker was ludicrously flamboyant himself in a bright red shirt and multicoloured satin tie worn with a black and white checked jacket hanging open to reveal a substantial paunch. In his early-fifties, he was an older and smaller version of his son, though Wilf's features were sharper than Mick's, his face weatherbeaten and heavily wrinkled, his dark hair dusted here and there with silver.

Mick got the drinks and offered his cigarettes around.

'So, how are you getting on in your posh house among the nobs?' asked Wilf.

'We're doing all right,' said Mick, ignoring the implied criticism.

'Wife and kids okay?' enquired his father dutifully.

'Fine,' replied Mick, pretending not to notice his father's lack of interest.

'Good.'

'How's business, Dad . . . people still buying plenty of fruit and veg?'

14

'I'm not complaining.'

Not ten minutes ago Mick had felt like a man of power and influence. Now he felt like a gormless schoolboy.

'I've got my new Jag outside,' he announced, knowing he would be made to regret having mentioned it but unable to resist the temptation to show off. 'Do you wanna see it?'

Wilf didn't reply but the cronies seemed keen to take a look so he couldn't refuse without appearing churlish.

'Now that *really* is some motor,' said one of the men as they stood around the vehicle.

'You must be doing well,' said another.

Wilf said nothing.

'Well, what do you think, Dad?' asked Mick.

'Very nice,' he said with noticeable indifference.

'Glad you like it,' said Mick stiffly.

'Now that we've seen it, let's go back inside, eh, lads?' said Wilf, turning away from the car and walking back to the pub.

'We want to hear the rest of that story you were telling us,' said one of the men as they drifted away, Mick's car forgotten.

He caught up with his father and took him to one side.

'What is it with you, eh, Dad?' he demanded. 'Why don't you ever show an interest in anything I do?'

Wilf shrugged his shoulders.

'Afraid I might steal some of your limelight, is that it?' pressed Mick.

'Coming round here flashing your money about isn't gonna do that,' he said. 'All that does is put people's backs up.'

'You just can't bear anyone else to have any attention, can you?'

The pub door opened and one of his cronies called, 'Come on, Wilf . . . we're all waiting to hear the rest of the tale.'

'New cars and posh houses won't bring you popularity,' said Wilf, moving towards the door.

'Depends what sort of people you mix with,' replied Mick lamely.

'Are you coming?' asked his father, ignoring Mick's remark. 'They're waiting for us.'

'They're waiting for *you*,' he said bitterly. 'I'll give it a miss.'

'Suit yourself,' said Wilf nonchalantly and sauntered back into the pub, leaving his son outside feeling deflated, as usual.

God knows he ought to be used to it but it hurt just as much now as it had as a boy when his father had mocked and discouraged him whenever he'd shown promise or initiative. Wilf Parker was a man who refused to be upstaged for a second, especially by his own son.

In the office Mick found the catalogue he needed, glanced through it then sat down with his feet on the desk, smoking a cigarette and staring absently through the office window into the warehouse, stacked from floor to ceiling with boxes and packages on rows of high metal shelving.

He was still feeling unsettled by the meeting with his father which was why he'd sat down to calm himself with a cigarette instead of going straight home to Jane.

Thinking back over it, he decided that he probably had his father's enormous ego to thank for the existence of Parker Supplies, because the need for attention he'd never had from his father had made him determined to make something of himself. The spotlight had never shone on Mick or his sister Marie when they were growing up. Wilf's overbearing personality had pushed everyone else into the shade. Poor old Mum still lived in his shadow now.

It was pathetic really, he admonished himself. He would be thirty next year and still he wanted approval from his father. Still he longed to have his own love reciprocated, even though he would never admit it to anyone, not even Jane.

The thought of her immediately made him feel better. She thought he was wonderful merely because he breathed. So why was he sitting here thinking about his father when he had a diamond like her waiting for him at home?

He put his cigarette into the ashtray while he rolled up the catalogue and stuffed it into his jacket pocket, eager now to get home and remembering with some annoyance that he had promised to call on his father-in-law. Shutting the door of the office rather too forcefully behind him in his haste, he hurried down the aisles of stock to the exit.

Unbeknown to Mick, the slamming of the office door caused the cigarette he had left balanced on the ashtray to fall on to a pile of invoices on the desk . . .

Joe Harris opened the door to his son-in-law in pyjamas and dressing gown.

'Blimey, Joe, it's a bit early for bed, even for you,' said Mick.

'I'm not going to bed yet,' explained Joe, a thin man in his early-fifties with brown receding hair and a snub nose like his daughter's. 'I'm watching a play on the telly and I feel more comfortable when I'm dressed like this.'

'You and that blooming telly,' teased Mick, going inside. 'We'll never get you away from it when colour television comes in. They reckon it'll be starting next year.'

'Yes, I was reading about that in the paper,' said Joe, his pale brown eyes troubled, for unexpected visitors unnerved him.

'It'll seem funny seeing things in colour instead of black and white, won't it?' said Mick. 'We'll get to see what the celebrities really look like.'

'Yes. I bet the sets will be expensive, though,' said Joe conversationally.

'Bound to be when they first come on to the market,' agreed Mick. 'I'll be one of the first to have one, though, whatever they cost.'

17

His father-in-law didn't doubt it.

'Can I offer you anything?' he dutifully invited as they went into the living room, soberly furnished in beiges and browns with a few tasteful nick-nacks dotted about.

'No, thanks. I'm not stopping,' said Mick, amused at the look of relief on his father-in-law's face. 'Jane asked me to call in as I was in the area but I can't stay long, so don't panic.'

'I wasn't.'

'Ooh, not much!' boomed Mick, laughing loudly. 'I know you can't wait to get rid of me so you can get back to the telly.'

Still smarting from the meeting with his father, he was being even more exuberant than usual in an effort to restore his own confidence. Without his even being aware of it, the volume of his voice had risen to an irritating level for someone of a quiet disposition like Joe.

A model of working-class respectability, he worked as a clerk in the offices of a food-processing factory. He had never been gregarious and since losing his wife had retreated even further into his shell. His son-in-law was always a bit too full of himself for Joe's taste and tonight Mick was being particularly exhausting. Joe longed for him to leave.

'Have you been to see your folks?' he asked politely.

'Yeah. Dad was in the pub, having everyone in fits as usual.'

Joe nodded.

'He's a real comic . . . the most popular man on the manor.' Praising his father to other people was something Mick felt compelled to do. It helped assuage his guilt about his true feelings.

'Yeah, I can imagine,' said mild-mannered Joe who actually thought Wilf Parker was a boring, self-opinionated git and avoided him whenever possible. He wouldn't tolerate him at all if it weren't for the fact that Jane was married to his son.

'Anyway, Jane said I was to tell you we'll see you on Sunday for lunch . . .'

Joe frowned. Even after all this time, he still felt shattered by his wife's death and found company difficult. 'I'm not really sure . . .'

'She told me to tell you she won't take no for an answer. The children will be disappointed if you don't come, too.'

Although Joe loved his grandchildren, he never felt able to amuse or control them. Everything seemed so difficult since his wife had fallen victim to a heart attack. All his zest for life had gone along with her. But he knew he must make the effort for the sake of his beloved daughter.

'Okay, Mick, I'll be ready.'

As they headed for the front door, Mick just had to mention the car.

'I bought a new Jaguar today.'

'A Jag, eh?' said Joe, pretending interest. 'What *will* you come up with next?'

'Ah, that's all part of my charm, innit? You never know what I'm gonna do next.'

That's a fact, thought Joe, but said, 'What does Jane think about the new car?'

'You know Jane – she likes what I like, and goes along with anything I decide to do.'

'That's true.'

In fact Joe often wished that Jane would assert herself more with her husband, who had squeezed her personality almost out of existence. Mick was a good husband and a wonderful provider, no one could deny that. But he had sidelined his wife into becoming a mere extension of himself, in the same way Wilf had with Rita.

Because Jane was Joe's only child and meant more to him than anyone else in the world, it was painful for him to see her so thoroughly dominated, even though in fairness it didn't seem to worry her.

'No point in asking you to put your coat on and come

down and see the car, I suppose?' said Mick.

'I'll see it on Sunday.'

'Okay.'

What was the matter with these people? Mick asked himself. Didn't they realise what a huge achievement becoming the owner of a new Jaguar was for someone from his background? Surely he deserved a little more enthusiasm?

'I'll see you on Sunday then . . . pick you up around midday.'

'Okay, mate. Thanks for coming.'

'No problem.'

'See you, Mick.'

'See you.'

When the door had finally closed behind him, Joe heaved a deep sigh of relief and went back to his armchair. He could only take his vociferous son-in-law in very small doses.

'Hello, love,' said Jane sleepily when Mick came into the bedroom.

'Still awake then, babe?' he said, unbuttoning his shirt.

'Only just.'

'Sorry I was so long.'

''S'all right.' She peered at him drowsily over the sheet, the bedside light gleaming on her naked shoulders. 'Well, were they all suitably impressed with the new car?'

'My mum and dad thought it was terrific,' he said, because he couldn't bear to admit his father's true reaction, not even to Jane.

'Did you get to see my dad?' she asked, yawning heavily.

'Yeah. He was all ready for bed so he'll see the car on Sunday.'

'Was he okay?'

'I think so . . . he isn't much of a talker, though, is he?'

'No, not really.'

20

'Don't worry about your dad, babe. He's fine. He was watching the telly.'

'Thanks for going to see him.'

'That's okay.'

Mick went into the bathroom. When he got into bed he smelled of toothpaste and aftershave.

'You smell nice,' said his wife, snuggling up to him.

'So do you.'

Mick was a very passionate man. When he made love to Jane, all his self-doubt was swept away by an all-consuming sense of power. Tonight he was so rough, she had to ask him to take it easy.

'Hey, Mick. What's got into you?' she asked when it was over. 'I'll have bruises like beetroots tomorrow.'

'Sorry, babe, I didn't mean to hurt you,' he said, gently drawing her to him. 'I must have got carried away because I love you so much.'

'I know,' she said, instantly forgiving him. 'I love you too.'

The intimate mood was shattered by the shrill sound of the telephone ringing on Mick's bedside table. It was the police to tell him that his warehouse was on fire.

By the time Mick got to Brentford the fire was almost out and the warehouse reduced to a smouldering ruin. He wasn't allowed to go inside because the firemen were still clearing up in there but he could see from behind the police cordons that the building was completely gutted.

'Any idea how it started?' he asked one of the firemen who was rolling up the hose near to where Mick was standing.

'Can't say for sure, mate.'

'You must have an idea, though,' he said, devastated by what had happened. He thought it must be the work of an arsonist. How else could a fire have got started when the premises were empty and closed for the night?

'We reckon it started in the office.'

'Faulty wiring?' Mick suggested in a sudden burst of inspiration.

'We didn't see any evidence of that,' said the fireman.

'No?'

'No. It was more likely to have been someone being careless with a fag.'

'Any sign of a break in?'

'No.'

'Oh . . . so it must have been started by someone with access to the place, then,' muttered Mick, almost to himself.

'S'pose so, mate,' said the fireman. 'But it isn't my job to work out the cause.'

'No, 'course not.'

An uneasy feeling nagged at him and grew into a ghastly suspicion. Mick turned hot, sweat drenching his skin then turning ice-cold. *He* had been in the office earlier. Had he been smoking? Yes, he remembered putting a cigarette into the ashtray while he rolled up the catalogue and stuffed it into his pocket, just before he left. Surely he would have picked it up again, though?

With a burning rush of shame, he recalled lighting a cigarette immediately he'd left the building, which meant he must have left the other one in the ashtray. So he himself was to blame for the fire! Thousands of poundsworth of stock destroyed because of his own carelessness.

But he alone knew the truth and he had no intention of admitting it to anyone. He would have to be honest about being in the office earlier this evening, of course, but not a damned soul could prove he'd been smoking in there.

He stared miserably at the bleak scene around him. The building was still steaming, the firemen's voices echoing eerily in the damp and misty night air. Mick's throat and chest felt sore from the smoke and he retched painfully as he coughed, eyes streaming.

Cold with fear as the ghastly implications of this disaster registered fully, he walked away from the scene of devastation and headed for his car with his handkerchief held to his face.

Chapter Two

'So, Mick's still waiting for the insurance money to come through then,' said Jane's sister-in-law and close friend Marie, who was visiting with her offspring, Melanie and Roy, of a similar age to Davey and Pip.

'That's right,' replied Jane, setting down a tray of tea and biscuits on an occasional table and handing her guest a cup. The children were making the most of the sunshine on this fine June afternoon and playing outside in the garden, which meant the two women had the lounge to themselves.

'It's certainly taking them long enough to pay out,' snorted Marie, angry on behalf of her beloved brother. 'It must be all of three months since the fire.'

'I suppose they must still be checking it out,' said Jane.

'Standard procedure, probably,' said Marie. 'For the insurance company to make sure there's nothing dodgy about the claim ... that the fire wasn't started deliberately or anything,' she said, helping herself to a digestive biscuit and dunking it in her tea. 'It still seems an awfully long time to have to wait, though.'

'Yes,' agreed Jane, sipping her own tea.

'When they do pay out, they'll reimburse him for loss of profits while his business isn't functioning, won't they?' said Marie. 'So he won't lose out in the long run.'

'I imagine that would be in the terms of his insurance policy but I never question him about business matters, as you know.'

'He's bound to have taken care of that, I should think.'

'Sure to,' said Jane, nodding. 'He says his standing

25

with the bank is good, too, so there's no real problem.'

'Good.'

'I thought perhaps we'd have to pull our horns in until he gets the insurance money but he says there's no need for anything like that.'

'That must be a relief?'

'Not really,' said Jane. 'It wouldn't hurt us to live more frugally for a short time.'

'Talking about banks,' said Marie on a lighter note, 'have you heard about this bank card thing that's just come in? You can use it to buy things on credit, apparently.'

'Yes, I remember reading something about that in the paper the other day,' said Jane. 'They're talking about having cash-dispensing machines outside banks eventually, too.'

'You mean like chocolate machines?'

'Yeah. Apparently you put the card in and out comes the dosh.'

'That's incredible! I can't see that ever becoming a reality.'

'It does seem a bit unlikely,' agreed Jane. 'No prizes for guessing who'll be one of the first to have a card, though.'

Marie's expression softened affectionately. 'Mick's probably already arranged to have one, if the truth be told.'

'That's our Mick,' said Jane fondly. 'If it's the latest thing, he has to have it.'

'Has he had any luck finding another warehouse?'

'Not so far as I know.'

'It's a good job he was only renting the other place. At least he doesn't have the responsibility of getting the fire damage put right,' said Marie. 'That must be a relief to him.'

'He hasn't said much about it, actually,' said her sister-in-law. 'You know what Mick's like for keeping his business affairs to himself. He just says everything is under control and I'm not to worry.'

'That's Mick for you,' said Marie evenly. 'He's always been very protective of you . . . even before you were rich. He put you on a pedestal right from the start.'

'I don't know about a pedestal but he is very protective,' admitted Jane.

'I wouldn't mind some of that sort o' pampering myself now and again,' declared Marie jokingly. 'My Eddie, bless him, doesn't have a romantic bone in his body.'

'Mick isn't so much romantic as macho!'

'Sees himself as a bit of a caveman, I think,' agreed Marie, and they both hooted with laughter.

'Your Eddie's a good sort, though, isn't he?' said Jane.

'Oh, yes.' A tall, angular woman with similar colouring to her brother, Marie's face softened with a smile, her dark eyes shining with warmth at the thought of her bus-driver husband. 'Eddie's the best,' she said warmly. Her large features were emphasised by the fact that she wore her black hair taken back rather too severely into a pleat.

'You wouldn't really want him to be as masterful as Mick, would you?' said Jane, because Marie always seemed to be the more assertive partner in her marriage.

'Seriously, I think it would drive me nuts. Anyway, Eddie's just an ordinary working bloke on a set wage and we live in a different world from you and Mick, in our little council house,' said Marie. 'He brings home his wages and we work out our budget together.'

'Quite different from us,' said Jane.

Marie nodded then sipped her tea, pondering. 'To be perfectly honest,' she said, 'I rather like the idea of its being a joint effort. There isn't much left over for treats when the essentials have been paid for, but at least I know exactly what we can afford. I don't have exciting surprises like you do, with flash new cars suddenly appearing on the drive.' She glanced around the room which was light and airy with mint green walls and a soft carpet, patches of sunlight striking the wall above the marble fireplace. 'Or a beautiful house like this to

27

live in – but at least I feel in control.'

'I've got so used to Mick's taking care of our finances, I wouldn't have a clue where to start,' admitted Jane.

'Doesn't that make you feel a bit . . . sort of ineffectual?'

'I don't really think about it,' confessed her sister-in-law. 'It's become a habit after all this time.'

'I suppose it would do.'

They lapsed into a comfortable silence, nibbling biscuits and drinking tea.

'So where's Mick now?' enquired Marie after a while. 'Out looking for another warehouse?'

'I'm not sure. He doesn't say much about where he goes during the day,' said Jane. 'Just says he's out on business.'

'Let's hope he's back in business properly before long.'

'He will be, don't worry. This *is* Mick we're talking about.'

'All this waiting about is getting him into a bit of a state, though, isn't it?' said Marie, frowning. 'I thought he seemed very edgy when he called at our place the other day.'

'Who wouldn't be on edge after losing all their stock and having the aggravation of having to set up in business somewhere else?'

Marie was right, though. Mick *had* been extremely tense this last three months. Bad-tempered and moody. And she knew he wasn't sleeping properly.

'Have they found out how the fire started?' asked Marie.

'Not so far as I know. Mick seems to think it must have been caused by faulty electrical wiring.'

'That makes sense. The electrics in these old buildings can be lethal.'

'More tea?'

'Please.'

Jane poured them both another cup and they moved on to more general matters.

'So what time would you like me to have the kids here for Davey's birthday party on Saturday?' asked Marie. 'I know it says three on the invitation but I expect you'd like me to get here earlier to give you a hand?'

'That would be lovely,' said Jane. 'Come as soon as you can after lunch.'

'Sure.'

When Marie had finished her tea, she yawned and stretched.

'Well, as much as I'm enjoying this relaxation, it's time I was making tracks . . . or there'll be no dinner on the table when Eddie gets in.'

'I'll run you home in the car, if you like?' offered Jane. 'To save you waiting for the bus back to Chiswick.'

'Well . . . if you're sure?' said Marie. 'I don't want to put you out.'

'You won't be, and Davey and Pip will enjoy the ride,' she said brightly. 'I'll go and call them all in from the garden and we'll go whenever you're ready.'

Mick was home when Jane got back from Chiswick. He was sitting in an armchair in the lounge, staring blankly at the television set.

'Hello, love,' she said, leaning over and kissing the top of his head. 'Had a good day?'

His reply to that was a gruff, 'Where have you been?'

'Taking Marie home,' she told him. 'She came for the afternoon.'

'Oh.' A pause. 'Are you making tea?'

'I wasn't going to. I'm about to start getting the meal . . .'

'Make me some tea first,' he demanded in a tone that didn't invite argument.

She felt irritated by his command, which was unusual for her because normally she waited on him without giving it a second thought.

'Okay, I'll put the kettle on,' she said, tight-lipped.

Delighted to have their daddy home so early, the

children hovered around his chair, chattering to him excitedly and vying with each other for his attention.

'Roy and Melanie got into big trouble with Aunt Marie today, Daddy,' announced Pip, climbing on to her father's lap.

'Did they?' he said absently.

'Yes.' She fidgeted, snuggling closer to him and smacking a wet kiss on his cheek. 'They were being ever so naughty . . . quarrelling about whose turn it was to go on the swing.'

'Is that right?' His daughter wriggled and squirmed, arms around his neck, hugging him. 'Sit still, Pip, please, or you'll have to get down.'

'Mel and Davey were naughty too,' she continued, sitting still now. 'Davey called Mel a show-off and she said he was smelly.'

'Don't tell tales, Pip,' rebuked Jane, on her way to the kitchen.

'She's always telling tales,' chanted Davey, who was watching Jackanory with half an eye.

'No, I'm not.'

'Yes, you are.'

'Now then, no squabbling, you two,' said Jane, pausing for a moment at the door.

Davey clambered exuberantly on to his father's lap alongside his sister as he often did. But before he had a chance to settle, both children were forcibly removed and thrown roughly on to the settee.

'*Sit there and be quiet!*' thundered Mick, glaring at them red-faced, eyes blazing, voice clipped with temper.

Two pairs of startled eyes stared at him.

'I won't have you climbing about all over me like a couple of monkeys!' he raged. 'You're little savages, the pair of you.'

They looked bewildered because normally he encouraged them to sit on his lap and never shouted at them. After a few moments' stunned silence, Pip began to howl and Davey stared warily at his father, the darkness of his eyes emphasised by a deathly pallor.

Hearing the commotion, Jane hurried in from the kitchen.

'What on earth's going on in here?' she wanted to know.

Pip ran over to her mother and clung to her legs, sobbing.

Davey followed and stood at his mother's side with his mouth trembling.

Mick observed his wife sheepishly, putting his hand to his brow as though his head hurt and that was the excuse for his behaviour.

'Isn't a man entitled to some peace in his own home?'

'What did they do to upset you?'

'They were using me as a sofa,' he told her, voice ragged with rage. 'All I wanted was to sit down quietly in the armchair for a while.' His fury seemed to increase with every syllable. 'But there's no chance of that in this house, is there? Bloody kids jumping all over you . . .'

Jane stared at him in amazement. This incident was quite unprecedented. Disciplining the children was usually left entirely to her. Mick couldn't get enough of them as a rule and was patient to a fault with them normally.

'Come on, you two,' she said, taking them both by the hand. 'Let's leave Daddy to some peace and quiet.'

They went with their mother into the kitchen where Jane pacified them and suggested they play in the garden. Pouring Mick a cup of tea, she took it into him and put it rather forcefully on the coffee table near his chair.

'Look, I know you're under a lot of pressure, waiting for the insurance money to come through and everything,' she said, standing in front of him with arms folded, 'but there's no need to take it out on the children.'

'I wasn't,' he denied irritably. 'They were jumping all over me and I stopped them, that's all there was to it.'

'You've always encouraged them to get on your lap. They're not to know . . .'

'So I'm not in the mood today,' he cut in heatedly. 'Why must you make such a big drama out of it?'

31

'Because you're becoming impossible to live with, that's why,' she told him. 'Take your frustration out on me if you must, but not on the children.' Her mouth was dry and she was trembling because she wasn't used to standing up to him. 'I know you've a lot on your mind at the moment but you really must try not to be so bad-tempered.'

'Stop moaning, woman, and give me a break, will you?'

Mick got up and paced over to the french windows where he stood with his back to her, looking into the garden where the children were playing on their tricycles. Seeing the rigid set of his shoulders and guessing he was feeling wretched, she went to him, eager to put things right between them.

'Is there anything I can do to help?' she asked, slipping her arms around him from behind.

'No.'

'Don't shut me out, Mick,' she pleaded. 'I want to help.'

'I don't need help.'

'Would you like me to phone the insurance company for you?' she suggested. 'Find out what's causing the delay. Someone different enquiring might encourage them to hurry things along.'

She was quite unprepared for the violence of his reaction.

'Oh, for God's sake, stop babying me,' he said, swinging round and pushing her away. 'I'm a grown man, not a child.'

'But I . . .'

'I'm not Davey or Pip, you know,' he said grimly. 'I'm the breadwinner of this family. The head of the house. *I* run things around here and *I* know what I'm doing.'

'I've never suggested otherwise . . .'

'You stick to cleaning the house and keep out of things that don't concern you.'

'Mick, I . . . I was only trying to help.'

His eyes narrowed in accusation.

'What's the matter? Don't you trust me to look after my own family?' he ranted. 'Is that what's bothering you?'

'Of course I trust you,' said Jane, shocked by this outburst.

'Why interfere then?'

'I love you, Mick, and when I see you worried, naturally I want to help . . .'

'Well, you can forget it,' he said. 'Because I don't need it.'

'Perhaps if we made a few economies until everything is sorted out . . .'

'No, no, no!' he bellowed. 'How many more times must I tell you that nothing is going to change? So far as this family is concerned, everything is exactly the same as it was before the fire. So will you just shut up about it? Shut your big mouth before I do it for you!'

Shrinking back as though he'd already hit her, hot tears burning beneath her lids, she turned and walked away from him.

Mick came after her and pulled her to him, holding her close, full of remorse.

'I'm sorry, babe . . . so sorry,' he said, gently smoothing her hair from her face with his hands and kissing away her tears. 'I didn't mean to upset you. All this waiting about and not having a business to run is really getting to me. But you're absolutely right, I shouldn't take it out on you and the kids.'

'I'm glad to hear you admit it.'

'I don't want to hurt you,' he said, stroking her face. 'Will you forgive me?'

'Oh, Mick. You know I will.'

'I do have everything under control, you know,' he told her. 'There's nothing for you to worry about at all.'

'I'm not worried about the money, it's you I'm concerned about.'

'I'll try to be better tempered in future, I promise.'

'I hope you mean that?'

'I do . . . I really do.'

'You'd better.'

'But you must trust me to take care of everything and leave the insurance company to me.'

'Okay, Mick,' she said. 'You won't hear another word about it from me.'

Over his shoulder, she could see the children peering in through the french windows at their parents embracing. They looked subdued and uncertain.

'I think you should make your peace with the children too,' said Jane. 'Let them know you still love them.'

'Yeah, sure,' he said. 'I could slit my own throat for being such a pig.'

Peeling the potatoes in the kitchen a few minutes later, Jane heard shrieks of laughter coming from the garden as Mick and the children became friends again. That was more like it, she thought, smiling. But a niggling knot of tension remained because she had a horrible suspicion that this period of calm was only temporary.

Davey's fourth birthday party was in full swing. Tea was over and there was a boisterous game of musical chairs in progress in the Parkers' lounge.

There had been the usual catalogue of disasters among the under-fives: squabbles, screaming, spillages – none of which was helped by the rain which kept everybody indoors. But things had calmed down after tea and now it was going well.

It was a real family occasion. Mick was in charge of the record player while Jane, Marie and Eddie were removing the chairs and organising the children. Mick's mother and Jane's father were washing the dishes in the kitchen. Wilf Parker was busy with his round and hadn't come.

The music stopped, and after the scramble for seats a row erupted.

'It isn't fair!' wailed a golden-haired little girl called Jemima. 'Roy pushed me out of the way so he could get the chair.'

'No, I didn't,' denied Roy, his bottom safely planted on the chair.

'You did, you did!' she yelled, and thumped him in the back.

'Now then, Jemima,' intervened Marie, patience stretched, 'that's not very nice, is it? Not very nice at all.'

'He cheated,' she said, sobs gathering momentum. 'I'm still in the game.'

'You're not,' said Roy.

'I am,' screamed Jemima.

Jane finally ended the dispute by putting another chair in the line and asking Mick to start the music again.

'Is it nearly time for party bags and home to Mummy?' Marie whispered to Jane with a chuckle.

'Judging by the state of my nerves, I should think it must be!'

When the music stopped and Jemima failed to get a seat again, all hell broke loose. The child argued with anyone who would listen and finally proceeded to scream her head off. Jane was still trying to pacify her when Mick put the music back on.

'Hey, hang on a minute, Mick,' she shouted to make herself heard above the shrieking child. 'We're not quite ready yet.'

The music stopped and the room resounded to Mick's booming voice as he embarked upon the second outburst of the week.

'Get this bloody lot out of here!' he shouted to his wife.

'Mick . . . shush!'

'Bugger off, the lot of you,' he barked to the children, who stared at him, horror-struck.

'Stop it, Mick . . .' Jane tried again.

'You're like a lot of wild animals.' He moved towards the centre of the room and flapped his hands at the children as though shooing away a flock of pigeons. 'Get out of my house, the lot of you. *Out, out, out!* You horrible little tykes.'

'Daddy!' gasped Davey, mortified as his friends

huddled together, pale with fright, not sure what they were supposed to do next. Jemima had stopped crying and was looking at Mick with a bemused expression.

'Don't be so ridiculous, Mick,' said Jane, moving closer to him and speaking in a hushed voice. She could have strangled him for embarrassing their son in this way. 'These children are only four years old. They can't go home until their parents come to collect them – not unless we take them. Anyway, they're our guests and they aren't going anywhere until the end of the party.'

'In that case, *I'll* go,' roared Mick before the stunned gathering. 'I'm not staying in this bear garden a moment longer.'

Without another word, he marched from the room. The front door slammed, followed by the sound of a car driving away at high speed.

Some of the children were giggling, others crying. Davey had disappeared. Leaving the other adults in charge, Jane found her son in his room, sitting on his bed. He was near to tears.

'Hey, come on now, love,' she said, sitting down beside him. 'Cheer up. We'll finish the party without Daddy.'

'It's all spoiled,' said Davey tearfully.

'No, it isn't,' she reassured him, slipping her arm around him. 'We'll soon put everything right. Just you wait and see.'

'I want them all to go home.'

'It isn't time for their parents to come for them yet,' Jane explained gently. 'So we have to carry on entertaining them until then.'

'I don't want to.'

'We have to, love. It would be very rude of us not to finish the party properly.'

'Why is Dad so grumpy?'

'He has things on his mind. He doesn't mean it.'

'My friends will think he's horrid now. They'll say I've got a horrible dad.'

'Of course they won't,' Jane soothed. 'All daddies have bad moods.'

'Not like that.'

'I bet they do.'

'Honestly?'

'Yes, honestly,' she reassured him. 'Anyway, your pals will forget all about it once we get another game going. How about pass the parcel? Everyone likes that.'

'I don't want to go down there.'

'But you're the birthday boy. You can't hide away up here.'

'I'm not going down.'

Jane went down on her haunches, looking into his face and wiping his nose.

'Come on, Davey, you're the guest of honour. The party's nothing without you.'

'I don't wanna go down there.'

'Better you come down and face your friends now,' she said. 'Or you might feel silly about it when you see them tomorrow.'

He thought about this.

'Please, Davey . . . I'm relying on you to help me make the party end with a swing.'

'Oh, all right then,' he said reluctantly.

'Good boy.'

He looked her directly in the eyes and said vehemently, 'But I *hate* Daddy . . . I really, really *hate* him.'

At that precise moment, Jane was having similar thoughts about Mick herself. But she said, 'I'm sure you don't mean that? Not after all the things he does for you.'

'He used to be nice,' said the boy solemnly. 'But not any more.'

Jane's nerves were so taut, even the ticking of the clock on the mantelpiece registered with painful clarity as she waited for Mick to come home that night. All the guests had gone and the children were asleep in bed. Eddie and Marie had taken Rita Parker and Jane's father home in their Ford Cortina. Everyone had been very supportive towards Jane, doing their best to cheer Davey up and make the party end on a happier note. They had all been shocked by Mick's behaviour, though.

'I shall have a few strong words to say to him when I next see him, I can promise you that,' declared his mother.

'It was disgraceful behaviour,' exclaimed Jane's father.

'He's got a lot on his mind at the moment,' said Marie, who had always been very close to her brother and tended to make excuses for him.

'Trust you to stick up for him,' said her husband Eddie. 'I could murder him for spoiling Davey's party.'

And now Jane was sitting in the armchair in the lounge, wrestling with her own confused emotions. She was furious about the contretemps, worried about her husband's state of mind that had caused it, and filled with dread that he would confirm the suspicions with which she now knew she must confront him.

As the time passed and he didn't come home, she wondered what sort of a state he'd be in to be driving a car, because he was sure to be in a pub or drinking club somewhere. And it wouldn't occur to him not to drive home. Mick had never been responsible about that.

At ten o'clock she watched the news but about the only thing that registered, albeit vaguely, was the fashion designer Mary Quant getting an OBE.

When Mick did appear soon after that, it wasn't booze he was full of but contrition.

'That's all very well, Mick,' said Jane after he'd apologised and begged her to forgive him. 'But this is the second time this week you've blown your top and upset the children, and not in a minor way, either.'

Had there been another such incident earlier in the week? He couldn't remember. He was becoming alarmingly forgetful lately. This afternoon he'd found himself at a club in Hammersmith with no knowledge at all of getting there or why he'd gone. It had scared him half to death. Eventually he'd remembered storming out of

Davey's party but the images were very muddled and vague.

'All right, don't go on about it,' he said, because he wasn't prepared to admit his memory lapses to Jane and have her think he was losing his marbles. 'I know I've done wrong.'

'What you did to Davey this afternoon was unforgivable.'

'I've said I'm sorry and I meant it,' he said, looking very ashamed. 'I'll make it up to him, don't worry.'

'You can't put a thing like that right with just a few kind words,' she told him. 'One of the most painful things you can do to a child is to embarrass them in front of their friends.'

'He's too young to be seriously affected by a thing like that, surely?'

'I'm not so certain. I think he was properly humiliated. The poor kid wanted the floor to open up and swallow him.'

'Oh, Gawd!'

'You'll have to make a real effort to win back his confidence.'

'I feel such a bastard.'

'And so you should . . .'

'I know.'

'Where have you been all this time, anyway?' Jane wanted to know.

'At a drinking club in Hammersmith with some old mates.'

'So how come you're not legless?'

'I went on to tomato juice quite early on. Thought I'd better not come home drunk . . . on top of everything else.'

'Well, that's something in your favour, I suppose.'

'Thank God there's something!'

They were sitting to either side of the fireplace, handsomely adorned with a large vase of fresh flowers. Although he longed to make love to his wife, Mick knew better than to make any sort of physical approach to her while things were so delicate between them.

'I'm glad you're not drunk because I think it's time we had a proper discussion about the situation,' said Jane.

He looked pained.

'Oh, no, not again. I've told you, there's nothing to talk about.'

'Oh, but I think there is, Mick,' she said firmly. 'And I want the truth.'

'The truth?'

'There is no insurance money due to you, is there?' she said.

The blood drained from Mick's face, leaving him ashen.

'Of course there's insurance money due to me,' he blustered.

'I don't believe you.'

'Oh, that's nice, that is. My own wife calling me a liar!'

Her gaze didn't falter even though her heart was doing somersaults and her chest felt as though it would burst with tension. She didn't utter a word or move a muscle, just sat where she was, looking at him and waiting.

'Honestly, you don't half get some weird ideas, Jane.'

'Be man enough to answer me truthfully, please, Mick.'

Getting up, he took a cigarette from the packet on the mantelpiece and lit it with his gold lighter. Then he paced restlessly about the room, eventually standing with his back to the window across which the curtains were drawn. He experienced a fleeting feeling of unreality, as though the room was unfamiliar to him and he didn't know who he was.

'I don't know what gets into you sometimes,' he prevaricated.

She didn't reply, just looked at him, the intensity of her gaze demanding the truth.

'I've told you, everything's fine. You've nothing to worry about,' he said, puffing agitatedly on his cigarette.

'Yes, you have told me that, and I don't doubt you will continue to look after us all. But there isn't actually any insurance money to come, is there?'

He stared at the floor for what seemed a long time. When he raised his head and looked at her, she knew she'd been right.

'No, there isn't,' he admitted, sounding very subdued.

Jane's heart lurched but she managed to stay calm.

'So, why won't the insurance company honour your claim?'

Mick's shirt looked snow-white against the red velvet curtains; his hair gleamed darkly as he stood, casually smoking, his shirtsleeves rolled up.

'There is no claim,' he said, eyes not quite meeting hers. 'I didn't have any insurance on the business.'

Biting back recriminations, Jane waited for him to explain.

'I kept meaning to get insurance cover when the business got bigger and I began carrying a large amount of stock,' he explained. 'In the early days it didn't seem worth it. As I only rented the premises, I didn't need to insure the buildings. Then . . . later on . . . I just never got around to it.'

'But you were carrying thousands of poundsworth of stock?'

'Don't remind me,' he said ruefully. 'I intended to take out insurance eventually. But I was on a winning streak . . . everything I touched was so successful, I thought it would go on forever.' He exhaled slowly, producing a cloud of smoke, reminding himself to keep to his original story about faulty wiring and not let slip to Jane the real cause of the fire. 'You know how it is? You never think these things are going to happen to you.'

She could have told him how thoroughly irresponsible he'd been but since he must already be aware of this, there was hardly any point. Hysterics wouldn't solve anything either.

'So what are you going to do?'

'Start again, as I said I would.'

'How?'

'All taken care of,' he said quickly. 'The bank's behind me. They're going to fund the new business once I've found suitable premises and got everything organised.'

'Just like that?'

'They know a winner when they see one,' Mick was quick to point out.

'Oh?'

'Of course. Having watched me build the last business up from nothing, they're only too happy to do so again. They know they can't lose.'

'Why have you been on such a short fuse lately, then, if there isn't a problem?'

Mick shrugged his shoulders. 'Dunno. I suppose it's because I can't get things moving fast enough. You know me, I like everything done yesterday. But these things take time.'

'True.'

'Well, don't look so worried, it isn't the end of the world.'

'I know that.'

'What's the matter then?'

'You lied to me.'

'I didn't want you to worry.'

'I'm your wife, Mick,' she pointed out emphatically. 'We're supposed to be a team. Your problems are mine too. We should work things out together.'

'There *are* no problems.'

'Why lie to me about the insurance money, then?'

'Because I knew you'd only see trouble where there is none,' he explained. 'I just wanted to spare you.'

She believed him about that anyway.

'What about all the letters and phone calls from the bank?'

'They've been chasing me about the paperwork for the funding of the new business,' he told her. 'Figures to be agreed, forms to be signed . . . all that sort of thing. But it's more or less finalised now. As soon as I find the right premises, Parker Supplies will be up and running again.'

'I see.'

'I won't let you down, Jane.' He waved his hand, indicating the room, the subdued wall lighting casting a gentle glow over the elegant furniture and fittings. 'All of this . . . the house, our cars, everything . . . it's all safe.'

'These things aren't the be all and end all to me, Mick,' she said, her voice thick with emotion. 'Can't you understand that you and the kids are what is important to me? Whatever happens, good or bad, we face it together. But I don't want you to lie to me, no matter how well-meant.'

Her words brought tears to his eyes. What a wonderful woman she was – so good, so caring. She looked so small and feminine sitting there, the light bringing out the golden tones in her hair, it was no wonder he wanted to protect her.

'Oh, babe,' he said, moving towards her.

Drawn to him by the force of her love, Jane got up and went into his arms.

'No more lies, Mick . . . promise me?' she entreated.

'I promise.'

He kissed her passionately, then moved back and gave her one of his most melting looks.

'So, am I forgiven for what happened this afternoon?'

When he looked at her like that, his dark eyes somnolent with passion, she found it hard to refuse him anything.

'It was Davey you hurt,' she said. 'He's the one you need to talk to.'

'Yeah, of course. I'll do something about it tomorrow.'

'If you don't, you'll have me to answer to,' Jane promised him. 'And I won't be easy on you.'

Later that night when Jane had fallen asleep in the afterglow of lovemaking, Mick lay awake in the dark, listening to her even breathing and mulling over the actual situation, which was entirely different from the version he had given her.

The truth was, he was in a mess and that was why he

43

was so bad-tempered. But how could he let Jane even suspect he was in trouble financially? How could he tell a woman who worshipped him as a man of credibility and power that the bank was threatening to foreclose on him, and that he spent all his time outside the house begging them for more time and trying to raise money?

For a month or so after the fire, the bank hadn't pressurised him. But as his overdraft had soared under the strain of high living expenses, heavy mortgage and hire purchase payments, with no income to service them, they began to give him a hard time, especially since he'd been forced to admit that there was no insurance money due to him.

As things stood at the moment, he had one week in which to restore their confidence in him by paying money into his account – or they would close it. Everything would go if that happened. The house would be reclaimed by the building society and the bank would take what was left over after the mortgage had been settled, to repay the overdraft. The cars and everything inside the house would be taken by the finance companies.

He'd managed to spin his bank manager a convincing yarn about an uncle who was willing to back him in a new business, and had promised to credit the account within the time limit.

The amount of money Mick needed to get him out of trouble couldn't be obtained from an ordinary job or the welfare state. But cash *would* go into his account as promised. Oh, yes. He was determined not to lose the lifestyle he had worked so hard for. He couldn't go back to being a nobody after being someone of substance. It would kill him!

Having people – especially his wife – think he was tough and invulnerable was meat and drink to him. Jane admired him for what he'd achieved and had become accustomed to living as the wife of a rich man, even though she claimed that money wasn't important to her. Well, she wasn't going to see him go under, not while he had a brain in his head and breath in his body!

Money would be credited to his account first thing on Wednesday morning, he could guarantee it. Because on Tuesday night he was going out on a job with two old mates from the Berrywood Estate who earned their living outside the law. There was no way he could get out of this mess legally.

Just thinking about the path he was about to tread made his head throb and tightened the tension in his stomach that had been bothering him ever since the fire. He just couldn't lie still.

Careful not to disturb his wife, he got out of bed, felt his way across the room in the dark and crept down the stairs. On his way to the kitchen, he went into the hall cloakroom and took a bottle of tranquillisers from the inside pocket of his leather jacket which was hanging up. Sitting gloomily at the kitchen table, smoking, he swallowed two tablets with a cup of tea.

When he was feeling calmer, he went back upstairs, replacing the tablets on the way. No one would discover them there. He dreaded to think what would happen to his macho image if word got out that he'd consulted the doctor about his nerves.

Anyway, he only needed something to help him temporarily, just to get him through this agony until Wednesday. With money in the bank he would feel more like his old self again.

Of course, his share from this one job wouldn't be enough to solve his problems in the long term. But it would buy him time with the bank. Time to work out what to do next . . .

Chapter Three

Mick was in Paddington, at the wheel of a parked Ford which had been stolen for the getaway. His eyes were glued to the service-station opposite where his mates Terry and Pete, who were in the back of the car, would soon go into action. Sick with fear, the rapid beating of his heart reverberated through Mick's body and thundered in his ears.

Sticky with sweat, and panic stricken as his mind went blank, he reached into his jacket pocket for the bottle of tranquillisers, quickly replacing it as his memory returned and he thought of the possible consequences of becoming too relaxed. He reminded himself that nothing could go wrong, that the job was a doddle. The forecourt attendant on the evening shift was being given a cut for supplying information which had enabled them to make their plan fool-proof . . .

When the garage closed for the night, the proprietor, who also owned other service-stations in the area, would arrive with his minder to collect the day's takings. This was his last call and the cash from his other collections would be locked in the boot of his car. The two men would go into the office to collect the money and when they emerged, Terry and Pete, wearing stockings over their heads, would be waiting.

As well as the cash, they would snatch the keys of the proprietor's car and grab the rest of the money from the boot. The boys would have to rough them up a bit in the process, of course, but nothing too violent, Mick had been given their word on that.

His job was to drive the Ford on to the forecourt at

the appropriate moment for the getaway. They had arranged to abandon the car a mile away where Pete's vehicle was parked, then drive to his place in Hammersmith to share out the loot. Afterwards Mick would get into his own Jaguar and go home, a saved man, his wife thinking he'd been out on business as usual.

Now the attendant was putting the 'Closed' signs up and turning the forecourt lights off, leaving just the square of light in the office shining from the darkened building. Inside the Ford, the three men watched and waited.

'Here he comes, boys, dead on time,' said Pete as the Mercedes swept on to the forecourt and stopped to the side of the petrol pumps.

As soon as the two men disappeared into the office, Terry and Pete got out of the Ford and hurried across the road, shadowy figures in the amber glow of the street lights.

With his hands damp and trembling on the wheel, Mick waited with the engine running, his eyes never leaving the scene. The car radio was playing low and an item of news about someone being sentenced to eighteen years in prison for his part in the Great Train Robbery registered like a fist in his guts. It was three years since that notorious event and they were still bringing the villains in, he thought. You weren't safe even after all that time. What sort of stretch would this job carry? he wondered fearfully.

Across the road things were happening. The two men came out of the office and were immediately leaped on by Pete and Terry. Now it was time for Mick to play his part . . .

But as he was about to turn into the forecourt, his mates came tearing towards him with owner and minder in hot pursuit.

'Put your foot down, mate, or we'll all go down for attempted robbery and assault!' said Pete as he and Terry fell into the back of the car, panting.

'What the hell happened?' asked Mick with a sinking heart.

'That henchman only swung a bag of coins at me, didn't he?' said Pete. 'Hit me right across the head with it an' all. The spiteful bugger could have killed me!'

'The other bloke threw a wacking great bunch of keys at me,' said Terry. 'Caught me right in the face . . . he's probably broken my nose.'

'Did you get *any* of the money?' asked Mick in desperation.

'Not a penny, mate,' answered Pete.

'Don't tell me I've been through all this for nothing?' complained Mick, who was shaking and wanted to be sick.

'Could you have done any better in the circumstances, then?' growled Terry.

'You've done enough jobs . . . surely you knew what to expect?'

'How were we to know they'd pull a stunt like that?' complained Terry.

'You planned the job . . . you should have anticipated the unexpected.'

'You were there when we planned it,' Pete pointed out. 'If you're so clever, why didn't you predict what might happen?'

'I don't have the experience,' said Mick.

'Exactly . . . so don't criticise us.'

'There's no point in arguing about it,' said Terry as Mick pulled up in a back street and they all piled into Pete's car.

'There's nothing we can do about it now anyway,' said Pete. 'We'll just have to put that one down to experience.'

'But I really need that dough,' moaned Mick, in the back of Pete's car now.

'Don't we all, mate, don't we all?' said Pete, not sounding too concerned.

'Some you win, some you lose,' said Terry. 'That's the way it goes.'

Mick sank back into the misery of his own black world, isolated from his mates by the seriousness of his dilemma. Pete and Terry were small-time crooks who

lived from day to day and had no real financial commitments. The failure of the robbery didn't spell disaster
for them as it did for him.

His last hope had gone. There was no way out. What
was he going to do?

'Daddy's home, Daddy's home!' cried Pip excitedly,
seeing her father's car on the drive when Jane parked
beside it the next day at lunchtime.

Having been to the supermarket while the children
were at nursery school, Jane had been out all morning
and Mick had still been in bed when she'd left. Since the
fire there was no set routine to his day and she never
knew what his plans were. She'd been asleep when he'd
got home last night and he'd been none too happy when
she'd taken him a cup of tea in bed this morning so she
hadn't risked asking him what he was doing today.

Pip trotted round the side of the house to the back
door while Davey 'helped' his mother unload the shopping. Weighed down with carrier bags, Jane was heading
for the house when Pip came to meet her with the news
that she couldn't find her father.

'He isn't in any of the rooms downstairs.'

'He's probably still in bed or in the shower or something,' said Jane.

'Shall I go and look?'

'No. Leave him be, Pip . . . just in case he's still asleep.'

She got the rest of the shopping from the car and
went upstairs to the bedroom, expecting to find her
husband in bed. He wasn't there. Nor was he anywhere
else in the house, the garden or garage. He must have
gone out for a walk, she thought, which struck her as
odd because Mick would take the car to the end of the
road to get a newspaper rather than go on foot. Was he
in with one of the neighbours, perhaps? Most unlikely
because all the men were out at work. Maybe one of his
mates had picked him up and taken him out somewhere?
But that wasn't Mick's style. He liked to be in the
position of control, in the driver's seat. Anyway, he

wouldn't have left the back door unlocked if he was going out for any length of time.

Putting the shopping away and getting the children's lunch, Jane felt uneasy, mostly because it was so unusual for Mick to go anywhere without his beloved car. There was something strange afoot, she could feel it. Mick wasn't the sort of man to account to her for his every move but neither was he given to disappearing without a word. She phoned his mother and sister; they had neither seen nor heard from him.

The afternoon passed. She took Davey to a friend's house to play and collected him later. Still no sign of Mick. She got the children's tea and prepared the vegetables for her and Mick's meal. She bathed the children and put them to bed and cooked a meal as though everything were normal.

Drying her hands in the hall cloakroom, she brushed against Mick's leather jacket and a rattling sound caught her attention. Tracing it to the inside pocket, she put her hand inside and drew out a bottle of prescribed valium. So, he'd been to see the doctor – unheard of for Mick. He would consider being on tranquillisers to be a sign of weakness which must be why he hadn't told her about it.

Hating herself for invading his privacy but feeling compelled to do so in the light of this new development, she checked the other pockets and found his wallet containing paper money and his cheque book.

He couldn't have gone far without these essentials. So where the devil was he?

'Marie, it's Jane.'

'Hi. Your timing's perfect. The kids are in bed and I'm in the mood for a chat.'

'I haven't phoned for a chat.'

'No?'

'No. I think something's happened to Mick.'

'Still not back?'

'No, he's disappeared. I haven't seen him since before

51

I went out this morning to take the kids to nursery school.'

'Oh, come on, Jane,' said Marie in friendly tones. 'I hadn't seen Eddie since this morning until just now when he got in from work . . . you can hardly call *that* a disappearance!'

'But this is different.' Jane explained about the car and the wallet. 'It's as though he's disappeared into thin air. He couldn't have intended to be gone long or he'd have taken his wallet.'

'Mick always carries a fair amount of money in his trouser pocket,' Marie reminded her. 'You know him, he's always got a wad of notes on him.'

'Yes, there is that.'

'There you are then.'

'But it feels wrong,' said Jane through dry lips. 'Perhaps he's been taken ill or something? He usually phones me when he's out for any length of time, if I don't know where he is.'

'I'm sure you're worrying unnecessarily,' said Marie. 'He'll be home in a minute and you'll feel daft for having got yourself so worked up.'

'Yeah, course he will,' said Jane, only slightly reassured by Marie's confidence. 'I shouldn't have bothered you.'

'Don't be silly . . . if you can't ring your best friend when you're worried, who can you turn to?' Marie assured her kindly.

'Thanks.'

'It's odd him not getting in touch, I admit, but I'm sure there's no cause for alarm. Phone me when he gets in.'

'Will do.'

An hour later, Marie phoned Jane to find out if Mick had turned up.

'No, and I think I ought to phone the hospitals.' Jane sounded desperate now.

'I don't think that's necessary but if it'll put your mind at rest . . .'

None of the hospitals had admitted anyone answering to his description.

'Do you think I should call the police?' Jane asked Marie when she called again.

'And tell them that your husband's gone out and is late back?' she said with a touch of friendly cynicism. 'I don't think so, Jane. They'll just say, So what? You and a million other wives.'

'I suppose so.'

'While you're telling them all about it, he'll turn up.'

'I'll murder him when he does!' said Jane. 'For getting me into this state.'

'He'll have been held up . . . got involved somewhere,' said Marie. 'You know what men are like, they get talking and forget the time.'

'I've phoned all his usual drinking haunts and no one's seen him.'

'He'll be propping up a bar somewhere, though, you can bet your life on it, especially as he hasn't got the car with him,' said Marie, keeping her mood light so as not to alarm Jane, though she genuinely believed there was no cause to worry at this stage. She was annoyed with her brother for causing his wife such anxiety, though. He'd made Jane far too dependent on him, which made her panic when he wasn't around. 'He was probably feeling a bit down because the insurance money hasn't come through and decided to go on a bender. He'll be back when he's sobered up.'

Loyalty to Mick prevented Jane from telling Marie the truth about the insurance money.

'He's never been out of touch for this long before,' she said.

'Yeah, well, he's been under a strain since the fire, hasn't he?' Marie pointed out. 'It's changed him. The way he carried on at Davey's birthday party is proof of that.'

'I suppose so.'

'Why don't you make yourself a nice cup of coffee and watch the telly, love?' suggested Marie. 'It might help to take your mind off things.'

'I doubt it.'

'Give it a try. It'll calm you down and help you to sleep.'

'Sleep . . . you must be joking!'

'The best thing you can do is go to bed at your usual time and forget about him, Jane,' Marie strongly advised.

'How can I?'

'Relax. You know Mick. He'll be there beside you in the morning, large as life and sleeping off a giant hangover.'

'You could be right, I suppose,' said Jane, sounding doubtful.

'He'll be there,' said Marie. 'I know my brother, he'll come home when he's ready.'

Jane didn't go to bed. She wandered around downstairs, in and out of the silent rooms, then sat rigid in an armchair waiting for him, every creak inside the house and rustling sound outside jarring her nerves. When tension made it impossible for her to sit still, she got up and stood by the window, staring out into the avenue at the dark shadowy trees swaying gently in the breeze in the pale glow of the street lights. The beauty of the night with its starry sky and pearly moon only added to her pain as she stood there, aching to see Mick striding towards the house and silently begging the telephone to ring.

In one way time seemed to stand still as she waited for the silence of the night to end. But every hour that passed without news, passed too quickly. Mick wouldn't stay out this long without contacting her unless something was terribly wrong.

When the sky lightened with the dawn, Jane knew she could no longer pretend that this was an ordinary situation. With fear and desolation in her heart, she telephoned the police.

'He could be dead or dying in a ditch somewhere,' she told a policeman that same afternoon, her nerves in shreds after what had been the most terrible day of her life.

'Try not to let your imagination run away with you, Mrs Parker.'

'It's difficult not to!'

'I know,' he said sympathetically. 'But getting into a panic won't help anyone.'

Policemen had been coming and going all day to keep her informed. Every time Jane saw a uniform she braced herself for the worst. But there had been no news of Mick at all. They were searching the neighbourhood, apparently, and the Chiswick police were looking for him in the Berrywood Estate area. But they had been honest with her and admitted that it was a very difficult task, finding a missing person in a place as heavily populated as London.

She had answered so many personal questions about her life with Mick, she was beginning to think the police suspected her of doing away with him. Having not slept at all the previous night, she couldn't think straight by now and her eyes and head were sore. Her legs were aching, too, because she was too tense to sit down for any length of time and had been walking about aimlessly for hours.

Marie was looking after the children. Jane had taken them to her place straight from nursery school to protect them from the drama here at home. Her sister-in-law had offered to have them for the night but Jane thought they needed the security of their mother's presence. Eddie was bringing them home later on because Jane was afraid to leave the house in case there was some news.

'Are you sure he hasn't just, er . . . left?' the policeman was saying.

'There isn't another woman, if that's what you're getting at.'

'I wasn't . . . not especially.'

'No?'

'No. But he might just have gone off. You said he'd been under stress since the fire, mentioned finding tranquillisers . . .'

'If my husband were alive and well, he'd have been in touch with me,' she stated categorically.

'You think so?'

'I *know* so. He would never just go off and leave me and the children . . . we're his whole life. He wouldn't have me worrying like this if he was all right.'

'It wouldn't be the first time a man has left home without any word of warning,' said the policeman, meaning to be kind and keep things in perspective because the lady's imagination seemed to be running riot. 'It happens every day . . . a chap goes out for a packet of fags and doesn't come back.'

'You don't understand,' said Jane, brushing her tired brow with her hand. 'My husband and I are very close. We've been together since we were teenagers and we don't have any marital problems.'

'Even so . . . sometimes things get too much for people and they feel the need to go away for a while. Often they turn up after a few days,' said the policeman, wanting to reassure her. But this case had all the classic signs of a straightforward desertion. In these cases the abandoned party often had no idea, or didn't want to admit, that anything was wrong with their marriage.

'Something's happened to him, I know it has,' said Jane, her voice quivering with emotion. 'You have to find him . . . please.'

'We're doing everything we possibly can, my dear,' he said patiently.

'For how long will you go on looking?' she asked, picking at her finger-nails nervously.

'Until we think there's no point in continuing,' he replied. 'But your husband will be put on the missing persons' list so he won't be forgotten.'

She moistened her lips which were dry and chapped.

'You can't call off the search!' she declared, her voice rising hysterically, anguish making her unreasonable. 'It's your job to find him. It's our taxes that pay your wages.'

'I'm aware of that. But we don't have unlimited man-power,' he explained calmly. 'There are other cases to be attended to. We can only give this case priority for so long.'

'Yes, of course, I'm sorry,' she said, holding her throbbing head.

'Try not to worry, Mrs Parker. Our chaps are out there looking for him as we speak,' said the policeman, moving towards the door. 'We'll let you know as soon as we have any news.'

'Thank you, you're very kind,' she said, seeing him out.

When Eddie brought the children back, they wanted to know when their daddy was coming home.

'When he's finished the job he's doing in another place,' fibbed Jane, catching Eddie's eye and detecting a hint of disapproval.

'What should I have said to them?' she asked as he joined her for a cup of tea in the kitchen while the children played in the garden on this warm evening. 'That I've no idea where their father is . . . that he's probably lying dead somewhere?'

Eddie was a down-to-earth type of man, thickset with straight brown hair and honest grey eyes. He looked grave because he was worried about Jane and the children. He'd never had any time for his wife's brother. Mick Parker was too fond of himself for Eddie's liking.

'No, of course not, but . . .'

'But?'

He hated to be harsh with Jane but thought that for her own sake she ought to face up to the most likely explanation for Mick's disappearance. There was no point in deluding herself.

'Shouldn't you prepare yourself and them for . . . the other alternative?'

'Which is?'

'That he's simply walked out and won't be coming back.'

'Oh, no, Eddie,' she said with a vigorous shake of the head. 'Mick would never do a thing like that. You're as bad as the police. That's what they've been suggesting.'

'It must have occurred to you?'

'Not for a moment,' said Jane, and it was true. 'I'm surprised you can even think such a thing . . . you know how close Mick and I have always been?'

'Yes, I do know that.'

'Well, then?'

'I can look at the situation objectively,' he said. 'You can't and neither can Marie because she and Mick have always been so close.'

'And the situation as you see it is . . . ?'

'Well, Mick is young and healthy so he isn't likely to have dropped down dead somewhere. And if he'd been in an accident or been taken ill the hospitals would know about it. Even if he has no identification on him, they'd know from the description you've given the police. That leaves murder and we both know that really is delving into the realms of fantasy. So what else is there except desertion?'

'Okay, Eddie, I accept you have a point,' Jane conceded. 'But *why* would he leave us?'

'I don't know, Jane,' he replied gently. 'I really don't know.'

The next morning, while the children were at nursery school, Jane had a visit from Mick's bank manager. Having been unable to contact Mick by telephone, he had decided on a personal visit because of the serious nature of this business. Jane had been too distracted to do more than tell callers that Mick wasn't at home when she'd answered the phone this past couple of days. The last thing on her mind was his funding for the new business.

But when she admitted the awful truth to the bank manager, that Mick had gone missing, he was honest with her too. He told her that the bank could no longer support her husband. As from today his bank account would be frozen – no more payments would be made, no more cheques honoured.

In her husband's absence Jane was thoroughly enlightened about the parlous state of his finances. The bank manager had no choice since she was about to become homeless and destitute.

For a long time after he'd left, she sat by the french windows, staring into the garden and trying to make the dreadful news sink in, too stunned to move. She cast her eye over the pretty patio fringed with potted geraniums, the neat lawns edged with roses and marigolds, all tended by a gardener. She glanced around the expensively furnished room and through the wide archway to the dining room where a polished suite stood resplendent, a blade of sunlight striking the solid silver candelabra at the table's centre.

None of this had ever been theirs. It all belonged to people foolish enough to lend her husband money. The man she had so admired for having the courage and tenacity to better himself had proved to be of no real substance, so greedy for the glory of material success that he'd been spending money he didn't have on the strength of a business he hadn't even bothered to insure! Even if the fire hadn't happened, they would have lost all of this eventually because he was hopelessly over committed. The bank manager had been very definite about that.

It was the deceit that hurt. The fact that he'd lied to her even when he'd known they were on the brink of disaster. Most painful of all was the fact that he'd left her to discover the truth in such a humiliating way and to face the problems alone.

There must be another explanation, her heart told her. Mick would never be *that* cowardly. Perhaps he was trying to put things right and would be back when he'd done so? But she knew she was clutching at straws. The man she had thought she'd known so well now seemed like a stranger to her.

No wonder he was on tranquillisers! He'd known how close they were to losing everything and had not been man enough to tell her. But he wouldn't have lost her, he must have known that. She'd already told him it wasn't the money that mattered to her, just him and the children. No matter how great the hardship, there was nothing she couldn't face with Mick by her side.

But he wasn't here. He'd known how much she loved him and hadn't cared enough to stay and see this through with her. As agonising as it was, she forced herself to face up to the truth: that Mick had run away from troubles of his own making and wasn't coming back.

After years of protecting her so completely, he'd gone without a word. Left her feeling frail and helpless without him. That was his gift to her – total vulnerability. She hated him for that. But she hated him even more for leaving his children. How could a man who had professed to love his family do a thing like that?

A sudden memory surfaced with such clarity it startled her. It was so vivid she could smell his spicy aftershave and taste the tang of his exotic cigarettes when he'd kissed her before going out on the evening of the fire, the night that had proved to be such a watershed. He'd been singing the Beatles hit 'We Can Work It Out' as he'd gone out of the door, she remembered it well. That was the last time they'd been happy.

Recalled to the present by the realisation that it was time to collect the children from nursery school, she wiped the tears from her eyes and left the house, painfully aware that her pleasant daily routine was at an end. Along with everything else they had enjoyed in Maple Avenue, expensive luxuries such as nursery school were no longer available to the Parker family.

There were fresh tears in her eyes as she greeted her children, her love for them even stronger in the knowledge that their father had abandoned them. Deserted and vulnerable she may be but she was all Davey and Pip had.

Somehow she had to find the strength to bring them up alone and make a good life for them. She bent down and held them close, feeling their soft skin against hers as she put her face to theirs. Then she helped them into the car and headed for home, to the beautiful house they would soon be forced to leave.

Chapter Four

'Stop bothering your granddad, you two,' commanded Jane, hurrying into her father's living room from the kitchen, having perceived a definite note of irritability in his response to the children's relentless efforts to capture his interest. 'He's trying to watch the telly.'

'Will you play a game of I-spy with us, Granddad?' asked Davey, disobedient in his dogged pursuit of attention.

'Not now, son,' said Joe, looking harassed because he had just got home from work and was hoping for a peaceful half-hour in his armchair to watch the early-evening news.

'Oh, please, Granddad!' Pip chimed in.

'No,' said Jane's father more sharply. 'Now, please be good children and go and amuse yourselves while I watch the news.'

'Come into the kitchen with me while I get the supper,' intervened Jane, riddled with guilt for having disrupted her father's life by moving in with him, and exhausted from constantly being on edge about the children's destroying his much-needed relaxation.

'I wanna go outside to play,' declared Davey in re-calcitrant mood, lingering by his grandfather's armchair.

'You know very well you can't do that,' replied Jane through clenched teeth. 'You've been living here long enough to know that Granddad doesn't have a garden. So go and get something to play with and come in the kitchen with me.'

'I wanna play in the street!'

'No, Davey.'

'We wanna go outside,' whined Pip, uniting with her brother against authority. 'There's nothing to do in here.'

'You are *not* going out,' said Jane, clinging tenaciously to her overtaxed patience.

'Why?' asked Pip.

'Because of the traffic. It's too dangerous for you to play out there. I've told you a hundred times . . .'

'Other children play out there, we've seen them,' announced Davey knowingly.

'They're older than you.'

'Not all of them.'

'Some of them are smaller than us,' argued Pip petulantly.

Jane was so tense, her shoulders ached and her throat was constricted. She could understand her father's being tetchy. It couldn't be easy to adjust to the noise and exuberance of young children about the place at his age, especially in a small flat like this one. But she felt sorry for Davey and Pip too, being so restricted after what they'd been used to. The upheaval had certainly taken its toll on their behaviour. They never used to be this difficult.

'You are *not* playing in the street,' she hissed at them. 'And I don't want to hear another word about it! Either come into the kitchen with me or go and play in the bedroom. But leave your granddad to watch television in peace.'

'I don't like you,' whined Pip, tears forming. 'I want my daddy.'

'I hate Daddy,' said Davey, pausing as though digging around for the most effective insult before adding, 'He smells.'

Joe released a loud eloquent sigh then got up and marched over to the television set and turned up the volume.

Jane hastily grabbed her children, took them forcibly into the kitchen and closed the door.

'Now listen to me, both of you,' she said, keeping her voice down, 'Granddad's tired when he gets home from work and likes some peace and quiet for a while. So leave him alone.'

'I hate living here,' moaned Pip. 'I wanna go back to the house with the garden . . . where Daddy lives. I wanna ride my bike.'

'We can't go back there, silly,' said Davey, 'Mummy's told you we can't. Anyway, Daddy doesn't live there any more. He's gone away.'

'I wanna see him.'

'Well, you can't, so shut up about it,' said her brother with an air of finality.

Resorting to bribery, Jane went down on her haunches before them.

'Look, if you're very good and play quietly until supper's ready, we'll take a picnic to the park tomorrow afternoon. Would you like that?'

'With Mel and Roy?' queried Davey.

'Yes. I'll ask Aunt Marie if they'd like to join us,' she promised.

This seemed to pacify them. Davey got a couple of his toy cars and sat at the table with them. Pip got some crayons and paper and sat opposite him, drawing squiggly patterns and moon faces with spiky hair. All was quiet while Jane continued grilling sausages and cooking potatoes to make into mash.

Three months had passed since Mick's departure and they were living here until the council found them a place of their own. Jane had stayed at the house in Maple Avenue only long enough to clean the place from top to bottom.

She'd been told by the Department of Housing that it could take as long as a year to house her. It depended on movement within the system. The waiting list for council accommodation was very long in this crowded borough. Jane thought that another year of the present arrangement would put them all into an asylum and regularly scoured noticeboards and the accommodation section in the local paper.

There were places to be had privately but none she

could afford or that would accept children. Had Davey and Pip not already suffered such a blow when their father left, she might have considered finding someone to look after them and getting herself a full-time job to improve her finances. But she believed it was important to be with them during the day at this time. Rather than relying on state benefit, she gained the means to support them by doing an early-morning stint of office cleaning while they were still asleep, and a shift in a sweet factory every evening when they were in bed.

Her biggest fear was that the powers-that-be at the council would realise how overcrowded they were here in the flat and take the children into care until a home could be found for the three of them together. Her father said she was worrying unnecessarily but they both knew that such things did happen even if they didn't get into the newspapers.

Although Joe was sometimes impatient with the children, he'd been wonderfully supportive to Jane and hadn't hesitated for a moment about taking them in or babysitting while she was out working. He pretended not to mind having Davey and Pip sleeping on camp beds in his bedroom while Jane slept on the put-u-up in the living room. He tried not to complain if they left their toys around for him to trip over. He did his best to stay patient when they were being loud and boisterous. But he *was* only human and at an age to prefer young children in small doses.

Jane's emotions were in a permanent state of conflict. While she still felt bitter towards Mick for leaving them, she wanted him back with painful urgency. Most nights she cried herself to sleep in her lumpy, makeshift bed, this being her only time to herself. She tried not to let the children see her cry. Outwardly she was indomitable, in reality she felt lost without Mick to look after her.

Apart from Jane, Marie and his mother, nobody had a good word to say for Mick. Despite Jane's fury towards him, she had an irrational instinct to leap to his defence and make excuses for him, frequently saying he couldn't have been in his right mind to have done such a thing.

'Don't kid yourself, love. He knew what he was doing, all right.' Her father was adamant. 'He knew what a mess he'd got himself into and he scarpered and left you to it, there's no more to it than that. The man's a coward, and the sooner you accept that, the easier it will be for you to get over him. And if he were ever to come back, you'd be a fool to let him get a foot in the door after what he's done.'

Jane's salvation had been Marie whose house had become a second home to her. The four children had always been more like siblings than cousins and Jane and Marie were close, having been friends long before they were ever related.

Marie was ardent and inflexible in her defence of her brother.

'Never in a million years would Mick have done a thing like that had he been in a normal frame of mind,' was her categorical opinion. 'He adored you and the kids. He must have been in a very disturbed state to have left like that . . .'

By now Jane had creamed the potatoes, opened a tin of baked beans, and was ready to serve the meal.

'Okay, kids,' she said. 'Who wants supper? It's sausages and beans.'

'Hooray!' they shouted.

'Put your toys away then, so I can set the table.'

They smiled up at her, Davey dark like his father, Pip with light brown hair like her mother and the same rich velvety eyes. In an overwhelming rush of love for them, she abandoned the supper preparations to hug them tight. With Mick gone, they were her reason for living.

'If we had more room, you could move in with us,' Marie said to Jane the next day as they sat on the grass in the park, eating cheese and tomato sandwiches and discussing Jane's unsatisfactory living arrangements. 'But we're pushed for space as it is. I don't think Eddie could cope with any more people about the place.'

'Don't worry. I can't think of a better way of ending our friendship than for us to move in with you,' said Jane. 'If Dad wasn't my father he'd probably have fallen out with me by now!'

'It must be difficult for him, having his home invaded.'

'I know, and I really feel for him,' said Jane, 'but it isn't easy for the children either, after what they've been used to.'

'And you're caught in the middle?'

'Exactly.'

It was a glorious autumn day, warm sunshine beaming from a hazy blue sky and bathing the green and pleasant parkland. The children had finished eating and were playing hide-and-seek nearby. The bright sunlight emphasised Jane's pallor and the dark shadows under her eyes.

'You look worn out, love,' remarked Marie with concern.

'I don't feel too good, as it happens,' she confessed. 'It must be a reaction to the trauma of Mick's leaving and the tension of living at Dad's, I suppose. But I've been feeling very tired lately, and generally out of sorts.'

'Everything that's happened is bound to have had an effect on your health.'

'Mmm. If I could find somewhere else to live, it would help,' Jane said dolefully.

'Have you been to see the council housing people lately?'

'I'm always pestering them.'

'And they can't help?'

'They're doing what they can. We'll get a place when they have one vacant, that's the situation. And I daren't go on too much about how the kids are suffering in case they let the Children's Department know and some overly conscientious social worker decides they'd be better off elsewhere – without me.'

'There is that.'

'I keep looking out for somewhere private, just to tide us over.'

'Too expensive and kids not welcome, I suppose?'

'That's right.'

'I've been keeping an eye out for you too,' said Marie.

'Thanks.'

'I thought I'd struck lucky the other day, actually.'

'Oh, really?'

'Yeah. I saw an advertisement in a newsagent's window for a furnished flat,' she explained. 'It would have been absolutely ideal for you . . . a flat in a widower's house. A professional man. It said a very low rent in exchange for light household duties.'

'Ooh!' said Jane. 'That would suit me down to the ground. Where?'

'Lang Road.'

'It's nice round there.'

'Mmm.'

'So what was the catch?'

'Mature woman, it said at the bottom of the card, retired professional lady preferred,' explained Marie gloomily. 'Which basically means he doesn't want kids about the place.'

'What a shame,' said Jane.

'I was disappointed too.'

'Still, there would have been a problem with my early-morning cleaning job without Dad on hand to listen for the kids.'

'You might not need to do that if the rent was low enough,' explained Marie. 'You could just have done your evening job. I'm sure your dad wouldn't mind babysitting in the evening. And I could always help out when Eddie isn't on late shift.'

'That's nice of you but it's all just hypothetical, as I don't meet the criteria.'

'True.'

They went on to talk about other things as they finished their lunch, eventually strolling over to the kiddies' playground.

'Thank goodness for parks and your back garden,' said Jane, watching her children enjoying themselves on the swings in the sunshine. 'I don't know what I'd have done without them since we lost the house. At least Davey and Pip can play out in the fresh air sometimes.'

'The houses in Lang Road have decent-sized back gardens,' remarked Marie wistfully.

'Do they?' said Jane, who hadn't been able to get that advertisement out of her mind either.

'Yes, I've noticed them when I've been out walking round that way.'

Jane pondered on this.

'You don't remember what number Lang Road it was, do you?'

'I do, as it happens,' said Marie. 'It was number twenty. It stuck in my mind because I was sure it would suit you until I saw the mature woman bit at the bottom.' She gave Jane a wicked grin. 'Why, are you gonna dust your hair with flour and keep the kids hidden in the wardrobe?'

'No, but I *am* going to go round there to see if I can talk my way into that flat somehow,' she said, laughing. 'I'll leave a bit early for work tonight and call in there on the offchance that he's in.'

'It did say mature woman,' Marie pointed out, fearing disappointment for her friend.

'People have been known to change their minds, you know,' said Jane. 'Anyway, it's worth a try. And I've nothing to lose but the time it'll take to go and see him.'

'Good for you,' said Marie heartily. 'I'm amazed at how quickly you've learned to stand up for yourself after being mollycoddled by Mick for so long.'

'I'm surprised too,' admitted Jane. 'But there's nothing quite like desperation to motivate you.'

Number twenty Lang Road was a traditional pebble-dashed detached house in quiet, residential surroundings. The middle-aged man who answered the door to Jane that evening seemed to blend with his background perfectly, being grey-haired and bespectacled, quietly spoken and dressed in a dark business suit.

She explained why she was there and he invited her in, which she thought was a promising start since she obviously didn't meet his requirements.

'The flat is still available then?' she said, standing in the hall by an old-fashioned, semi-circular table in dark mahogany which housed a telephone and a dusty pot plant.

'Yes, but . . .'

'You're looking for an older woman?'

Pale-skinned, with anxious but oddly penetrating eyes, he said, 'Well, yes . . . as it says in my advertisement.'

Deciding that timidity wasn't an option she could afford to consider, Jane went on, 'Won't you entertain the idea of anyone younger?'

'Not really.'

'Oh.' Since he had invited her in, knowing why she was here, his answer surprised her. 'Is there any particular reason for that?'

He seemed startled by her forthright manner but said, 'Yes. Someone of a similar age to myself would be more companionable.'

'Yes, of course.'

'Also, I want a tenant who'll stay for a while at least,' he explained. 'Not some youngster who'll just get settled in and then meet a fellow and leave to get married.'

'It isn't because you don't want children in the house then?'

His brows rose.

'No, not at all,' he said, as though the thought had never occurred to him.

'I'd like to be straight with you, Mr . . . ?'

'Ashton.'

'I'll be perfectly honest with you about my situation, Mr Ashton,' said Jane with a boldness that would have been beyond her before Mick's departure. 'My husband has left me and I have two children below school age. We're living with my father at the moment in his flat and things are difficult to say the least because it's very small. My father needs peace and the children need a garden

71

and space to move about in. I'm very sensible and mature in my outlook – and I really am desperate for somewhere to live.'

'Oh.' He seemed quite bewildered by this flow of information. She got the impression that he was a very nervous man.

'My children aren't angels by any means but they're quite well-behaved as kids go,' she went on. 'And it isn't as though they're babies who'd cry at night and keep you awake.'

He remained silent, looking at her, small grey eyes studying her through his spectacles. Considering her as a tenant, she hoped.

'I wonder if I might . . . er . . . if I could possibly see the flat?' she said, knowing she was chancing her arm outrageously.

'Yes, all right,' he said, which she thought was a hopeful sign.

She followed him upstairs to the flat which comprised a bedroom, living room, kitchen and bathroom. It was quite shabby with only the most basic furnishings but perfectly adequate for her present needs.

'It's quite self-contained,' he said as they stood in the living room, his attitude seeming to change, as though *she* was the one in the stronger position and *he* was trying to persuade her to take the flat. 'The only thing the tenant has to share with me is the hall.'

'Yes, I see.'

'You'll have noticed that there's only one bed in the bedroom but the settee in here opens up into a double bed.'

'That's fine.' She went to the window and looked out into the back garden which was secluded and lawned with a profusion of mature shrubs. 'Would the children be allowed to play out there?' she asked, turning to him, growing more confident with the way the interview was progressing.

'Yes.' He cleared his throat and she got the impression he had great difficulty in asserting himself. 'So long as they don't make too much noise and disturb the neighbours.'

'I'd make sure they didn't do that.'

'The washing line can be used by the tenant,' he told her.

'Good. These light household duties?' she said, almost as though she was interviewing him. 'What exactly do they consist of?'

Again she sensed a fearfulness about him which struck her as peculiar since he was the one in the position of power.

'Keeping the whole house clean, including my flat and the hall and stairs,' he explained. 'And preparing an evening meal for me during the week. I cook for myself at weekends and see to my own laundry.'

'Well, that sounds fair enough to me,' she heard herself say, almost as though the flat was already hers which she sensed, somehow, it was. She couldn't believe her luck in finding it. It seemed too easy because arrangements like this were practically non-existent. 'I'm surprised the flat hasn't already been snapped up?'

'It takes time to find someone suitable when you're letting a part of your house.'

'What happened to the previous tenant?' she asked casually.

He didn't reply; seemed uneasy. She wondered if she had pushed her luck too far and made him angry. But he just said, 'She went to live with her sister in the country. She was getting on a bit in years and found the housework too much.'

'I see.'

'I had the top floor made into a flat after my wife died, three years ago,' he seemed keen to explain. 'The house is too big for me on my own and I didn't want to move away.'

She nodded.

'I'm a partner in a firm of accountants in the City and I'm out all day which is why I need help in the house,' he said as though he needed to justify himself.

'I've only just got home this evening, as a matter of fact. Anyway, the housework is reflected in the rent which will just be a token amount and will include gas and electricity.'

Better and better, she thought, but said, 'Well, the arrangement would suit me perfectly. And the house would be kept spotless, I can promise you that.'

'In that case, you can move in as soon as you like.'

'Oh, that's wonderful.' Jane felt quite lightheaded with relief. 'I'll move in at the weekend, if that's all right with you?'

'That's fine.'

'Good,' she said, beaming.

Closing the front door behind her, the smile faded from Mr Ashton's lips because he had let the flat to the young woman very much against his better judgement. He really should have waited for a mature lady to apply.

It would be nice having her in the house, though. Her and the kiddies. He'd always regretted the fact that his marriage hadn't been blessed with children.

Going into his front living room, he stood at the window, unseen behind the net curtains, watching Mrs Parker swing down the front path, an attractive figure in jeans and a sweater. She turned at the gate and looked towards the house, smiling.

He frowned, chewing his lip. She wouldn't be so eager to move in if she knew why all the previous tenants had moved out, he thought. But this time it was going to be different, he promised himself.

Jane's kitchen at Lang Road had been a box room before the house was converted, and overlooked the back garden. Washing the dishes after lunch one Sunday a couple of weeks later, she took pleasure in looking out of the window to see Davey and Pip enjoying themselves in the fresh air. The garden was aflame with colour, the shrubs bright with plump red berries, the lawn covered with fallen leaves.

The children were 'helping' Mr Ashton, who was clearing the leaves from the lawn with a rake. He was raking them into a pile and they were gathering them up into a bucket and carrying them to the compost heap in the corner of the garden, spilling most of them on the way. She smiled and felt a surge of gratitude to him for his patience. He would obviously get on a whole lot faster without their assistance.

He'd been wonderful. So helpful to her and kind to the children. Her brow creased into a frown as a wave of nausea forced her to wonder how he would feel if he knew she was expecting a baby.

It was only the last few days she had faced up to the fact that she was pregnant. She'd put the sickness and exhaustion down to the stress of Mick's departure, which had left her too stunned to keep proper track of her periods. Even when she'd realised she had missed, it was easier to put it down to tension rather than confront the real problem. Because, from a purely practical viewpoint, another baby was a major disaster and Jane didn't know how she was going to manage. But for all that, she wanted it *so much*. It made her feel as though she hadn't lost Mick altogether, somehow, having his child growing inside her.

Had she realised her condition before she'd moved into the flat, she would have been honest with Mr Ashton. But at that time, the biggest problem in her life had been getting the children housed and the symptoms hadn't been identified. Now she was putting off telling her landlord in case he asked her to leave.

After all, having two entertaining children of a civilised age in your house was one thing; having a brand new baby with all the attendant noise and chaos was quite another. But the children were so happy here at Lang Road, she was loath to uproot them again. And there was no need to say anything to Mr Ashton for a while yet. She wasn't even four months down the road if her reckoning was correct and she had conceived on the night of Davey's birthday party.

She didn't intend telling anyone until it became embarrassing not to. Her father was going to be very upset. This would be yet another stick to beat Mick with. Leaving a wife with two children was bad enough; add pregnancy to the scenario and her normally even-tempered father would explode.

Thinking of her father recalled her to the present for they were going to visit him this afternoon for tea, calling in on Marie on the way. Jane finished the dishes and went down to the garden where she found Davey and Pip kneeling on the grass stroking the tummy of Tibs, Mr Ashton's marmalade cat, who was rolling around on his back with his paws in the air, purring.

'Time to come in and get ready, you two,' she said, the sunshine feeling pleasantly warm on her face.

'Do we have to come in?' asked Davey.

'Yes.'

'Why?' put in Pip.

''Cause we're going to see Granddad and you have to get ready,' Jane explained.

'Can we take Tibs with us?' asked Pip.

'No, darling.'

'Why?'

'He'd get lost,' put in Mr Ashton helpfully. Tall and thin, dressed in a baggy brown sweater and corduroy trousers, he was standing on the lawn, resting his rake on the ground.

Davey squinted up at him. 'Why?'

'Because he'd go off somewhere. You can't stop cats straying like you can dogs. And cats can't find their way home when they're in a strange place. They have to have time to get to know the area.'

'Oh. We'd better not take him then,' said Davey, convinced.

'Indoors, quick,' said Jane, clapping her hands and smiling. 'We're going to see Roy and Melanie on the way to Granddad's.'

That got them moving. They trotted to the back door and Jane removed their muddy shoes in the small lobby, whereupon they ran into the house, squealing with high spirits and trying to beat each other up the stairs to the flat.

'Thank you for being so patient with them, Mr Ashton,' she said from the back door. 'It's very kind of you.'

He walked towards her and leaned the rake against the wall of the house.

'It's a pleasure, my dear,' he said. 'I enjoy having them around. They're nice kiddies.'

She glowed. A compliment to her children was always more appreciated than one to herself.

'Thank you.'

'They seem to have settled in very well here,' he remarked, walking towards the back door.

'We all have,' she said, stepping into the kitchen so that he could get into the lobby. 'It's so much better for all of us, including my father.'

'Good.'

'How about you?' she enquired conversationally. 'Are you happy with us as tenants?'

He nodded.

'No complaints about the housework then?'

'None at all, my dear,' he said. 'It's all worked out very well.'

He took his gardening shoes off, left them in the lobby and put on his slippers. From upstairs came the thunder of running feet.

She raised her eyes.

'I hope that racket doesn't bother you too much?' she said, moving towards the door to the hall which stood open.

'Not at all.'

'That's good.' Jane was finding it difficult to get away because he seemed to want to chat. It wasn't the first time this had happened and she guessed he was very lonely.

'It's just youthful high spirits.'

'I'm glad you see it that way,' she said, inching nearer

to the doorway. 'Anyway, I must be going . . . I have to get the children looking presentable for visiting. Dad likes to see them on a Sunday.'

'He's a lucky man,' said Mr Ashton wistfully. 'To have grandchildren.'

'You don't have a family, then?'

'No. My wife and I would have liked children but they just didn't come along.'

'That's a shame.' She was beginning to feel *really* uncomfortable. He seemed so terribly sad and alone. Some sixth sense warned her not to be too sympathetic, though. There was something about him that gave her the creeps. 'I'll be off, then. See you . . .'

As she turned to go, he passed her on his way to his living room and brushed against her, lingering for a moment, stroking her bottom. Stunned, she moved away quickly, cheeks flaming.

'You keep your hands to yourself!' she said, but he was already walking away.

'Mr Ashton,' she called, feeling that she couldn't let the matter pass.

Turning, he said casually, 'What is it, my dear?'

'You heard what I said.'

'Did I do something to offend you?' he asked innocently.

'You know very well you did.'

'I'm sorry, did I nearly knock you over in my hurry to get past?' he said. 'There's something I don't want to miss on the radio.'

He was so convincing, she thought she must have imagined it.

'It's always a bit of a squash in this hallway,' he continued briskly. 'I do apologise.'

And before she could say another word, he disappeared into his living room and closed the door, leaving her feeling embarrassed for having overreacted.

Surely she must have misjudged his intentions? she told herself on the way upstairs as she replayed the incident in her mind. Mr Ashton was a perfect gentleman, he wouldn't have deliberately touched her up. It must have happened accidentally.

The celibate life is giving you delusions, Jane admonished herself, and hurried up to the flat to get the children washed and changed. But she felt uneasy just the same.

Finally she resolved to put it out of her mind. She had quite enough real problems to cope with, without imagining more.

Chapter Five

In common with people all over the world, Jane and Marie were deeply affected by the disaster in Wales when a slag heap slipped down a hillside, burying the local school and killing a hundred and sixteen children and twenty-eight adults.

'When you've kids of your own, it really brings something like that home to you, doesn't it?' said Marie to Jane one wet and windy morning in late-autumn soon after the tragedy, when the two women were having coffee and a chat in Jane's kitchen.

'Makes me want to weep every time I think about it,' she said, spooning instant coffee into mugs on the makeshift worktop.

'The one place you do expect your children to be safe is at school,' said Marie, sitting at the kitchen table.

Jane nodded in agreement.

'A major disaster like that makes your own problems seem small in comparison, doesn't it?'

'Compared to the people of Aberfan, we don't have any.'

'Well, actually,' began Jane hesitantly, turning to face her friend, 'I have something to tell you . . . something you might see as a problem for me.'

'Oh?'

'I'm pregnant.'

The howling wind and rain lashing against the kitchen window filled the silence as Marie digested this news.

'Well, I can't pretend it isn't a bit of a shock,' she said at last, in a low voice because the children were next-door in the living room and the kitchen door was open.

'It was to me too!'

'Since Mick's been away for four months, you must be quite far gone?'

'Yes, I am. I only admitted it to myself a couple of weeks ago, though,' said Jane, leaning against the sink unit waiting for the kettle to boil.

'That must be why you've been off colour lately?'

'And I was putting it down to stress.' Distractedly, she ran her fingers through hair that had grown out of its stylish bouffant and now hung heavy and uneven to her shoulders. 'I suppose I just didn't want to face up to the truth.'

'Too late to do anything about it now,' said Marie.

'I wouldn't anyway,' said Jane, shocked at the suggestion.

'All right. No need to jump down my throat,' said Marie. 'I was only thinking how difficult it's going to be for you in the circumstances.'

'Oh, it'll be that all right,' she said, quickly adding, 'can you keep it to yourself for the moment? I don't want my dad to know until he has to. He'll be worried to death.'

'I suppose you must be a bit miffed about it yourself.'

'I was when I first realised 'cause of the sheer worry of having another mouth to feed. And I daren't even think about how I'm gonna keep my job at the factory with a new baby to look after,' she confessed. 'But I'm thrilled to bits now that I'm used to the idea. Makes me feel as though Mick's still a part of my life.'

Marie was worried about her friend. She'd been through so much and looked permanently pale and exhausted. She had coped with the trauma of Mick's leaving better than anyone had expected, considering the fact that she and her husband had been like one person. The way Mick had protected her and made her so dependent on him, it was a wonder she hadn't fallen apart. But she'd kept her head and been strong for the children. Marie was full of admiration for her. A new baby, though. How would she stand up to the added problems that would bring?

'It won't be easy for you, though, Jane,' said Marie gravely.

'I know . . . but I'll manage.'

'I'll do what I can to help, of course.'

'Thanks, Marie.' Tears sprang to her eyes at the warmth of the other woman's friendship. 'I don't know what I'd have done without you this last few months.'

'I'm only too pleased to help,' she said. 'It's the least I can do since my brother isn't where he should be.' She paused, shaking her head. 'My God, he's got a lot to answer for! Just wait till I get my hands on him. I'll throttle him!'

Jane threw her a sharp look. 'There isn't much likelihood of your ever being able to do that, though, is there?'

'He'll be back.'

'You reckon?'

'Oh, yes.'

'What makes you so sure?'

'Being around the two of you since your very first date, I suppose,' said Marie thoughtfully. 'I've never seen a man so much in love with a woman as Mick has always been with you. I'd almost go so far as to say he was obsessed.'

'Which makes his going away even more of a blow to me.'

'Yes, I can understand that.' Marie pondered a moment. 'But that sort of feeling doesn't just disappear. He'll be back as soon as he's got things sorted. There's no way he'd stay away from you and the kids permanently.'

'You seem certain that I'd take him back?' Jane commented evenly.

'That's because the two of you are a natural pair,' said Marie. 'You belong together.'

'I know you and Mick have always been very close, Marie, and it's hard for you to see any wrong in him,' said Jane reasonably, 'but it was a rotten thing to do, running out on me.'

'You don't have to tell me that! As I've said, I could kill him for what he's done to you. But I still think that what you and he have between you is very special and worth hanging on to.'

'I always thought so, too, and that makes it even harder to bear.'

Jane turned away and made the coffee to hide the fact that she was struggling against tears as the pain of missing him cut deep, intensified by the new life growing inside her. The kitchen felt damp and smelled musty, the windows steamy and running with condensation. The poky little room had an ugly old gas cooker and kitchen fittings consisting of one bent and crooked formica top next to the sink. Thoughts of how different this was from the luxury kitchen Jane had grown used to inevitably led to memories of her life with Mick, adding to her wretchedness. Biting back the tears, she added milk to the coffee, determined not to break down and cry in front of Marie because she didn't want to upset her.

'Anyway, despite all the practical problems it will cause, I *really do* want this baby,' she said, putting two mugs of coffee on the table and sitting down opposite Marie.

'In that case, I'm pleased as well,' she said, reaching across the table and giving Jane's hand a friendly pat.

'I don't know how my landlord will feel about it, though,' said Jane with a wry grin. 'He seems happy enough having Davey and Pip in the house, but I'm not sure how he'll feel about having a new baby about the place.'

'Another baby will move you up the council waiting list, if he does give you notice, though,' Marie pointed out hopefully.

'That's true.' Jane sighed. 'But this place suits me for the moment because paying such a low rent means I can feed us without tearing my hair out. It will be a bit crowded when the baby comes, but it won't be too bad until it starts running around.'

'And you don't find Mr Ashton's housework too much?'

'It's no trouble at all. He's out all day so I do it in my

own time.' She paused. 'I told you he lets me use his washing machine, didn't I?'

'Yeah, you do that while he's out too, I suppose?'

Jane nodded.

'It's almost like having my own house during the week,' she said. 'And I try not to get in his way in the evenings and at weekends.' She paused thoughtfully. 'Though he often seems to want to chat to me. He's a lonely old boy... never seems to have any visitors.'

'He seems like a real gent, from the little I've seen of him,' said Marie who had met him when she and Eddie helped Jane to move in.

'I thought he was a groper the other day,' she said lightly. 'He brushed past me in the hall and I thought he'd touched me up.'

'He didn't, though, did he?' asked Marie, sounding concerned.

'No, 'course not. He touched me accidentally as he passed and I started imagining things.'

'So long as he didn't,' said Marie seriously. ''Cause you can't stay under the same roof as someone who's that way inclined, no matter how convenient it is.'

'He's harmless enough,' said Jane. 'I just hope he doesn't notice my waistline thickening, for the time being.'

'Make sure you wear baggy clothes until you're ready for people to know.'

'Don't worry, I will, not least to keep it from the parents. They're gonna do their nuts when they know there's another baby on the way,' said Jane. 'Except, perhaps, for your mum who never makes a fuss about anything.'

'A fully trained doormat,' said Marie.

'That isn't very kind.'

'It's true, though. I'm always telling her to be more assertive. But she's let Dad walk all over her for so long, she seems to have lost the will to do anything else now.'

'She's nice, though.'

'One of the best,' agreed Marie. 'She deserves more

from life than waiting for Dad to come home so she can wait on him hand and foot.'

'She seems happy enough doing it, though,' remarked Jane.

'Yeah, I suppose so.' Marie gave her a warm look. 'She's ever so pleased you still take the children to see them.'

'Why wouldn't I?' asked Jane. 'They're her grand-children.'

'She thought you might turn against her and Dad, because of what Mick's done?'

'That's the last thing I'd do,' Jane assured her. 'Mick's a grown man. They're not responsible for his actions.'

'No . . . but he *is* their son and what he does reflects on them,' she said. 'They feel really bad about it. I do too, come to that.'

'You've no need.'

'Well, you know how it is with family.'

'Yes, but in this case it isn't necessary.'

'My dad will have a field day when he hears about the baby,' said Marie. 'There's nothing he likes better than finding fault with Mick. There's always been friction between those two.'

'Mick's spent his whole life trying to impress your father.'

'The trouble is, they can't both be the centre of attention,' said Marie.

They fell into a comfortable silence, drinking their coffee.

'Of course, a new baby means you won't be able to get a daytime job when Davey and Pip go to school, doesn't it?'

'Not for quite a while.'

'I'm going to try to find some sort of employment once mine are off hand,' said Marie. 'But it isn't quite as easy as you might think, not if you want something to fit in with school hours.'

'Perhaps you could help with the dinners at the school?'

86

'Everyone has the same idea so there's a waiting list.'

Finishing her coffee, Marie got up and mooched idly over to the window. She cleared a patch of condensation with her fingers and looked down into the wet garden, the rain trickling through the trees and bushes, soaking the lawn and forming puddles on the concrete paths and patio.

'You've a nice set-up here,' Marie remarked. 'It isn't what you were used to with Mick but at least you've a garden for the kids to play in . . . and your own part of the house.'

'Yeah.'

'It'll be a pity if you do have to leave when the landlord finds out about the baby.'

'I think so too.'

Jane's loneliness was suddenly all-consuming. Oh, Mick, if only you'd had the courage to stay with us, she thought, we'd have worked things out together somehow.

One evening the following week, when Jane got in from work and her father had gone home, she went downstairs to the garden to get some washing off the line, having taken advantage of the dry, blowy day. When she came back inside with the clean washing in a plastic basket, Mr Ashton was in his kitchen.

'Everything all right?' he asked because she hardly ever came downstairs of an evening. She left his meal ready for him to heat up.

'Yes, everything's fine. I'm sorry to disturb you,' she said, looking flushed and windswept because it was cold and windy outside. 'I didn't get around to getting the washing in before I went to work. The children both have heavy colds and have been a bit fretful so I was busy keeping them occupied. Sorry to come down here so late.'

'No need to apologise, my dear,' he said amicably. 'I just wanted to make sure all was well when I heard you come down.'

'That's thoughtful of you.'

87

'Were you able to see what you were doing out there in the dark?'

'Just about, in the light from your kitchen window,' she said, shivering. 'Ooh . . . it's cold out there, though, and blowing a gale.'

'Yes.'

Something about the way his eyes lingered on her brought an earlier incident back to mind, sending a shiver up her spine.

'I'll be glad to get back upstairs by the fire,' she said uneasily, hurriedly moving towards the door to the hall.

He moved back to let her pass and as she did so he put his hand firmly on her bottom. *This time she definitely hadn't imagined it.* Slamming the washing basket down on the floor, she swung round and slapped his face.

He stood in the doorway with his hand to his cheek, looking wounded and bewildered.

'Whatever's the matter?' he asked, as though nothing had happened.

'You know perfectly well . . .'

'I don't.'

'So touching up a relative stranger is normal to you, is it?'

'I didn't deliberately . . .'

'Yes, you did,' she cut in. 'And not for the first time, either.'

'I really don't know what you're talking about.'

'Don't give me that. I suppose you thought that because I didn't make a fuss the first time, you could take liberties again,' said Jane, ignoring his denial. 'Well, the only reason you didn't get a kick in the groin before was because you made me think I'd imagined it. But I didn't imagine it *this* time.'

As she headed for the door, he closed it and stood in front of it, blocking her path. Oh God, she thought, sweating with fear and averting her eyes as he unzipped himself.

'Come on,' he said persuasively, moving towards her,

fully exposed. 'You need a man just as much as I need a woman.'

'Ugh, you're sick!' she gasped, pushing him away as he tried to grab her arms.

'I'm not going to hurt you,' he said, advancing towards her again. 'I only want us to make each other happy.'

'Get away from me!'

'We live in the same house . . . so where's the harm in it? No one would know and there would be no strings attached.'

'You touch me and you'll wish you never had,' she said vehemently.

'Don't be like that . . .'

'I mean it,' she gasped, shrinking back against the wall as he grabbed her arms roughly and moved his face nearer hers.

'All I want is a bit of comfort.' His grip tightened. 'Surely you won't deny me that.'

She looked him directly in the eyes, her face pinched with pain from the pressure on her arms. 'If you don't let me go this instant, I'll make sure everyone in Lang Road knows what you get up to. You won't dare put your head outside the door when I've finished. I'll have nothing to lose 'cause I won't ever be coming down this street again.'

'You wouldn't,' he said fiercely.

'I would,' said Jane.

He moved back and dressed himself, his attitude suddenly changing to one of grovelling remorse.

'I'm so sorry,' he said, standing by the door so she still couldn't pass.

'Not half as sorry as I am, mate,' said Jane, feeling sick and shaky. 'Now let me pass.'

'Please let me explain,' he said, and he was trembling too. 'I didn't mean to offend you.'

'Oh, for God's sake,' rasped Jane. 'What sort of woman do you think I am?'

'I didn't intend . . .'

'Let me through that door!'

'Please don't move out,' he begged. 'I give you my word that nothing like this will ever happen again.'

And to her utter astonishment, he dissolved into tears.

Nauseated, and wanting only to escape, she said, 'Of course I can't stay. Not now. I wouldn't feel safe here after this.'

'But I can't bear to live in an empty house,' he sobbed, tears running down his face.

'You should learn to behave yourself then, shouldn't you?' she said, guessing that this had happened before and that was the reason the flat had been so easily available. 'Now let me go upstairs to my children . . . please.'

'I promise you that nothing like this will ever happen again if you stay.'

'I'm *not* staying.'

'Please let me do something to make it up to you, to show you how sorry I am?'

'There's nothing you can do, Mr Ashton,' she said gravely. 'It happened and that's all there is to it.'

He stared at her a moment longer then opened the door and rushed up the hall to his living room, shutting the door after him, leaving Jane to go upstairs, sadder and wiser. She pitied him because he obviously had a problem, but she was also aware of the dangers of offering him sympathy.

Upstairs, she went into the bedroom and stood looking at the children fast asleep in the large double bed, the landing light shining into the room. She began to cry silently – for them. They were happy here and liked Mr Ashton. But once again they must have their lives disrupted. Jane would endure most things for her children, but to stay here would put them at risk too. Who could say what a weirdo like that might do? She wouldn't dare turn her back for a minute.

She bent down to kiss each of them and gently pulled the covers over them. 'I'm so sorry, loves,' she whispered to the silent room. 'I'm so sorry to give you more up-heaval. Someday I'll find a place for us to live that will be a proper home . . . somewhere we'll feel like a family again.'

Mr Ashton sat in his armchair by the electric fire, staring at the floor and sobbing into his handkerchief. So the nightmare had happened again. He had spoiled a perfectly good arrangement and lost pleasant company around the house, and all because of his lack of control.

Why, oh why, hadn't he stuck to his original plan and opted for someone safe and elderly who wouldn't bring him to shame like this? He couldn't bear to recall how many times the same thing had happened since he'd lost his wife. He never intended it to, being driven by uncontrollable urges when he was in a situation of close contact with a young female. After the last tenant, who had not been elderly at all as he'd led Mrs Parker to believe, he'd vowed to leave the flat empty.

But the desolation of an empty house had driven him to place another advertisement, making sure he stipulated someone of advanced years whom he'd hoped would become a companion of the platonic sort. He and his wife had been so self-sufficient, they'd had no need of friends, which had left him unable to communicate socially after she died. So outside of working hours he saw no one.

From time to time he'd toyed with the idea of placing an advertisement in the lonely hearts column of the newspaper but had never had the courage to go through with it. Letting the flat had been his only chance of company and now he'd ruined it yet again.

Thank God nothing like this had ever happened at the office! The shame of that really would be too much to bear. He felt different, somehow, at his place of business. There he was a figure of importance, set apart by his superior position from the young female members of staff with whom he came into contact during the course of the working day.

It was only here at home that his needs overpowered him so disgustingly. Maybe because it was here he felt

91

so crippled with loneliness and had time to listen to the promptings of his body.

Oh, well, he couldn't put things right with young Mrs Parker but there must be plenty of other women out there in need of accommodation.

Drying his tears, he went over to the writing bureau, sat down and began to compose another advertisement. This time it read: 'Only mature, retired professional woman need apply'.

'So what happened at Lang Road to make Jane move out in such a hurry?' asked Eddie the following evening when he got home from work to be told by his wife that Jane had moved back in with her father. 'I thought she liked it there?'

'The landlord tried it on,' Marie explained, checking a meat pie in the oven then digging a fork into the potatoes boiling in a saucepan on the gas stove.

'Oh, no!'

'Awful, innit?' she said, poking the bubbling greens with a fork. 'He got her cornered in his kitchen apparently.'

'Dirty devil,' said Eddie in disgust, going over to the sink to wash his hands. 'Did he actually try to rape her?'

'No, it didn't go that far. But he did expose himself.'

'The pervert!'

'That's what I thought.'

'So what happened then?' asked her husband.

'Jane said he backed off and was really ashamed of himself when she threatened to ruin his reputation. But obviously she can't stay there.'

'I should say not!'

Marie gave him an anxious look.

'Don't tell anyone about it, though, will you? Jane doesn't want her dad to find out in case he goes charging round to Lang Road to give Ashton a pasting, and gets himself hurt in the process. She reckons she's caused her father more than enough worry this last few months.'

'He must have wondered why she left Lang Road?' said Eddie, washing his hands at the sink.

'She told him the landlord found it too much having children in the house.'

'Poor Jane,' he said, taking a towel from a hook on the door and drying his hands. 'She's certainly having more than her fair share of trouble lately.'

'You can say that again.'

'Is she okay?'

'Well, she's not exactly on top of the world after having some old bloke disgrace himself to her, and she's disappointed at having to move out,' said Marie. 'But you know Jane, she isn't the sort to make a big fuss about anything. I think the thing that's upsetting her most is having to uproot the children again.'

'Poor little things.'

'I know,' she agreed sadly. 'It's really awful for them.'

'She shouldn't have to go through all this,' said Eddie hotly, because he thought Jane was a nice woman who'd deserved better than Mick Parker. 'That husband of hers should be with her, taking care of her and the children.'

Marie and Eddie agreed about most things but not about Mick.

'Yes, well, there's no point in going on about him,' she said sharply. 'He isn't here and that's all there is to it.'

'I know what I'd like to do to him if I could get my hands on him . . .'

'What right have you to judge him?' she blurted out, unable to help herself. While she felt entitled to criticise her brother, she couldn't bear anyone else to do so, not even Eddie. It was all to do with blood ties and primal instincts, she supposed.

'I've a right to give my opinion,' he said. 'Any man who does what Mick did needs a good smacking – which is what he'll get from me if I ever set eyes on him again.'

'You know Mick would never have gone if he'd been in his right mind.'

'Why can't you face facts, Marie?' he said. 'Your precious brother didn't have the guts to stay and see his problems through!'

93

'How dare you call him a coward?' she said emotionally. 'He must have had a very good reason for going off.'

'He *did* have a very good reason,' said Eddie sarcastically. 'He was skint and didn't have the bottle to stay and face up to it.'

'You've never liked him.'

'You're right, I haven't,' he was quick to agree. 'He's a bighead and a poseur, always has been. Even at school he'd do anything to be the centre of attention. These last few years he's been unbearable, always being Mr Big and trying to make everybody else feel inferior to him.' He gave a humourless laugh. 'The joke is, he had nothing to boast about, if the truth be known . . . it was all talk.'

'Now be fair, Eddie,' she said, cheeks flaming. 'Mick did have a very good business and worked hard for it.'

'He did well to get a business of his own, I'll admit that,' he said. 'But it couldn't have been all it was cracked up to be or he would have managed to stay afloat. Anyway, what kind of an idiot doesn't insure against fire?'

'That was careless, I admit, but it could have happened to anyone.'

'Not to the shrewd businessman he pretended to be,' Eddie disagreed. 'Mick was all top surface. The minute he got the smell of success, he had to have all the trappings of a rich man – when he didn't have the money to pay for them.'

'He was generous to us,' she reminded him. 'Always giving the kids expensive presents and offering to take us out.'

'Only to make himself look big and rub my nose in it.'

'That isn't fair!'

Eddie knew he had gone too far and was sorry. It was bad enough for Marie that her brother had left, and only natural she would defend him. Eddie had grown up on the Berrywood Estate and had known the Parkers all his life. He knew how close Marie and Mick had always been, which wasn't surprising with an egomaniac like Wilf Parker for a father.

Wilf didn't need money to get attention because his personality made him stand out wherever he went. That was something money couldn't buy for Mick so he'd tried to compete with things that could be bought. And it had all come to nothing. It was rather sad, really. But Eddie couldn't find it in his heart to feel too sorry for Mick when Jane was having such a tough time.

'You're right, love,' he said. 'I shouldn't have said that. I'm sorry.'

'I should think so, too.'

'Am I forgiven?'

'Yeah, 'course you are,' she said, because she wasn't the type to bear a grudge. Neither was Eddie and it was rare for bad feeling between them to linger.

Marie removed the meat pie from the oven and put it on the working top, then strained the vegetables in the colander at the sink.

'The kids are quiet,' he remarked.

'There's only one thing that keeps them as quiet as this.'

'Batman on the telly?'

'Exactly.'

They smiled in unison, the tension between them giving way to warmth and companionship. Eddie was so pleased to be home. It might be only a council house but they had made it comfortable and, more importantly, he could afford the rent. He had no cravings for the posh house and classy car that his brother-in-law had just lost. Eddie's old Ford suited him well enough. It might not be in the first flush of youth but it *was* paid for.

He was content with his lot. They could have done with a bit more money coming in, but they managed. So long as he had his wife and children, he was happy. He couldn't imagine any circumstances which could make him act as Mick had done.

'Make yourself useful and lay the table, will you, love?' said Marie in a friendly manner.

'Sure,' he agreed amicably. 'Then I'll go and see the nippers.'

'You probably won't get a word out of them until Batman's finished.'

'I'll watch it with them.'

'You'll get hooked on it if you're not careful,' she laughed.

Feeling utterly blessed, Eddie went to the cutlery drawer, thinking of Jane and what a rough time she was having lately. Just when things were beginning to improve for her, some dirty old sod had to go and spoil it. Men like that made him *so* angry.

Later that same evening, after the supper dishes had been washed, when the children were in bed and Eddie and Marie settled in front of the television, he got up suddenly and said he was going down to the pub for a quick one. But he didn't go anywhere near the pub. Instead he went to Lang Road to pay Mr Ashton a visit.

As a direct result of Eddie's visit, he decided to sell the house in Lang Road and move to an area where he wasn't known. To make a new start in a smaller place more suited to a widower like himself. A house without a flat to rent out.

The sooner he moved away from this house of shame the better he would like it. He would go to an estate agent's office and talk to them about putting the property on the market – just as soon as his bruises had faded sufficiently for him to feel comfortable about going out to face people.

Chapter Six

On the afternoon of NewYear's Eve, Jane, Marie and the children went out walking by the river. It was a cold and blustery day with intermittent bursts of watery sunshine gilding the bleak landscape and tinting the muddy waters of the Thames. The river was at high tide, a sharp wind ruffling the surface from time to time. Swathed in woolly hats and mufflers, they found the temperature invigorating and walked at a steady pace.

'Are you all right, Jane?' enquired Marie, because her sister-in-law was now more than six months pregnant. 'Don't be afraid to say when you've had enough.'

'I'm fine at the moment, thanks . . . let's just go as far as Kew Bridge, shall we?' Jane sensibly suggested for she was carrying a lot of extra weight. Her pregnancy was now generally known and she was booked into hospital for the birth. As predicted, her father's reaction to the news had been explosive, but he was now used to the idea of another grandchild.

'Okay,' agreed Marie. 'We'll probably all have had enough by then.'

Full of high spirits, the children had gone on ahead, running and skipping and stopping every so often to watch the swooping seagulls or the ducks riding the waves, staring with interest at the occasional boat passing by.

'It's good to see Davey and Pip enjoying the fresh air instead of being cooped up in Dad's flat,' remarked Jane. 'The bad weather is hellish with us all stuck indoors.'

'I can imagine.'

'They're of an age now to need some sort of organised

play, for part of the day at least,' remarked Jane. 'They used to really enjoy going to nursery school.'

'Mine are the same,' said Marie. 'Still, Davey and Mel will be starting proper school in September, won't they?'

'True.'

'A new stage in their lives.'

'Yes. Sad, really. I know that Davey's ready for it but I'm dreading that first day,' confessed Jane. 'It'll be like sending him out into the big wide world for the first time.'

'I know what you mean. We'll probably both weep into our coffee that morning!'

They laughed and walked in silence for a while, so at ease with each other that words weren't necessary.

'Today doesn't feel a bit like New Year's Eve,' remarked Jane after a while. 'It'll be very different for me this year.'

'We shall all miss your New Year's Eve party,' said Marie. 'It was almost as much a part of the festive season as Christmas pud.'

'It certainly was.'

Jane and Mick had entertained on New Year's Eve ever since they'd been married. It had begun with just a few friends in their bedsit in the early days and had grown along with their circumstances, progressing from bedsit to self-contained flat to a small semi for a while, before they'd moved into the big house in Maple Avenue where New Year's Eve had been a lavish occasion.

'You're welcome to come round to our place tonight,' invited Marie. 'We're not doing anything special but we'll stay up to see the New Year in with the telly and a few drinks. We can put Davey and Pip top and tail in bed with our kids . . . and I'll make up a bed for you on the sofa.'

'Thanks for asking me but I think I'll stay home and keep Dad company.' Jane was dreading tonight and wanted the painfully emotive time to pass with the minimum of fuss. 'He might be lonely if I go out. He's always spent the New Year with Mick and me up until now.'

'Well, you'll be more than welcome if you change your mind.'

'I'll keep it in mind . . . and thanks.'

They caught up with their offspring who were gathered around a scraggy black cat perched on a garden wall. This area on the Chiswick side of the river near Kew Bridge was threaded through with narrow lanes and alleys leading off the foreshore, which was fronted by quaint old cottages as well as some very imposing houses. The cat, obviously a stray, leaped off the wall and streaked along the towpath. The children followed, disappearing around a corner.

'I'll go on ahead and keep an eye on them,' said Marie. 'You follow in your own time. We can't have you running about in your condition.'

Jane didn't argue and plodded on at a slower pace as Marie dashed off. She was feeling much more bloated and uncomfortable with this pregnancy than she had with either of the others. She'd positively glowed with health then. This time she'd felt tired and unwell from the beginning, which wasn't too surprising considering the strain she'd been under.

'Mummy, Mummy, come quick . . . come and see!' shouted Pip excitedly, appearing from the turning and tearing towards Jane.

'Hey, you mustn't run off like that, Pip,' Jane warned her sternly. 'How many more times must I tell you?'

'But we only went round the corner . . . and guess what?'

'What?'

'We've found the pussy cat's house.' She tugged at her mother's hand excitedly. 'He lives there all by himself.'

Jane allowed herself to be led down a narrow paved street called Tug Lane. It was flanked to either side by a hotchpotch of old properties, some houses, some pretty little cottages, most of them well-kept with tiny front gardens. When they reached the end, past a pair of shabby semi-detached dwellings called Vine Cottages,

99

they turned the corner and made their way along an alleyway backing on to the rear of the houses in Tug Lane.

Following her daughter, Jane went through a creaking wooden gate with a rusty number one nailed to it and into the back garden of a derelict property she assumed was number one Vine Cottages. Here she found Marie and the children peering into the cottage through the dusty windows.

'Whatever do you think you're doing?' Jane asked in a hushed voice. 'We mustn't come in here, we'll get into trouble for trespassing.'

''Course we won't,' said Marie. 'No one lives here except the cat. The place is a ruin. Who's to know or care who's here?'

'Come and see the pussy, Mummy,' said Davey, turning from the window with a serious expression. 'He's ever so sweet, isn't he, Aunt Marie?'

'Yes, he is, love. The poor thing's half starved by the look of him,' she said, glancing round at Jane only briefly before turning and looking through the window. 'He's obviously a stray who uses this place as a shelter.' She pointed to a broken window. 'He gets in through there, I expect. Come on, Jane, come and have a look.'

She picked her way through the overgrown garden, almost tripping over a rusty old mangle hidden in the undergrowth, and eventually reached the cottage which, like its partner, was of rust-coloured and grey brick, patched with ivy. The other cottage was also empty and in a state of neglect.

'There's the cat, look,' said Marie, her face pressed to the window. 'He's sitting on the bottom stair washing himself.'

'Aah, isn't he lovely?' chimed Davey.

'Puss, puss,' called Pip. 'Come out and see us, puss.'

'It's a wonder he's got the strength to move about, he's so thin,' said Marie. 'He's very friendly, though, for a stray, letting the kids stroke him back there. Some stray cats are feral and won't let you get anywhere near them.'

'Why isn't anyone looking after him?' Davey wanted to know.

'I don't know, love. Perhaps his owners got fed up with having him around and took him out and dumped him,' said Marie. 'Some people can be very cruel.'

Jane cleared a patch on the grimy glass with her glove and peered in, finding herself overwhelmed by an unexpected surge of emotion. For some reason she found the scene inside unbearably moving: the emaciated cat sitting in a patch of sunlight, managing to survive, unloved but sheltered in this ancient cottage which, to Jane, exuded a feeling of warmth and friendliness.

'Cor, what a dump!' said Marie, breaking into her thoughts. 'Whoever put the "To Let" sign up must have a warped sense of humour.'

'I think it's lovely,' said Jane.

'You're joking?'

'No, I'm not.'

Clearing some more dust off the window, Jane peered in again. She was looking into an unfurnished room that had been empty for some time judging by the amount of dust and cobwebs. It was larger than she'd expected and had an old-fashioned iron fireplace set into one wall. She could see bow windows and a door in the opposite wall at the front of the house, which meant this room ran the full depth of the cottage. In the corner, a wooden staircase curved to the upper floor. Through an open door towards the back of the property Jane could see into a room she guessed was the kitchen, which looked quite roomy and jutted out, making the building L-shaped at the back.

'Just look at the pretty brickwork!' she enthused. 'And feel the character of the place.'

'All I can feel is dust in my throat,' was Marie's response. 'About the only thing this place is fit for is a cat to live in.'

'I think it has terrific potential,' declared Jane.

'Only as a shelter for down and outs!'

'Now you really *are* exaggerating,' said Jane lightly.

'It might have been all right donkey's years ago,' said Marie dismissively. 'But it certainly isn't fit for human habitation now.'

'Oh, I don't know so much about that,' said Jane with a lift to her voice her sister-in-law hadn't heard in a very long time.

Marie shot her a look, waiting for her to elaborate.

'With a bit of paint and polish, it would be ideal for me and the kids,' Jane said, standing back and looking at Marie.

'You can't be serious!' she exclaimed, frowning darkly.

'I am.'

'But you can't live in a place like this,' said Marie, looking towards the cottage. 'It's nothing short of a hovel.'

'It does need cleaning up, I admit,' said Jane with a wry grin.

'It needs a whole lot more than that!'

'I'd have to get rid of all that dark, old-fashioned wallpaper, of course, and paint the walls a light colour,' Jane murmured almost to herself. 'But at least it would be a place of our own and the children would have a garden to play in.'

'This isn't a garden, it's a wilderness!'

'Nothing a bit of effort with a good pair of garden shears won't cure.'

'A bulldozer would be more appropriate.'

'The garden isn't a bad size for London,' said Jane, ignoring her sarcasm.

'I can't believe I'm hearing this,' said Marie with blistering disapproval. 'You really must be desperate if you'd even consider living in a place like that.'

'But I am desperate, aren't I?' she said. 'We both know that.'

'But if you wait a bit longer, the council will get you a place,' Marie pointed out persuasively. 'Don't forget you'll be given more priority once the baby arrives.'

'I'd rather live here,' said Jane, eyes glued to the window again. 'And it would probably work out cheaper than a council place. The owner can't possibly charge much rent because of the state it's in.'

'Do yourself a favour and forget it, Jane, please.'

'I don't *want* to forget it. I have a real feeling about this cottage,' was her immediate response. 'Just imagine what that fireplace would look like if it was cleaned up.'

'It's hideous,' said Marie, who had no eye for anything old-fashioned.

'I think it's beautiful.'

'And I think we'd better go home before you lose your marbles altogether.'

'I've never felt more sane in my life.'

'You mustn't even contemplate living here,' said Marie. 'It's too awful.'

But Jane had moved away from the building and was staring up at the roof.

'Oh, look, there's an attic,' she said, flushed with pleasure. 'That could be used as another bedroom eventually. It already has two rooms upstairs, you can tell by the windows.'

The conversation came to a sudden halt when the cat sprang through the broken window and shot up a tree at the bottom of the garden, delighting the children who fought their way through the long grass and stood at the bottom of the tree.

'An apple tree,' cried Jane. 'Oh, how absolutely perfect!'

'Oh, God,' muttered Marie, despairing of her friend.

The cat was sitting on a branch, staring down at them, its coat dull and matted, greenish-yellow eyes resting on them soulfully.

'He's so thin,' said Jane. 'A mere shadow of a cat, really.'

'Yes,' agreed Marie, eager to be gone because Jane's interest in the cottage worried her. 'It's very sad. But be that as it may, it's time we were on our way. It's freezing, standing about here.' She shivered and stamped her feet as though to emphasise the point. 'Come on, kids, time to go.'

'But we can't leave Shadow up the tree,' said Davey,

103

christening the animal. 'He might not be able to get down.'

'He'll get down, don't you worry about him,' said Marie.

As though to confirm this, Shadow shot down the tree and darted back into the house.

'Can we come back and see him tomorrow?' asked Melanie.

'We could bring him some food,' suggested Roy hopefully.

'Stray cats will always find food,' said their mother briskly. 'I know he's thin but he'll survive. Cats are known for it.'

'Oh, please, Mum!'

'Now we've started something,' said Marie under her breath to Jane. 'They'll have us round here every day to feed the damned thing.'

'Can we come back and see him tomorrow, Mum?' requested Davey.

'I don't know about tomorrow, love, but we'll definitely come and see him again sometime soon,' Jane promised.

Walking back along the riverside, Marie said worriedly, 'You weren't serious about wanting to take that cottage on, were you?'

'I'm serious about loving it,' said Jane. 'And I know the children and I could be happy there.'

'How can you know a thing like that?' asked Marie, baffled.

'It's just a feeling I have, really. Nothing I can actually put my finger on,' said Jane. 'All I can say is, the place felt right for us and I'm certain I could make it into a real home, given a little time. I want to give the children back the sense of security they lost when Mick went. Living in someone else's place just isn't the same.'

'I can understand your feeling like that but it wouldn't be wise to take on anything so dilapidated, especially not in your condition,' cautioned Marie. 'Think of all the hard work getting it clean enough to live in. I dread to think what sort of a state the plumbing is in too. And you know what these old places are like for damp . . .'

Her negative attitude was beginning to have an effect on Jane. It wasn't easy for a deserted wife to stay confident about striking out on her own and doing something different, especially when she was hard up and pregnant.

'You're probably right,' she agreed with a sigh, surprised by the depth of her own disappointment. 'It's a nice idea but not a practical one. Not when you really think about it.'

In the early hours of the next morning, Jane lay awake listening to the children's gentle breathing in the camp beds beside her. The sleeping arrangements had altered as soon as her father knew she was pregnant. He'd insisted that she have his bedroom until after the baby was born while he managed on the bed settee in the living room. She felt guilty about depriving him of his bed but he was adamant.

Looking back on the last few hours, she decided that this had been the strangest and saddest New Year's Eve she had ever experienced and she was thoroughly glad to see the back of it. The sensible thing would have been to ignore the ritual altogether. But she had felt it was something she had to face up to, so she and her father had gone through the motions with the celebrations on the television.

'Auld Lang Syne' always moved her to tears. Mick used to tease her about it. Tonight her father had hugged her and he'd been crying too because it had made him think of all the New Years he'd seen in with his wife. They'd drunk a toast to Jane's mother and Jane had secretly sent her thoughts and wishes to her husband, wherever he was. Soon after that they had gone to bed, each wanting to be alone with their own private sorrow.

Quite a contrast to New Year celebrations of the past when she and Mick had fallen into bed tipsy in the small hours and made love. Closing her eyes tightly, she conjured up a vivid image of his face which made her cry. She wondered if he'd thought of her on this New Year's Eve, their first apart since they'd been teenagers.

Mulling things over, Jane thought that she was probably coping with life as well as anyone in her position could be expected to. But missing Mick never seemed to get any easier. The feeling clung to her like a lasting illness, dragging her down and shadowing her life.

Recalled to the present by her demanding bladder, which sent her to the bathroom umpteen times during the night at this stage of her pregnancy, she got out of bed and felt her way across the bedroom in the dark to avoid disturbing the children by switching on the light. As she crossed the hall, she noticed from the clock on the wall that it was past three o'clock, which meant she would be dead on her feet all day tomorrow.

Back in bed, her spirits rose unexpectedly at the thought that it was a new day and the first morning of the New Year. A time for hope and resolution. All right, so she was deserted, pregnant and poverty-stricken. But she was also young and healthy with two beautiful children and a new life growing inside her.

Mick had torn their family apart and broken their hearts. It was up to her, as the children's mother, to give them security and a sense of family without their father. She must find the courage to follow her instinct which told her that she could best do this for them at number one Vine Cottages, Tug Lane. Despite all the difficulties that Marie had so sensibly pointed out, Jane was convinced that that cottage was right for her and her children.

Being so taken with the place, she had made a mental note of the letting agents in Chiswick High Road. Now she would pay them a visit to find out if it was possible for her to rent it.

Once that decision was made, she felt happier and more positive than she had in a very long time. It was almost as though she was about to embark upon a new life . . .

Jane's faith in her own judgement was tested to the limits over the next few days because she met with strong opposition from all sides about the cottage. Even her normally peaceable father was fierce in his objections to it, threatening to go to the council and demand they house her to prevent her from moving into such a hell-hole. Her proposed move drew a similar response from Mick's parents and from Marie and Eddie.

But, nonetheless, a week or so later, she was in possession of the key, having persuaded her father to lend her the required month's rent in advance which she would pay back in instalments. He'd also agreed to come round and babysit in the evenings while she was at work at the factory, and insisted she have the bed settee and the camp beds and various other bits and pieces of furniture that weren't essential to him.

Although extremely doubtful about the project, Marie did what she could to help. Rita Parker suddenly decided to have new curtains in her living room and insisted on adapting her old ones for Jane to use until she could afford better. She also agreed to look after all the children so that Jane and Marie could clean the cottage. Even Wilf Parker made a contribution in the form of a paraffin heater he used to heat his van, saying he had been going to replace it soon anyway.

'You've all been wonderful,' Jane said to Marie as they worked together to make the cottage habitable. 'I'm sure I don't deserve it.'

'You're right, you don't,' agreed Marie playfully. 'Giving us all forty fits by moving into a place that ought to be demolished, not lived in. But since you're determined, someone's got to give you a hand.'

'It's really good of you to come and help me clean it up.'

'You can count it as a mark of true friendship,' said Marie, affectionately teasing her. 'I don't like cleaning at the best of times. But you can't move in as it is, and you can't do it all on your own . . . not in your condition.'

Jane was genuinely touched by her friend's help and knew Marie's blunt comments were her way of coping with the emotional moment.

Standing back for a moment from the ancient gas cooker she was cleaning, Jane cast her eye over the kitchen walls which were covered in heavily patterned floral wallpaper which had browned with age and was dominated by enormous, once-yellow sunflowers, now a mucky beige shade, their green leaves khaki and resembling food stains.

'Dreadful, isn't it?' said Marie, who was washing the kitchen door.

'Hideous,' agreed Jane. 'I can't wait to get the walls stripped.'

'Well, you're going to have to wait for a while, aren't you?' Marie reminded her with a warning look.

'Don't worry, I haven't forgotten,' said Jane, because she had promised her worried relatives that the actual painting and decorating would have to wait until after the baby was born.

'That wallpaper will take some living with, though,' said Marie.

'The ruddy stuff is all over the place like measles,' said Jane. 'I think the owner must have had a thing about sunflowers.'

'I think they must have too,' laughed Marie. 'I quite like them myself in the garden but not all over the walls.'

'The whole place will be so much lighter when the wallpaper has gone,' said Jane thoughtfully. 'Don't you agree?'

Her friend nodded, wringing out her cleaning cloth in a bowl and looking around.

'What sort of colours do you fancy?' she asked casually.

'Sunshine yellow in here, definitely,' said Jane, glancing around the kitchen which was much roomier than it looked from the outside.

'What about the other rooms?'

'Well . . . maybe a warm peach colour in the living

108

room. The children can choose what colours they want in their bedroom.'

'Sounds good.'

'It will be when it's all finished,' she said, 'but it will have to be done very gradually because of the expense.'

'Mmm.'

'I shall haunt jumble sales and junk stalls in the market to get a few bits of furniture and nick-nacks to make it more homely.'

'It's the only way.'

'I'm going to try to get a cleaning job where I can take the kids with me,' said Jane, 'to add to my earnings from the factory.'

'You might get something in one of those big riverside houses.'

'That's what I'm hoping.'

'You'll have to have some time off for the baby, though, won't you?'

'Of course, and it's worrying me to death because I can't afford not to be earning for long. I'll just have to wait and see how it works out.'

They continued working for a while longer, then ate a companionable lunch of cheese sandwiches and coffee from a flask, the paraffin heater taking the chill off the house. They sat on the stairs feeding titbits to Shadow who had been adopted as a family pet and was already showing the benefit of regular meals.

When they left that afternoon, Jane felt as though they had really made progress.

'Another few days and we'll have done enough for me to be able to move in,' she said as they sat on the bus back to the Berrywood Estate, to collect the children from her mother-in-law's.

'Then for the difficult part,' laughed Marie.

'How do you mean?'

'Actually living there.'

'Oh, Marie . . .'

'Only teasing,' she said. 'I think you're crazy but I admire your guts.'

Jane was most uncomfortable in bed that night. She was churning with excitement about moving into the cottage but, as well as that, her tummy felt odd and unsettled. Adding to her discomfort, too, was the fact that she couldn't lie on her side because of her enlarged proportions; she was also being driven to the bathroom every half hour because of the effects of pregnancy.

Fortunately the children were fast asleep. Rita had taken them to the park and worn them out. But sleep still eluded Jane. She felt achy and sick and had a dragging pain in her stomach and back which she'd had quite often lately. She hoped she wasn't going down with anything. She didn't have time to be ill – not with the cottage to be finished.

Her eyes were itchy and sore with tiredness but she just couldn't go off to sleep. She propped the pillows up behind her to see if that would help. It didn't. Eventually nature took its course and she drifted into a fitful sleep.

When she came to with a start she thought she'd been asleep for ages, but a glance at the luminous hands on the alarm clock told her that only an hour had passed. Through the muddled mists of drowsiness she realised she was feeling really ill now. The stomach ache was worse. It couldn't be the baby – not yet. She wasn't even seven months.

Realising that she must yield to nature yet again, she heaved herself out of bed and made her way cautiously to the bathroom in the dark so as not to disturb anyone, switching on the light only when she got inside.

Emerging a few moments later, she was shaking all over and deathly white. She staggered into the living room and turned on the light. Her father stirred on the put-u-up.

'What's going on?' he muttered.

'Dad, can you go to the phone box and call an ambulance, please?' she said, keeping her voice down and trying not to show how frightened she was.

'Ambulance?' he said, leaping out of bed. 'Why, what's the matter?'

'I'm bleeding . . . quite heavily,' Jane explained through dry lips. 'I need to get to hospital – urgently.'

Chapter Seven

The new admission in the bed next to Jane's in the gynaecological ward was extremely chatty, which was irritating because all Jane wanted was to be left alone to recover from the strain of putting on a cheerful front for the visitors who had just left. She felt utterly drained, as though she'd lost every vestige of energy as well as her baby, and the last thing she wanted was a conversation with someone she didn't know.

'You have two lovely children,' said the woman of whom Jane knew nothing except that her name was Margaret.

'Thank you. I think they're pretty special,' she said, warming at the mention of her children who had visited her this evening along with her father, Marie and Rita.

'At least you already *have* children,' remarked Margaret.

'Well, yes,' said Jane, not sure what she was getting at.

'I suppose that must help . . .'

'Help?'

'Make you feel less bad about losing one,' she explained.

'It doesn't work like that,' snapped Jane.

'Sorry . . . I didn't mean to be rude.'

'It doesn't matter,' she said wearily.

Jane lay back and closed her eyes, hoping her neighbour would take the hint and leave her alone with her thoughts. The staff here were very kind and understanding. They said she was bound to feel low. Losing a baby was a very traumatic thing. And she'd had a full anaesthetic for the routine post-miscarriage D and C operation, which could also have a depressing effect.

She had blamed herself for the miscarriage, thinking she had overdone it when working at the cottage. But that wasn't the reason apparently. The doctor had said she would have miscarried anyway. They had discovered that the baby hadn't been progressing as it should.

It was as though she had been plunged back into hell after recovering slightly from Mick's departure. Two days ago she'd been looking forward to the future in the cottage with Davey and Pip and their new brother or sister. Now there was no new baby, only emptiness and pain. It had been a boy, apparently. Another little boy. Oh, how she would have loved him!

She tried to find comfort in the thought that it was all for the best because the pregnancy had never been right, had not felt right from the beginning. But it didn't help.

Hot tears swelled beneath her lids and meandered down her cheeks. There was nothing she could do to stop them. She turned over on to her side away from Margaret and cried quietly, hiding her face in the pillow. The other women in the ward diplomatically excluded her from their chatter now. Eventually she dozed off from sheer exhaustion and was woken by the nurse bringing round the cocoa.

'Feeling better?' asked the loquacious Margaret when Jane sat up to drink her cocoa.

'A little,' she said drowsily.

'I'm sorry to have upset you earlier,' she said with genuine concern. 'That was the last thing I intended. I don't think before I speak, that's my trouble.'

'You didn't upset me.'

'Oh, I thought I'd made you cry?'

'That wasn't your fault,' said Jane, eager to reassure her because she sounded so worried. 'It's probably the after effects of the anaesthetic making me so weepy.'

'It was insensitive of me, though.'

'Don't worry about it.'

'I really envy you,' said Margaret, cradling her cocoa mug in her hands.

'Me?' said Jane, who at the moment couldn't feel less like a figure of envy.

'Yes. I suppose that was what made me say such a silly thing earlier . . . about your feeling less bad about your miscarriage because you already have children. I'm so desperate for a baby, I tend to see everything from my own point of view.'

'You don't have any children, then?'

'No. We've been trying for a family for ten years without success.'

'What a shame.'

'Yes. That's why I'm in here, actually, for some adjustments that might help. They can't guarantee anything, of course, but even if it increases my chances only fractionally, it's worth doing.'

'If it means that much to you . . . well, yes,' agreed Jane.

'Time's getting on for me,' the other woman continued. 'If it doesn't soon happen, it will be too late.'

Jane kept a diplomatic silence.

'It's a terrible feeling when you can't have a child,' Margaret went on. 'It takes over your whole life.'

Turning to look at her properly, Jane thought she was probably in her late-thirties, a rounded woman with soft golden-brown eyes and a look of kindness about her. Jane felt bad about having been so sharp with her earlier.

'I'm sure it must be awful,' she said in a much more sympathetic manner. 'But there's still time left for you.'

'It's running out fast, though.'

'Perhaps this operation will do the trick?' said Jane, wanting to reassure her, her own sorrow seeming suddenly less all-consuming.

'Oh, if only that were true . . . I'd be the happiest woman alive!'

'You wouldn't be in here if they didn't think there was a very good chance, would you?' Jane pointed out. 'They wouldn't waste their time. Busy people, doctors.'

'Yes, there is that.'

They chatted around the subject for a long time with Jane making a real effort to boost Margaret's confidence. When the conversation turned to Davey and Pip, she felt truly blessed.

'I feel a lot better for having a chat,' said Margaret as they settled down for the night.

'Me too,' said Jane. 'In fact, talking to someone has really helped.'

'Good.'

She fell asleep thinking about Davey and Pip and longing to be back with them. The loss of her third child was a bitter disappointment but the others were alive and needed her. How lucky she was!

She was reunited with her children a few days later when Marie and Eddie came to collect her from the hospital in Eddie's car, and brought them along.

'It's ever so good of you to bring me home,' said Jane, after hugs and kisses had been exchanged and she had settled into the back of the car with the children. 'I hope you didn't have to take time off from work 'specially, though, Eddie?'

'I'm on late shift today so it worked out very well.'

'Oh, good.'

'We've left Mel and Roy with Mum,' explained Marie. 'I thought four kids might be a bit too much for someone just out of hospital.'

Jane was grateful to them for that because she did feel rather frail. She'd been told to take it easy for a few days, which was virtually impossible with two young children to look after. Now that she was out of hospital, she found herself worrying about all the work left to do on the cottage before they could move in. She certainly didn't feel up to tackling it at the moment.

They were all so busy chattering, Eddie missed the turning to the Berrywood Estate.

'You've passed the turning to Dad's place, Eddie,' Jane told him.

Everyone was very quiet suddenly.

'We're going to . . .' began Pip, but was silenced by Davey who told her to 'Shush'.

'We've got a . . .'

'Shut up!' admonished her brother.

'What's going on?' asked Jane.

'Nothing,' said Davey, giggling.

He was joined by his sister and they rocked and squealed with laughter.

'See how happy they are to have their mother back,' said Marie with a smile.

Jane smiled too, from the sheer joy of being with them.

'Have you got to go somewhere else before taking me home?' she asked when Eddie didn't turn back towards the Berrywood Estate.

'Something like that,' replied Marie.

They seemed to be heading towards the river, Jane noticed. When Eddie drew up in the street near the cottage where he usually parked the car because Tug Lane was too narrow, Jane was really concerned.

'Eddie, I'm staying at Dad's place until I've time to get the cottage ready to live in,' she reminded him. 'I should have mentioned it before we set off but I thought you already knew? Now you've come all this way for nothing.'

The children were convulsed and Jane could see from Marie's quivering shoulders that she was laughing too. What *was* the matter with everyone?

'No, I haven't,' said Eddie, and he had a smile in his voice too. 'Have you forgotten that moggy of yours? He needs feeding.'

'Oh, of course,' she said, because he'd promised to go to the cottage every day to feed Shadow while she was in hospital, having got the key from her father.

'Are you coming in to say hello to the cat?' he asked lightly.

'I don't think I can face the mess in there until I'm feeling a bit stronger.'

'Oh . . . all right,' he said, sounding disappointed for some reason. 'The kids will come in with me, won't you?'

There was an affirmative cry.

'Come in for a minute, Mummy,' said Davey. 'Just to see how much fatter Shadow is getting now that we're feeding him properly.'

'Please, Mummy?' added Pip.

'You might as well,' said Marie, getting out of the car.

'Okay, you've twisted my arm,' said Jane.

'Don't worry about the mess,' advised Marie as they walked around the corner to the front entrance of the cottage. 'We'll get cracking on it together once you're back on form.'

Eddie opened the front door and hurried inside, followed speedily by Marie and Pip and Davey, everybody rushing ahead of Jane which struck her as rather odd. The reason soon became obvious, however, as she stood transfixed in the doorway which led directly into the living room.

Gone was the ugly old wallpaper. The walls were now plain and a delicate shade of peach, which emphasised the wooden beams. The floorboards had been scrubbed, the murky green paintwork was now pure white, and there was a log fire glowing in the gleaming fireplace.

'Well?' said Marie to her stunned friend. 'Do you like it?'

'Like it? I *love* it . . . but who . . . how?' She shook her head, her heart so full she could hardly speak. 'I just can't believe it.'

'Marie organised it,' said Eddie. 'She's been behind us with a whip.'

'Eddie and me and your dad did the work between us,' she explained, looking very pleased with herself. 'We've spent every spare second here. My mum's been looking after all the children so we could get on with it and have it finished in time for your homecoming.'

'Oh, Marie . . . I just don't know what to say.' Jane looked from one to the other. 'But thank you *so very much*.'

'We were planning to do it while you were in hospital having the baby,' she explained. 'So we had to change our plans a bit lively.'

Jane grinned at her.

'So that's why you were so interested in what colour scheme I fancied?'

Marie grinned.

'The kids will show you what they chose for their bedroom,' she said. 'I had to take a chance on yours. I was afraid you'd suspect something if I asked any more questions.'

'*You've done upstairs too?*' Jane cried in astonishment.

'That's right.'

'And the kitchen,' put in Davey. 'It's yellow like you wanted.'

'The curtains aren't a very good fit,' said Marie, glancing towards the shiny clean windows where a pair of Rita's old curtains were drawn back. 'But they'll do for the moment to keep you private when you've got the lights on.'

'It's all absolutely perfect,' said Jane, recognising some bits and pieces of furniture dotted about. Her father's put-u-up and his kitchen table, three odd chairs from different sources among the family. Incongruous, but adding a cosy touch by the fire, was a red and white striped deck chair she'd seen in Marie's garden in the summer.

'It's all a bit basic but I think the place is just about habitable.'

'Oh, thank you all so much! I'm so lucky to have such lovely people around me,' said Jane, hugging them all in turn.

'Isn't it great here, Mum?' said Davey.

'Yeah,' said Pip.

'It's wonderful,' she said. 'I'm so very glad to be home.'

And this place really did feel like home. Never mind the bare floorboards and lack of creature comforts; number one Vine Cottages was more of a home than the house in Maple Avenue ever had been.

The full flow of her emotions would be suppressed no longer and Jane sobbed with joy and love and gratitude for the kindness of these dear people.

'Hey, come on, that's enough o' that,' reproached Marie, her own eyes also shining with tears. 'You're getting me at it now.'

But she was smiling. Every minute of the hard work had been worthwhile just to see the look of pleasure on Jane's face. Marie hoped this was the beginning of better times for her. If anyone deserved a break, it was Jane.

Chapter Eight

'My throat hurts, Mummy,' wailed Pip. 'And I think I'm going to be sick.'

'There, there, darling,' soothed Jane, a bowl poised ready before her ailing daughter. 'Mummy's here . . .'

'My head aches,' moaned Davey, his cheeks unhealthily suffused. 'And I want to be sick, too.'

'It'll be your high temperature making you feel sick,' muttered Jane almost to herself as she kneeled between the two camp beds which she'd moved downstairs by the fire when the children fell ill a few days ago. The doctor had been and informed her that they had the latest 'flu virus, and she was to treat them with junior Disprin and plenty of fluids.

At this moment, however, simultaneous vomiting was keeping her busy.

'You should feel a bit better now, for a while at least,' she said when they had finished and she was settling them back against their pillows, both looking very washed out.

When she had comforted them, supplied them with a drink, cleared up with disinfectant, fed the cat and let him out, she took a Beecham's Powder to relieve her own raging 'flu symptoms which had begun to trouble her that morning and grown steadily worse throughout the day. Having both children poorly at the same time was difficult enough, without feeling like death herself.

It was late-afternoon on this cold February day and the light was already fading. Going back into the living room from the kitchen, she stirred some life into the fire with the poker, put the light on and read the children a story, hoping to lull them off to sleep. They'd been too ill to do much of that this last few days.

'I want to go to Granddad's or Aunt Marie's to watch the telly,' wailed Pip.

'We can't go today, love,' said Jane patiently.

'Why not?' she asked, pouting.

'Because you and Davey aren't well enough to go out,' she explained gently. 'Anyway, Melanie and Roy aren't well either so Aunt Marie doesn't want visitors.'

'I want to live at Granddad's,' said Pip, her condition making her irritable. "Cause there isn't a telly in this house and we can't see Batman.'

Jane's eyes smarted with tears and she was forced to question her judgement in bringing her children here to live. After that wonderful homecoming from hospital six weeks ago, when she'd been so full of optimism, life had been difficult in the extreme. The weather had been bitter, the children had picked up one bug after another, which had made them rundown and tetchy, the pipes kept freezing up and the property had been colder and damper than she could possibly have imagined before moving in.

Having secured a few hours' cleaning in the mornings for a professional woman who lived in a big house on the riverside, was out at business all day and didn't mind Jane taking the children along with her, she seemed to be continually letting her employer down because the children were sick. She was afraid the woman would lose patience and give her notice.

'How about another story or a game of I-spy?' she suggested, bone weary for she'd been up with the children this last two nights, her whole body aching as the virus took hold.

'I-spy,' said Pip.

'A story,' said Davey.

'We'll have a game of I-spy first, then I'll read you a story.'

'I want to see Shadow,' wailed Pip, who wasn't normally this petulant.

'He's gone off somewhere, darling,' said Jane, staying patient because of her daughter's condition but close to breaking point from her demands. 'He'll be back when he's ready.'

'Can he sleep on my bed tonight?' asked the little girl.

'I want him to sleep on mine,' said Davey.

'He sleeps in the kitchen, you both know that,' said Jane, moving on quickly. 'Now . . . I spy with my little eye, something beginning with . . .'

Within a few minutes, both children had fallen asleep. She went out into the kitchen and let the cat in because he was wailing demandingly on the window sill, no longer the meagre moggy they'd taken in out of pity but a healthy cat they all adored with a fine glossy coat and bright eyes. Jane was planning to have a cat-flap fitted into the kitchen door as soon as she could afford it, so that he could come and go as he pleased.

Hot and shivering at the same time, she tidied the kitchen, which seemed to be in a permanent state of chaos with illness in the house, lit the paraffin heater to boost the heat from the coal fire and went out to the garden to fill the coal scuttle from the ramshackle coal shed before the temperature dropped with the onset of evening. Then she made up the fire, changed the water in the children's hot water bottles and started on the backlog of ironing. She wasn't planning on going back to work at the factory until the children were better because she didn't think it would be fair to them or her father.

With all the chores done, she made herself a mug of Oxo and sat in the deck chair by the fire next to her two sleeping children, the effects of the medication beginning to ease her aches and pains. The cat settled down in his usual position at her feet by the fire and purred loudly. Sipping her hot Oxo, she experienced a moment of utter joy and tranquillity as the cosiness washed over her.

She knew in that moment that she had not made an error of judgement in coming to the cottage. How could that be so when the place had such a sense of welcome about it? For all its disadvantages, Jane didn't want to live anywhere else. And neither would her children by the time she had finished.

The winter seemed endless. Jane didn't know which was worse, the bitter frosts of February or the high winds of March which rattled the doors and windows, sent whistling draughts right through the house, and drove the rain against the window with such force it seemed as though the glass would break.

Winter hardships strengthened her, though, and her morale was high once they'd all recovered from 'flu. She began to feel as though she was actually living her life without Mick, instead of just existing from day to day. No longer having her father under the same roof, she was forced to stand on her own two feet and was bringing her children up in her own way and making a life for them. As lonely and difficult as it was at times, *it was a life*.

The lack of money made homemaking something of a challenge. But much to her surprise, Jane enjoyed it more than ever before. Cooking became a new experience and she found fulfilment in concocting nourishing meals on a shoe-string, searching for the cheapest cuts of meat and making them go further by using plenty of vegetables. No longer able to buy cakes, she enjoyed making her own. In fact, baking cakes and pastries in the cottage kitchen became one of her greatest pleasures. She was very creative, adapting basic recipes to make them more interesting. The children loved baking days and would squabble over who would lick the spoon and bowl when she'd finished.

To fill the gap left by television in the evenings after the children were in bed, Jane joined the library and discovered the joy of losing herself in a book. She enjoyed novels in particular and found herself becoming more informed about all sorts of things, her interests widening in the process. The transistor radio that had been a present from Mick, and was one of the few personal items she'd been allowed to keep, sat on the kitchen window sill, keeping her entertained and up to date with the latest news and views.

Some day she would get a television set and all the other home comforts her little family had been used to – when she had found a way of earning some decent money without disrupting her children's lives. She still couldn't bear the idea of farming them out while she went to work all day. Not while they needed her so much.

Having to think for herself, Jane found that her opinions were changing – or, more accurately, she was forming opinions of her own rather than sharing Mick's. She was becoming more assertive than she used to be, too. You had to be when you didn't have a man to lean on.

This was something that was happening almost subconsciously and Jane constantly surprised herself. Never more so than one Saturday evening in late-March when Wilf Parker called at the cottage with some fruit and vegetables for her, something he'd been doing regularly since she'd moved into the cottage, prompted, she guessed, by his wife.

'Are you sure you won't take any money for this stuff?' she asked as he put a small wooden crate down on the kitchen table. He never allowed her to pay him anything. 'I mean, you do have a living to earn. I'm sure you can't afford to give your stock away.'

'In the normal run, of course I can't, but it's different when it comes to you,' he said, grinning broadly to show nicotine-stained teeth.

'It's very kind of you.'

'Take it as my contribution to my grandchildren's welfare.'

'Thanks again.'

'It's the least I can do for you, since that no-good son o' mine's legged it to Gawd knows where.'

'Would you like a cup of tea?' asked Jane, stifling her irritation at his criticism of his son.

'I'll have a quick one if you're making some, ta, love,'

said Wilf, removing his sheepskin coat and putting it over the chair.

Jane filled the kettle and put it on the gas stove to boil. He stood in the kitchen doorway watching her, wearing a light brown, heavy cotton coat-style overall with a multicoloured scarf knotted at his neck gypsy-style. He looked windblown, his cheeks pink and blotchy from being outside.

'Have you just finished your round?' asked Jane to make conversation.

'Yeah.'

'Working late then?'

'Saturday is always a busy day and I've been chasing up some of my regulars who pay me at the end of the week.' He glanced towards the stairs. 'Are the nippers in bed?'

She nodded.

'Peace, perfect peace, eh?'

'Not half. Why don't you go and sit down in the living room?' she suggested courteously. 'I'll bring the tea in to you.'

'Righto.'

When Jane took the tea in, he was sprawled out in the deck chair so she sat on one of the hard chairs.

'It's a novelty anyway,' Wilf grinned, referring to the deck chair.

'Yeah, it's great. I can sit by the fire and imagine myself on a sunny beach somewhere.'

'It's about the nearest you'll get to it, now Mick's buggered off,' said Wilf with glaring insensitivity.

'Oh, you never know,' she replied, determined not to be cast down by his complete disregard for her feelings which had offended her many times in the past, even though she had never said so or even admitted it to herself until now. 'I might manage to take the kids on holiday one of these days.'

'I don't see how, love,' he said, casting a critical eye around the room. 'You've got your work cut out just keeping this place going.'

'I don't intend to use a deck chair in my living room for the rest of my life, you know,' Jane told him firmly. 'Once Davey and Pip are a bit older, I shall get a job.'

'You shouldn't have to, though, should you?' he said. 'That bigheaded son of mine should be here looking after you.'

This was greeted with stony silence.

'The bloody fool!' Wilf went on angrily. 'If he hadn't tried to be Mister Big the whole time, he wouldn't have got himself into bother he couldn't cope with – and you wouldn't have to live in a dump like this!'

'You're only living in a council flat yourself,' Jane heard herself say, on the defensive. 'It's hardly a palace.'

Wilf's bushy brows rose in surprise because it wasn't like his daughter-in-law to be so disrespectful.

'At least I've never pretended to be something I'm not,' he said. 'I've never got my wife and kids used to a lifestyle they can't keep, then cleared off when the going gets tough.'

'I like living here, actually,' said Jane. 'I like it a lot.'

'You don't like having bare boards, though, do you?' he said. 'And no comfortable chairs to sit on?'

'Of course not, but the place is clean and as comfortable as I can make it for the time being.'

He gave her a sharp look.

'There's no need to defend yourself 'cause I'm not having a go at you, love,' he said. 'That's the last thing I would ever do. I think you're a ruddy marvel, the way you've coped, being left with two kids to bring up on your own and losing the baby on top of everythin' else. No, it's that son of mine I'm talking about . . . bloody waster! Always putting on a show and trying to be something he wasn't.'

Jane couldn't imagine ever being so much against her children, whatever they had done. Wasn't it an inherent part of parenthood to defend the young, no matter what? Apparently not in Wilf's case.

'There's nothing wrong with trying to better yourself,' she said evenly.

127

'But Mick hadn't bettered himself, had he?' Wilf pointed out, putting his tea on the floor and waving his arms emphatically. 'The damned great house and fancy car didn't even belong to him. Why the hell he couldn't have settled for being ordinary like the rest of us, I do not know.'

'Maybe if you'd given him some attention instead of hogging it all yourself, he wouldn't have been so desperate to make something special of himself,' Jane replied, shocked to be uttering the words but realising she had wanted to say something like this for a very long time.

'I don't know what you mean,' he said, affronted. If there was one thing Wilf couldn't bear, it was a forceful woman. This was a side of his daughter-in-law he hadn't seen before.

'Oh, come on,' she said reprovingly. 'If Mick is nothing else, he *is* his father's son. You both have the same need to be the centre of attention. It wouldn't have hurt you to stand aside for him every so often.'

'Are you suggesting it's *my* fault he got into debt over his head and ran off?'

'No, of course not,' she said, amazed at her own confidence because she'd always been very much in awe of Mick's father. 'But I *am* saying that he spent his whole life, ever since I've known him anyway, trying to please and impress you. And you wouldn't give him that satisfaction . . . your own son.'

'That isn't true!'

'Oh, but I think it is,' she said. 'And having children of my own, it's something I find very hard to understand.'

'And I find it hard to understand why I'm under attack when all I've done is bring you some fruit and veg?'

'I'm very grateful to you for that and I'm not attacking you,' Jane was quick to deny. 'I'm just saying what I believe to be true. I'm not suggesting you deliberately set out to hurt Mick. But I do think a little encouragement now and again wouldn't have gone amiss.'

'Mick was born wanting to be a bigshot.'

'Because he takes after you.'

Wilf's mouth curled cynically.

'Me want to be a bigshot? That's a new one on me. I've never been the slightest bit ambitious. I've always been quite content with my greengrocery round and a little council place to live in.'

'I meant socially,' she said. 'You like to be the big man at parties . . . in the pub. Mick didn't have the personality to compete with that so he tried to go one better another way. He thought material success would bring him status and respect . . . and it did with everyone except you.'

Wilf lit a cigarette, looking aggrieved.

'All this psychology rubbish is beyond me,' he said, inhaling deeply. 'So far as I'm concerned, Mick was a grown man when he ran out on you and I'm ashamed of him for it. The blame doesn't lie at my door.'

'I wasn't suggesting it did,' said Jane, amazed that he was still listening to her. It was a wonder he hadn't taken umbrage and stormed out at the first sign of opposition. Maybe he was just too shocked by someone having the temerity to tell him the truth?

'Sounds like it to me.'

'I'm just pointing out one aspect of Mick's background that might have contributed to the man he turned out to be, that's all,' said Jane with an air of finality because she thought enough had been said on the subject. She stood up. 'Another cup of tea?'

'No, thanks,' said Wilf, also rising. 'I'd better be getting off home or Rita will skin me alive when I get in.'

'I'd like to see her try,' said Jane, managing a smile.

'Yeah, well . . . it's just a figure of speech, innit?' he said, grinning as though to indicate he wasn't going to hold her comments against her.

'Thanks for the fruit and veg,' she said at the door. 'I really do appreciate it.'

'You're welcome.'

Closing the door behind him, she found herself

trembling from reaction at having spoken her mind, but pleased with herself too. What she'd said was long over-due. Over the years she had put up with Wilf Parker's arrogance and pretended to be amused by his crude jokes and vulgarity because he was Mick's father. As Mick's wife she had had no identity of her own – she could see that now. In fact, she had been too devoted to him to *want* a mind of her own.

But having to fend for herself and her children had changed all that. Wilf would think twice before talking down to her again. She doubted he'd accept hospitality from her next time he called in case she said anything else he didn't want to hear. Wilf Parker wasn't used to a woman asserting herself when he was around!

When the weather improved Jane got busy in the garden. Chopping down knee-high vegetation with shears borrowed from Eddie, she discovered flat, grassy ground which she worked on with the mower she received as a joint birthday present from her father, Marie and Eddie. With garden tools on loan from Eddie and a book from the library about basic gardening, flower beds were freshly dug and plants put in; paths were swept and fences painted. She even learned how to deter slimy marauders from gorging themselves on her fresh young plants.

The children thrived in the fresh air and Shadow shot up and down the apple tree as though revitalised by the onset of spring. The sound of children at play filled the air. As the adjoining cottage was empty, Jane didn't have to worry about their disturbing anyone with their high spirits. This was particularly useful when Marie and her family came to visit and all the children played in the garden.

The riverside was vibrant with new life too. Grassy banks were patched with daffodils and crocuses beneath the leafy willows. Gulls soared whitely against the light spring skies which were reflected on the sun-dappled river. Coming out of hibernation, pleasure craft cruised among the commercial river traffic and the rhythmic splash of oars could often be heard. Jane found walking along the riverside a joy.

She was on her way round to Marie's place one afternoon when she saw a notice on the door of the community hall in one of the side streets between the river and Chiswick High Road. It was a handwritten announcement about a social group for mothers and pre-school children that was held there two afternoons a week for a very small fee.

Because it was within their means, Jane and Marie decided to give it a try, especially as Pip and Roy would still be at home for a year after the other two started school.

The group proved to be fun, providing plenty of new company for the children and shared interests between the mothers. Joy Goodall, who ran the group, had begun it when she found herself lonely at home with young children and missing the company of her work colleagues. A natural organiser with boundless energy who involved herself in many causes, it was obvious from Joy's general demeanour and the fact that she had her own car that she was in a wealthier social class than Jane and Marie.

One afternoon she suggested that the group have some sort of event to raise funds to buy toys for the children to play with at the hall. A jumble sale was the most obvious solution and this was agreed upon unanimously. Jane said she had plenty of jumble but she wore it or used it. Instead she suggested a cake table and offered to organise one and make her contribution that way.

The jumble sale, with other attractions including a lucky dip and raffle prizes, took place one Saturday afternoon in the late-spring and was a huge success, Jane's cake table being the star of the show. A lot of people, it seemed, wanted home-made cakes. She'd sold out within the first hour.

At the next group meeting, the main topic of

conversation was the sale which had made them enough profit to buy a range of indoor toys.

'I hope we have another one sometime soon,' laughed Jane. 'I thoroughly enjoyed organising the cake table. It was great fun.'

'Yes, that was an outstanding success,' agreed Joy. 'It just proves people still love anything home-made, and with so many women going out to work these days, they don't have the time to do it themselves. I was glad I bought something from you early because when I went back later the table was empty.'

'I was amazed by the speed at which they disappeared,' agreed Jane.

'That spicy apple cake was one you contributed yourself, wasn't it, Jane?' asked Joy.

She nodded. 'Why, did it give you indigestion or something?'

'Far from it. It was absolutely mouthwatering. In fact, I want to talk to you about that after the meeting, so don't rush off.'

'Okay,' said Jane, intrigued.

When they'd tidied all the chairs and cleared the hall, Joy took Jane aside and put a surprising proposition to her.

'I was wondering if you could make me another one of those cakes, well . . . a couple actually if you could manage it? I've got guests coming for tea on Sunday and I'm not much of a cook myself. I can just about manage not to poison the family with my basic cooking, dinners and so on. But all our cakes are shop bought. If I could have something home-baked for Sunday, it would make it really special.'

Although Jane was flattered to be asked and wanted to do it, she looked doubtful, thinking about the cost of the ingredients.

'Oh . . . are you too busy?' said Joy, disappointed at her reaction.

'It isn't that . . .' She bit her lip, feeling embarrassed.

'I wouldn't expect you to do it for nothing, of course,'

said Joy, catching on. 'Naturally I would pay you.'

'I have no idea what to charge,' said Jane. 'I only make cakes for the family.'

'Well, that's easily solved. Work out the cost of the ingredients and the gas or electricity, then add your time and expertise to that,' Joy suggested. 'And don't be mean to yourself, either. I'm only too happy to pay a decent price for a quality product.'

Jane was thrilled with the idea of getting paid for doing something she enjoyed, and immediately planned to spend the few shillings she would make on a treat for the children.

'You'd like two large cakes then?'

'Yes, please, to make sure they each have a decent slice,' Joy said. 'And if there's any left after the guests have gone, it won't go begging, I can promise you that!'

'Okay, you're on.'

'Wonderful.'

'Do you want one spicy apple and one of another sort?' asked Jane. 'A sponge or a light fruit cake, perhaps . . . and I'm told my chocolate cake is delicious.'

Joy thought about this.

'No, two spicy apple, I think. It's got such a special taste,' she said. 'I'll try the others the next time.'

'Fine.' Jane's thoughts were racing ahead. 'Can you collect them from my place, though? Only I don't have transport. I'll have them ready for you on Saturday afternoon.'

'Certainly, just let me have your address,' said Joy, smiling.

'Well, fancy that,' said Jane to Marie as they left the hall with the children. 'I can't believe anyone would actually want to *pay* me to make a cake for them.'

'I can,' said Marie. 'I'm always telling you your cakes are fab . . . and that apple cake really *is* special.'

'Let's hope the ones I make for Joy are up to my usual standard.'

They were. In fact, when Jane saw Joy on Tuesday at

the group meeting, she had another order for her. This time it was for four spicy apple cakes!

'Not all for me this time,' she explained. 'My mother and sister and a friend were all smitten with them. Definitely a case of once tasted, never forgotten.'

Jane was astonished. The most she'd hoped for was a compliment. She hadn't expected more orders.

'Can you do them then?' asked Joy.

'I'll be delighted.'

'You'll be setting up in business if this continues,' said Marie.

'I only wish I could,' said Jane. 'But it'll probably just be a five-minute wonder.'

It wasn't just a five-minute wonder. The orders snowballed as word spread about Jane Parker's delicious cakes, especially the spicy apple one. People even began to call at the cottage to place their orders. She was soon selling more than thirty cakes a week and was able to buy Davey a toy garage for his birthday to replace the one he'd had to leave behind when they'd left the house in Twickenham in such a hurry. She could even afford a tea party for him with his cousins and new friends he'd made at the playgroup.

After tea the children played in the garden under the apple tree in blossom. Watching them enjoy themselves from the kitchen window as she and Marie washed the dishes, Jane's eyes misted with tears of joy. She had thought her children would never be happy again after their father left.

'I might be able to use the apples from the tree for the apple cakes in the autumn if we get a decent crop and they're the right kind,' she remarked casually.

'It'll save you the cost of buying them anyway.'

'Yes.' Jane paused thoughtfully. 'Actually, Marie, I've had a germ of an idea and I'd like to talk to you about it.'

'Oh?'

'Well, I think I can turn my cake-making hobby into a proper business.'

'Really?'

'Yes, but I can't just rely on word of mouth for orders. Not if I'm to make a living at it eventually.'

'So?'

'So I need to go out and sell.'

'I agree, but how exactly?'

'I've found out that you can rent a pitch for just Saturday at Southall market,' she explained. 'And I'd like to give it a try.'

'A market, eh? That's very brave of you.'

'Yes, well, I thought I'd throw myself in at the deep end. It's the only way I'm going to find out if there's enough of a market for my cakes to build a proper business.'

'True.'

'I do need your help, though,' said Jane. 'Yours and Eddie's.'

'In what way?'

'I need you to look after the children while I do the market,' she said. 'And I need Eddie to drive me to the market with the cakes.'

'You know I'll have the kids for you,' said Marie. 'And I'm sure Eddie will drive you there, so long as he isn't working.'

'I'd pay you.'

'Don't be silly . . .'

'No, listen, Marie,' she said ardently, emptying the bowl and drying her hands, 'this isn't like I'm ill or anything and you're looking after the kids because of a crisis. This is business, and if I make a success of it I'll need you to look after the children on a regular basis. 'Cause if Southall market goes well, I'd like to do Kingston on a Monday too, where you can also have a pitch just for one day. I wouldn't want to leave the children on a daily basis but a few hours a couple of times a week won't hurt them. And it isn't as though they'd be with a stranger.'

'You've certainly been doing your homework?' Marie smiled.

'That's because I'm really serious.'

'I've gathered that.'

'Anyway, if I'm earning money, you're entitled to be paid, and so is Eddie for taking me there. So let's have no more talk of freebies, not when it comes to business.'

'You're the boss,' said Marie jokingly. 'But what happens if you don't sell anything?'

'Then I'll have to pay you in stock.' She grinned. 'So let's hope you're not living on cakes for weeks afterwards!'

'I might have guessed it would be raining,' said Jane to Eddie the following Saturday as they unloaded the cakes from the car at the market.

'Shall I take you back home again, then?' he said, teasing her.

'Not on your life,' she said. 'I'd see this thing through if there was snow on the ground and a gale blowing.'

But she did feel very apprehensive when Eddie had gone home and she was standing by her stall in the pouring rain. The cellophane-wrapped cakes were sheltered by the awning but the general atmosphere was damp and miserable.

'Talk about flamin' June,' said the woman on the clothes stall opposite.

'Typical British summer,' replied Jane, who was wearing a white 'wet look' raincoat over her summer dress.

'Let's hope it brightens up later on,' said the woman, glancing at the heavy clouds.

'I'm banking on it,' said Jane. 'I don't want to take this lot home again. I can't keep my stock for long like you can.'

'If a drop of rain kept the punters away, we'd all have gone out of business long ago, with weather like ours,' said the woman. 'The crowds will be here later, rain or not.'

'I do hope so,' said Jane, heartened.

The woman, who was middle-aged and had a weatherbeaten face and dark hair poking out from under a scarlet headscarf, said her name was Rose. She'd been working the markets all her life, apparently. She and her husband travelled all over the country. She said he would be along later on to do a stint on the stall.

'If your cakes taste as good as they look, you'll do a roaring trade,' she remarked. 'I'll have something off you myself later on, to eat with my coffee.'

Jane had made quite a variety. Jam sponges, chocolate cake with butter filling, fairy cakes she'd packed in cellophane bags of six, lemon madeira. But the largest number was of her spicy apple cake.

People passed by in macs, heads down against the rain, heading straight for the fruit and vegetable stalls without even giving Jane's wares a second glance. They were only interested in essentials this morning. Perhaps it was too early in the day to think about cakes unless you were familiar with the products and bought regularly. The thought gave her an idea. Taking one of each of the large cakes, she cut them into small taster portions and arranged them on a plate at the front of the stall for people to try.

To let the punters know what was on offer, she called out. 'Lovely home-made cakes . . . taste before you buy . . . all freshly made . . .'

She felt a bit foolish at first but soon forgot her inhibitions when a woman stopped for a taste.

'Ooh, this is really good,' she said of the apple cake. 'I'll have one o' those.'

The thrill of her first sale was like nectar to Jane, especially as others quickly followed.

'Here, let's have a taste,' said Rose after noticing the sales gather momentum.

Jane gave her a piece of each one.

'They're all nice but that apple cake is really moreish. Give us one before they all go,' she said, handing Jane her money.

By midday she had sold out of apple cake and by two o'clock everything else had gone. She would need to produce more for next week – a lot more, she thought excitedly.

She had finished so much earlier than expected, she had a couple of hours to kill before Eddie was due to collect her. But no sooner had she got all her trays and cloths ready to load into his car, prepared for a long wait, than he appeared with Marie and all four children.

'We thought we'd surprise you,' said Marie. 'Davey and Pip wanted to see their mummy at work. Seems we're too late, though?'

'Where are all the cakes?' asked Davey.

'All sold, love.'

'None left for us?' said Pip.

'I'll make something special for you tomorrow,' Jane said, beaming. 'In the meantime let's find a cafe and I'll buy you all something nice to celebrate my first day in business.'

'Calm down, you lot!' shouted Marie across the garden of Jane's cottage to the four cousins who were squabbling about whose turn it was to go on the new swing, bought from Jane's profits and erected by Eddie near the apple tree on which fruit was beginning to appear. Shadow was peering down through the foliage at all the excitement with a look of feline disdain.

'They're all really wound up about the swing,' said Jane.

'I'll take it down again if you're going to argue about it,' threatened Eddie.

This produced instant quiet and they began taking it in turns.

'I suppose it's a bit late in the year to put a swing up, really,' said Jane. 'But they so wanted it, and they used to have such a lot of fun with the one we had in the garden at Maple Avenue.'

'There'll probably be quite a few nice days yet before winter sets in,' said Marie. 'Anyway, it'll be there ready for the spring.'

It was late-afternoon on a glorious Saturday in early-September and Jane and Marie were sitting in the sunshine drinking tea. Children's toys were dotted about on the lawn – bikes, scooters, a doll's pram. Eddie had erected the swing while Jane had been out at the market. Later on, they were all going for supper in a burger bar, a treat for the children as Jane's cake business was doing so well and this was the last weekend before Davey and Melanie started school.

'This time next week Mel and Davey will be school-children,' remarked Marie.

'Yes,' agreed Jane wistfully. 'And so a new era begins . . .'

'Mmm.'

'There have been so many changes lately.'

Marie nodded.

'You've proved us all wrong about this place anyway,' she said. 'When you moved in here in the depths of winter, I never dreamed that by the summer we'd all be sitting in a civilised garden with a lawn and flower beds.'

'Neither did I,' Jane admitted. 'Though I always knew the cottage was right for us.'

'It's almost like having a detached house, isn't it?' remarked Marie, looking towards the adjoining cottage. 'With next-door being empty.'

'Yes, we've been incredibly lucky,' said Jane. 'Davey and Pip wouldn't have nearly so much freedom if someone were living next-door. I'd spend all my time keeping them quiet.'

'Let's hope no one moves in then.'

'I notice that the "To Let" board has changed to "For Sale",' remarked Jane. 'The owner has obviously given up hope of ever letting it and thinks he'll stand more chance of finding a buyer. Some people see these old places as an investment . . . they do them up and sell them at a large profit.'

'Yes.'

'There's only so much you can do when you're renting,' Jane continued. 'I can make my place more comfortable with carpets and furniture but as the tenant I can't do anything much beyond painting and decorating. Whereas if you owned a cottage like this, you could make it into a little palace. Not that I could ever afford to buy this place and do anything like that, but still . . .'

'Who knows what the future holds?' said Marie. 'The way your business is going, anything is possible.'

'I'm flattered by your faith in me, but I'm a very long way from being a property owner. My biggest aim for the moment is to have a telly installed by Christmas.' She put her finger to her lips. 'Not a word, though. I want to surprise them.'

'I'm sworn to secrecy.'

It was very satisfying for Jane to be able to buy home comforts for the cottage and to clothe and feed the children decently. No one had been more surprised than she was by the demand for her products. She had quite literally baked her way into a full-time business and no longer went out cleaning or to do the evening shift at the factory. She now had a regular pitch at the Monday Kingston market as well as Southall on Saturdays, and was selling a wide range of cakes, though her most popular line was still the spicy apple cake. She was thinking of expanding further by trying to get her cakes into some of the small grocery shops and cafes where they did afternoon teas.

But now the sun was sinking in the hazy blue sky. It was very still and the air was tinged with autumn, the faint scent of woodsmoke, and plump wasps buzzing lazily around the hollyhocks that grew along the dividing fence to the overgrown garden next-door. The cat whizzed down the tree and jumped on to Jane's lap, inclining his head meaningfully. She fondled him absently, absorbing the scene around her: the children playing happily with their cousins, their uncle pushing them on the swing.

Sorrow overwhelmed her unexpectedly as she became sharply conscious of a vital missing element in this happy family scene. Mick should be pushing his children on the swing, not Eddie. Mick should be giving his son encouragement as he embarked upon a new phase in his life as a schoolboy.

The first anniversary of Mick's departure had passed unmentioned but not unnoticed by Jane three months ago. Although nowadays she was too busy to dwell upon his absence unduly, she often found herself overcome by a longing to see him, to touch him, to feel his arms around her. This was one such moment.

Inevitably, as time passed, she had become accustomed to not having him around. The children rarely mentioned him now, Davey hardly ever. Pip occasionally said she wanted her daddy but she didn't persist. Jane sometimes thought it was probably just as well that children of that age didn't have long memories.

'A penny for them?' said Marie, looking at her friend.

'I was thinking about Mick, actually,' confessed Jane.

'Aah . . .'

'He doesn't deserve it but I still miss him,' she said sadly. 'Sometimes I want him so badly, I think I'll go mad.'

'You're bound to feel like that at times.'

'I can go for days without thinking about him . . . then suddenly it hits me again.'

'He'll be back.'

'You don't still believe that?'

'I'm convinced of it,' said Marie. 'You two belong together and that's how it will be again. I don't know when . . . I just know it *will* happen.'

Chapter Nine

One evening in November of the following year, Ron Beach sat alone at a corner table in a pub in the seaside resort of Bognor Regis, smoking a cigarette, drinking beer and reading the newspaper. An item of news about someone called Margaret Thatcher being appointed as shadow transport minister didn't interest him in the least. As someone who was living hand to mouth outside the system, politics was of no concern to Ron. A piece about the arrest of Bruce Reynolds, the last unapprehended Great Train Robbery suspect, leapt off the page at him though. He wondered why it made his stomach churn? Could it be that he himself was a criminal of some sort?

Finishing his drink, he went to the bar and ordered another. If he'd had any mates he'd have stood at the bar and chatted but he didn't know anyone well enough to do that. He had a nodding acquaintance with some of the regulars because he'd been using the pub for over two years; he even occasionally made up the numbers at darts. But he didn't have friends. A man in his position daren't get too pally with anyone.

Realising, without much interest, that he ought to eat something, he bought a steak and kidney pie and took it back to the table with his drink. He could count the number of times that he'd bothered to cook for himself in his bedsit on one hand. A fried egg sandwich now and again, nothing more. Had it not been for the fact that this was his night off, he would have had a meal supplied at the hotel where he worked in the kitchen, washing up. The job was strictly casual labour, cash in hand, the only sort of employment available to someone without a P45 or National Insurance number, which he didn't have because Ron Beach didn't exist so far as officialdom was concerned.

When he'd finished eating and drinking, he left the pub and walked along the seafront, a rough-looking man in a shabby duffel coat which he'd bought secondhand. He pulled up the hood against the weather, the cold wind taking his breath as it howled across the promenade. He preferred it along here out of season, though, because he felt less of a misfit without the colour and gaiety of the holiday crowds around him. Being so close to the elements soothed him too: the cutting wind on his face, the salt taste in the air, the angry sound of the sea roaring out of the darkness. It was deserted but for him, the lit windows of the big hotels shining anonymously into the bleakness, the smaller establishments having closed for the winter.

His thoughts drifted back to the day he'd first arrived here nearly two and a half years ago. It hadn't been winter then. It had been a beautiful summer's evening when he'd found himself on the beach with no idea of who he was, how he'd got there or why.

At the memory of how terrifying that blankness had initially been, his heart beat faster. He'd felt hysterical at the time, hadn't known what to do. Stricken with panic, he'd headed for the nearest police station or hospital, whichever he came across first. But before he'd reached either, some sixth sense made him wonder if it would be wise to make himself known to the authorities, a feeling that he might be in trouble of some sort haunting him.

So he'd gone instead to a pub and calmed himself with a good few whiskies which he paid for with the money he had found in his pocket. With enough alcohol inside him, he was able to believe that everything would come back to him after a night's sleep.

That first night he'd slept on the beach and although his memory hadn't returned the next morning, he was sufficiently in control by then to deal with the situation.

Inspired by his surroundings, he'd renamed himself Ron Beach, booked into the cheapest boarding house he could see and set about finding work in case his memory didn't return before his money ran out.

His most fruitful source of casual labour had been hotel kitchens, and garages where he'd wash cars. He'd stayed on at the boarding house until the end of the season then moved into a bedsit which gave him more privacy. Convinced that some sort of adversity lay in his unknown past, he lived in fear of being recognised.

From time to time, he'd had flashes of memory. Hazy images of a woman and two children, and a man with dark, greying hair. Sometimes he saw a house with a Jaguar on the drive. But he couldn't hold on to the pictures long enough to analyse them. He didn't recognise the people but the images made him sad and frightened, and he had no idea what any of it meant.

But now he turned off the seafront into the town and a street of Victorian houses where he rented his room. He shuffled along with his head down, a habit that came from the insecurity of a lost identity. Slowly, he made his way up the stairs to his room, the bare floorboards creaking beneath his step. He passed another tenant on the landing, a young man with a drug habit. They acknowledged each other only with a nod.

Ron's room was sparsely furnished with a single bed, an armchair, a wooden table and chair, and a wardrobe with a tarnished mirror. In the corner was a cracked sink, a food cupboard and a gas-ring. The floor was covered with brown linoleum and there was a rug by the gas fire which was so stained the pattern was barely distinguishable.

The room was so cold he was shivering violently as he held a match to the gas fire, then shambled about the room with his coat on. When he eventually took it off and laid it on the bed as an extra blanket, he caught sight of himself in the wardrobe mirror and was startled to see himself smiling and wearing smart clothes. He narrowed his eyes at the distorted reflection, trying to hold the image in his mind, guessing it was a flashback to how he had once been rather than just wishful thinking.

As the illusion faded, Ron stared gloomily at himself as he really was: a man with dark eyes and black hair which he cut himself with scissors to save the cost of a barber, a pathetic figure wearing a shapeless old jumper and trousers he'd bought from a junk stall. He didn't know who he was but instinct told him that he wasn't meant to be a loser. He might be living in squalor now but inside he was someone of importance. A conviction of this filled him with a sense of frustration and power-lessness that sapped his strength.

Sitting down in the armchair by the fire, he switched on the portable radio he'd bought in a secondhand shop and listened to the Pete Murray Show. He enjoyed pop music. It made him think of being at the wheel of a car somewhere, feeling good about himself.

When his shillings ran out in the gas meter, he had a quick wash at the sink, went to the communal toilet on the floor below then came back and got into bed, to escape from his bewildering and miserable life in sleep.

'So . . . you're going to be having some next-door neigh-bours at last then, Mrs Parker?' said Mrs Robinson, a formidable lady of advanced years with blue-rinsed hair and small, darting eyes who lived with her husband in the big house opposite. She had waylaid Jane one January afternoon as the latter came out of her front gate in high black boots and a short scarlet coat, on her way round the corner to the alley behind Tug Lane where she parked her car.

'We are?' said Jane in a questioning tone because she had heard nothing about anyone moving into the cottage next-door.

'A young couple came to look at the property while you were out the other day,' explained Mrs Robinson, who was generally known as a gossip. Conservatively clad in a long grey coat and heavy boots, she was clutching the handle of a basket on wheels full of shopping.

'Really?' said Jane.

'Yes. They seemed very keen to go ahead. They want to do the place up, refurbish and modernise it quite substantially, apparently.'

'You're very well informed?'

'I just happened to be on my way to the shops when they were coming out of the cottage,' she explained. 'The agent had given them the key and left them to it by all accounts. They were very pleasant . . . and really quite chatty.'

Which roughly translated meant she had seen them arrive and lain in wait behind her net curtains ready to approach them when they emerged. Jane tried to be tolerant and remember that nosiness was better than cold indifference and that every neighbourhood had its busybody, but Mrs Robinson's superior attitude made this very difficult. Fortunately, Jane didn't often run into her because she usually went out the back way to her car; she hadn't done so today only because the back path was somewhat waterlogged from this morning's heavy rain.

'Oh, well, I shall meet them in due course,' she remarked, eager to go because she was on her way to collect the children from school.

'Teachers,' announced Mrs Robinson as Jane began to walk away.

'Pardon?'

'Schoolteachers,' she declared triumphantly. 'They're both schoolteachers.'

'Oh, really?' Jane was already edging away. The weather was raw and penetrating and she didn't want the children to be kept waiting at the school gate. She was taking Melanie and Roy home in the car, too, as it was so cold.

'They work at the Gram . . .'

'That's interesting.' Jane had recognised the note in the other woman's voice, the implication being that Jane, as a deserted wife who baked cakes for a living and sold

147

them from a market stall, should feel threatened by having members of the professional classes living next-door to her. Stifling the urge to throttle her neighbour, she arranged her features into her sweetest smile. 'I can't wait to meet them.'

'Oh.' Jane's refusal to be ruffled made Mrs Robinson even more determined to make her point. 'At least they'll bring some respectability to the area.'

Jane looked her straight in the eyes and said, 'I'm really pleased to hear that.'

Mrs Robinson was clearly disconcerted by this implied challenge to her position as Tug Lane's arbiter of good taste. Before she could utter another word, however, Jane had bidden her a hasty farewell and was off round the corner, boots clicking on the pavement, shoulder-length hair swinging.

Driving away in the old green Morris Traveller she'd been forced to buy for business reasons, she couldn't pretend to be thrilled at the prospect of having school-teachers living next-door. They were bound to be crusty and authoritative. They would want peace and quiet around them – not easily attainable with two lively youngsters in the adjoining house and garden.

Having had no one next-door for so long, Jane and the children had become spoiled. They were bound to feel more restricted when the new people moved in because Jane was determined to be a considerate neighbour.

Stopping at the traffic lights, she turned on the heater, thinking what a treat it was to have a car on a bitterly cold day like this, especially as she spent so much time going to and from the school now that both children were there. Transport had become essential to Jane as her business grew, especially when she began to supply shops and cafes, who expected to have the cakes delivered. This runaround was by no means new but Eddie said that the mechanics were sound and should give her a few years' service yet.

With the growth in output, Jane had been forced to

spend money on other things too – an industrial food mixer and a second oven. As her kitchen became home to a thriving cottage industry, a telephone also became essential.

Now that she had been in business for a year and a half, she was making a steady living. She wasn't rich by any means but the cottage now had carpets on the floor, decent furniture and a television set. They were also able to live to a reasonable standard. That was all she had ever wanted from her business: to be able to provide for her children properly. She had never been interested in empire-building.

She didn't hanker after the material acquisitions it had been second nature to want when she'd been with Mick: the latest gadget, the smartest car, the swankiest house in the road. In fact, she couldn't imagine ever wanting to move from the cottage she adored. When she came indoors, a sense of belonging washed over her, and she believed the children had come to feel that way too.

Inevitably her life with Mick had receded into the past. She thought about him less often now and was used to being independent and making her own decisions. Life no longer held many fears for her but she often felt lonely in a way that the children couldn't help.

Oh, well, you can't have everything, she thought, smiling as she drew up outside the school just in time to see a stream of youngsters begin to pour out of the gates.

Because of the Saturday market, Friday was a very busy day for Jane in her cottage kitchen. She was up early and had already done some baking before taking the children to school. When she got back, she worked flat out until it was time to collect them, breaking off only to have a sandwich at lunchtime and feed the cat.

With her livelihood depending on producing a certain number of cakes, interruptions were anathema to her during these vital hours. So when the doorbell rang one Friday morning a few days later, while she was spooning mixture into tins ready for the oven and had one batch almost ready to come out and go on to cooling trays, she marched to the door with an apron worn over her jeans, in no mood for Jehovah's Witnesses or door-to-door salesmen.

A man stood on the doorstep. He was about thirty, she thought, tall and fresh-complexioned with brown curly hair and an athletic look about him. He was wearing a navy blue duffel coat and a blue and white striped muffler around his neck; not the usual attire of a salesman.

'Hello,' he said with a warm smile.

'Hi.' Jane's tone was abrupt. He might very well be gorgeous but whatever he was selling, she didn't want any.

'Sorry to disturb you . . .'

'I *am* very busy.'

'Oh.'

She removed her hand from the door handle, looking meaningfully at the sticky mess of cake mixture deposited there.

'Look, I really am very busy and I don't want any central heating or double glazing at the moment, thank you.'

'That's just as well 'cause I don't have any to sell you,' he said with a wicked grin.

'Neither do I want to talk about the bible . . .'

'Nor do I.'

'What *are* you selling then?'

'Nothing. I just dropped by to introduce myself,' he told her. 'My wife and I have bought the cottage next-door and we'll be moving in soon.'

'Oh, dear.' She opened the door wider, her head at an angle as she looked suitably contrite. 'Is there a hole I can sink into?'

'Don't worry. Perhaps I have the hungry look of a salesman about me?' He laughed, warm brown eyes twinkling.

'When strangers come to the door, they're usually selling something . . .'

'I know. Your reaction was perfectly understandable.' He offered his hand, smiling. 'Giles Hamilton.'

She shook it.

'I'm Jane Parker. But do come inside so we can introduce ourselves properly over a cup of coffee.'

'I don't want to impose,' he said. 'Not if you're busy?'

'We can talk while I work,' she said, ushering him inside. 'At least give me a chance to show you that I do have some manners.'

They entered the kitchen to a blast of warm spicy air. Every surface was covered in cakes at different stages of production – in various-shaped tins, on wire cooling trays, in uncooked form in the mixing bowl. The radio was on and someone was talking about the recent tragedy when an airliner crashed into houses near Gatwick, killing fifty people.

'Makes you go cold to think about it, doesn't it?' she remarked.

'Yes, it's terrible,' said Giles, slowly shaking his head.

Jane speedily removed some tins from the oven.

'Oh, just in time,' she said. 'Another few minutes and they'd have been overdone . . . dry and horrible and fit only for the bin.'

He looked bewildered.

'I make cakes for a living,' she explained.

'Ah, I see. No wonder you don't want people coming to the door.'

'Present company excepted, of course.' She pointed to a chair. 'Take a pew. I'll just get this lot out of the oven and another lot in then I'll make us some coffee.'

'Tell me where things are and I'll do it?' he offered.

She took up his suggestion without hesitation. She felt as though she'd known him for years. It was extraordinary!

'You're a very busy lady then?' he remarked as they waited for the kettle to boil.

'Phew, not so you'd notice!' She grinned, getting another tray of small cakes into the oven then easing some cooked ones out of their tins on to the cooling trays. 'But I like having plenty to do and I really enjoy my work.' She did a mental check around the kitchen. 'Now I can take a short break with my coffee.'

They went into the living room, carpeted recently in a rich red and furnished comfortably in pretty cretonnes. Jane turned up the electric convector heater which she used during the day until she lit the fire for the children to come home to.

'We're having central heating put in before we move in next-door,' Giles told her, making himself comfortable in an armchair.

'Oh, lucky you! I'd love that but I can't have it done even when I can afford it because the cottage isn't mine.'

He explained that he and his wife were currently living in a modern semi in Hammersmith but wanted something with more character.

'We bought the cottage at such a low price, we can afford to spend some money on it. We'll do what we can ourselves and have professionals in for anything we don't feel able to handle.'

'That's sensible.'

'I'll have to get the garden into a civilised state before the good weather or I'll be in dead trouble with my young son if he can't kick his ball about out there.'

'You've a son?' she said with Davey in mind. 'How old is he?'

'Seven in June.'

'Well, I'll be blowed,' said Jane, delighted. 'I've a little boy of the same age.'

'That's great,' said Giles. 'They'll be company for each other.'

'Indeed.'

'My wife will be delighted to know that Kevin is going to have company,' he said. 'There are plenty of kids around where we live now and he'll miss that. Being an only child can be lonely.'

She nodded. 'You and your wife are both teachers, then?'

He looked puzzled for a moment, then said, 'Ah, the lady opposite.'

'Mrs Robinson, Tug Lane's very own broadcasting service,' she said with a wry grin. 'She told me that you both work at the Gram.'

'That's right.' His face seemed to light up when he spoke of his wife. 'Lena only works part-time now, though. She went back to work when Kevin started school. Does two and a half days a week. We first met through work.'

'What are your subjects?' Jane asked in a conversational manner.

'Lena teaches French, I'm the PE master, but I also teach history.'

'The games master, eh?' she said lightly. 'No wonder you look so fit.'

'It goes with the territory.'

They talked about this and that. Jane had rarely met anyone with whom she felt so quickly at ease. The thing that was most noticeable about Giles was his enthusiasm for life. He was obviously a family man and devoted to his wife and son.

'I'm looking forward to meeting your wife,' she said when he was about to leave.

'I'm sure you'll like her . . . everyone does. It'll be nice for her to have someone of the same age living next-door.'

'For me too.'

'She'll be coming over to the cottage soon and I expect she'll pop in to introduce herself to you,' he said as they stood at the front door. 'We'll both be to and fro a lot before we move in, for various reasons. She's working today or she'd be with me now. I came to have a look round, to see exactly what needs doing and in which order of priority.'

'You're not working today then?'

'I managed to get the morning off but I'm going back now.'

They both noticed the curtains twitching in the house opposite.

'Mrs Robinson is on duty.' Jane grinned.

'So it seems.'

'I usually come in and out the back way as the car is parked in the alley,' she said. 'The poor thing is probably quite distraught because she can't see me come and go.'

'Spoilsport!'

'Aren't I just? But anyway, if there's anything I can do to help . . . if you want me to let workmen in or anything, just let me know.'

'Thanks. I'll bear that in mind . . . cheerio.'

''Bye for now.'

Jane went back to her work smiling. If Giles's wife and son were as pleasant as he was, having next-door neighbours wasn't going to be so bad after all. In fact, she was looking forward to it.

Ron Beach wasn't due at the hotel kitchen until lunch-time that day so he stayed in bed to keep warm. January was sheer hell in this freezing bedsit. Every morning he scraped ice off the inside of the windows, and at night went to bed fully dressed with a hot water bottle – and was still kept awake by the cold.

He was passing the time listening to the radio on which there was a discussion of the air crash near Gatwick. Wanting to escape from the misery of the subject matter, he sat up and twiddled the knob to find something a bit more cheerful and came across the Jimmy Young Show. The programme wasn't a favourite of Ron's but at least it was more entertaining than hearing about a plane crashing into people's houses.

Jimmy Young played an old Beatles hit, 'We Can Work It Out'. For some reason the song made Ron feel emotional and a lump gathered in his throat, tears flooding his eyes. He began to sing along with it but fell silent suddenly, buffeted by a vivid flashback to another time when he'd been singing that song.

For the first time since the onset of his amnesia, he was able to hold on to a memory. It stayed in his mind and expanded. Like a blow to the head, he suddenly remembered who he was . . .

For a long time he lay back, holding the rough blanket around him, physically weak from the shock, his head aching as he struggled to remember more. It came in confused fragments at first, then in a flood, everything he'd longed to know for such a long time tumbling into his mind. God, what a mess! He'd been better off not knowing.

His thoughts lingered on that terrible summer's day, the one after the failed robbery on the service-station. Now he understood his reaction to the arrest of the train robber.

He could remember not having slept that night and being in bed in the morning in the empty house after Jane and the children had gone out. He recalled the black hopelessness as he'd searched his mind for a solution to his problems. But there had been no way out. He was about to lose everything and his wife knew nothing about it. There had been a moment when he'd contemplated suicide with an overdose of tablets. But that must have been just a passing thought because the next thing he remembered was finding himself on Bognor beach with no knowledge of the journey there. That was still a complete blank.

With a burst of energy, he leaped out of bed in a state of high agitation. He must get back to Jane. She would think he'd deserted her. *He had deserted her.* But not in the way she would think. He had to go home and put things right – tell her he'd had some sort of a breakdown and didn't even remember leaving. He'd been away far too long.

In a frenzy, he washed and shaved and pulled on his clothes, bursting with urgency to get home, both excited and terrified at the prospect. He brushed his hair in the mirror, smiling for the first time in ages. He'd known all along he wasn't a loser. He was Mick Parker, well-known entrepreneur, not Ron Beach – odd jobber and nobody.

As he looked in the mirror his animated expression faded as reality nudged him and his adrenaline drained away. He couldn't go back, not as a failure. He couldn't face Jane, not after walking out on her. He didn't even know where she was now – she certainly wouldn't still be living in Maple Avenue. He knew that this was just an excuse because he could easily trace her through her father or his sister. But he realised it was a terrible thing he'd done and was too ashamed to see her – to see any of them.

He could imagine what had happened after he'd left. He would have been the talk of the manor. His name would be mud with the family for running out on his wife and children. And even worse than that, he would be a laughing stock among his mates for losing everything.

Oh, yes, there were plenty of deadbeats from the Berrywood Estate who would have been only too glad to see him go under. His father would have had a whale of a time doing him down too.

Well, no one was going to get the opportunity to gloat! They'd have had a field day behind his back but they weren't going to get the chance to do it to his face. They'd love the fact that he'd had a breakdown, that really would raise a laugh. Oh, no, nobody was going to put Mick Parker down. Ron Beach might be an easy target for mockery but not Mick Parker.

One of these days he would go back and take his rightful place with his wife and children. But not now, not until he had regained his former prestige and had something to offer Jane, which would also protect him from scorn. She couldn't possibly respect him as he was now. And he'd sooner not have her at all if he didn't have her admiration.

Completely taken up with thoughts of himself, he had few for Jane's welfare. He wanted to see her with aching desperation, and for things to be as they were before the warehouse fire. He longed to touch her, to hear her voice, to feel her soft, warm body next to his. But any concern for how she must have felt when he'd left, or how she was actually managing to survive without him to provide for her, was far outweighed by concern for his own reputation.

Mick paced the room, feverishly planning his next move. Now that he knew who he was, he could get back into the legitimate system and back into business. But he couldn't do that here in Bognor. It just wouldn't be feasible suddenly to become the strong and capable Mick Parker in a place where he was only known as feeble Ron Beach.

Anyway, he needed a busy place with plenty of opportunities to earn real money. He had no idea how he was going to do it but he was determined, somehow, to regain his former status. One thing he did know for certain: he was *never* going to wash up other people's greasy dinner plates for a living again.

Should he go to a different area of London where he wasn't known? he wondered, and decided that that was a bit too close to home at this stage. What about Brighton? There was always a lot going on there. Plenty of opportunity for someone with a bit of savvy to do well.

Fired with a strong sense of purpose, he began to stuff his meagre belongings into a shabby holdall.

Things will look up once you get away from here, Mick, old son, he told himself. Brighton is the place for you. But only as a stepping stone back to where you really belong, with Jane and the children.

Chapter Ten

'You must be Lena?' said Jane, getting out of her car in the alley just as a slim, dark-haired woman was locking a Ford Anglia parked by the back gate of the cottage next-door.

'And you must be Jane?' said Lena Hamilton, smiling warmly and offering her hand. 'I'm so pleased to meet you. Giles has told me all about your little chat the other day.'

'Fancy a coffee?' invited Jane, who was just back from taking the children to school.

'I'd love one,' her new neighbour said. 'But I don't want to hold you up. Giles said you work from home and get very busy.'

'I don't have a market tomorrow so this isn't one of my frantic days,' Jane explained. 'I've some orders to get on with but I can spare half an hour for a coffee and a chat.'

They went into her cottage and Lena sat down at the kitchen table while Jane made the coffee. Shadow immediately jumped on to Lena's lap and made himself comfortable.

'You're gorgeous, aren't you?' She fondled his head and said to Jane, 'I adore cats.'

'He was here when we moved in,' she said. 'A scruffy little stray, taking shelter in an empty house. Now we are all enslaved to him. He went missing for a couple of days once . . . we were all demented. He breezed back as though he'd never been away.'

'That's cats for you, come and go as they please.'

As her husband had been, Lena was very easy to talk

to. She had an educated accent without sounding affected and was attractive in a natural sort of way, with very little make-up and her dark hair worn in a simple bob. Being tall and willowy with striking green eyes, she looked especially good in her cream, thick-knit sweater and denim jeans.

'You're not working today then?' remarked Jane, putting two mugs of coffee on the table and sitting down opposite her.

'No, it isn't my day for school so I thought I'd take the opportunity to measure the windows next-door for curtains.'

'You must be very excited about moving in?'

Lena threw back her head and emitted a deep-throated laugh.

'I'm not sure if excited is quite what I'm feeling,' she said. 'Scared stiff of what we've taken on would be nearer the truth. I'm dying to get on with it, though. Giles and I both enjoy a challenge.' She chuckled. 'There wouldn't be much point moving in next-door if we didn't. There's so much work to do in there. It'll be years before we get it the way we want it.'

'It'll be quite a change for you, if you're used to a modern house.'

'It certainly will,' said Lena, sipping her coffee. 'The place we're in now is comfortable and convenient but it just isn't us. It has all mod cons but is very boxy and on an estate of others all exactly the same. We fancy something a bit more interesting . . . and these cottages are certainly that.' She glanced around. 'Yours is lovely.'

'Thank you. There's only so much I can do to it as I rent,' explained Jane, 'but I love it here. I wouldn't want to live anywhere else.'

'I can understand that.'

'Everyone thought I was off my rocker to move in here with my kids, though,' said Jane ruefully. 'The place was in a terrible state . . . and I'm on my own, you see.'

'I see.'

'My husband left me.'

'Oh, dear.'

'It was pretty grim at the time. I thought I'd never get over it,' she heard herself say, surprised to be revealing this to a stranger. 'But I survived. He'll have been gone three years this June, so I'm used to it now.'

'Bound to be.'

'Anyway, once the family realised that I was determined to rent this place, they were really supportive. Even though they thought I was crackers.'

'We're getting a similar sort of reaction too,' said Lena. 'But Giles's family think we're a bit touched anyway.'

'Really?'

'Oh, yes. Well, all of them except his mother, who is also reckoned to be a bit potty by the rest of the family.' She gave a wide grin. 'But I adore her. She's a real one off.'

'Why do they think she's potty?' Jane couldn't help asking. She already felt as though she and Lena were old friends.

'Because she's very unconventional.'

'Oh?'

'A theatrical type.'

'On the stage?'

'Not as a professional. She never managed to get into showbiz proper but has always been involved as an amateur. Local drama groups, that sort of thing,' Lena explained. 'When her children had grown up and left home and she had time on her hands, she started a showgroup which is still going strong. All the members are women of a certain age. "London Lights" they call themselves. They put on shows at old people's homes and hospitals: singing, dancing, comedy sketches and monologues. Sometimes they do supper shows to raise money for charity.'

'Your mother-in-law sounds to me like a woman with a heck of a lot to offer,' said Jane, 'rather than someone who is slightly deranged.'

'I agree with you,' said Lena. 'But I suppose the family expected her to retire gracefully into the background

161

and spend her days playing bridge. When people don't do what's expected of them, they're usually considered to be a bit barmy. Giles and his mother are two of a kind. As I said, the rest of them think he's touched too.'

'Would it be too rude of me to ask why?' enquired Jane, intrigued.

'Of course not,' Lena said chirpily. 'Giles's family are well off . . . they own a brewery.'

'Not Hamiltons' beers?'

'Yes, that's the one,' said Lena. 'Giles and his brother Clement both went into the family business with their father as soon as they were old enough. It was expected that they would. Clement took to it but Giles isn't cut out for business and hated it from the word go. In the end he left and did a teacher training course, which was what he'd wanted to do all along. His father was alive then and he was furious. He couldn't understand how anyone would want to give up all the material benefits of working in a successful family business to go into something as poorly paid as teaching. This was all long before Giles and I met, of course.'

'So who's running the company now?' asked Jane, keen to have an insight into this family background which was so different from her own.

'Giles's brother,' she said. 'He's a real chip off the old block . . . lives and breathes business, just like his father used to.'

'So he did well out of Giles's leaving the business, then?'

'Oh, yes. The company is his, lock, stock and barrel, and he's filthy rich . . . beautiful house, kids at private school. He and his wife think Giles and I are real odd-balls because we're not interested in money, over and above what we need to live in reasonable comfort. We hardly ever see them. It isn't that we don't like them . . . but we have nothing in common.'

'Do you ever have the tiniest regret that Giles turned his back on the family money?'

'No, I can honestly say I don't,' said Lena without

hesitation. 'Which probably makes me some sort of loony. But I'd never been used to money like Giles had . . . boarding school and all that. My people are very ordinary, and what you've never had, you don't miss.'

'That's true.'

'Anyway, I would never have met him if he hadn't gone into teaching,' she said, adding on a more serious note, 'I truly believe it was the right thing for him to do. He's a natural for the job. You should see him in action with the kids . . . he's wonderful.'

'Did his mother take his side?'

'Oh, yes. Trudy is a great believer in freedom of choice.'

'She doesn't think you're mad to buy the cottage, then?'

'No. But she does think we're mad not to let her help us pay for the alterations,' confessed Lena. 'She's very well off. Giles's father left her more than comfortably provided for.'

'I can understand your not wanting handouts,' said Jane. 'I'm just the same. Not that my father has any spare cash to give away, bless him.'

'Giles feels very strongly about it,' explained Lena in a serious tone. 'When he left the family business he knew exactly what he was giving up. He says it would be wrong to sponge off his mother now, no matter how well off she is.'

'It's quite a story,' said Jane.

'Yes.' Lena gave her a warm look. 'I can't believe I've talked so much to anyone at a first meeting, but I feel so at ease with you. I suppose it's because you don't run with the pack either.'

To Jane the Hamiltons were fascinating because they were so different from anyone else she knew. Whereas she'd always thought of herself as very conventional and ordinary.

'I don't?' she said enquiringly.

'I'll say you don't!' said Lena emphatically. 'I mean, how many women on their own take on a cottage in a derelict state and make it into a home, then bake cakes for a living to bring their kids up?'

'Not many, I suppose,' agreed Jane. 'I hadn't thought of it like that.'

They went on to talk about other things until Lena said she ought to be going.

'I didn't realise I'd been here so long,' she said, looking at her watch.

'Nor did I.'

'Neither of us will get anything done when I move in, if this is anything to go by.'

They both laughed.

'Still, better that way than our not hitting it off at all,' said Jane.

'I'll say,' agreed Lena, going to the back door. 'But I think you and I are going to get along like a house on fire.'

'Me too,' said Jane, seeing her out.

The warm feeling of having made a new friend stayed with her all morning.

Chapter Eleven

'You will be coming to the football match on Wednesday night, won't you, Granddad?' Davey said one Sunday in August when Joe was having tea with them at the cottage.

'Not if *that woman* is going to be there,' replied his grandfather adamantly.

'Trudy Hamilton is sure to be there as she's Giles's mother and Kevin's grandma,' said Jane, passing him the salad.

'Sorry, son,' said Joe, looking at Davey sheepishly.

'Surely you're not going to let a thing like that stop you going to see your grandson play football?' said Jane with a hint of reproof.

'Please come, Granddad,' urged Davey. 'It *is* the Riverside Juniors' first proper match.'

'Yes, and Giles has worked very hard to get this team together,' added Jane. 'The least we can all do – as relatives of the boys – is go along to their first game and support them.'

Sighing heavily, Joe served himself with salad.

'I know all that and of course I want to go to the match . . . but that woman will accost me!'

'Honestly, Dad . . . you don't half exaggerate.'

'I like Kevin's grandma,' declared Davey. 'I think she's great.'

'So do I,' added Pip.

'And so she is,' said Jane, who thought Giles's mother was one of the warmest and most interesting people she had ever met. 'She's only being friendly when she makes a fuss of you, Dad.'

'She's *too* damned friendly – too loud, too bright, and too much altogether.'

'It's just Trudy's way,' said Jane. 'She's friendly towards everyone.'

When Lena Hamilton had described her mother-in-law as a one off, she hadn't been exaggerating. Jane had never met anyone like Trudy before. Neither had Joe, which was why he felt so intimidated by her, especially as she seemed to have taken a shine to him and blatantly pursued him when they were both visiting their offspring at the same time. Dad just couldn't cope with her gushing personality and dazzling clothes, which wasn't surprising since she wasn't like any woman he was ever likely to meet on the Berrywood Estate. His attempts to avoid her had become something of a joke between Jane and Lena and Giles.

The Hamiltons had moved into their cottage during the Easter holidays and had completely transformed life for Jane and the children. Far from restricting them, their new neighbours added another dimension to the Parkers' lives and they had quickly become good neighbours.

Davey and Kevin became inseparable almost from day one. Not having a daughter of her own, Lena made a great fuss of Pip and her friendship with Jane progressed as she had hoped it would after that first meeting. They were the same age and had a similar point of view about things. It was all very casual. The two families didn't stand on ceremony with each other and felt free to use each other's back doors without causing offence.

The Hamiltons were cultivated and urbane but enormous fun to be with. They were well-read and interested in the world around them. Their pleasures were simple, though, Jane noticed. Walking, reading and listening to music seemed to be their favourite pastimes, when they weren't busy with some community or charity project for they were both active voluntary workers.

Not having any other educated friends, Jane was surprised by how much she had in common with them.

166

Being in their company helped to broaden her mind, something that had been happening gradually ever since Mick left anyway. Conversation took on a whole new meaning for Jane now. She even began to like classical music because of the influence of her new friends.

Although they were obviously devoted to each other, Jane never felt excluded when she was in their company, and enjoyed many happy suppers with them after the children had gone to bed. The three of them had stayed up all night, glued to Jane's television set, on that momentous occasion in July when two American astronauts had taken the famous giant leap for mankind by being the first men ever to set foot on the moon. Having stimulating adult company so close to hand was a positive delight for Jane.

Giles was something of a hero to Davey and his friends and it wasn't difficult to see why. He was energetic and sporty and able to communicate with children authoritatively while appearing to stay on their level. His getting a football team together for the younger children of the area had been inspired by Kevin and Davey's love for the sport. Giles had worked tirelessly to get it organised, while still finding the time to work on his cottage. Throughout the summer he'd spent hours on the playing fields coaching the boys and had arranged for them to play other teams during the season, which was due to start on Wednesday evening. Now, as Davey tried to persuade his grandfather to attend their first game, Joe remained adamant that he wouldn't go if Trudy was there.

'She's not as friendly to others as she is towards me,' he insisted. 'She's after me . . . keeps trying to rope me in to help with those damned shows she puts on.'

'Doing what?'

'She asked me to take tickets at the door at some charity show she's organising in the autumn,' he said. 'I said no, of course.'

'It's all in a good cause, you know,' Jane pointed out. 'And it would do you good to get out more.'

'I'm out at work all day.'

'In the evening, I mean.'

'You can forget it, 'cause I'm not getting involved with a lot of silly old women,' he declared. 'And that's an end to it.'

'Trudy's only about your age.'

'Exactly,' he growled. 'She should grow old gracefully, not go about like some reject from the set of a horror film.'

The children found this riotous and roared with laughter.

'Now you really are going too far, Dad,' admonished Jane sternly. 'You're being very rude about Trudy. I like the way she looks . . . she's a very attractive woman.'

'Mutton dressed as lamb,' he snorted. 'I don't know who the daft cow thinks she is, carrying on like some West End producer.'

'The shows she puts on give pleasure to a lot of people,' said Jane.

'I'm not denying it, but all Trudy Hamilton gives me is a whole lot of grief,' he complained. 'I can't even come to visit my own daughter without fear of her barging in.'

'She probably thinks you're lonely and could do with a friend,' suggested Jane. 'You should be flattered that she's bothering with you. She has more than enough to do with her time.'

'Well, I'm not flattered, and I can do without her friendship, thanks very much.'

'I think you're being most unkind about her,' announced Jane firmly. 'And we'll all be very upset if you don't come to the football match on Wednesday after work.'

Joe looked pained.

'Oh, Gawd,' he said with an eloquent sigh. 'My life isn't my own.'

'It never is when you've a family. You should know that by now,' said Jane, secretly applauding Trudy Hamilton for trying to force her father out of the rut he'd dug for himself after his wife died.

It was a fine evening and the dying sunshine spread its golden light over the playing fields where twenty-two little boys were running their legs off on the football pitch. A sprinkling of spectators gathered on the touch line to cheer them on, Jane among them, having a wonderful time and yelling with the rest. It was so good to see Davey enjoying himself, and for her to participate in the community spirit that was so palpably present here this evening.

'The kids love it, don't they?' remarked Marie at half-time as she and Jane idly watched Lena go on to the pitch to take a plate of orange wedges to the players.

'They certainly do.'

'Roy's so excited actually to be in a football team.'

'I know, it's great for the younger boys to get a game. I think Giles's aim is to involve as many children as possible. It's only a bit of fun but it teaches them team spirit and gives them something to look forward to outside school hours.'

'They'll have to have the games at the weekend when the nights draw in.'

'That's right,' said Jane, suddenly aware of the earthy chill of autumn as evening fell. She could hardly believe they were on the brink of another winter, her third at the cottage.

'She's very attractive in an unobvious sort of way, isn't she?' remarked Marie, watching Lena walk back across the field, having delivered the half-time refreshments.

'I think she's lovely.'

'She's got a touch of class about her, that's for sure.'

'They both have.'

'He really is one to leave home for,' said Marie jokingly as Giles, wearing a bright blue tracksuit, bounded across the pitch to speak to Eddie who had been enlisted as linesman.

'Not half,' agreed Jane in a frivolous manner.

Marie looked at her sharply. 'You don't really fancy him, do you?'

'I'd be wasting my time if I did.' Jane grinned. 'He only has eyes for Lena. They're besotted with each other.'

'Yes, but supposing he *was* available. Would you be interested then?'

'I don't know,' she replied truthfully. 'As it isn't likely to happen, I'm not even going to think about it.' She gave Marie a questioning look. 'But you started all this. Are you having fantasies about him yourself?'

'Don't be daft,' she was quick to deny. 'I was only wondering about you. I can't imagine you ever being interested in anyone in that sort of way, except Mick.'

'I think I might be eventually,' Jane remarked thoughtfully. 'I don't suppose I'll spend the rest of my life alone.'

'You won't have to because Mick will come back one of these days,' said Marie swiftly.

Jane felt uneasy. Although her comment had been made lightly, Jane sensed that Marie was trying to make a point. Her sister-in-law had made her views known on this subject many times. She still assumed that if Mick did return to Jane, everything would be as before, after the recriminations were over. There had been a time when Jane had shared the same opinion. But Mick had been away a long time now, and she had made a life for herself without him. She honestly didn't know how she would feel if he were to come back into her life.

Guessing that Marie's devotion to her brother would make it difficult for her to understand this, she just said, 'Well, we'll just have to wait and see, won't we?'

'Yeah.'

They turned their attention back to the Hamiltons as they waited for the referee to blow the whistle for the second half. Lena ran over to her husband on the line and said something to him. He leaned his head close and spoke to her. Even from a distance you could see the intimacy between them.

'You're right about those two being besotted with each other,' said Marie.

'I know.'

'When I see them together, it reminds me of you and Mick.'

Jane didn't reply because she didn't want to argue with Marie. But Lena and Giles had a vastly different sort of relationship from the one Jane had had with Mick. Although the Hamiltons were closely bonded, they gave each other space. They had many shared interests and did lots of things together, but also pursued individual activities. Lena belonged to various women's groups and quite often went out in the evening without Giles, as he did without her. It obviously did wonders for a relationship, keeping it fresh and full of variety. Jane could see now how one-sided her relationship with Mick had been. He'd had a life outside the home but wouldn't have allowed his wife the same privilege.

Her thoughts were interrupted by Trudy, looking stunning in a billowing kaftan-style dress in multi-coloured cotton, and a scarlet turban-type hat worn with a few wisps of her tinted blonde hair poking out at the front.

'Hello, girls,' she said, kissing Jane's cheek then doing the same to Marie, whom she had met several times before. 'Nice to see you both.'

'You've missed the first half,' said Jane, after greetings had been exchanged.

'I know and I feel awful about it. But my showgroup meeting went on longer than I expected and I just couldn't get away.'

'Never mind, there's still the whole of the second half to come.'

They concentrated on the game as boys in varying degrees of muddiness tore about the pitch, falling over and excavating the field with the studs on their boots.

'Oh, I see your father standing up there by the goal, Jane,' said Trudy, sounding pleased.

'Yes.'

'He looks lonely up there on his own,' she said. 'I'd better go and keep him company . . . the sweet old thing.'

'Don't worry about Dad,' advised Jane, in an attempt to protect her father from annoyance. 'He likes his own company, especially when he's watching a soccer match.'

'Even so . . .'

The conversation was halted by the appearance of Pip and Melanie who were bored by all the boyish activity.

'Can we go and play on the swings, Mum?' asked Pip.

'Not now, love,' said Jane.

'Why?'

'Because you can't go on your own, and Aunt Marie and I want to stay here and watch the rest of the match.'

'Why can't we go by ourselves?' Melanie wanted to know.

'Because the playground is too far away for us to keep an eye on you,' said Marie.

'I'll go with them,' offered Trudy, turning to Jane and Marie. 'So long as that's all right with you?'

'Perfectly all right,' said Jane, smiling. 'In fact, we'd be very grateful.'

Trudy clutched the girls by the hand.

'Come on then, dears. The swings it is. Let's just go across and say hello to Pip's grandfather on our way, though, shall we?'

As she sallied forth with her charges, Jane said, 'She'll be about as welcome with Dad as the drugs squad at a rock festival.'

'It's a shame,' smiled Marie, who knew all about Jane's father's feelings towards the ebullient Trudy. ' 'Cause she's a smashing woman. It's a wonder she bothers with any of us. I mean, it isn't as though we're in the same class.'

'She's quite down to earth, though,' said Jane. 'The same as Giles. I suppose they must have got used to mixing with the hoi-polloi, with him turning his back on the family money and teaching in an ordinary state school.'

'Mmm.'

'I mean, I doubt if soccer was the game he played at

his own school. They all play rugby at these posh boarding schools, don't they? But it hasn't stopped him
throwing himself into the game of the masses for the
local kids.'

'It certainly hasn't.'

Glancing around, Jane was suddenly filled with
warmth towards the people she cared about. A frown
creased her brow as she thought of two of them who
were missing from this gathering.

'It doesn't look as though your parents are going to
make it, does it, Marie?'

'No. Dad does his midweek late round on a
Wednesday,' she explained. 'I told Mum to come without
him, said we'd bring her in the car with us. But he likes
her to be at home with his dinner on the table when he
gets in from work. And you know my mother. She won't
do anything to put him out.'

'It would have been nice for her to come along,
especially as both her grandsons are playing,' said
Jane.

'That's what I said to her but it's like talking to a
brick wall, trying to get her to stand up to my father,'
said Marie.

'I can imagine.'

Their conversation came to an abrupt end when
Davey scored a goal and both women jumped about,
shouting and cheering.

'Hello, Joe dear,' said Trudy.

' 'Lo.'

'How are you?'

'Mustn't grumble. You?'

'Fine. Enjoying the game?'

He nodded.

'I'm taking the two girls over to the swings for ten
minutes or so. They're bored stiff with the football.'

'Mmm.' He kept his eyes fixed firmly on the game in
the hope that the dratted woman would clear off and
leave him alone.

'It's nice to see the boys enjoying themselves, isn't it?' she remarked casually.

'Yeah.'

'It certainly helps to work off some of the excess energy they have at that age.'

'That son o' yours has done well by the lads,' he felt forced to admit, unable to avoid looking at her and hoping she didn't see his comment as an invitation to involve him in a lengthy conversation. He was heartened by the fact that the little girls were eager to go to the swings and were agitating to that effect.

'Yes, Giles is never happy unless he's organising something.'

No prizes for guessing who he gets it from, thought Joe.

'Anyway, we'll wander off to the swings now,' said Trudy.

Thank God for that, he thought, but said, 'Okay . . . enjoy yourselves then.'

'I'll give you a go on the see-saw, if you want to come with us?' laughed Trudy.

'Oh . . . no!' His face was a picture as he stared at her in horror. 'I think I'm a bit past that sort of nonsense.'

Trudy let out a deep throaty laugh that seemed to start at her toes and erupt through her body. What a fool he was not to have realised that she'd just been joshing with him!

'You know what your trouble is, don't you, Joe Harris?' she said, still chuckling.

'No . . . but I've a horrible suspicion you're going to tell me,' he said with a straight face.

'You take yourself far too seriously,' she told him cheerfully. 'You ought to lighten up a little.'

'Oh, grow up, woman, for goodness' sake,' he said gruffly.

'If growing up means never having fun, and sitting at home letting the world go by when there are so many things to do out there, then I hope I never do grow up,' she told him. 'I'm certainly not planning to.'

'Humph.'

'Come on then, girls,' she said. 'Let's go and have fun in the playground.' She threw Joe a parting smile, her complete lack of umbrage making him ashamed of his own boorishness, 'Who's going to be first up the slide?'

'Me,' they chorused.

Watching her stride purposefully across the field towards the playground area, swinging hands with the little girls and turning every so often to talk and laugh with them, he felt a stab of envy for her appetite for life and ability to be carefree. How good it must be to laugh so easily and have the confidence to do new things. Joe had never let his hair down in his life. Neither had his dear wife. Hardworking people like them had quite enough to do making ends meet to waste time on point-less merrymaking. Trudy Hamilton might have the time and money to make a fool of herself, but Joe Harris hadn't.

Seeing her enjoying herself, though, it seemed as if she reached out for the sunshine of life while he stayed put in the shade. He found himself wanting to be in the sunlight too, warm and happy and having fun. This line of thought shocked him. It wasn't like him to be envious, especially of some batty old woman who dressed like a cross between an ageing Eastern Queen and a hippy.

He must be going dotty in his old age or something because he felt an overwhelming urge to run across the grass and join Trudy and the girls in the playground. He wanted some of that sunshine that Trudy Hamilton found in such abundance. Admonishing himself, he turned his attention back to the game. But the restless feeling lingered.

Lena and Giles were having a bit of a lie-in as it was Saturday. They were both awake, though, and having a good-humoured battle about who was going to go down-stairs and make some tea.

'I suppose I'd better do it,' he said with mock sorrow. 'If I wait for you to get out of bed, I'll wait forever.'

'Thank you, Giles,' said Lena, burrowing under the covers. 'You're so good to me.'

'Flannel, nothing but flannel,' he said, getting out of bed and dragging on his dressing gown. 'But what's a chap to do . . .'

'I'll do the early-morning tea lots of weekends running to make up for you doing it now,' she bargained with him. 'When the weather gets a bit warmer.'

'I'm in for a long wait then,' he said. 'Seeing as it's only December.' Grinning, he pulled the covers back to reveal her face. 'Anyway, it isn't cold in the cottage . . . we had central heating put in so it wouldn't be.'

'During a bitter cold spell like this, it's cold despite that.'

'Rubbish!'

'I'll make the tea tomorrow . . . I promise.'

'Oh, look, there's a fleet of pigs coming in to land,' he said, waving his hand towards the window.

She threw a pillow at him and disappeared under the covers.

'If I wasn't certain that Kevin would walk in here at any minute, I'd be back in that bed to make you pay for that.'

'Promises, promises,' came her muffled retort from under the covers.

Giles went over to the window and opened the curtains with a flourish and an exaggerated deep breath for his wife's benefit. But he was silenced by what he saw outside. The landscape was white with frost. It was as though it had been carefully sprayed on to the bare winter trees and rooftops and dusted over the garden lawns and privets, just enough so that some of the green showed through. Everywhere was still and silent. Giles had seen a million frosty scenes before, but for some reason this one seemed ineffably beautiful to him this morning.

'You've gone very quiet,' said his wife, peering at him over the top of the sheet. 'What's out there that's shut you up?'

'Just nature,' he said softly.

'What particular aspect of it?'

'Get your body out of bed and come over here and have a look.'

She sat up slowly.

'You'll try anything to get me out of bed,' she said warily.

'You can go straight back afterwards,' he said. 'I won't renege on the tea-making, I promise.'

'Is it snowing or something?'

'Come to the window and see for yourself.'

'It had better be good,' she muttered, swinging out of bed and pulling on her dressing gown.

'It is.'

'Oh, yes, you're right,' said Lena, looking out over the rime-covered garden, glistening in the early sun. 'All we need is a robin redbreast and we'd have the pukka Christmas card scene.'

Giles slipped his arm around her.

'Our first heavy frost in the cottage,' he said softly.

'Yes, I know,' she said, her tone becoming more serious. 'I'm so glad we decided to buy it.'

'Me too. I really love it here.'

'Even though it's been such a lot of hard work and we're still not at the end of it?'

'Even more so because of that,' she said. 'I'm enjoying getting it how we want it. I've never felt so much at home anywhere.' She paused. 'Jane feels like that about hers, too. There's something about Vine Cottages that makes you never want to leave. It's funny.'

'And talking of Jane . . .'

Their eyes focused on the garden next-door as Jane marched down the path carrying a bucket of steaming water. She went to her car in the alley and began melting the ice on the windows with a cloth dipped in the hot water. She was wearing a black winter coat over trousers with a bright red woolly hat and matching muffler around her neck.

'That's the downside of a morning like this,' Giles remarked.

'Yes. The frost will probably have melted by the time we need to go to the supermarket in the car, though.'

'We're lucky. It's Jane's day for market so she has to go out early,' said Giles.

'She takes the children to her sister-in-law's first, too.'

'I certainly don't envy her working in a market on a day like this.'

'It's enough to give her double pneumonia standing about in the cold for hours on end,' remarked Lena as they watched Jane rubbing at the windscreen.

'I suppose market people get used to it,' said Giles.

'I think they must do.'

'Jane is very courageous in her way, don't you think?' he said.

'I'll say she is,' Lena agreed wholeheartedly.

'She seems to tackle life head on, almost daring it to do its worst.'

'Yes. I get the impression that whatever obstacle fate puts in her way, she'll never allow herself to be beaten. She doesn't make a fuss, just gets on with what must be done.'

'I get that impression too,' he said. 'She has a quiet kind of courage.'

'That's the perfect way to describe it,' declared Lena.

They watched Jane in silence for a while as she worked her way around the car, her breath turning to steam, cheeks glowing.

'She's very attractive,' said Lena.

'Yes. Never any sign of a boyfriend, though, is there?'

'No, there doesn't seem to be. I think she's probably a bit wary . . . I mean, after her husband going off and leaving her.'

'Something like that is bound to have an effect.'

'She was pregnant when he left, did you know?'

'No, I didn't.'

'It came out in conversation the other day,' said Lena. 'She lost the baby quite late in the pregnancy, apparently.'

'Poor Jane.'

'Oh, no, she'll never be that, Giles,' said Lena with strong emphasis. 'Brave Jane, gutsy Jane, but never *poor* Jane.'

'I only meant in that it was a rotten thing to happen to her,' he said. 'But I know what you mean about her. She definitely isn't poor, not in any sense of the word.'

Jane was trudging back up the path, her face almost as red as her hat. She saw them up at the window, their heads close together, and smiled and waved. They waved back.

'I'm really glad she lives next-door to us,' said Lena.

'Me too,' said Giles. 'I think in Jane we have a true friend.'

Going back into the house, Jane was thinking much the same thing about the Hamiltons; how much she enjoyed having them next-door and how she valued their friendship. But she was thinking these thoughts with an aching heart. She was going to miss them dreadfully. It was a bitter disappointment to her that she couldn't continue to be their neighbour. She would give a lot to be able to stay on here at Vine Cottages!

But something had come in the post the other day that had shattered her life yet again. She'd had a letter from her landlord, politely informing her that he was planning to put her cottage up for sale in the New Year so she would have to look for alternative accommodation!

Chapter Twelve

Around midday on that same December Saturday, Mick Parker walked briskly along the Brighton seafront, well turned out in a dark overcoat, white silk scarf and leather gloves. He was on his way to a pub in the Lanes where he was a lunchtime regular. It was bitterly cold with a deceptive sun beaming down on the stucco-covered houses, the overnight frost lingering in shaded places that didn't catch the sun.

Mick would be the first to admit he was more likely to be inspired to pleasure by a lucrative business deal than anything nature had to offer. But since he'd been in Brighton he'd grown to enjoy living by the sea. He liked the feel of the ocean nearby, its salty winds and special tang, particularly in winter when it was wild and dark or glinting icily in the heatless sun, as it was today.

Brighton had been good to him this last year and he seemed to have found a niche for himself here, albeit temporarily. There was a lot to be said for the history and architecture of the town, its fine squares and sweeping crescents. But Mick related more to its life, its colour, its criminal element – which was proving to be very useful to him.

He was now back in business and doing well, in a smaller way than he'd been in London but at least he was able to rent a decent flat and run a car. He still had a lot of ground to cover before he could afford to go back to Jane but he'd get there in the end. Thanks to some contacts he'd made in the pubs in the area, he was heading for big money.

When he'd first arrived here, he'd tried to go straight

for a while, selling household goods and cheap clothes door-to-door; he'd even had a go at encyclopaedias. It had given him a living but not enough of one to supply the capital he needed to set up in business properly.

Then one day he'd got talking to a man in a pub who'd introduced him to a much more profitable type of employment – handling stolen goods from regular sources. This soon earned him enough to rent a small warehouse. Finding buyers who didn't ask questions had been no problem at all because the cheap prices he was paying for the stuff meant he could afford to sell low. Mick never took anything hot unless he was sure he could shift it in double quick time.

His trade in dodgy goods was fronted by a legitimate wholesale operation and it worked like a dream. He would rather have done the whole thing straight, of course, but what choice did he have if he couldn't make money fast enough that way? When he'd got enough dough behind him to feel secure, he'd leave the hot gear alone and concentrate on straight stuff, maybe . . .

Working outside the law hadn't been nearly as frightening as he'd expected, considering that he'd been scared witless on the service-station job. His confidence was boosted by the fact that his set-up was more or less foolproof. So far as anyone except his criminal colleagues was concerned, he was running a squeaky clean wholesale business. He wasn't known to the police so there was no reason for them to check him out.

Walking through the narrow paved streets of the Lanes, in an area of ubiquitous jewellery shops, he slowed his step, attracted by the window displays. Christmas was drawing near. For the first time since he'd left home he could afford to buy Jane a decent present. There were some lovely dress rings on offer here, and beautiful gold watches. This was all classy gear – more unusual than the stuff that could be bought in the High Street jewellery chains. These were the trading outlets of small jewellers whose styles were more individual, many of them dealing in secondhand and antique jewellery.

With enthusiasm for Christmas growing, he became quite excited and thought of getting presents for the children too. When he'd finished here, he'd have a look round the big shops in the town centre at the toys.

'Can I help you?' asked the man standing behind the counter as Mick strolled into a shop.

'Yes, mate. I'm looking for something special for the wife . . . for her Christmas present,' he explained, finding it strange to be referring to his wife again after all this time. Jane and the children were outside the shady world he now inhabited so he never mentioned them.

'A necklace, perhaps . . . or a watch?' The man looked through the glass-topped counter into the showcase beneath. 'I've a lovely lady's watch here.' He pointed to a small gold cocktail watch. 'Guaranteed to keep you out of the doghouse with the wife until Easter.'

'Yeah, it's lovely,' muttered Mick, but his enthusiasm was already fading as he realised he would have to send the gifts by post. The parcel would be postmarked with this area and could lead to trouble. As things stood at the moment, Jane had no idea where he was. If she had an inkling of the district, she might try to trace him. And he didn't want that. He didn't want to see her until he was ready.

'Swiss made,' the jeweller was saying, taking the watch out of the showcase and laying it on the counter. 'Just look at that beautiful craftsmanship.'

'Sorry, mate, I've changed my mind,' said Mick, and hurried from the shop leaving the jeweller frowning.

He could hardly believe how careless he had almost been. That was what came of missing Jane so much. It had made him reckless. Oh, God, how he wanted her! The possibility that she might not want him back didn't even occur to him because he knew Jane wouldn't look at another man. Of course, with her not being in possession of the true facts of his leaving, he was going to be in trouble initially, until he'd explained what had happened. But she'd be so pleased he'd come back to rescue her from poverty and to look after her again, he didn't envisage any long-term problems in that direction.

But he wasn't going back until he could afford to reinstate them in their old lifestyle, in a lovely house like the one in Maple Avenue filled with good quality furniture, and a decent car for them both to use. Jane was a very special lady – she deserved the best. He experienced a rare pang of guilt at the thought of her living less well than she had when he'd been with her but he was soon able to dismiss it. After all, the state didn't let people starve these days, and he'd make it up to her when he got back. He was disappointed at the thought of another Christmas away from his family, though.

The alleyways in the centre of Brighton, were lively and bustling on this winter Saturday. Mick passed antique shops, boutiques, craft shops, emporiums selling fancy goods, his heels clicking on the cobble-stones. Passing a well-known oyster bar, he walked on through this maze of quaint old buildings with overhanging upper stories until he came to the Drake's Arms.

A blast of warm air and cigarette smoke greeted him as he pushed open the doors and he was instantly cheered. In here there were familiar faces – mostly men, many of them small-time villains. A lot of Mick's business deals were done here because this was a pub patronised by the sort of people who wanted to buy or sell with no paperwork or questions asked.

He nodded to a few men on his way to the bar where he ordered a scotch.

'You're not new to this game, are you, love?' he said to a barmaid he hadn't seen before, noticing what a sure touch she had with the optics.

'Not so's you'd notice, no,' she said with a friendly smile. 'I've been pulling pints for so long I could do it with my eyes shut.'

'Is that so?'

'Yeah. I've been working at the Fiddlers Inn for quite a while,' she informed him. 'This is my first day at the Drake's.'

'I knew I hadn't seen you in here before . . . I would have remembered.'

'My name's Patsy.'

'I'm Mick Parker and I'm glad to have you around,' he said, grinning at her as he gave her his money, noticing how good-looking she was in a brash sort of way.

'You're a regular then?' she said, handing him his change.

He nodded.

'I hope the rest of 'em are all as friendly as you,' she said.

'They're bound to be to a girl with lovely blue eyes like yours.'

He was stretching it a bit calling her a girl because she was well on the way to forty. And it was the contents of her tight-fitting sweater he'd noticed rather than the colour of her eyes. But she was a tasty sort with bright red hair, vivid blue eyes and a warm smile.

'Is that the best you can do in chat-up lines?' she asked.

He wasn't chatting her up, the silly cow. He was merely talking to her the way most blokes talked to barmaids. She'd be lucky!

But he heard himself say, 'I can try to improve on it, if you like?'

'No. Don't waste your time, love,' she told him lightly. 'I was only teasing you. I've heard 'em all in this job. And I never trust the smooth operators.'

'Very wise, Patsy,' he said, sipping his whisky.

She moved away to serve other customers and he found a space at the end of the bar and lit a cigarette. A man who had seen him come in and had checked with the landlord as to his identity, appeared at his side.

'Mick Parker?' he asked.

'That's right.'

'I hear you might be interested in a spot o' business?'

'I might be,' said Mick cagily, looking at the man who was thirtyish, tall and painfully thin with protuberant eyes and a long hairstyle like Mick Jagger's. 'I'm always willing to listen to any business proposition.' He paused meaningfully. 'So long as it's legit. I don't touch anything chancey.'

'Bristle Sharp gave me your name,' the man said meaningfully. 'He told me I'd find you in here.'

'Bristle Sharp, eh?' said Mick, his attitude changing at the mention of a well-known local villain with whom he regularly did business.

'That's right.'

'In that case, let's go and sit down, mate,' said Mick. They sat at a corner table.

'Sheepskin coats,' said the thin man, who was known ironically as Podge. 'Men's and women's. They'll go like a bomb in this weather.'

Mick knew this would be a good earner if he could get the coats cheap enough. But it wasn't in his best interests to seem eager.

'I might be interested,' he said. 'But I'd have to see the goods before I could say for sure.'

'Fair enough.'

'Bring a sample out to my warehouse on South Street,' he said. 'If I like what I see, we can talk price.'

'It's top-quality gear,' said Podge.

'It's also hot,' said Mick. 'I'd be taking a risk. I won't touch 'em at all unless I get 'em at a rock bottom price.'

'Plenty of people will be willing to take 'em off me,' said Podge.

Mick drew slowly on his cigarette, looking unconcerned.

'Feel free to let them go then, mate,' he said with feigned indifference. 'But if you've still got 'em on your hands next week and you wanna do business, come and see me at the warehouse.'

'Righto.'

Each man was aware of the other's tactics. They both knew they would eventually do business. It was just a matter of who would win on the question of price. They chatted about business generally while Podge finished his drink, then he left.

Mick went back to the bar and ordered another whisky.

'Have one yourself, Patsy,' he said pleasantly.

'That's very nice of you, Mick,' she said. 'But I'll miss out this time, if you don't mind. I've already got one lined up. There's still quite a while to go until closing time. Daren't get squiffy, not on my first day.'

He grinned. 'We can't have you rolling home, can we?'

'No fear.'

He noticed she wasn't wearing a wedding ring but pretended innocence as a way of extracting information.

'You'd be in dead trouble with your husband if you did that.'

'I'm not married, dear,' she said breezily. 'Not any more. I've been divorced for five years.'

'A boyfriend?'

'Not at the moment.'

'Oh.'

'You married?' she asked.

Mick hesitated before replying. To his surprise he found himself wanting to bare his soul to her. He hadn't responded to anyone on a personal level since he'd left home but Patsy's warmth touched him for some reason. There was something about her that he found appealing. God, he was lonely. He needed someone. It had been so long since he'd been with a woman.

'Separated,' he said at last.

'We're two of a kind then.'

'That's right.' He drank his whisky. 'What are you doing when you finish here?'

'Going home to have something to eat and put my feet up before it's time to come back for the evening session. Why?'

'I was wondering if the two of us might go somewhere,' he said, feeling oddly nervous. 'Seeing as we're both on our own. Perhaps we could go and have a bite to eat together?'

'Yeah, that'll be smashing, Mick,' she said with a beaming smile. 'I'll look forward to it.'

They went to a fast food place and had steak and chips because they were too late to get lunch anywhere classier. It was hardly luxurious but it was bright and cheerful and the food was excellent. Patsy was such good company it was impossible not to get along with her. Even at this early stage he could tell that she had a very easy going nature. She told him she was originally from London and had come to Brighton to make a new life for herself after the break-up of her marriage.

'He went off with my best friend,' she explained over coffee. 'A double betrayal, I think they call it. It meant I lost the two people closest to me.'

'Must have been awful.'

'It was a real blow. I had to get away somewhere . . . away from all the pity that was being dished out to me. I was demoralised enough. I didn't need people feeling sorry for me.'

'I can understand that.'

She gave him a querying look. 'How about you? Are you getting a divorce?'

'Oh, no!' he exclaimed in horror, because even the suggestion caused him pain.

'Well, don't look so shocked,' she said lightly. 'It's what separated people usually do eventually, isn't it? Get divorced.'

'Not Jane and me,' Mick said firmly. 'Ours is only a temporary separation.'

'Oh, I see,' she said knowingly. 'It's just a trial thing, is it?'

'Something like that.'

She drew on her cigarette, looking at him. 'Well, I hope it works out for you.'

'It will, it will . . . there's no doubt about it,' he insisted with far too much emphasis. 'It's just a matter of time.'

'You're lucky.'

'You'd like to get back with your husband then?' he said.

'Oh, no. I don't want that bugger back . . . not ever.' She looked thoughtful. 'It's just that . . . well, it does sometimes get awfully lonely, going home to an empty place.'

'A woman like you doesn't need to be lonely, surely?' he said. 'I mean, with looks and a personality like yours.'

'I get plenty of offers,' she said, 'but I don't go in for one-night stands with married men who get a kick out of laying the barmaid in their local.'

Mick knew she had said this as a warning to him. Oddly enough it wasn't a one-night stand he wanted with her. He didn't know quite what he did want from her but it was more than just sex. He needed someone to ease his loneliness until he was ready to return to Jane and the children.

'You may find it hard to believe but I don't go in for one-night stands either.'

She didn't say anything, just looked at him with a half smile. Her face was large and round and heavily made-up. She looked cheap and tarty but there was a gentleness in her eyes, despite the thick mascara. He knew instinctively that he could trust her.

Maybe it was because she was a stranger; perhaps it was because she had such a warm and comforting way about her. But whatever the reason, he found himself telling her the bizarre story of how he came to be here in Brighton – the whole sorry tale. It was a huge relief to unburden himself at last.

'That's some story,' she said finally.

'You're not kidding,' said Mick. 'I'm just living for the day when I can go back to Jane.'

She chewed her lip, worried because it seemed rather a naive thing to say.

'Don't you think you should have gone as soon as you got your memory back?'

'Oh, no, I can't go back to Jane while I'm a loser.'

'But, Mick, she'll have gone through hell when you went missing,' Patsy pointed out. 'Don't you think you owe it to her to let her know you're alive and well?'

'No,' he said firmly. 'I'm not going back until I'm ready.'

'How long have you been away?'

'Oh, it must be more than three years now,' he said. 'Yeah, it'll be four years next June.'

'And you're quite certain she'll have you back?'

'Positive.'

'You don't think she might have found someone else by now?'

He shook his head. 'Not Jane. I'm the only man for her.'

Which was perfectly understandable for a woman married to Mick Parker, thought Patsy, who had fancied him rotten the minute she'd clapped eyes on him. She thought he was gorgeous with his swarthy complexion and dark, melancholy eyes. If he hadn't had such an obsession about his wife, there might have been a chance of something worthwhile developing between them. But even after such a short acquaintance, she could tell he was a troubled man with a definite fixation.

'While you were there with her, I expect that was how things were,' she said, because she thought he needed to face facts. 'But you've been away a long time and she doesn't know that you're planning to go back. I mean, you couldn't blame her . . .'

'You can take my word for it, Patsy,' he interrupted with emphasis, '*I'm* the only man Jane wants.'

'The sooner you go back to her the better then,' was her answer to that.

'I can't . . . not yet.'

'But how is she going to feel when you do go back and she realises you've had your memory back for some time?' she asked.

He didn't even want to think about that so just said, 'I'll worry about that when the time comes.'

'Anyway, you don't seem much like a loser to me,' said Patsy.

'Compared to what I used to be, I am,' he said. 'I mean . . . I run a secondhand car and live in a rented flat. It isn't much for someone who used to have a big house and two new cars on the drive.'

'Are those things really so important to you?' she asked.

'Aren't they to everyone?'

'Not to me,' she said without hesitation. 'So long as I've a roof over my head and enough money to live on and pay my bills, I'm happy.'

For a moment Mick almost envied her. But not for long.

'What you've never had, you don't miss, I suppose,' he said. 'But I've been up there in the money and I want to be there again.'

'Oh, well, each to their own, I suppose,' she said mildly.

They lapsed into silence, each lost in their own thoughts.

'Well, that was a most enjoyable meal,' she said after a while. 'But I must go when I've finished this coffee and cigarette.'

'So soon?' said Mick, who felt happier than he had in ages and wanted it to continue.

'Afraid so.' She drank her coffee. 'I have to be back at the pub at half-past five and I need to do a bit of shopping before I go home.' She smiled at him. 'Thanks ever so much for lunch, Mick . . . it made a nice change.'

'I've enjoyed your company.' He stirred sugar into his coffee slowly, looking at her. 'You've really cheered me up.'

'I could win medals for cheering people up,' said Patsy.

'I can quite believe it . . . but I can't believe I've told you so much about myself.'

'It'll go no further.'

'I know that.'

They left the cafe soon after and went their separate ways, making no further arrangements. But that evening Mick couldn't get to the Drake's Arms quick enough.

'I was wondering,' he said to Patsy as she served him with a whisky, 'if you fancy going somewhere after you've finished here tonight? We could go to a club, if you like.'

191

She turned to the cash register and put his money through the till. When she turned back to him she was smiling.

'Why not?' she agreed casually, and he wondered if anything ever rattled her. 'We might have a few laughs.'

They went to a club called the Orange Tree which was in a smoky cellar. There was a small dance floor surrounded by tables and a band playing in the corner. They dined on chicken in a creamy sauce followed by chocolate gâteau and a good few drinks. When they smooched around the dance floor, Mick felt as though he had rejoined the human race after a very long absence. It felt so wonderfully normal to be holding a woman in his arms again.

'Fancy coming back to my place for a nightcap?' he whispered into her ear.

Patsy didn't come over all coy, or ask what he had in mind. She simply said, 'I thought you'd never ask.'

They were two lonely people, reaching out to each other for comfort. There was no more to it than that. They both knew Patsy wouldn't leave until the morning but neither of them had any thoughts beyond that. It was enough to feel happy for now.

'But, Jane, you can't do this to us,' said Lena one evening a few days later when Jane went next-door to tell her neighbours she was looking for somewhere else to live. All the children were playing upstairs, safely out of earshot.

'Whatever will we do without you?' said Giles, sitting on the sofa moving a pile of exercise books.

'I'm absolutely devastated,' said Jane who had been offered a chair by the fire opposite Lena, sitting with her legs curled under her. They were all drinking coffee which Lena had made as soon as Jane appeared.

'I bet you are,' said Giles.

'For some reason it had never occurred to me that the landlord might want to sell the cottage one day. I suppose it should have come into my mind when this one was put on the market.'

'Property prices are shooting up at the moment, especially in London,' said Giles. 'I suppose he wants to get in on the boom.'

'I haven't told the children yet,' said Jane. 'They'll be heartbroken.'

'So will Kevin,' said Lena gloomily. 'To lose his best pal, Davey.'

'He won't lose him,' said Jane. 'We'll be staying in the area and the kids will be going to the same school. I'm determined not to uproot them any more than I have to. I just hope I can find a decent place to rent not too far away.'

'It won't be the same for the boys as living next-door to each other,' said Lena.

'It won't be the same for any of us,' put in Giles sadly.

'We were only saying the other day how much we value having you next-door, weren't we, Giles?' said Lena.

He nodded.

Jane glanced around the room which was furnished country-style with tapestry-covered chairs, brasses on the walls and polished wood floors.

'I feel the same about you,' she said, looking from one to the other. 'It seems as though we've been neighbours forever.'

'What sort of a place are you looking for?' enquired Giles.

'I'm going to try for a house rather than a flat,' she said. 'If I can find one I can afford. But they charge the earth for houses to rent in London.'

Lena nodded. 'It's almost as much to rent as to buy these days.'

Giles looked at Jane. 'Have you thought of buying your cottage?'

'No, of course not.'

'Why not?'

'It wouldn't be within my means,' she said, adding thoughtfully, 'Would it?'

'I don't know what your financial position is, of

course, but you have a business which should stand you in good stead as regards getting a mortgage. And as a sitting tenant, you'd get the place below the asking price because the owner would save on agent's fees as well as all the trouble of trying to find a buyer. You'll probably have to pay a bit more for yours than we paid for ours because prices have gone up, even since we moved in. And yours isn't in such a bad state as ours was. But it still doesn't have central heating or luxury fittings so he'll have to keep the price within reason. The mortgage repayments probably won't be all that much more than the rent on another place.'

'Don't you have to pay a huge deposit, though?' said Jane, who could hardly believe she was having this conversation. Her a home owner? It wasn't possible. She had managed to save a bit from her profits, though.

'Not necessarily huge. The first thing you need to do is see the landlord. Find out how much he's asking for the place,' said Giles. 'If you need anyone to bargain with him for you, I'll be only too happy.'

'You've certainly given me food for thought,' she said.

'Well, don't think about it for too long in case he gets an offer,' said Giles.

'Don't worry, I won't,' said Jane excitedly.

The opposition Jane had met from the family when she'd first told them she was going to rent the cottage was as nothing to the outcry she received when she said she was thinking of buying it.

'You can't be serious?' declared her father, who was of a class and generation who thought only in terms of renting living accommodation.

'Why not?'

'Because owning property is a mug's game for anyone,' he stated categorically. 'And for a woman on her own it'll be a disaster.'

'I don't see why.'

'It's a huge responsibility. It'll be nothing but a millstone around your neck.'

Jane had purposely kept quiet about it until she had some solid facts because she knew what the family's reaction would be.

'I've enough saved for the deposit and the mortgage repayments won't be much more than I'll have to pay if I rent a place.'

'But it's an old property, Jane,' Joe reminded her. 'What about when the roof needs fixing or the place needs rewiring? There won't be a landlord to hand the bill to. It'll all be down to you.'

'I'll worry about that when the time comes,' she said.

'Things are bound to go wrong in a property of that age,' he insisted. 'You'll be better off in rented accommodation. You could always approach the council again.'

'That isn't what I want, Dad,' she told him firmly. 'I've made up my mind about the cottage and I'm going ahead.'

'On your head be it then.'

Marie and Eddie were just as negative.

'It'll be nothing but trouble,' said Marie. 'It isn't as though you've a man to lean on when the pipes burst or you get rising damp.'

Wilf and Rita were full of gloom too.

'If you must buy a place, why not get something more modern?' suggested Wilf. 'Something with all mod cons that won't give you any headaches.'

If it hadn't been for the Hamiltons, Jane might have been put off going ahead. But their attitude was entirely different.

'I'm so glad you're staying on next-door,' said Trudy warmly. 'We were all dreading the idea of your leaving.'

'Me too.'

'You can do what you like with your cottage once you become the legal owner,' said Trudy. 'Isn't it exciting!'

At a small drinks party at Jane's cottage on Christmas morning, her father and Trudy got quite heated when Trudy expressed these views to him.

'She's making a rod for her own back,' declared Joe. 'And you shouldn't be encouraging her.'

'She's building something solid for the future,' argued Trudy. 'It's a first step on to the property ladder. Even apart from the fact that she loves living in the cottage, it will be an investment if she ever wants to move away. Property prices are rising. These cottages will fetch a good price one day.'

'Cost her a fortune, more like.'

'Rubbish!'

'She'd be much better off renting a place,' he objected. 'It isn't as though she has a husband to turn to.'

'I don't have a husband either but I don't have a nervous breakdown every time something needs doing to my house.'

'It's different when you've got money . . .'

'Your daughter isn't exactly helpless, you know,' said Trudy forcefully. 'She has a very good business. You should have more faith in her.'

'I do have faith in her, but buying an old place like this . . .'

'She'll have a survey done before she signs anything.'

'Humph.'

Despite the minor altercation, that Christmas was one of the happiest Jane had ever known. Her father spent Christmas Day with her and the children and they visited Mick's parents in the afternoon as usual. On Boxing Day they all went to Marie and Eddie's as always. But everything was enhanced, somehow, by the Hamiltons being next-door. They were out visiting friends and relatives, too, but popped into Jane's in between times to compare notes.

Lena and Giles and Kevin spent New Year's Eve with Jane. Her father declined her invitation in favour of his local pub and Trudy had a party to go to, so it was just the three of them and the children for a buffet supper and party games.

As it was the end of a decade, they allowed the children to stay up until midnight. The boys managed it but Pip fell asleep on the sofa and was carried up to bed by Giles. For the first time since Mick's departure, Jane enjoyed the New Year's Eve celebrations.

She felt very positive about the New Year, too, and looked forward to becoming the legal owner of number one Vine Cottages. 1970 was going to be good for her, she could feel it in her bones . . .

One Saturday afternoon in high summer, Patsy Brown and Mick Parker were sitting on a bench on Brighton's Palace Pier, eating a fish and chip lunch from the paper and enjoying the sunshine. They had come here instead of going home when Patsy finished her midday session at the pub.

The crowds were out in force, a heaving mass of day trippers here for one purpose only: to eat, drink and be merry, with the emphasis very much on the latter. Many of the local residents preferred to stay away from the seafront during the summer when their town was taken over by strangers, especially since the mods and rockers had come a few years ago and wreaked havoc.

But Patsy loved the raucous gaiety of the holiday crowds and enjoyed watching them flock past, gorging themselves on candy floss and ice-cream and toffee apples.

'Plenty of people about this afternoon, aren't there?' she remarked.

'Plenty of pigeons an' all,' said Mick as crowds of the feathered variety strutted and pecked around their feet.

'Look at all the seagulls,' said Patsy, pointing to a row of birds perched like ornaments on top of the white-painted handrail through which the West Pier could be seen across a shimmering stretch of water. Some of the gulls had taken up residence on top of the lamp standards too. Patsy had never seen so many birds all in one place. 'They're not a bit put off by having us humans around them, are they? Living proof of the peaceful coexistence of the civilised and the untamed.'

'You can say that again,' said Mick, as a gang of youths walked by, shouting and laughing, their transistor radio blaring.

Patsy burst out laughing, giving him an affectionate nudge.

'Oh, Mick, you are awful,' she said. 'You know I meant the birds.'

'The seagulls aren't the only untamed creatures in Brighton today,' he said, smiling into her eyes.

'Oh, you,' she admonished playfully, grinning back at him.

This last six months or so had been bliss for Patsy. After going to Mick's flat that first time, she'd only been back to her own place once, to settle her bill and move her things out of there. She believed that Mick was happy with her, too, in his way, but he would never admit it because he was still hankering for his wife.

He'd been honest with Patsy and she appreciated that. He'd told her he liked her a lot and wanted her to live with him but it would never be a permanent relationship. Knowing that, it was up to her whether or not she moved in. He didn't want to mislead her in any way.

Smitten with him as she was, she hadn't hesitated, and had fallen ever more deeply in love with him as time passed. Theirs wasn't a lovey-dovey relationship and she never told him how much he meant to her for fear of driving him away. She lived for the moment and didn't dwell on the future.

It wasn't in Patsy's nature to make a fuss or complain too much about anything. From a poor home in London's East End, she was no stranger to hardship. And with a failed marriage behind her she was realistic about what life had in store for her. She took each day as it came and didn't expect too much. Meeting Mick had changed her life, though. They were really good together and had a lot of laughs. She wasn't blind to his faults. He was vain and selfish. He didn't respect the law in his business dealings and was greedy for money. But he was kind to her, was a wonderful lover, and when she could get him to relax he was entertaining company.

After all, she wasn't much to write home about herself. She was thirty-eight and didn't have any money behind her or any particular skills. Barmaiding was about the only thing she was any good at and that would never make her rich. Patsy didn't care about that but she did care about Mick, more than was good for her. She spoiled him, she knew that. She acted as his unpaid housekeeper and was always on hand with sympathy and support, of which he needed plenty. Five years older than he was, her concern for him was almost maternal at times. She worried a lot about him. His lust for money had already given him some sort of a mental breakdown. She was afraid it would do so again – that and his obsession about his marriage to which he naively believed he could return and pick up where he had left off. Being a realistic sort of person, she tried to suggest to him that things might have changed for Jane, that it might not be quite so easy as he expected. But he was deaf when it came to his wife, and painted a picture of a human being Patsy had yet to meet: someone without fault or defect.

So why did Patsy stay with him as glorified house-keeper, mother and lover all rolled into one? Because she was crazy about him. It was as simple as that. In her heart, she truly believed that if only he could let go of the past, he would learn to love her too.

'Have you finished, Pats?' Mick asked, screwing his chip paper into a ball ready for the litter bin.

'Yeah.'

'Let's have a wander then, shall we?' he suggested.

Having deposited their rubbish in the bin, they walked arm in arm to the end of the pier, past oriental domes and fancy metalwork arches, whelk and mussel stalls, souvenir sellers, palm readers, amusement arcades, and a host of other entertainments.

At the end of the pier they leaned on the handrail near some fishermen, looking across the turquoise waters to the shore – the pebble beach a pale biscuit colour in the distance, dotted with people; the hotels gleaming whitely in the sun.

Patsy drew a deep breath.

'Oh, it smells good, doesn't it, the sea?' she said.

'What you can smell of it above the hot dogs and hamburgers.'

'Don't be so unromantic, Mick,' she said, slapping his arm playfully. 'You know you're enjoying yourself.'

'If you say so. All I know is I used to be able to stay home and sleep off my Saturday lunchtime beer in peace until you came along and started dragging me out.'

'This is better than laying about at home on a lovely summer's afternoon.'

He looked down into the sea for a moment, then surprised her by turning to her and saying, 'Yeah, it is, as a matter o' fact. I'm glad you bully me into doing things like this.'

'Someone has to organise you or you wouldn't go anywhere at all outside of work, except to the pub,' she told him.

'I know.'

'Blimey, what's got into you today?' she said teasingly. 'I mean, actually admitting that I'm right about something.'

'Perhaps I'm going soft or something,' he said, but his tone was gentle.

'I think you must be.'

They both stared down at the calm waters in silence, listening to the lap of the waves and the gulls crying.

'Do you know something, Pats?' he said after a while. 'I'm really enjoying my life here in Brighton with you.'

'I'm glad 'cause I enjoy it too.'

Turning to her, Mick rested his large hand on her plump small one on the rail.

'You're one of the best,' he said. 'You're very good to me.'

'Now I know you're going soft,' she said, touched by the tenderness in his eyes.

'Maybe.'

They lingered for a while longer, thoroughly content in each other's company. Then Patsy said they ought to

think about going home because she had to get ready
for her evening shift at the pub.

Chapter Thirteen

Jane was busy in her garden collecting windfalls of apples from the lawn. It was a fine autumn morning with gentle sunshine filtering from a hazy blue sky, the windless air sweet with the scent of the fruit.

In contrast to the weather, Jane herself was in turbulent mood. She told herself she was imagining things about Lena and Giles Hamilton's attitude towards her; tried to make herself believe that they hadn't become deliberately cold. She clung tenaciously to the possibility that their manner must be due to their being busier than usual which was why Lena had stopped calling in for a chat, and why they both gave Jane short shrift when she called at their door or saw them in passing. After all, their normal routine did seem to have altered lately. Lena was not around a lot of the time now, and Giles seemed to come and go at odd times during the day when he would normally be at school.

But for all this sensible reasoning, there was no denying the fact that the once warm and friendly couple had drawn into themselves and didn't want Jane around. What she had done to offend them, she couldn't imagine. She'd wracked her brains for a clue but had drawn a blank.

The children had perceived a difference in their neighbours too. Davey said that Uncle Giles had been grumpy at football training and Pip claimed that Auntie Lena had gone off her. Jane wondered if personal problems were making them offhand. Marital troubles perhaps? But the fact that they were so united in their exclusion of Jane and her children made this most unlikely. Jane and Lena had become close friends. If she had a problem that didn't concern Jane, surely she would have confided in her about it?

Deeply hurt by their behaviour, Jane had felt obliged to stop calling on them since it was obvious she wasn't welcome. She felt awkward when she saw either of them in the garden or if she happened to be parking her car at the same time as they were. They both looked so strange, so different – sort of grim and absorbed in themselves.

Having this valued friendship come to an end without a word of explanation was very hard to take. The two families had enriched each other's lives in so many ways since becoming neighbours. Had it not been for the Hamiltons' encouragement, Jane would probably not have had the confidence to go ahead and buy her cottage, something she didn't regret for a second even though the current situation with Lena and Giles made living here most uncomfortable.

With all the fallen apples gathered into her basket, she sat on a wooden bench on the lawn, kicking off her sandals and tickling Shadow's tummy with her toe as he rolled about on his back, his fur warmed by the sun, eyes half closed with pleasure. The apples on the tree had proved to be eaters and unsuitable for use in her cake recipe but were crispy and delicious nonetheless. Jane gave them away to family and friends at this time of year; Lena and Giles, too, when they'd still been approachable.

The feel and smell of autumn pervaded her senses, filling her with melancholy at the passing of summer when they spent so much time in the garden. Now the lawn was covered with leaves, the bushes aflame with berries, the air tinged with the chill of advancing winter, despite the sunshine. With everyone inside behind closed doors, contact with her neighbours would be even more difficult.

Living here without the Hamiltons' friendship indefinitely was a depressing thought. With a sudden burst of determination, Jane decided she wasn't prepared to let it end like this. The least they could do was to tell her what she'd done to bring about their sudden change of heart.

Hearing their car draw up in the alley, she tensed, realising that here was an opportunity to bring things out into the open. She didn't know which one of them it was because she couldn't see over the back fence into the alley from this angle but she guessed it would be Lena as her husband would be at school.

With nerves jangling, she waited for the garden gate to open, surprised after all to see Giles and not Lena. Taking her courage in her hands, she went over to the dividing fence.

'Hello there, Giles.'

'Hi,' he said indifferently.

'I've plenty of apples if you'd like some?'

'Oh.' He had a grey, preoccupied look about him and didn't sound in the least bit interested in what she had to say. 'Thanks . . . er, it's kind of you to offer but I can't stop at the moment.'

'Kevin really loves them.'

'Yes.' He scratched his head, seeming distant and anxious to get away. 'I'll see you about it another time, if you don't mind?'

'Can you spare a minute to answer a question . . . please, Giles?' she said boldly.

'Some other time,' he said. 'I have to collect some books, then go straight on to school. I've had a lot of time off lately.'

Biting back tears at yet another rejection, Jane blurted out, 'Please tell me what I've done to upset you and Lena? Surely I deserve that much?'

'Upset us . . . you?' He looked baffled. 'You haven't upset us.'

'Oh? Then why am I being given the cold shoulder? If I've unintentionally done something to offend either of you, I'd like the opportunity to put things right.'

He clasped his head in both hands and, to her amazement, she saw tears in his eyes.

'Oh, Jane,' he said with feeling. 'It isn't you . . . not you at all.'

'No?'

'Absolutely not.'

'Why then?'

'We've been so wrapped up in our own troubles . . . neither of us realised how much we've been neglecting you.'

'Troubles?'

'Yes.'

'Giles, I know you're in a hurry but you look as though you could do with a coffee,' she said, perceiving his distress.

He looked at his watch.

'I suppose another half hour won't make much difference,' he said, and made his way into her garden through the gap in the fence they all used as a short cut.

'We should have told you what was going on,' Giles said, his hand trembling slightly when she handed him a cup of coffee. 'But we've had the most ghastly shock and neither of us has felt like talking to anyone except each other. It's even been an effort putting up a front for Kevin.'

With fear in her heart, she waited for him to continue.

'I can see now that we must have seemed offhand,' he said. 'I'm so sorry about that, Jane. But . . . well, the truth is, Lena and I have been locked in a world of our own.'

'Why, Giles? What's the matter?'

He didn't seem able to reply. His face was grey with tension, his eyes bloodshot and deeply shadowed as though he hadn't been sleeping. It was the first time Jane had been this close to him for weeks and she hadn't realised just how much his physical appearance had altered.

'Are you ill, Giles?'

'No.' His voice was tight, lips dry and pale. 'I'm not. But Lena is.'

He was sitting in an armchair in Jane's living room. She stood nearby, dry-mouthed and terrified of what he was about to tell her.

'She has a tumour on the brain,' he managed to utter at last. 'They say she has two months . . . maybe less . . . three at the most.'

It was as though he had slammed his fist into Jane's face. Her legs almost gave way and she wanted to be sick. But she knew she must control herself for his sake.

'Oh, Giles. I don't know what to say.'

'There isn't anything to say . . .'

An awkward silence hung between them. Jane searched her mind for the right thing to say or do and knew there wasn't one.

'How is Lena?' she said, hearing her words ring with foolishness. 'A silly question . . . I mean, how is she bearing up?'

'Not so good at the moment.'

'Oh, dear.'

'I've just taken her to the hospital for treatment,' he explained. 'I'll collect her later on, after school. We've been to and from the hospital all the time this last few weeks, that's why I've been home at odd times.'

'She doesn't actually have to stay in hospital then?'

'Not now. She has been in for a spell but she's an out patient at the moment. She wants to stay at home as long as she can.'

'That's understandable.'

He raked his hair back from his brow with his fingers, shaking his head in disbelief.

'Who would have thought this could happen? Just a few months ago we were planning the future . . . now there isn't one.'

'It does seem so terribly sudden.'

'She'd been having bad headaches but we weren't worried at first . . . I mean, everyone gets headaches from time to time.'

'Of course.'

'But hers became unbearable so she went to see the

doctor. He sent her for tests and that was it . . . all over for Lena at the grand old age of thirty-two.'

'And while you were trying to come to terms with this crushing blow, I was fretting because I thought you'd both gone off me,' said Jane humbly. 'God, it seems so petty now.'

'You weren't to know,' he said. 'We shouldn't have shut you out. But we've been too shattered to think straight. It's been almost as though the rest of the world had ceased to exist . . . we've been feeling so sorry for ourselves.'

'Who wouldn't?'

'It's just as well you've brought things out into the open, though,' he said, looking at her gravely. 'Because I should hate to lose you as a friend, and I know Lena feels the same.'

'It's been ages since she and I have had a natter and I've really missed her.' Jane paused then added with feeling, 'Tell me what I can do to help, Giles . . . please?'

His brow was deeply furrowed.

'Just be there for her.'

'I will be, you know that.'

'You'll have to be patient, though,' he explained. 'Because she doesn't want to see anyone. She's gone right into herself.'

'Oh, dear . . . that isn't like her.'

'No, it isn't. She doesn't even want to see my mother and you know how she feels about Trudy.'

'I do indeed.'

'The trouble is, Lena is very tearful at the moment, and doesn't want people to see her like that.'

'I shall just have to be persistent then, won't I?'

'The doctor has told me that this weepy stage will pass.'

They lapsed into silence, each locked in their own sorrow.

'If there's anything at all I can do to help either of you, you only have to ask,' Jane said.

'Thanks.'

'Perhaps I can look after Kevin . . . especially later on when things get more difficult?' she suggested. 'Being with Davey and Pip might help to take his mind off things, and he's just like one of the family with us.'

'Thanks again,' said Giles, finishing his coffee and getting up to leave. 'I'll bear that in mind.'

After he'd gone, Jane went into the kitchen to wash the coffee cups. She'd planned to experiment with a new cake recipe this morning. Now all she wanted to do was howl. She turned on the radio out of habit. They were playing 'Bridge Over Troubled Water' by Simon and Garfunkel. Tears poured down her cheeks. She knew she would never be able to listen to that beautiful song again without remembering the desolation of this moment and wanting to cry.

The following afternoon, when she knew Lena was at home alone, Jane armed herself with magazines and nipped through the gap in the fence to rap on the Hamiltons' back door with her knuckles. No reply. She knocked several more times and, when this didn't produce a response, opened the door warily and went in – something she would have done without a second thought a few months ago.

'Coo-ee, Lena, it's me, Jane,' she called into the house. 'I've just popped in for a chat.'

Silence. She could almost hear Lena holding her breath and hoping her visitor would go away. Chancing her arm but trusting her instincts, Jane went into the living room to find her friend sitting in an armchair by the fire, wearing ski pants and a sweater. She was pale and had lost weight but still looked lovely.

'I've got some front, I know, just walking in like this.'

'You said it,' said Lena cuttingly, regarding Jane with unveiled hostility.

'I thought you might like these magazines?' she said, putting them down on the coffee table.

'So I can read about next season's fashions?' said Lena bitterly.

'Oh, Lena, I'm so sorry,' cried Jane, her voice full of compassion.

'Not half so sorry as I am,' she said, her voice hard and brittle.

'I can imagine.'

'About the last thing I need right now is someone bursting with health and with a future ahead of them, feeling sorry for me!'

Jane swallowed hard.

'I can't help feeling sorry, Lena,' she said, voice quivering. 'I'm not being patronising, honest.'

Lena's eyes brimmed with tears which she managed to control. 'Oh, get out of here . . . just go and leave me in peace.'

'I want to say the right thing but I don't know what it is.'

'There's nothing you can say that will make me feel any better, so get out of here before you become as depressed as I am.'

'Oh, Lena, please don't shut me out,' begged Jane, venturing closer to her chair. 'I'm your friend, don't deny me that.'

'What use are friends to me now?'

'You may not need *me* but I need *you*,' said Jane firmly.

'Oh.' This clearly took her by surprise. 'I can't see why, since you're not the one who's going to die.'

'If you can't see why, then you're not the person I thought you were.'

Lena looked at Jane, her green eyes huge in her emaciated face. Then she stood up and opened her arms to her friend.

'Oh, God, Jane, what am I doing? I just can't seem to shake off this wretched self-pity. I shouldn't take it out on you.'

They hugged each other, sobbing.

'Why me?' asked Lena, when they were both calmer and sitting in chairs by the fire. 'Why should it happen to me?'

'It's a mystery,' said Jane shaking her head. Lena was

too young, too lovely, to be facing death. It didn't make sense.

'You can't possibly understand what it feels like to know that I won't see my son grow up.'

'I can't know but I *can* imagine,' replied Jane.

'I want to be brave but I can't fight my way out of this awful blackness.'

'You asked me what use friends were to you? Well, I can't do anything to change your destiny but I can promise to do what I can for Kevin. I know he has his father and his grandmother and all your other relatives. But I want you to know that I'll always be there for him as well, close at hand next-door. He'll want to be with Davey, he'll need his friends, and my house will be home to him for as long as he needs it.'

Lena didn't reply but Jane saw a hint of the old warmth in her eyes.

'That means a lot to me, Jane,' she said eventually in a soft voice. 'Thanks for coming in to see me.'

'I'm glad to see you again,' said Jane. 'I've really missed you.'

'I'm sorry I've neglected you, I've been in shock.'

'Don't worry.'

'I'll make us some tea.' She threw Jane a warning look. 'And don't you dare offer to do it for me. You might have to later on but until that time comes, I'm in charge around here.'

'Okay.' Jane grinned.

'Come into the kitchen with me while I do it, though, and tell me what's been going on around here while I've been out of circulation? I'm really out of touch.'

Jane guessed Lena was only putting up a front but at least some of her old spirit was back now.

It was bitterly cold and misty when Jane collected the children from school that terrible November afternoon.

'Is Kev coming to our place again, Mum?' asked Davey.

'Yes.'

'Brilliant,' said Davey.

'Hooray,' cheered Pip, who adored her brother's friend and irritated the life out of them both by trying to join in their games.

'We can finish that game of table soccer we started last night, Kev,' said Davey.

'Is Daddy at the hospital again, Auntie Jane?' asked Kevin.

'Yes, I'm afraid so, love,' she told him, her heart breaking.

'Oh.'

'You'll be all right with us until he gets home, won't you?'

'Sure,' he said, sounding subdued.

'I'm sorry your mummy is ill, Kev,' said Pip, patting his hand sympathetically, unaware of the seriousness of the situation. 'But it's really great that you're staying at our house so much. It's like having another brother, but better 'cause you're not as bossy as Davey.'

Lena was in hospital, in a coma and not expected to last the night. For a while after Jane's reconciliation with her, she had seemed quite well. Jane had spent as much time as she possibly could with her. Between Trudy, Jane and Lena's mother, the sick woman hadn't lacked for company while Giles was out at work. Knowing this was the case, he could go into school with an easy mind, so at least Jane felt she was making some sort of contribution.

Most of the time Jane and Lena had talked about all the usual things – men, marriage, kids, clothes – just as though everything was normal. It struck Jane as odd that they could be this ordinary at such an extraordinary time. But sometimes Lena's bravery deserted her and she became almost hysterical with the unfairness of it all. Jane also wanted to scream at the injustice but knew this would only upset Lena even more. Jane didn't know how best to behave so followed her instinct which seemed to be telling her to keep things as normal as possible. It was an appalling strain but she had to go on being there for as long as Lena needed her.

Then about a week ago her friend's condition had worsened suddenly and she'd been taken into hospital. True to her promise, Jane concentrated on helping Kevin through this terrible time in the only way she knew how, with kindness and love. Giles wanted to spare his son the agony of seeing his mother at the end, and Jane had told Giles that if he needed to stay at the hospital overnight at any time, she would put Kevin to bed with Davey.

Now, giving the children their tea, Jane managed to behave normally though sick with dread, waiting for what she knew must come. Every time the telephone rang, her heart lurched. When tea was over, the children watched the television for a while then went upstairs to play in Davey's bedroom. They were all unusually subdued. The boys even tolerated Pip's company without making a fuss which was an indication of how they were feeling.

When Jane had finished washing the dishes, she went into the living room and sat down in an armchair with the newspaper, in an effort to take her mind off things. But the fact that the first year of Mr Heath's Conservative government had been marked by more working days lost by strikes than at any time since 1926 seemed trivial compared to the drama taking place here. The item about missiles being thrown at the stage by protesters during the recent Miss World contest didn't hold her interest either.

She was just beginning to think about getting the children ready for bed when Giles came in at the back door. She could tell by the stricken look on his face that it was over.

'It was quite peaceful,' was all he said.

'Oh, Giles!'

She wanted to put her arms around him and comfort him but he looked so grim, so distant and unapproachable.

'You look done in. Come into the living room and

have a cup of tea . . . or I might be able to find something stronger?'

'No, thanks, Jane. I have to take Kevin home. I have to tell him.'

'Yes, of course,' she said. 'He's upstairs. I'll call him.'

'Thanks for having me, Auntie Jane,' said Kevin at the door.

'It was no trouble at all, love,' she said. 'See you soon.'

It was a sad moment for Jane, watching father and son go off together to struggle with their loss. She wanted to be with them, to make them feel better somehow. But for the time being she could not; they needed to be alone together with their grief.

'What's the matter, Mum?' asked Davey as she closed the door after them and turned into the kitchen, crying. 'Has something happened?'

'Yes, I'm afraid it has,' she said sadly. 'Kevin's mother has died.'

'Oh,' he gasped, looking frightened. 'Does that mean she's never coming back?'

'That's right.'

'Poor old Kev,' said Pip, her eyes filling with tears.

Davey was thoughtful, his dark eyes faraway.

'Do you think if I gave him one of my table soccer teams it might cheer him up?'

Jane very much doubted it but it was such a kind thought.

'It might do,' she said, holding both her children close to her as the fragility of life was brought starkly home to her.

Jane and her father both attended the funeral on a dark November day with mist swirling around the graveside. It was a large gathering of friends, relatives and colleagues. Giles had allowed Kevin to be there to say his final goodbye and the two of them stood close together.

It seemed strange to see Trudy looking subdued in black. But she still managed to stand out, albeit unintentionally, in an enormous black hat and fashionably long dark coat.

'It should have been me, not her,' Jane heard her say to Joe when the funeral party gathered at Giles's cottage afterwards.

'You mustn't think like that,' he said with unusual kindness towards her. 'If it was meant to be that way, that's how it would have happened. It isn't for us to say how these things should be.'

'Poor Giles,' said Trudy with a worried sigh. 'God knows what he's going to do without her.'

'He'll manage,' said Joe, reminded of his own loss and also that Trudy had lost her husband. 'We all do, somehow.'

'Kevin's young . . . and children are very resilient,' she went on, almost as though he hadn't spoken. 'But Giles . . . I mean, he and Lena were everything to each other. I just don't know how he's going to come through this.'

Hearing this conversation, it was as though Jane's own thoughts were being spoken aloud. This was something that had been keeping her awake at nights, too.

Giles withdrew into himself. He avoided conversation with Jane whenever they met, which was often because Kevin spent most of his time outside school hours in Jane's cottage. She collected him from school every day with Davey and Pip to save him waiting for Giles to finish at the Gram. Kevin usually had tea with Jane's children and stayed until bedtime. Giles seemed relieved to shed this responsibility so that he could nurse his own personal grief.

His zest for life died with Lena. He lost interest in the Riverside Juniors and left the running of the football team to a pal of his who had previously been his assistant. Once a great walker, whatever the weather, he didn't even do that now. So far as Jane could gather, he didn't do anything except go to work and care for Kevin in a distant sort of way. It was obvious Giles's behaviour was having an effect on the boy who never seemed to want to go home.

What could Jane do? It wasn't her place to interfere. She thought of inviting him to join them for meals occasionally but Giles made it so obvious that he wanted to be left alone, she felt to do so would be an imposition. She included Kevin in her own family outings, but on Saturdays when Davey and Pip were with Marie, while Jane was at the market, he was always at the window waiting for them when they got home. Her heart went out to him.

As Christmas drew near and Giles showed no sign of emerging from his depression, she was really worried. Jane cared about him as she had cared about Lena. She knew he had to go through this grieving period but wished she could do something to help. She hated to see him so lost and alone.

She was in the kitchen getting supper ready one Saturday evening after a busy day at the market when he came to the back door with a package he had taken in for her from the postman. She ushered him inside, hastily putting the parcel out of sight in the first place to hand – the larder. She offered him a cup of tea which he declined.

'It's lucky the kids are in the other room because that parcel is full of Christmas presents for them from my mail order catalogue,' she explained, putting some hamburgers under the grill. 'If they knew they were in the house, they'd have the place upside down looking for them every time my back was turned.'

'Oh, I see,' Giles said dully. ' I thought the larder was an odd place to put a parcel.'

'They have eyes like hawks when it comes to Christmas presents,' she said. 'I expect Kevin is the same?'

'Mmm,' he muttered vaguely.

'I'll open the parcel to check the contents when they've gone to bed, then hide it properly,' said Jane chattily. 'I've got stuff hidden all over the house.'

'Of course, Christmas is almost upon us now, isn't

it?' he said, sighing heavily as though the mere thought of the festive season made him feel even more miserable.

'It won't be long,' she said, frying chips in the chippan. 'I've ordered quite a few bits and pieces from my catalogue. It's very handy at this time of the year.'

Giles looked stricken.

'I suppose you could do without Christmas this year?' she said quietly, standing back from the cooker and looking at him.

'You could say that.'

'Still, you'll have to make an effort for Kevin's sake, won't you?' Jane opened a tin of baked beans and emptied them into a saucepan. 'Children are very therapeutic. They force you to keep going. I know mine did when Mick left, even though all I wanted to do was die.'

He didn't reply and when she turned she was disturbed to see that his face was contorted and he was crying silently.

'Oh, Giles,' she said, putting her arms around him and holding his quivering body close to hers.

'I'm sorry,' he spluttered. 'I'm being pathetic. I'll go.'

'Shhh,' she said gently.

'This is the first time I've actually let go and cried.'

'I guessed that.'

'I've tried to stay strong for Kevin. Now look at me.'

'Letting your grief out isn't a sign of weakness,' she said gently. 'You have to let it out, Giles, it's the only way forward.'

'I don't want to go forward without Lena,' he sobbed, his words barely audible.

'I know, I know,' she told him softly. 'But you have to carry on somehow . . . for Kevin's sake. He needs you. You have each other, you'll come through this together, believe me.'

He sat down at the table with his head in his hands, his body heaving as he sobbed uncontrollably, his cries deep and guttural. She left him alone, saying nothing and busying herself by turning the supper down and making a pot of tea. When the children came in in search of food, she shooed them away with a biscuit and a request to make themselves scarce for a while.

Giles wept for a long time and when he finally managed to compose himself, Jane poured tea for them both and sat opposite him at the table.

'What must you think of me?' he said. 'I'm sorry to be so weak.'

'You haven't been weak,' she assured him. 'Keeping a stiff upper lip indefinitely was doing you no good at all.'

'I don't know what came over me . . . once I started, I just couldn't stop.'

'You'll be all the better for it,' she said. 'I've been so worried about you. You've been going about like a robot.'

'Sorry.'

'Stop apologising,' she urged him. 'I'm your friend, remember?'

'Oh, Jane,' he said, contrition emerging through his grief. 'I've been so wrapped up in myself, and you must have been suffering too, having lost a dear friend.'

'I do miss her terribly . . .'

'You've been so good to me, having Kevin as a more or less permanent house guest. It's been an effort having him around because I've been feeling so wretched.'

'We enjoy having him. He's just like one of the family. But it's you he really wants. Losing his mother must have traumatised him.'

'I've been neglecting everything except what I actually have to do at school,' said Giles, his voice husky from weeping. 'The football team, my after-school gym club . . . but, more importantly, I haven't been giving Kevin the attention he needs.'

'I can't disagree with you about that. But don't be too hard on yourself,' she said. 'This is a very bad time for you. You'll do all the things you should . . . eventually.'

'I have to pull myself together, though.'

'Yes, you must, for Kevin's sake.'

'Easier said than done.'

'I know this might seem to be suggesting the impossible, the way you're feeling now,' she said, 'but if you force yourself to take up your old commitments again, the football team, the gym club and so on, it might help.'

'I've been feeling too lethargic and lacking in heart to do anything.'

'I know the feeling.'

'You do?'

'Oh, yes. I didn't lose my husband through death but it felt as though he'd died after he left me,' she said. 'Some days I didn't know how to put one foot in front of the other, I felt so dreadful. But I had to keep going for the sake of the children. They gave my life a purpose and helped me through it.'

'I'd forgotten that you've been through a similar sort of experience,' he said. 'You've been so organised ever since I've known you, it's hard to imagine it was ever any different.'

'It was, I can assure you. And I had all the humiliation and rage to cope with too, the anger with him for walking out on me,' she explained. 'God, I felt so demoralised.'

'I've been feeling angry, too,' Giles said. 'Angry with God for letting her die, angry with her for leaving me. Stupid, isn't it?'

'Irrational, not stupid. But I've heard that's quite a common reaction when someone you love dies. I suppose it's a response to being so powerless against a higher force.'

'Yes.'

'There was nothing irrational about the fury I felt when Mick walked out and left me and the kids penniless, though,' she said. 'I was angry, hurt . . . completely shattered. I'd never have thought he could do such a thing. Still, they say you can never really know anyone, don't they?'

'And now?'

'The anger has more or less burned out after all this time.'

'Good.'

'I still wonder about him, though . . . where he is, what

219

he's doing. We were very close, you see. Until he disappeared I could never have imagined life without him. I was very reliant on him which made it even more difficult for me to adjust. But I'm used to living without him now and think about him less often as time goes on. Inevitable, I suppose.'

Davey came into the kitchen wanting to know how long they had to wait for supper because he and Pip were really hungry.

'Not long now,' she told him. 'I'll call you when it's ready.'

'I'd better go and leave you to it,' said Giles when Davey had gone. 'Kevin and my mother will be wondering where I've got to. I told them I'd only be a minute.'

Jane looked at him, wondering.

'Why don't the three of you join us for supper?' she suggested impulsively.

'Thanks but . . .'

'We're only having burgers, beans and chips but I can easily make a bit extra,' she persisted. 'And we'd really love to have you.'

Giles still looked doubtful.

'We're having one of my spicy apple cakes to follow,' she said, to make light of it and try to bring some ordinariness back into his life.

'Well, in that case, how can I refuse?' he said, managing a watery smile. 'I'll just pop next-door and get them.'

'Brilliant,' said Jane, smiling.

Chapter Fourteen

'What would you say if I was to tell you that I'm thinking of opening a shop?' Jane asked Giles one Sunday afternoon in the early-summer of the following year when they were out walking in Richmond Park with their offspring, who had gone on ahead to watch some children flying a kite.

'Instead of the markets or as well as?' he enquired.

'Instead of.'

'In that case, I'd say it's a very good idea.'

'You don't think I'm being a bit too ambitious then?'

'Not at all. At least you wouldn't be so completely at the mercy of the weather, especially in the depths of winter.'

'With the amount of clothes I wear, that isn't really a problem.'

'Even so . . . it can't be pleasant when it's bitterly cold.'

'It isn't. I'll be sorry to give the markets up, though,' she told him thoughtfully. 'I enjoy the lively atmosphere and I usually get a few laughs with the other traders.'

'Now that you've been in business for a while and have proved there's a steady demand for your cakes, a shop would be more sensible.'

'Yes, it does seem to be the most logical thing to do,' she agreed. 'And I'd have more time with the children at weekends.'

'How's that? Surely you would open the shop on a Saturday?'

'Of course. But I'm thinking of having staff working in the shop while I concentrate on the actual cake-making,' she explained. 'I think it's time I stopped being a one-woman operation.'

'You're planning a major expansion then?'

'I'm not planning on opening other branches and becoming a chain, or anything like that,' she said. 'But I would like to put my business on a more stable footing.'

'Good idea. But would you do the baking at the shop?'

'Oh, no. To do that would mean I'd be away from home more rather than less,' she said. 'I'd rather continue to make the cakes in the cottage kitchen . . . as long as I have big enough ovens.'

'I still don't see how you'll be able to take the weekends off, though?'

'Well, as things are at the moment, because I like the cakes to be as fresh as possible, I bake on Fridays for the Saturday market and on Sunday for the Monday market. On other days I'll be working on the orders for shops and cafes and customers who order from me direct.'

'And you're out working on Saturdays at the market.'

'Exactly. I shall have to work until late tonight to make up for the fact that I've taken this afternoon off, for instance. But if I had a shop, I wouldn't open on a Monday which means I wouldn't have to bake on a Sunday. If I had the shop staffed I would be free on Saturdays too. Obviously, there would be occasions when I'd have to work at the weekend – staff sickness and holidays, special orders and so on – but at least I wouldn't be quite so tied as I am now. And as I wouldn't have to go out selling cakes, I'd have time to experiment with new recipes, so that I can improve existing favourites and introduce new lines.'

'You won't change the recipe for the spicy apple cake, I hope?'

'No fear! That's still my biggest seller. I seem to have got the taste and texture of that just about right.'

'I can vouch for that.'

'I'd like to develop the occasion cakes side of the business too . . . birthday cakes and so on. I have to turn orders away at the moment, 'cause I just don't have the time.'

Giles looked puzzled.

'Surely you'll be even busier, though, won't you?' he said. 'I mean, if you have a shop trading five days a week, you'll need to produce more cakes than you do now.'

'Lots more,' she said. 'But I'm thinking of offering my sister-in-law Marie a job . . . working with me in the kitchen.'

'Ah, now that really *is* a good idea.'

'I know she could do with the extra money and we get on really well together, having been friends for so long. I trust her to keep my recipes to herself, too.'

'An important factor.'

'Oh, yes.'

'What about the school holidays as regards her children?'

'No problem. She can bring them to work with her. They're quite at home at my place, anyway, with Davey and Pip. It wouldn't be practical to give her a job in the shop because they would be in the way there.'

'Well, it sounds to me as though you have it all worked out and have already decided to go ahead.'

'I have, more or less. I just needed actually to say it out loud to someone – someone who can view the idea objectively. I can't talk anything like this over with my father because he's too personally involved. He gets worried for me, thinks I'm getting in too deep.'

'Like he did when you bought the cottage?'

'Yes. But once a thing becomes a fait accompli, he calms down.'

'It's only because he cares about you that he puts up opposition.'

'Yes, that and the fact that he isn't used to women being in business for themselves or owning their own house.'

The discussion was halted by the children who had seen enough of the kite-flying and were now eager to take a look at the deer who lived in the park. So they all tramped on, chattering and laughing, lingering for a while by the sun-splintered waters of Pen Ponds where legions of waterfowl splashed about on the surface:

ducks, swans, herons – a flock of geese pecking for insects on the grassy banks.

The little group trekked on through thickly wooded areas of ancient oaks and beeches, ash and willows, eventually coming to Spanker's Hill Wood where they observed a herd of deer from a safe distance.

'There you are, kids,' said Giles as they watched the magnificent creatures. 'Straight from Santa's workshop.'

The two boys tutted and raised their eyes with youthful scorn.

'There isn't really a Santa Claus, Uncle Giles,' explained Pip earnestly. 'It's just an ordinary man dressed up.'

'Is that right, poppet?' he said, teasing her affectionately. 'Where do all the presents come from at Christmas then?'

'They come from people, silly,' she informed him patiently, not quite old enough to catch on to the joke. 'Your friends and family give them to you . . . if you're good. Everyone knows that.'

'Does that mean I'll have to be good if I want some presents this Christmas?'

'You won't get any if you're not,' she said in the manner of an indulgent parent pacifying a child.

Jane smiled. She usually felt a warm glow when they were all together like this, almost as one family.

They walked on and climbed the hill to the highest point in the park where, through the trees, they could see St Paul's Cathedral, twelve miles away. They sat on a bench in the sunshine for a while to recover, then the children were promised ice creams from the van in the car park when they got back.

'I'll have leg muscles like an athlete before long,' remarked Jane as they made their way back down the hill.

'Why's that?' asked Giles.

'Because of all the extra walking I've been doing this last few months,' she explained. 'A gentle stroll by the river was about the most strenuous exercise my legs had to contend with before you started dragging me out for killer marathons like this.'

'Go on with you, you know you feel better for it,' he said.

'Just teasing.'

'Good. I should hate to think I was twisting your arm.'

'You're joking,' she said heartily. 'Striding through Richmond Park has become one of my greatest pleasures.'

It was true. Over the last six months or so she and Giles and their children had spent a lot of time together. After he'd joined them for supper that first time after Lena's death, Jane had felt able to suggest that they team up again, for meals and outings. At first he needed coaxing but after a while he'd seemed to find the Parkers' company as enjoyable as his son did. He even began to take the initiative and organise things for them all to do together. It was lovely!

After sobbing his heart out in her kitchen last Christmas, he'd seemed to drag himself out of the doldrums, on the surface anyway. He'd resumed various commitments including the management of the Riverside Juniors until the end of the season, while Jane inherited Lena's job of laundering the team shirts. She also helped transport some of the boys whose parents couldn't get to the matches. Fortunately, most of the games were on a Sunday morning so she was available.

In helping Giles through this time of adversity, Jane found personal fulfilment. Whereas Mick had encouraged her to think of enjoyment only in terms of organised entertainment and material comfort, Giles opened her eyes to simple pleasures that cost nothing beyond a little effort. Although their relationship was platonic, he took far more interest in her as a person than Mick ever had. It was only in retrospect that she could see that her life with her husband had revolved around him entirely. She had been happy enough in his shadow because she had known nothing else. But life was much more satisfying for her now.

'Getting back to this shop idea of yours,' Giles said as the children ran on ahead, 'do you have any area in mind?'

'Well, actually, it's funny you should say that . . .'

'You've already found somewhere, haven't you?' he cut in, laughing.

'Yes, there's an empty shop for rent in Chiswick High Road that I think would be suitable. It used to be a sweet shop,' she explained. 'It's only small but big enough for what I need as I shall be doing the baking at home.'

'Will it cost very much to set it up as a cake-shop?'

'Not a huge amount, especially as I'm only going to rent the premises,' she said. 'But I will need some working capital.'

'More than you have to hand?'

'Yes. I seem to have poured all my money into the cottage since it became mine . . . what with central heating and other improvements.'

'Does the shop need much in the way of alteration?' he asked.

'Nothing major,' she said. 'Just a few modern shop fittings. And I want it painted inside from top to bottom. I shall continue to do the markets until the last minute so I won't lose the income.'

'What will you do about the working capital, though?'

'I shall just have to throw myself on the mercy of my bank manager.'

'I'd help if I could but a teacher's salary doesn't run to lending people money.'

'I wouldn't dream of borrowing money from you,' she said, aghast at the suggestion. 'I've a good track record with the bank so I'm hoping they'll support me in this new venture.'

'If you need any practical help, getting the shop organised, you can rely on me,' Giles offered. 'School finishes for the summer holidays soon, so I'll have plenty of time.'

He looked haunted suddenly, his face pinched with pain. She realised that the once-longed-for summer break was anticipated with dread this year, without his beloved Lena. Kevin was going to feel it too but he was of an age where friends could fill the gap, up to a point.

'It's kind of you to offer, Giles. I appreciate that.'

'I can't come up with the money you need but I do have plenty of muscle . . . and it's all at your disposal.'

'You don't know what you're letting yourself in for,' Jane said lightly, but there was more than a grain of truth in what she said because she had just thought of a way of helping him through his first long summer holiday as a widower.

'I like the white streaks in your hair,' teased Giles, coming down the ladder where he'd been painting the ceiling of Jane's shop while she worked on the walls. 'They're very fetching.'

'Oh, no! How could I have got paint in my hair when it's covered up?' wailed Jane, who was wearing her oldest jeans and a tee-shirt, a scarf tied securely around her head.

'Your hair's come out at the front.'

'Damn!'

'Come here,' he said, putting his paintbrush into a tin of turpentine. He dipped a small piece of rag into the chemical. 'Let's see if I can get it off with this stuff.'

Putting her paintbrush into the turps, Jane went over to him and waited while he rubbed at her hair, inwardly trembling with pleasure at his close proximity.

'Well, I've got most of it off,' he said after a while. 'You'll have to cut the other bits off or let the paint grow out.'

'Thanks, Giles,' she said, reluctantly moving away.

'My pleasure.'

'Time to break for lunch, I think.'

'The perfect moment for a rest,' he agreed. 'I've finished the ceiling.'

'Well done,' she said, looking up. 'You've made a good job of it.'

They sat on a couple of orange boxes in the shop area

and Jane produced a flask of coffee and some cold chicken and salad, with apple cake to follow because it was Giles's favourite.

'I wonder if the children are enjoying themselves?' she remarked.

'I shouldn't think there's any doubt about that as they're with my mother,' he told her. 'She'll spoil 'em rotten.'

'A picnic by the river at Runnymede today, isn't it?' said Jane.

'Yes, I think that's what she said was on today's agenda.'

'It's certainly been a great help, having her keep the children occupied while we get on with this.' Trudy had taken the children out somewhere most days so that Jane and Giles could work at the shop undisturbed. 'She's a brick.'

'Has she told you about her latest craze?' he asked chattily.

'Ballroom dancing, you mean?'

He nodded.

'Yes, I've heard all about that.'

'She loves it.'

'I think she would try to get my father to go along with her but he's safe this time because it's in the afternoon while he's at work.'

'When he retires there'll be no stopping her,' warned Giles.

They both chuckled because Trudy's dogged quest to get the reserved Joe Harris 'out of his shell' was still a standing joke.

Giles cast his eye around the shop with its neo-Georgian bow window, the walls that Jane had finished looking fresh and white.

'With any luck, Cottage Cakes will be ready to open on time,' he said.

'Yes. Thanks to you.'

She glanced around the empty shop, imagining how it would look with gleaming glass shelves and a modern

228

counter. It had a room at the back with a kitchen for staff use and all the usual facilities. The Georgian-style shop front was very pretty and stood out among the other shops in the parade.

Having persuaded the bank to support her in this project, Jane had had an exciting time setting it all up – all the more enjoyable because Giles had taken such an active part, helping her to choose shop fittings and new equipment for the kitchen. It was he who'd suggested they paint the shop themselves to save the cost of professional decorators. It had been great fun and she adored being with him. Between Trudy and Marie, the children were having a good time too, so everyone was happy.

'I've enjoyed working on it with you.'

'Really?'

'Yes, really.'

Giles was speaking the truth, albeit that enjoyment didn't have quite the same meaning for him now. When Lena was alive, it had meant a feeling of happiness and exuberance. These days it was simply a time when the pain of his grief was slightly less acute.

Helping Jane to set up her business had been therapeutic in that it had kept him occupied and given him something different to think about. It had also given him Jane's company, something he valued highly because she was so easy to be with. When he was with her he didn't have to pretend he wasn't still missing Lena because he knew Jane missed her too. With Jane he could talk about his late wife without causing embarrassment because she also wanted to talk about Lena. Jane was a terrific friend, he thought, looking at her with affection as she sat opposite him, smudged with paint, her big brown eyes resting on him warmly.

'As much as you can enjoy anything, eh?' she said, reading his thoughts.

'You're getting to know me too well.'

'Not really. But I do know how painful it is to lose someone you love,' she said, pouring him another mug of coffee and handing it to him.

Something about the warmth and caring in her tone touched Giles deeply and hot tears welled beneath his lids.

'Oh, dear, I'm sorry, Jane,' he said, rummaging in his trouser pocket for a handkerchief. 'It still hits me when I'm least expecting it.' He put his hands to his head. 'This great black cloud . . . Will it ever go away? Will I ever want to stop thinking about her?'

'It's still quite early days . . . not a year yet,' she reminded him.

He leaned forward and took her hand.

'You're so good for me,' he said. 'I don't know what I'd do without you.'

'You'd manage,' she said, feeling dangerously emotional. 'But I'm glad to be here for you. We help each other.'

Of course, he had no idea that she had fallen in love with him and wanted to be with him every second of the day. It seemed wrong to think of him in this way, some-how, almost as if Lena were still alive and Jane trespassing on her territory. Jane hoped that in time Giles would learn to love her too, but that wouldn't happen for a while because he was still besotted with his wife's memory. Jane sensed that even to hint at how she felt at this stage might bring their association to an end because Giles wasn't ready to cope with anything more than friendship just now. For the moment she had to make do with being his friend. And wait, and hope . . .

'You're a true friend, Jane,' he said, confirming her own thoughts on the subject.

'It isn't all one-sided, you know,' she said, smiling to bring some levity back into their conversation. 'Anyone who gives up a chunk of their summer holidays to help me paint a shop must be counted a true friend.'

They smiled at each other. The afternoon sun shone through the shop window, blurred by liquid cleaner that had been spread liberally on the glass to give them some privacy. The atmosphere became intimate. Jane felt so close to him she almost blurted out her true feelings.

'Come on then,' Giles said quickly, as though he was aware of the change of mood and made uneasy by it. 'Back to work.'

'Slave driver,' she said lightly, restoring the casual atmosphere, and they went cheerfully back to their work.

They were all there for the opening of Cottage Cakes at the end of August: Jane, Giles, Trudy, Marie and Eddie, and all the children. Even Jane's father took the morning off work to give her his support. Rita and Wilf Parker had been invited but didn't show up.

Jane had drifted away from Mick's parents over the years. She still took the children to visit them quite regularly but her parents-in-law made no effort to pursue a close relationship with her. Without Mick there seemed no point as he had been their only common interest.

Davey and Pip thought it was very exciting, their mother having a shop of her own. Jane had to admit to a moment of pride too, when the fruits of her labours were put on show, looking colourful and appetising; iced cakes, apple cakes, sponges, fruit cake, chocolate gâteaux and a range of dairy cream items in a refrigerated display cabinet.

'Well . . . to Cottage Cakes,' said Giles, cracking open a bottle of champagne in the staff room just before they opened the doors.

Congratulations and good wishes abounded. But the party ended as business began.

'Now for the difficult part,' said Jane as customers began piling in. 'Making sure the punters keep coming back for more.'

'If you'll pardon the pun,' said Giles with a wicked grin, 'it'll be a piece of cake for someone like you.'

There were groans all round.

'Well, what do you think of it, then, Pats?' asked Mick Parker eagerly.

'It's very nice,' she said in her matter-of-fact way, shivering against the cold.

'*Nice?*' he echoed with disapproval. 'Is that all you've got to say about it?'

'What else can I say, Mick?' she replied, hugging herself and stamping her feet to stop them going numb. 'It's a car, not the flaming Crown Jewels!'

'It isn't just any car.'

'Okay, it's a very smart motor,' she said, teeth chattering. 'Now can we get in and go home, please? I'm frozen solid, standing about out here. I hope to God there's a heater in it.'

'Of course there's a heater in it,' he said irritably. 'As if they'd sell a car of this quality without a heater.'

It was a bitter night the following January and Mick had come to collect Patsy from her late shift at the pub. He usually spent most of the evening in the Drake's Arms and he and Patsy went home together. Tonight he'd been later because he'd been to buy a Jaguar from a man in Worthing.

'Get the doors open and let's get the heater working, then,' she said.

'But look at those lines, Pats,' said Mick, still gazing at the vehicle in the pale glow from the street lights. 'Beautiful, innit?'

'Yeah, yeah, it's lovely, Mick,' she said, impatient because she was so cold. 'But I can be a lot more enthusiastic from the inside of a car on a night like this! So stop going all poetic and let me in, or I'll get a cab to take me home.'

He opened the door at last.

'Ooh, thank Gawd for that,' she said, settling into the passenger seat. 'What with aching feet and frostbite, I'll be glad to get home.'

'We could go to a club for an hour or so to unwind, if you like?'

'No, I'd sooner go straight home tonight, thanks, Mick.'

'Okay.'

He started the engine and they rolled away.

'Do you like the colour?'

'What of?'

'The car, of course.'

'Oh, yeah. Blue, innit? I couldn't see properly in the street lights.'

'Not just blue . . . *metallic blue.*'

'Nice.'

'There you go again, calling it nice,' he rebuked. 'Nice isn't a word normally associated with a Jaguar. Fabulous, fantastic, terrific . . . nice is what you call cream buns!'

'You should know me by now, Mick,' she said, still shivering because the car hadn't yet warmed up. 'I'm not the sort of person to go over the top about things.'

'You can say that again!'

'Anyway, I don't know one car from another. So long as it gets me from A to B, that's all I'm really bothered about.'

'Doesn't it make you feel good to be seen in it, though?' he asked.

'Not really.'

'Honestly . . . you are the limit!'

'Look, so long as I enjoy going about in it, why should I give a toss what other people think about it?'

'Oh, I give up.'

To Mick there was something both infuriating and endearing about Patsy. The fact that it was impossible to impress her with possessions made her the most undemanding of women to be with. On the other hand, it was rather discouraging for him, as he aspired to better things, to find that Patsy couldn't give a damn and was just as happy with him at the bottom of the pile.

Even when he'd managed to get a foothold on the property ladder again by taking out a mortgage on a luxury flat in a classy block overlooking the sea, her plebeian attitude had coloured her reaction.

'It's a right little palace,' she'd said as she'd cast her eyes over the marble bathroom and dream kitchen. 'I hope we're not gonna be stuck with snobby neighbours, though?'

'There won't be any riff-raff in flats like these.'

'Except us!'

'Bloody cheek,' he'd said, outraged because he still had delusions of grandeur. 'I take that as an insult.'

'Oh, do be realistic, Mick dear,' she'd said. 'I'm a barmaid and you're a wholesaler dealing in dodgy gear. We're not gonna find it easy to make conversation with retired bankers or city solicitors who have a flat in Brighton as a weekend place.'

But the fact that she thought he was wonderful, rich or poor, gave him a lot of pleasure despite the fact that he still saw their life together as temporary. If things had been different and he hadn't been planning to return to his wife and children, he and Patsy could probably have made a go of it in the long term because they got on really well. He'd grown fond of her and enjoyed their rather offbeat life together; late suppers at clubs after she'd finished work, mixing with bohemian types and little-known seaside entertainers they got talking to in pubs and clubs. Sometimes she insisted on a spot of more traditional leisure, and they would drive out to the downs and have a drink in a country pub. She even got him walking sometimes too. No one had ever done *that* before.

Patsy might be as common as muck but she was quite a woman, he thought, taking a sideways look at her now, sitting beside him in her synthetic fur coat and excessive jewellery, some cheap that she'd bought herself, some expensive that he'd given her. Being able to buy such presents really marked his return to success and Mick revelled in it.

Of course, Patsy wasn't in the same league as Jane. How could she be when his wife was in a class of her own? Sometimes he couldn't get a clear image of her face into his mind. Leaving as he had, he didn't even have a photograph to jog his memory. He'd perfected a little trick though. He found that if he remembered the highlight of his day in his other life, coming home to Jane and the children after work of an evening, then he could picture her clearly, looking up as he went in at the kitchen door, or standing at the front door to greet him. In his mind's eye he saw her warm brown eyes, her shiny hair and gentle smile.

He longed to go back and still didn't doubt that she would have him. Any negative thoughts in that direction were instantly cast out in the same way as he dismissed anything that he found unpalatable. So far as he was concerned, there would never be anyone else for Jane, in the same way as there could never be any other woman for him. Patsy was just a stopgap. Once he had some real money behind him, he'd go back and face the music at home. A good few people would sit up and take notice when they realised that Mick Parker was back in the money and on the scene.

Sometimes he felt tired of the struggle. Occasionally he even envied Patsy her simple philosophy of life.

'You only want one roof to live under and one car to get about in,' was the way she put it. 'So long as you have food to eat and clothes to wear, why do you have to have more?'

'It's human nature to want better,' was Mick's answer to that.

'And when you get better, it's common sense to end it there.'

He didn't agree with that. Once you started being content, you were dead.

But now Patsy was saying, 'This motor must have set you back a bit?'

'I'll say it did . . . but I didn't pay for it outright.'

'Not many people do, not for expensive things like cars.'

'That's right.'

'Is it new?'

'Not brand new, no,' he said with a hint of apology.

'Don't sound so sorry about it,' she reproached him lightly.

'Well, the Jag I had before was brand spanking new.'

'You can always trade up later if it's that important to you.'

' 'Course I can.'

'Just enjoy what you have, Mick.'

'It won't be long before I can afford to trade this in for a better one, Patsy,' he said, voice rising excitedly. 'I'm on the up.'

'Yes, I know you are, Mick,' she said, sadness in her voice as they drove along the brightly lit seafront towards Hove. It was a pity success was so vital to him.

'You do?' He wanted reassurance.

'I'm not blind. Anyone can see you're going up in the world.'

It occurred to him that some women in her position might have used the term 'we', since she lived with him and shared his life. But Patsy knew she was only a temporary part of the equation. He made no secret of the fact that when he was ready, it would all be over between them.

Beside him in the passenger seat, Patsy was also thinking about the tenuous nature of her relationship with him and regarding it with a certain ambivalence. Because she loved Mick so completely, she empathised with him, even feeling anxious on his behalf in case Jane might not want him back. At the same time she was pinning all her hopes on that happening because if it did, he would come straight back to her, she had no doubt about that. Mick wasn't the sort of man who liked being alone.

Patsy was still of the opinion that he enjoyed his life with her, and believed with increasing conviction that if he wasn't so obsessed with Jane and his previous lifestyle, he might grow to love her – as far as Mick could love anyone except himself. Patsy had no illusions about that. He was one of the most self-centred people she had ever come across. Yet sometimes he could be the most tender and loving as well. There was no other man for her.

Because he didn't feel the need to prove himself to her, and was therefore relaxed when they were together, she had got to know Mick very well over the years. In fact, she thought she probably knew him better than he knew himself. Having this insight into his character led her to suspect that the idea of going back to Jane would probably be more palatable to him than the actual reality of a return. It gave him a goal to aim for, driving him onwards and upwards, and was something he felt he *must* do. Patsy didn't believe it was something he actually anticipated with any degree of pleasure. Maybe he had once, but not any longer.

Although she would never say so to Mick and he would never admit it to himself, Patsy thought that by his own standards and the things he considered important, he was a failure. He had got to the top the first time on credit; he was doing it a second time by breaking the law.

She didn't love him any the less for this. She just wished he would settle for an ordinary life without the need for a huge amount of money, and accept a good thing when he had it. But Mick measured success in purely financial terms and refused to believe that you could succeed simply as a human being.

It wasn't in Patsy's nature to bear grudges or feel used. So far as she was concerned, she enjoyed her life with Mick, so if it came to that *she* could be said to be using *him*.

There was no point in her trying to stop him leaving when he was ready to go. She would lose him forever if she did that. Neither would she turn him away if he wanted her back. Many women would think it degrading to her sex to have such a tolerant and forgiving attitude towards a man. But it wasn't in her to be otherwise, and so what else could she do? Trying to force him to stay wasn't the answer.

Anyway, he might never leave. His going back to Jane could be one of those things he would talk about forever and never actually do.

Many times she had suggested that he contact Jane, just to let her know he was still alive. He got quite uppity at this; said that when he contacted his wife it would be to tell her that he was going back to her. And when he did return it would be in grand style. He never seemed to give a thought to how Jane was managing, or how she must have suffered over the years, and got very cross with Patsy if she pointed this out to him.

But despite all of this, Patsy would stay with him until he no longer wanted her. And until that day came, she would make the most of every moment and not think about the future because she couldn't bear the thought of life without Mick.

Chapter Fifteen

The power cuts that were imposed throughout February 1972, as a result of the miners' strike, created havoc in the cottage kitchen. It was the beginning of March before the pay dispute was finally settled and things got back to normal.

'It's a treat to be able to work properly again, isn't it?' remarked Marie one morning, as she removed trays of small cakes from the enormous electric oven Jane had invested in when she'd opened the shop.

'Not half,' agreed Jane.

'It's bad enough trying to keep the kids warm and fed during the blackouts, but when you can't do your work either . . .'

'I think I'd have gone nuts if it had gone on for much longer,' said Jane for whom production had been seriously reduced by the electricity's being turned off for hours on end.

'Still, it's all over now . . . and these little chocolate chip cakes smell delicious,' said Marie, inhaling pleasurably.

'Let's spoil ourselves and have one with our coffee, shall we?' suggested Jane, tempted by the sweet aroma.

'Ooh, yes, please.'

Marie loaded the oven with more cake-tins while Jane put the kettle on.

'Shall I take a batch of cakes over to the shop when the next lot is ready?' Marie was able to suggest because she had learned to drive with the idea of helping with transporting the stock from cottage to shop.

'Yes, please. They've been on the phone from the shop

to say they've nearly sold out of apple cake already,' said Jane, spooning coffee powder into two mugs. 'But we'll have a coffee break first. We can both do with a sit down as we haven't stopped since first thing.'

'We never seem to do enough apple cakes, do we?' remarked Marie thoughtfully. 'No matter how many of them we make, they're always the first to sell out.'

'That was the cake that started this whole thing and it's still our most popular line.'

'My favourite.'

'Giles's too,' said Jane.

'Really?'

'Yes. He was never much of a cake eater until he tasted my apple cake. Now he's a complete addict. Never puts on an ounce of weight either. It's infuriating.'

'That'll be because of all the exercise he does.'

'Yeah . . . he's as fit as a fiddle. As well as the PE and games lessons at school, he also coaches the rugby team after hours.'

'Not to mention running the gym club and the Riverside Juniors in his spare time.'

'Mmm.'

Because the kitchen table was littered with the tools and ingredients of their trade, they took their elevenses into the living room where Shadow lay curled up on the mat by the fire, fast asleep, his silky black coat gleaming.

'That moggy certainly knows how to relax,' laughed Jane.

The cat twitched one ear, opened one eye – and went back to sleep.

'Talk about a life of luxury,' said Marie. 'I feel tired just looking at him.'

'They say cats are relaxing creatures to have around.'

The two women sat either side of the fire, eating cake and drinking coffee, the strong March winds roaring around the house and rattling the windows. A shaft of watery sunlight spilled on to the red carpet and glinted on a brass plate and copper pan on the wall.

'Compared to what my life was like before I got this

job, I sometimes feel as though *I* have a life of luxury,' confessed Marie.

Jane hooted with laughter.

'When do you ever get the chance of any Shadow-style relaxation?'

'I don't mean it in that way. I mean, being involved in something I enjoy,' she explained. 'It's made such a difference to my life, and I don't just mean the extra money.'

Jane sipped her coffee.

'I'm glad you're happy with the job.'

'I feel as though I'm part of the business rather than just a member of your staff,' explained Marie.

'That's the way I feel about it too.' Jane paused thoughtfully, cradling her mug in her hands. 'I must say, I'm pleased with the way the business is going. The markets were good – they got me started – but it makes more sense to leave the selling to others so that I can concentrate on baking.'

'Too true.'

'I'm thinking about a new line, actually . . . a ginger cake.'

'Sounds interesting.'

'I've been experimenting but I haven't got the flavour quite right yet. I tried it out on Giles the other day and we're agreed it needs something else to give it an edge over all the other ginger cakes on the market. I'm not quite sure what, though.'

'You still see a lot of your neighbour then?' remarked Marie.

'Yeah. It's inevitable really since Davey and Kevin are practically blood brothers.'

'Mmm.'

'And as Giles and I are both on our own, it makes sense to team up for outings with the children,' said Jane, suddenly feeling the need to justify herself to her sister-in-law.

'I suppose he must be over his wife's death by now?'

'I don't think he'll ever really get over it, but he's managing.'

'How long is it now?'

'Two years this November.'

'As long as that? I suppose it's time he got his life together.'

'For a couple like Giles and Lena, it's still early days,' said Jane. 'I've never come across two people as close as they were.'

'You and Mick took some beating in that respect.'

'We were close in that we'd been together a long time,' said Jane. 'And we got on well because I agreed with everything Mick said and did. But, looking back on it, I'm not so sure that we were actually all that suited.'

'I don't know how you can say that, Jane,' said Marie, frowning. 'There was never anyone else for either of you.'

'You're right about the physical side of it,' she agreed. 'But we never really talked about anything in any depth. It was all on the surface.'

'I'm surprised to hear you say that,' said Marie disapprovingly.

'What I'm trying to say is . . . Giles and Lena each had their own interests. They retained their own individuality but still stayed close. They worshipped each other.'

'So did you and Mick,' said Marie, becoming noticeably tense.

'Yes, we did at the time,' agreed Jane. 'But in the light of what happened, I don't think I ever really knew Mick.'

'Oh, Jane, how can you say that?'

'The man I thought I knew wouldn't have walked out and left me to cope with the mess he'd created,' said Jane. 'Nor would he have lied to me for months beforehand.'

'He only did that to protect you.'

'Maybe, but when it came to the crunch he wasn't there for me, was he?' she said firmly. 'He was off like a shot.'

'You still feel bitter about it then?'

'No, not really, not now. It's all such a long time ago.'

'Sounds as though you're resentful.'

'I'm not. Honest. I'm just being realistic. I think Mick and I being the perfect couple was just an illusion created by the fact that I was content to be dominated by him. I was never a partner with Mick, always a subordinate.'

'Oh, Jane . . .'

'I'm not blaming him,' she was quick to point out. 'It was just the way things were. I find it hard to identify with the person I was when we were together. You know, living for the sound of his key in the door and the next move up the ladder to that better house, the better car – all that dreadful one upmanship. In a way Mick did me a favour by leaving. At least it pushed me out into the world and forced me to find out about myself.'

'You've certainly made a life for yourself and the children,' said Marie, her dark looks contrasting with the white cotton mob-cap the women now wore for reasons of hygiene while they were working.

'It's amazing how you cope when you have to. I thought my life was over when Mick left. I was absolutely gutted and felt dead inside for a long time after. That's why I find it easy to understand how Giles is feeling, I suppose.'

'Yeah.'

'It hurts me to think of what that man must be going through.'

'You and he seem to be getting on really well?' said Marie meaningfully.

'Yes, we do . . . he's a great friend and neighbour,' said Jane lightly.

Marie kept her eyes fixed determinedly on the cat and Jane knew exactly what she had on her mind.

'I'm not sleeping with him,' she said.

'Did I suggest you were?' said her sister-in-law, looking up sharply.

'No, but it was what you were wondering,' said Jane firmly.

'Well, maybe I was,' said Marie, a flush suffusing her face and neck. 'I suppose it's only natural. I *am* Mick's sister, after all.'

243

'And he's been gone for six years,' Jane pointed out. 'Surely you don't expect me to stay celibate for the rest of my life?'

'Of course I don't,' said Marie, but it didn't ring true because she still had a blind spot when it came to Mick's place in Jane's life.

Jane couldn't tell Marie the truth about her feelings for Giles: that she was in love with him and hoped one day they would be more than friends. She couldn't tell her because Marie still harboured a dream that Jane and Mick would eventually get back together and they would all be one big happy family again.

As time had passed without word from him, Jane had tried to make Marie see how unlikely it was that he would ever return. But she was completely irrational when it came to her brother and couldn't accept the idea of Jane's finding happiness with anyone else. Occasionally Marie's attitude annoyed Jane but she didn't think it was worth making an issue of because she was very fond of her and they got on so well in every other way. Surely, as more time elapsed without sight or sound of Mick, Marie would face up to the fact that he wasn't coming back and that the Jane and Mick era was over?

'Mum . . . will you *please* tell Pip that she can't sleep in the tent with Kevin and me tonight?' Davey asked Jane who was in the garden pegging washing on the line. It was a fine Saturday morning in early-summer, a time of the week when she did battle with the backlog of domestic chores.

'Why can't she join you?' she asked, as if she didn't already know.

' 'Cause it's a boy's thing and we don't want any girls hanging around.'

'It isn't only a boy's thing,' protested Pip. 'Girls go camping as well as boys. I'll be going away to camp with the Girl Guides when I'm older.'

'Well, you're not sleeping in the tent with Kev and me tonight,' insisted Davey hotly. 'You'd only spoil it . . .'

'No, I wouldn't!'

'You would too! You'd be scared of creepy crawlies.'

Jane stopped what she was doing to resolve the problem.

'How about if you and Melanie sleep in the tent tomorrow night, if it stays fine?' Jane suggested to her daughter.

Pip thought about this. She was a leggy nine year old with big velvety eyes like her mother's and light brown hair tied back in a pony tail. The recent spell of warm weather had tanned her skin to a smooth nut colour.

'And the boys won't be allowed to come in?' she queried.

'No, just you and Mel,' promised Jane. 'Why not ring her up to see if she fancies it?' She paused. 'So long as her mother approves.'

Pip disappeared into the house while Jane continued pegging out the washing, enjoying the light breeze on her face and the sun on her arms. Pip reappeared, smiling, with the news that her cousin was all in favour of a night camping out in the tent. It was half term and the children had a week's holiday. Jane was hoping the good weather would hold. Camping out in the garden in the new tent Jane had bought for them was the latest craze. But they never stayed under canvas for long despite their very best intentions, and usually opted for the comfort and security of indoor living even before Jane had gone to bed.

She was on her way indoors when Giles appeared through the gap in the fence.

'You must be a mind reader,' she said. 'I'm just going to make some coffee.'

'Luck rather than telepathy,' he said casually, following her into the kitchen. 'I just called in to ask if you want anything from the supermarket, and to find out if Kevin can stay here with Davey while I'm gone? Save him dragging round the shops with me in such lovely weather.'

'No to the first 'cause I have to go shopping myself

later. And, yes, of course Kevin can stay here,' she said amiably.

'Thanks, Jane.'

'A pleasure.'

They sat in her living room with their coffee by the open french doors.

'I take it Kevin has your permission to camp out tonight?'

Giles nodded.

'Actually, while the kids are occupied and we're on our own, I've got something I want to say to you, something I've been thinking about for a while and have finally come to a decision about.'

Her heart pounded. On several occasions lately she'd felt as though their relationship was about to change course. A week or so ago when they'd all gone ice-skating at Richmond Ice Rink, she'd ended up on her bottom on the ice. Giles had helped her up and they'd laughed so much and the physical vibrations between them had been so strong, she'd expected something to happen then. But the moment had passed as had many other similar ones. They were on the verge of a love affair, though, she was sure of it.

'Well, don't keep me in suspense, then?' urged Jane excitedly.

'I'm moving away,' he said.

She was too stunned to speak, his words affecting her like a physical assault.

'Moving away?' she muttered at last, staring at him in disbelief.

'That's right,' said Giles in a controlled manner. 'I'm putting the cottage up for sale.'

'But why?'

'Too many memories for me here,' he explained. 'Lena is everywhere in the cottage. It's like living with her ghost.'

'Well, I must say, I'm surprised at your decision,' Jane said. 'I did think you might want to move away immediately after she died. But when you didn't, I thought

246

you'd decided to stay on indefinitely?'

'I had. I thought I could cope. But Lena's presence is still so strong! I can hear her laughing and talking about the place, and the pain of losing her is unbearable. Just when I think I'm over it, it all comes back.'

'I see,' said Jane dully.

'I think I need a new start somewhere else,' Giles explained. 'And there's a job going in Sussex. If I don't get that one there'll be others around the country. I really need to get away.'

'I'll miss you terribly, Giles.'

He stared fixedly into his coffee mug, avoiding her eyes.

'Yes, I shall miss you too.' There was no mention of their seeing each other after his move, she noticed. It was as though he wanted to make a clean break. 'But I have to move on.'

'Are you sure you're doing the right thing?' she said desperately. 'I mean, you have lots of friends here. It won't be easy starting afresh somewhere else.'

'I have to give it a try,' he insisted.

'Does Kevin know?'

'Not yet.'

'He'll be devastated,' said Jane with a sad shake of the head. 'So will Davey.'

'Yes . . . I know.'

'Oh, Giles, please reconsider? For Kevin's sake, if not your own,' she urged him impulsively. 'He's already lost his mother, don't make him lose his friends as well.'

'I have to do what I think is right for both of us in the long term,' he said gravely. 'People have far worse things to cope with than moving to a new area. Children are very adaptable.'

It struck Jane in that moment that she was going to have to fight to keep Giles. Being forced to imagine life without him had made her realise just how deeply she cared for him. She was sure he had begun to fall in love with her, too. He would probably admit it to himself in due course anyway, but now that things had taken such an unexpected turn, she wasn't prepared to wait and run the risk of losing him. Immediate action was definitely called for.

'Oh, well, I suppose you know your own business best,' she said mildly.

'Yes, I do.'

'Changing the subject,' she said casually, 'do you fancy joining me for a spot of supper tonight? After we've settled the boys in the tent and Pip has gone to bed?'

'I'd like that, Jane,' he said. 'Thank you.'

'You've gone to a lot of trouble with the meal tonight,' said Giles that evening as he and Jane sat at the candlelit table near the window in her living room, drinking wine and contemplating the lamb with redcurrant sauce that she had cooked for them. There was a small bowl of sweet peas from the garden in the centre of the table, their scent adding to the romantic atmosphere. 'And you're looking absolutely stunning.'

'Thank you, Giles,' she said, smiling and making him aware of how gorgeous she looked in her summery trouser suit in pale green, with her hair shining and her face enhanced with a touch of make-up.

'So what's the special occasion?' he enquired, because eating together was usually a casual affair. He deliberately made the tone of his next comment light because his awareness of her as a woman had been troubling him lately and he was anxious to defuse the situation. 'Are you planning to seduce me?'

If that was what it took, that was what she would do. But she said in a frivolous manner, 'What an old-fashioned word.'

'I'm an old-fashioned man.'

She cast an approving eye over Giles's tanned face which had a boyishness to it that belied his thirty-seven years. His thick wavy hair was neatly layered, his white open-necked shirt sitting well on his muscular frame.

'Conventional rather than old-fashioned, I'd say,' remarked Jane.

'That makes me sound really boring.'

'It certainly wasn't meant to.' Despite the banter, there was an underlying seriousness in the atmosphere. 'But conventional isn't a word normally associated with sudden impulses, is it?'

'Meaning?'

'Meaning that I don't think you want to move away from Tug Lane any more than I want you to go,' she said.

'We'll see each other from time to time,' he said evasively, and without a suggestion of any sort of commitment. 'The boys won't lose touch. I know you're worried about their being split up.'

'We've been so happy this last few months, Giles, you and me and the children,' she said. 'Why throw it all away?'

'I've told you why I have to go.'

'I don't believe that's the real reason you feel you have to leave.'

He looked at her. She was so lovely with the candlelight shining on her face, her lips full and pink, the warmth in her eyes embracing him. His heart turned over.

'You don't?'

'No. I think you're running away from me, not the cottage and all its memories of Lena.'

'Why on earth would I do that?' he asked, but she could tell by the guarded look in his eyes that she was right.

'Because you're falling in love with me, Giles, that's why.'

'Oh, so now we have to add mindreading to your many talents, do we?' he said tartly.

On impulse, she reached across the table and took his hand.

'Please don't be angry, Giles. The reason I believe this to be true is because I'm in love with you too,' she said. 'And like you, I feel guilty about it . . . because of Lena.'

He looked at her gravely, but there was tenderness in his eyes.

'Oh, Jane. It wouldn't be right,' he said in a tortured voice, clutching her hand in both of his. 'Not you and me. I'd feel as though I was being unfaithful to Lena.'

'In a few months' time, Lena will have been dead for two years,' she pointed out. 'Do you really think she wouldn't want you to be happy with someone else?'

'No, of course I don't,' he said. 'And if it was anyone else, it would be different. But you and me . . . I mean, you and Lena were such good friends. It just feels so wrong, like a betrayal.'

She removed her hand and looked at him solemnly, sipping her wine.

'Perhaps you need more time?'

He didn't reply but stared into his wine glass, running his fingers idly around the rim.

'I'm prepared to wait for as long as it takes for you to feel able to accept another woman into your life. But I *can't* lose you, Giles. You're far too precious to me.'

'Jane . . .'

'I'd offer to move with you to Sussex or wherever you go if I thought it would help. But moving away won't solve anything for you,' she said. 'Lena will always be in your thoughts, wherever you go and whoever you are with. You have to stop feeling guilty for being happy. She's gone, Giles.'

It hurt to see him wince but facts had to be faced.

'No one will ever take Lena's place in your heart . . . not me, not anybody,' she said. 'I know that and I wouldn't even try. But I also know that something special has grown between us.'

'I can't deny it,' he said, sipping his wine. 'And the guilt has been awful.'

'I know,' she said gently, looking into his eyes. 'But as harsh and cliched as it may sound, life does have to go on for you without Lena.'

'I'm not sure if I'm ready for another relationship yet,' he confessed, his shandy-brown eyes full of doubt.

'It wouldn't be fair to you if I didn't feel sure . . . didn't feel able fully to commit myself.'

'Let me be the judge of that,' she said. 'I know I've been forward in bringing things out into the open. But when you said you were selling up, I knew I had to speak up or risk losing you. Life's too short for pride and reticence, Giles.' She swallowed hard, emotion welling up inside her. 'We both know just how short it can be.'

'Yes.'

The atmosphere was highly charged. Jane could feel his desire for her drawing her towards him. But she could still sense uncertainty.

'I want you, Giles,' she whispered. 'Whenever you're ready, I'll be here . . .'

A scream from outside startled them, shattering the mood completely.

'The boys!' they gasped in unison.

They were on their feet and heading for the back door when Kevin burst through it, ashen-faced and trembling.

'Come quickly. Davey's cut his hand badly . . . his finger's hanging off,' he told them with a sob in his voice.

Kevin's description of the accident was a slight exaggeration, but only a slight one. The finger was not actually severed but his hand was quite badly cut – by a corned beef tin opened by torchlight. Giles and Jane found him sitting on the ground in the tent, looking as though he was about to pass out, with a handkerchief clutched to his hand, soaked with blood.

Giles took charge of the situation immediately, getting the trembling boy into the house and tying a tourniquet around his hand. Jane was busy calming Kevin and Pip who had been woken by the commotion and come downstairs in a fright. She was alarmed by the sight of so much blood.

'I'll take him to Casualty to get it seen to properly,' said Giles.

'I'll go,' offered Jane.

'No, you stay here with Pip and Kevin,' he said. 'I won't be long.'

And before she could say another word he was carrying Davey out of the house to his car, leaving Jane to comfort Kevin who was in a state of shock and crying silently. Apparently the corned beef had been appropriated from his father's larder without Giles's knowledge.

It was turned midnight by the time all the children were finally settled down and Jane and Giles flopped into armchairs in her living room to unwind with a glass of wine and some sandwiches, to make up for the meal that hadn't been eaten. Kevin had tried to keep awake for his father and Davey to get home from the hospital but had been so sleepy, Jane had made up a bed for him in Davey's room.

'So, we read the Riot Act to the boys in a big way tomorrow. . . yes?' said Giles.

Jane nodded.

'But I do think they've learned their lesson,' she said. 'I don't think they'll be opening any more tins for the time being.'

'Neither do I,' agreed Giles. 'They were both scared to death of all that blood.'

'So was I,' sighed Jane. 'Thank goodness it wasn't worse. I thought Davey would have to have more than a couple of stitches.'

'He told me he was sorry a dozen times at the hospital.'

'Kevin did the same to me.'

'If they wanted corned beef, why didn't they ask and we'd have opened the tin for them?'

'They obviously thought it would be more fun to do it themselves . . . more grown-up. They knew we wouldn't let them take the tin out to the tent and open it by torchlight.'

'Little horrors!'

'They never get to spend the whole night in that tent, do they?' she said. 'It's either too cold or too damp, they hear noises or see spiders . . . something always happens.'

'Not normally as dramatic as this, though.'

'No. Thank God.'

They ate their supper in companionable silence until Jane said, 'So much for my attempt at a romantic interlude.'

Giles couldn't help but smile.

'Kids certainly have a rotten sense of timing,' he said.

'Never a dull moment with our lot, that's for sure,' she laughed.

'You can say that again,' he said, thinking of all the incidents they had shared over the years, some happy, some worrying like tonight. He put his plate down on the coffee table and looked at her tenderly. 'How can I possibly move away from you, Jane?'

'I'm hoping you'll find it impossible.'

'Kevin and I will die of boredom without you lot next-door.'

'So . . . you'll be staying, then?' she said with a broad smile.

For reply, he stood up and opened his arms to her.

'Come here,' he said.

It was very much later when Giles crept across the moonlit garden and through the gap in the fence to his own cottage.

Summer became a time of intense pleasure and clandestine intimacy as Jane and Giles's love affair blossomed. Because Giles was a schoolteacher and Jane still technically married, they decided that discretion was essential, for the time being anyway. Despite modern attitudes to these things, many people still looked to teachers to set an example, not least the headmaster of Giles's school who held strict ideas about sexual morality and would be very upset indeed to discover that his games master was having an affair with a married woman.

Next year, when Mick had not been heard of for seven years, he would be presumed dead so far as the law was concerned and Jane could officially apply to remarry. Until the time when they could make definite plans to marry, they deemed it wise to keep their love a secret, though it wasn't easy. Brimming with happiness, Jane wanted the world to know.

Ostensibly they were two lone parents who spent time together because of their children. They went on family outings – Sunday trips to the seaside and walking in Richmond Park or by the river. They picnicked at Runnymede, took the children ice skating and swimming at the baths, on river trips and sightseeing in London now that they were old enough to take an intelligent interest in their heritage. Like a real family it wasn't all fun and laughter. There were the inevitable squabbles between the children and Jane and Giles didn't always see eye to eye.

But beneath the surface of this casual matiness, love grew and passion simmered. People seeing Jane and Giles together couldn't guess how much they longed to be alone. Only when the children were in bed at night did they steal a few precious, intimate moments. No one ever saw Giles slipping through the gap in the fence at frequent intervals to check on Kevin.

Jane felt positively reborn, her life transformed. She faced each day with renewed energy, enjoying her work all the more for having something special to look forward to outside it. Even the domestic chores didn't seem so tedious in her new happiness. She had thought she could never love anyone but Mick. Now she knew she hadn't known the meaning of the word until Giles had become her lover.

Loving Mick had meant domination and servitude, albeit she hadn't objected at the time. Loving Giles meant being loved and cherished but not restricted, either physically or mentally. They were equally matched, their relationship well-balanced. Jane had developed so much as a person the last few years, she felt no embarrassment about taking the sexual initiative with Giles, or refusing if she wasn't in the mood, something she would never have dared to do with Mick.

It wasn't all canoodling, though, even when she and

Giles were alone. The other side of their relationship could get quite sparky at times, especially when they were discussing current affairs. Whether they were debating the troubles in Northern Ireland or the expulsion of Asians from Uganda to Britain by General Idi Amin, Jane's views were taken seriously by him even though they sometimes got quite heated with each other. Mick had always been too busy making money to take any interest in anything outside his own personal ambitions, so this kind of discussion was new to her.

With Mick she had been limited and narrow. Now she fully embraced the world around her, enjoying the colour and richness of living life to the full. She sometimes thought how sad it was that Mick had never taken time to smell the flowers.

She and Giles took a keen interest in each other's work. Giles's job came especially into focus when school started in September because both Davey and Kevin would be candidates for selection to the Grammar School during this coming school year.

'Will you feel awkward having the boys at your school, if they do get in?' asked Jane one autumn evening as they sat together by the fire when the children were in bed and asleep.

'I won't but I'm sure Kevin will.'

'Because it'll make him seem different from the others?'

'Exactly. About the last thing a schoolboy wants around him at school is a beady parental eye.'

'Still it's quite a big school, you might not see much of him.'

'There is that. But I shall have to make sure that I treat him, and Davey for that matter, the same as any other pupil.'

'Any hint of favouritism would be fatal.'

'I'll say it would.' He seemed thoughtful. 'But here I am, talking about Davey as though he's my own son, the same as Kevin.'

'It's only natural that you would,' said Jane. 'I mean . . .

it's very much a father-son type of relationship you have with him.'

'Indeed.'

'I think he looks on you as the nearest thing he has to a father.'

'Does he?'

'Oh, yes. He's very fond of you.'

'I feel the same about him.'

'I wonder if the children have any idea . . . about us?'

'I'm not sure. Kids are pretty self-absorbed. And we *have* been very discreet.'

'It's hard to keep it secret when you're bursting with happiness.'

'Isn't it just?' he agreed. 'I thought my life was over when Lena died. Now I feel as though it's beginning all over again.'

'I'm sure the children will be pleased that we're all going to be one family.'

'I'm certain they'll be delighted . . . I only wish we could tell them.'

'To do that would be tantamount to broadcasting it on the BBC.' She smiled wickedly. 'Or telling our esteemed neighbour, Mrs Robinson.'

He laughed.

'Yes, they're too young to keep secrets at the moment.'

'If you weren't a teacher, it wouldn't matter . . . not these days.'

'That's true.'

'Still, next year we can bring it out into the open,' she said. 'We only have to keep it to ourselves for a while longer.'

'Yes.'

Although Jane was looking forward with pleasure to making their relationship public, she knew that the news wasn't going to be well received by everyone. In fact, she knew of one person in particular who was going to be very upset indeed!

Chapter Sixteen

'You're obviously not happy, Marie,' said Jane one October morning when the two women were working together in the cottage kitchen, and the pique that had been evinced by her sister-in-law so effectively during the last few days showed no signs of abating. 'So, why don't you tell me what's the matter?'

'I really don't know what you mean,' denied Marie huffily.

'Oh, *come on,*' said Jane with real concern. 'You've been going about with a face like thunder for days . . . and you've barely said a word to me.'

'There's nothing wrong with *me,*' she said with emphasis on the last word as she slammed a cake-tin down on the table ready to prepare for the oven.

'Oh, so I'm the one at fault, am I?' said Jane. 'In that case, tell me what I've done to upset you so that I can try to put it right?'

'Just leave it, will you?' said Marie through tight lips.

'No, I won't leave it,' objected Jane, distressed by her friend's attitude. 'You've been funny with me for days. And I think I've a right to know what I've done to deserve it.'

'Nothing,' declared Marie, the rigid set of her shoulders showing otherwise.

'Are you not happy with what I'm paying you for the job? Is that it?' asked Jane, who was peeling apples for the spicy apple cake.

'I'm quite satisfied with the pay, thank you,' said Marie starchily.

'Are you feeling overworked or something then?'

257

persisted Jane, determined to find out what was troubling her.

'It's nothing to do with the job,' said Marie sulkily.

'Ah, so there is something . . . you've just admitted it,' said Jane, pausing in what she was doing and turning to Marie who was greasing the cake-tin as though her life depended on it and refusing to look at her.

'Please answer me, Marie.'

No reply.

'Look, we've been friends for a very long time . . .'

'Humph,' snorted Marie. 'What do long relationships mean to you?'

'What's that supposed to mean?'

Marie shrugged her shoulders, her mouth set in a grim line.

'Oh, I've had just about enough of this,' said Jane crossly, patience weakening under the strain of Marie's mood. 'I'm being made to feel uncomfortable in my own kitchen and you won't even tell me what I've done wrong.'

Marie swung round, eyes flashing, cheeks brightly suffused.

'All right, you asked for it,' she rasped through clenched teeth. 'How could you, Jane? How *could* you do it?'

'How could I do what?'

'You and him next-door.'

'Oh, so that's what all this is about?' she said, putting the knife down and turning her whole attention to her friend. 'How did you find out?'

'I've suspected something was going on for ages but I refused to believe it,' she said. 'Then, the other day, I heard Davey telling Roy and Melanie, as bold as brass, that his Uncle Giles, whom he seems to think is the next best thing to Father Christmas, is his mother's boy-friend!'

'Oh dear,' said Jane, biting her lip. 'I'm sorry you had to find out that way. We obviously haven't been as discreet as we intended.'

'You don't deny it, then?' said Marie, the greaseproof

paper rustling in her trembling fingers.

'No, I don't deny it,' said Jane in a gentle tone because she knew this wasn't easy for Marie.

'Well!' she snorted.

'Look, I know how you feel about Mick and me. But there isn't really any reason why I should deny the fact that I'm seeing Giles.'

'Why have you been keeping so quiet about it then, if you don't feel guilty?'

'Because Giles is a schoolteacher and I'm still technically married.'

'Oh, so that fact hasn't been entirely forgotten then?'

'Of course it hasn't,' said Jane patiently. 'But we'd rather people didn't know about us until we're able to take steps towards getting married. And that isn't possible, legally, until next year when Mick will have been gone for seven years.'

Marie abandoned her task and wiped her greasy hands on her apron.

'You're sleeping with him, aren't you?' she said.

'I really don't think that's any of your business.'

'So you are,' she said in disgust. 'I can't believe you would do a thing like that.'

'Be fair, Marie. Mick has been gone for a long time. My having a boyfriend after all this time hardly makes me promiscuous.'

'So you're just using Giles for sex?'

'No, *of course I'm not*,' said Jane, insulted by the suggestion. 'I'm in love with him.'

'How can you say such a thing? To *me* of all people?'

'I don't want to lie to you about it . . . not now that you know we're together.'

'I never thought you would let anyone else take Mick's place.'

'And I haven't,' insisted Jane. 'What Mick and I had was very special and right for us both at that time in our lives. But he's long gone and I've fallen in love with someone else. It happens, Marie. Life sweeps us all along with it.'

Marie stared at her, accusation still burning in her eyes.

'I wasn't the one who walked out, remember,' Jane pointed out.

'Mick was under a strain . . . he'll be back.'

'Oh, for heaven's sake,' said Jane, angry now. 'You're being completely unreasonable. I know you love your brother but surely this is taking sisterly loyalty too far? You know what a hard time I had after Mick went. You're my friend as well as Mick's sister. Surely you should be pleased that I've found happiness with someone else?'

'Okay, so you think I'm unreasonable,' said Marie. 'But my first loyalty has to be to my brother.'

'Even though he deserted his wife and children?'

'Yes. Even though he did that.'

Marie had always had an unusually close bond with her brother. Now Jane realised just how unyielding that bond was.

'Surely you don't expect me to give Giles up just in case Mick turns up one day and we both still feel the same about each other?'

Her sister-in-law said nothing but the look in her eyes spoke volumes.

'It isn't even me as a person you object to having a boyfriend, is it?' said Jane sharply. 'It's the fact that *your brother's wife* has found someone else, that's what you can't take.'

'I can't, I admit it,' confessed Marie, her tone becoming more subdued. 'Okay, so I've no right to interfere . . . but I can't help it because you're the only woman Mick ever wanted.'

'Before he went away, that was perfectly true,' said Jane. 'But things have changed. He's probably found someone else by now, too.'

'Not Mick.'

'Be that as it may,' said Jane, 'I think you're being really unfair to me.'

'Maybe I am,' said Marie, shrugging her shoulders. 'But I can't help the way I feel.'

'I'm sorry you can't find it in your heart to be more understanding,' said Jane sadly. 'Because I intend to go ahead and marry Giles as soon as it's legally possible.'

'Well . . . don't bother to send me an invitation to the wedding,' rasped Marie.

'I won't if you'd rather not.'

'Oh, I'd rather not all right,' she cut in, her voice rising emotionally. 'In fact, I think you'd better find a replacement for me here, as well.'

'Oh, now you really are taking things too far,' said Jane, beset by a storm of emotions. She was angry, hurt, frustrated, and above all deeply sad. But she couldn't allow herself to be browbeaten. 'You just don't have the right to tell me how to live my life.'

'I know that.'

'I'm glad to hear you admit it,' said Jane with a glimmer of hope.

'But it won't work between us now that you have a new man in your life,' said Marie coldly. 'So it'll be best if I go.'

'So you are prepared to sacrifice your job and your friendship with me because of some misguided loyalty to your brother?' said Jane incredulously.

'There's no need to belittle my feelings,' Marie retorted. 'And, yes, I am prepared to give up those things.'

Jane was smarting from the knowledge that Marie would toss aside the friendship which had meant so much to both of them.

'Surely you don't really mean it?' she said in a softer tone.

'I do.'

'Let's talk about it, please?' said Jane in a conciliatory manner.

'What's the point when I meant what I said?' was the adamant response.

'Oh, well, if that's your attitude, don't let me keep you,' said Jane curtly, because she was so deeply hurt. 'You might as well go right away.'

'I don't want to leave you in the lurch,' said Marie, her voice trembling. 'I'm quite prepared to stay on until you find a replacement.'

'And make my life a misery with your constant disapproval? No, thanks,' announced Jane, struggling against tears. 'I'll manage on my own until I find someone suitable to replace you. I've done it before and I'll do it again. If your brother taught me nothing else when he walked out, it was how to fend for myself.'

'If that's the way you feel, I'll go this very minute,' said Marie, tearing off her overall and cap with sharp angry movements. 'And don't bother to collect my children from school in your car. I'll be picking them up myself in future.'

'As you wish,' agreed Jane, her heart breaking. 'I'll send your money on to you when I've worked out how much I owe you.'

'Fine. I'll see myself out,' said Marie, and marched to the hall to get her coat.

Jane stood where she was at the worktop, staring blindly at a pile of apple peel and wincing as she heard the front door slam. As well as her personal sense of loss, Marie had left behind a professional headache. The mild disorder of a commercial kitchen became chaos with a fifty per cent reduction in workforce. With half-done jobs to be finished all over the place and today's production target still to be met, there was no time to brood even though she wanted only to put her head in her hands and weep.

Forcing back the tears, she worked with a deft hand, mixing, pouring, chopping, loading and unloading the ovens, putting cakes on to cooling trays. She would probably meet her target but her heart wasn't in it.

After an utterly miserable afternoon, that evening Jane asked Giles if he could look after the children for an hour or so while she went round to Marie's to try to make her see reason.

Eddie answered the door and came out on to the path

to talk to Jane, looking grim and closing the door behind him.

'Marie saw you drive up outside and sent me to tell you that she doesn't want to see you,' he said with obvious embarrassment.

'I see.' Jane was gutted. 'She told you all about it, I suppose?'

He nodded.

'I came in the hope that we could patch things up,' explained Jane.

'She won't have any of it, not at the moment anyway,' he said. 'She's always had this thing about Mick.'

'It's so damned unreasonable and she must know that in her heart,' said Jane. 'She's an intelligent woman. So fair and rational in every other way.'

'She's never been clear-headed when it comes to that brother of hers,' he said sadly. 'It's an emotional thing with her.'

'I can't believe she doesn't want us to be friends any more.'

'She's devastated by what's happened, too, but she won't change her mind,' said Eddie, shaking his head slowly. 'I don't think she can help herself when it comes to Mick.'

'Surely she must realise she isn't being fair to me?'

'I think she probably does realise it, deep inside, but she won't admit it. She can't accept the idea of you and Giles, so she thinks it's best if she's out of your life.'

Jane's eyes filled with tears.

'I'm sorry, Jane.'

'So am I,' she said miserably. 'You can tell Marie that I'm very hurt that she's taken this attitude.'

'I'll tell her,' said Eddie with a sigh of resignation.

'Thanks. See you.'

'See you.'

His brow was deeply furrowed as he watched her walk down the path to her car.

The New Year of 1973 had been welcomed in with gusto

at Jane's cottage. Her father and Giles's mother had celebrated with them and were staying overnight with their respective offspring.

Joe had shown his usual reluctance to put in an appearance when he'd known Trudy was going to be there but had seemed to enjoy himself once he'd come. Both parents had been told of the situation between Jane and Giles and had agreed to keep it to themselves for the time being.

It had been a warm and friendly family evening consisting of a party-style buffet followed by a game of charades then some TV. The children had managed to stay awake until midnight and Davey, being the darkest, had first footed. After joining the television performers in 'Auld Lang Syne', they had all trooped outside to the garden to watch the sky lit with fireworks.

But now everyone had settled down for the night and Jane and Giles had slipped out for a walk by the river and a few precious moments alone together.

The stretch of river nearest to Vine Cottages was deserted but a vociferous crowd was doing the conga on Kew Bridge. The sound of partying drifted from some nearby pubs with extended licences, too. An occasional late firework exploded prettily into the inky black sky above the amber haze of town lights.

It was a clear night, the air permeated with smoke from the fireworks and the earthy smell of the river. Wrapped in coats and scarves, they stood on the lit promenade looking into the dark water, both in reflective mood after the festivities.

'I expect you've been thinking about Lena, haven't you?' remarked Jane.

'Yes, I have, actually... I hope that doesn't bother you?'

'Of course not.'

'The memories just came flooding in.'

'I hope they always do,' she said, squeezing his hand. 'New Year is a time for thinking about old loves and old friends. I often find the whole thing quite hard to take.'

'Have you been thinking about Mick?'

'Oh, yes, I always do at NewYear,' she confessed. 'You know, wondering where he is . . . what he's doing. If he's happy.'

Giles slipped a comforting arm around her shoulders and drew her closer to him.

'How would you feel if he ever came back?'

She didn't answer right away because she wasn't sure what the answer was.

'I don't know, Giles,' she said at last. 'I really don't.'

'I'm glad you feel you can be honest with me about it.'

'All I am certain of is that I'm in love with you,' she said. 'But obviously I still feel something for him, as you do for Lena.'

'Ghosts from the past.'

'I've been thinking about Marie too,' she said. 'I wish we were still friends.'

'Yes, it's a pity about that. Is there nothing you can do to put things right?'

'Only give you up and I'm not prepared to do that.'

'I should hope not!'

'That's the awful part about it, knowing I can't patch things up. As fond as I am of her, I can't let her dictate to me.'

'No.'

'I miss her, though.'

'Yes, it must be hard for you, losing your two closest women friends.'

'That's right. I was cut up about Lena, of course, but losing Marie is even more of a blow to me because we'd been friends for such a long time,' Jane told him. 'I miss her in the business too. She was such an asset in the kitchen.'

'Still, at least you managed to find another assistant.'

'It isn't the same,' she said wistfully. 'Marie and I knew each other so well we could communicate without words a lot of the time. I have to spell everything out for the woman who's working for me now. There isn't the same cosy atmosphere at all.'

'Maybe Marie will see things your way in time?'

'If only . . .'

'Anyway, it's New Year so let's look on the bright side,' he said.

'You're right . . . enough of looking back on sad things,' she agreed. 'We've plenty to look forward to this coming year.'

'We certainly have.' They looked at each other in the pale glow of the promenade lighting. 'Despite all the memories of Lena and the problems of having a secret affair, I really do love you.'

'And I you, Giles,' Jane said, lifting her face to his.

The New Year celebrations at the Drake's Arms had been predictably riotous and a good time had been had by customers and staff alike. The landlord had splashed out and hired a pop group for the night. They had played all the modern hits until 'Auld Lang Syne', after which the whole place had erupted into 'Knees Up Mother Brown'. A conga line had trailed out into the street.

'We didn't half shift some booze tonight,' Patsy said to Mick when they got home. 'The guvnor was well chuffed.'

'If a pub doesn't do well on New Year's Eve, they didn't ought to be in the business,' he said, pouring them both a scotch from a silver drinks tray on the sideboard.

'I really enjoyed myself,' said Patsy, leaning back in the armchair and kicking off her high-heeled shoes. 'It was bloomin' hard work but a lot o' fun too. Did you have a good time?'

'Not half.'

He handed her a drink and settled down in a chair opposite her by the imitation log fire set in an ostentatious marble surround. He wasn't exactly drunk but he'd had enough to make him feel happy and relaxed. Patsy had insisted that they leave the car at the pub and get a cab home.

'Christmas Eve and New Year's Eve are my favourite times at the pub,' she said thoughtfully. 'Even if my feet do feel as though I've walked to London and back without a break.'

'You should wear more comfortable shoes,' he suggested.

'Can you honestly imagine me in flat heels?' She grinned.

'No, not really,' he said with an affectionate smile.

'Neither can I.'

She looked like a tart, he thought, with her tight black skirt halfway up her thighs and her plunging neckline pulled down over one shoulder where she'd sat down awkwardly. Her brassy hair was wild, her make-up thick and bright. She wasn't the sort of woman you'd want to take home to Mother but she was great to have as a partner – amusing, undemanding and terrific in bed.

'You're a very good barmaid,' he remarked, sipping his whisky. 'Ever so popular with the customers.'

'Blimey, Mick, you must be drunk,' she said with a broad smile. 'It isn't like you to dish out the compliments.'

'Credit where it's due.'

'Thanks, love,' she said. 'It's nice to know I'm appreciated.'

'You are. Everybody at the pub thinks you're great. I'm the other side of the bar . . . I hear what's being said.'

They lapsed into a comfortable silence. Without any prior intention, Patsy found herself slipping into a serious frame of mind and mulling over something that had been bothering her rather a lot lately.

'Well, another New Year, eh, Mick?' she said. 'A time to make resolutions.'

'Not worth bothering with those,' he said. 'Nobody ever keeps 'em.'

'I'm going to make one this year,' she said, reaching a sudden decision.

'Oh, yeah?' he replied in a tone of amused affection.

'What are you giving up this year, ciggies or chocolate? If you say sex, you'll have me to contend with.'

'It's none of those things.'

'What then?'

'You, Mick . . . I'm giving you up,' she announced. 'I've decided to move out.'

Looking at her with a half smile, he said, 'You're having me on?'

'No, I'm not.'

'You've said nothing about it before,' he said, looking bemused.

'I've only just this second made up my mind,' Patsy told him. 'I've been meaning to talk to you for ages about the unsatisfactory state of our relationship, and the beginning of a New Year is the ideal time for sorting things out.'

'Oh, that's nice, that is,' he said, sobering up suddenly. 'That's a lovely start to the New Year, that is, you walking out on me.'

She sat up and leaned forward, looking at him earnestly.

'It's time you went back to sort your marriage out, Mick.'

'Oh, no, not that again.'

'Yes, that again.'

'Don't give me a hard time, Pats,' he said, frowning. 'I've told you, I have every intention of going back . . . when I'm ready.'

'That just isn't good enough,' she said determinedly. 'I've heard all about this wonderful woman you're married to. For years you've been telling me you're going back to her. But you never do a damned thing about it!'

'You know why that is.'

'I know what you've told me . . . that you want to wait until you're back in the money again,' she said. 'Well, you are now, aren't you? You're doing well. You run a good car, live in a decent flat . . . have plenty of dosh in your pocket.'

'I'm not sure if this is the time to go back, though . . .'

'You're putting it off because you're scared to death, and with very good reason,' she said. 'Your wife wouldn't be normal if she didn't give you a whole lot of grief. But it's your duty to go back and face up to it. The least you can do is to let the woman know you're alive.'

'So you've told me, many times,' said Mick impatiently.

'While I stay around, you'll never do it.'

'What's got into you, Pats?' he said. 'You're usually so easygoing, never one to nag or worry about the future or doing the right thing. That's why we get on so well, 'cause we're two of a kind.'

'I am easygoing, it's true,' she said. 'And I take each day as it comes, most of the time. But I'm only human and I like to know where I stand the same as anyone else. You told me when I first moved in with you that it would only be temporary.'

'Yes . . .'

'Well, it's time you either went back to your wife or put her out of your mind and made a go of it with me,' said Patsy. 'Either way, you must go and see her. Apart from anything else the children are your responsibility. Now that you can afford to contribute to their keep, that's what you should be doing. You can't stay away forever, ignoring your duty. And you can't expect me to live with the threat of eviction from your life indefinitely either. I'll be forty this year. Better I move out while I'm still young enough to make a new start . . . before I begin to feel permanently settled here with you. My leaving will give you a chance to sort yourself out.'

'But you don't have to move out right away, Pats,' he said persuasively.

'Oh, but I do. While I stay here, making life comfortable for you, you'll never face up to what has to be done.'

Mick was shaken to the core. It had never occurred to him that Patsy might leave. Control over their relationship had always seemed to be firmly in his hands. He could hardly believe she could be this assertive.

'Where will you go?' he asked because he knew she had made up her mind.

'I'll move into the pub . . . for the time being anyway. There's a room there I can have any time I like.'

'You've come to mean a lot to me, Pats,' he said, and meant it.

'Yes, I believe I have, Mick. But you're still in love with your wife.'

He nodded.

'I guess I always will be,' he said. 'It's just one of those things.'

'I know,' she said, trying not to show how down-hearted this made her. 'Because I've been so happy with you, I've let things drift on. I should have taken a stand a long time ago.'

'We've had some good times, you and me.'

'Not half. But I've never been happy with the idea of living with another woman's husband, even though you'd already left her before I came along.'

'My going back to Jane doesn't reflect on my feelings for you. You're one of the best and if things had been different . . . well, who knows?'

'I know.'

'It's just that I could never feel for any other woman what I feel for Jane. It's one of those rock-solid things for both of us.'

'I hope it works out for you,' said Patsy, swigging whisky to ease the pain. 'You know where to find me if it doesn't.'

'You mean, you'd have me back?'

'Only if your marriage was definitely over and you'd sorted things out properly with Jane.'

'You really are something else, Pats,' he said with genuine affection. 'You deserve someone better than me.'

'I know that,' she said, joshing. 'I'll go out and find myself someone better tomorrow, shall I?' She finished her drink and stood up. 'In the meantime, I'm going to bed. I'm absolutely shattered.'

'I won't be far behind you,' said Mick, getting up and

pouring himself another drink to help him over the shock of Patsy's decision to leave. He'd got used to having her around and was going to miss her. But that in itself might encourage him to make a positive move towards putting his marriage right.

'See you in a while, then,' she said with feigned cheerfulness and headed for the bedroom.

Closing the door behind her, she leaned against it, sobbing into her handkerchief so that Mick wouldn't hear. Forcing a watershed was something she'd known she would have to do sometime, and it was the right thing. But it was *so* hard. This way she would either lose him forever or get him back on a more satisfactory basis.

Either way, she would never be the love of his life but she'd rather be second best than not have him at all. How she was going to manage if he went back to Jane permanently was something she daren't even think about.

How perverse the fates were, she thought. Jane was the only woman for Mick and he was the only man for Patsy. But she couldn't go on as they had been, knowing he was constantly hankering for someone else. She dried her tears, for fear he would find her in this pathetic state. One of the things Mick liked best about her was the fact that she didn't make scenes, and she didn't want to lose points with him at this crucial stage.

When she was feeling a little more composed, she began to get undressed, deciding to move out of here tomorrow. Strike while the iron was hot, that was her motto. Further delay would only cause more pain. But, for all this sensible reasoning, just the thought of not being here with Mick tomorrow night made her want to cry again.

Chapter Seventeen

Jane left her car at the station and travelled into central London on the tube because of the parking problems in the West End. It was one of those deceptively sunny February days that felt warm through the windows of a heated house but which turned your toes and fingers numb as soon as you set foot outside. The weather was irrelevant to Jane, though, as she sat on the stale-smelling train, her stomach churning nervously, her heart beating erratically.

She'd been awake most of the night, reeling from the shock of hearing Mick's voice again after all this time. The telephone had been ringing at the cottage yesterday afternoon when she'd got back from collecting the children from school. He had got her number from Marie apparently.

Jane had been too stupefied to ask any more than the basic details, which were that he lived in Brighton and was staying in London in a hotel near Marble Arch. He wanted to see her urgently and said he would explain everything when they met.

Managing to gather her wits sufficiently to decide not to involve the children until she knew more about his intentions, she'd agreed to meet him for lunch at his hotel. It had meant reorganising her working day and leaving her assistant in charge in her absence, but Mick knew nothing of this and simply assumed she was free to fit in with his plans at any time. Having shattered her life nearly seven years ago, he was once again turning it upside down.

Walking to the hotel from the station in her

fashionably long tweed coat with a black fur collar and stylish black boots, Jane was feeling very confused and had no idea how she would feel about Mick when she saw him again. Naturally she was glad he was alive and well but a part of her wished he'd left her alone to continue with the life he had forced her to make for herself and which she'd grown to value. Just when she'd begun to look forward to a settled future with Giles, Mick had reappeared to complicate matters.

With her heart beating wildly, she went through the revolving doors and into the foyer where they had arranged to meet.

It had taken Mick nearly two months to pluck up courage to make contact with his wife. After Patsy had left, he'd felt lonelier than he could possibly have imagined and had spent a lot of his time at the Drake's Arms in search of company and business. But most of all he had gone there to see Patsy. The flat felt desolate without her chirpy presence. Despite his attempts to persuade her, however, she was adamant about not coming back. She wouldn't even consider it until he had sorted out his marriage one way or the other.

And now he was here in the hotel foyer, waiting for Jane and tingling with apprehension. When the smart woman with the smooth bobbed hair and air of confidence about her came through the doors, it didn't occur to him that she was his wife. Only when she drew nearer did recognition begin to dawn. But could this sophisticated lady really be his homely Jane? It was. *It really was!* How she had changed. He was mesmerised by her lustrous hair, her smooth skin, the classy look which was doubly obvious to him after being with Patsy for so long.

Emotion overcame him at the sheer joy of seeing her again. How could he have stayed away so long? How could he have left her in the first place? Thank God Patsy had forced him into coming back. This was where he belonged – with his beloved Jane. Dear old Patsy seemed positively tacky in comparison.

Jane was coming towards him and he could hardly breathe from the pleasure of it.

'Hello Mick,' she said evenly.

'Oh, Jane,' he said, tears in his eyes. 'It's *so* good to see you . . .'

He felt her stiffen against him when he kissed her, and she didn't seem to want to linger in his arms but drew back quickly.

'Shall we go into the bar and have a drink before lunch?' he suggested, feeling awkward with her.

'Good idea,' she said. 'Because you have a heck of a lot of explaining to do.'

'Yeah, I know,' he agreed breezily. 'So let's get settled with some drinks and I'll tell you all about it.'

Jane's first impression of Mick when she saw him in the foyer was that he looked different. He seemed flashier than she remembered. He wore his hair longer now and had thick, exaggerated sideburns which made him look rough. He was wearing a bright red shirt and a hideous multicoloured tie under a light grey jacket worn with black flared trousers. Was he more flamboyant than he used to be or was it simply that her tastes had changed? she wondered, as he came to the end of a rather unlikely story about losing his memory and living under a false name.

He still had the dazzling good looks and roguish charm that had first attracted her to him – but she wasn't attracted to him now. She had known the instant she'd set eyes on him in the foyer that her feelings for him had changed.

'It must have been some sort of breakdown caused by all the money worries,' he was saying. 'You can imagine how terrible I felt when I got my memory back and realised what I must have done to you and the children.'

'You don't actually remember leaving, then?'

'No, that's the strange part about it,' he said. 'I remember feeling desperate and not knowing which way to turn. I remember contemplating suicide. The next thing I knew I was on the beach at Bognor. I still don't know how I got there.'

'I thought you said you were living in Brighton?'

'I moved there later,' he said, careful not to be too generous with the truth about the time element. 'More scope for business.'

'Yes, I suppose there would be. It's a busy place.'

It was an incredible story which she knew many people would dismiss as a pack of lies. But she didn't disbelieve him. Such things did happen. She remembered reading about a similar case in the newspaper once. She also remembered finding the valium in his pocket after he'd gone, and how tense he'd been.

'You should have told me what a mess you were in financially,' she said.

'I just couldn't bring myself to.'

'It was a terrible shock when the bank manager came to see me and told me we were about to lose everything.'

'I'm sorry, Jane,' he said, tears in his eyes again. 'You must have hated me.'

'I didn't hate you but I was angry and hurt, naturally,' she said. 'Not knowing about the breakdown, I thought you'd just done a runner . . . left me to cope 'cause you didn't have the bottle to stay.'

'I bet your dad had a few choice things to say about me?'

'It's a wonder your ears didn't burst into flames!'

'Can't blame him, I suppose.'

'His reaction was perfectly normal,' said Jane. 'His daughter had been left homeless and penniless with two kids to bring up. We weren't to know you were ill.'

'Surely you must have known I wouldn't have gone if I'd been in my right mind? You and the kids were my life. Everything I did was for you.'

Most of what he'd done had been pure self-indulgence but she didn't have the heart to mention it as he seemed to have had such a bad time.

'At first I refused to believe you would just go off and

leave me,' she said. 'But when there was no word from you at all, and then when I heard the truth about your finances, that seemed to be the only logical explanation.'

'You must have been furious?'

'It was very hard for me, Mick . . . having no home and no income, and suddenly having to go out cleaning to feed the kids. And, yes, I did feel bitter at times. But I stopped feeling like that ages ago.'

'It took me a while to drum up enough courage to get in touch with you when I did get my memory back.'

'Yes, I think I can understand that,' she told him. 'What actually happened? Did it just come back all of a sudden?'

'Yes . . . sort of. Slow at first, then it came all of a rush.'

'When was that . . . a couple of weeks ago?' she said chattily.

He looked into her trusting eyes. If he told her the truth, that he'd had his memory back for more than four years, he could lose her forever. Although he felt perfectly justified in delaying his return until he had something to offer her, she might not see it his way. He daren't take the risk. He *must* have her back. Having seen her again, he knew he couldn't let her go. He wanted her now with a desire that by far outweighed anything he had felt for her when they had been together before.

'A couple of months,' he lied.

'As long as that?' she exclaimed, feeling very sorry for him. 'You must have gone through hell since then?'

'Yeah, it's been awful,' he said, knowing from her reaction that he'd done the right thing in hiding the truth.

'Poor you,' she sympathised. 'It must have felt very strange, not knowing who you were for such a long time.'

'I got used to it,' he said. 'I kept myself busy building a business.'

'It must have been very frightening, though.'

'It was terrifying at first,' he said, moving on quickly

to avoid more lies. 'But that's all over now. I'm back and that's all that matters.'

This made her feel uneasy because it sounded as though he expected to take up where they had left off. A few years ago, that was all she'd wanted. Now everything was different.

She looked at her watch.

'I think we'd better make a start on lunch,' she said. 'I have to get back in time to pick the children up from school.'

'Don't worry about that,' said Mick with an indulgent smile. 'I'll drive you home and we can pick them up together.'

'No,' she said, instantly protective of her offspring who had suffered so much by his going away. 'I'll need to prepare the children before you see them.'

'Oh . . . I see,' he said with obvious disappointment.

'Anyway, I've left my car at the station so I'll need to collect that.'

'A car . . . *you've got a car*!' he said in astonishment.

'Well . . . yes.' She threw him a puzzled look. 'Has Marie not told you anything about what's been happening while you've been away?'

'No. I only spoke to her for long enough to get your phone number,' he explained. 'I told her I'd go over to see her for a proper chat sometime soon.'

'You've not seen your parents either, then?' Jane surmised.

'I've not seen anyone yet,' he explained. 'I didn't want to see anybody else until I'd sorted things out with you.'

'In that case, I think we'd better go into the restaurant and have some lunch, Mick,' she said worriedly. 'And I'll bring you up to date with what I've been doing while you've been away.'

'You're running your own business?' he said incredulously when Jane had given him a brief account of how she earned her living.

'There's no need to sound quite so thunderstruck,'

she said, making a brave effort with the lemon sole she'd chosen because it was the lightest thing on the menu. 'Didn't you think I had it in me?'

'No, I didn't,' said Mick, whose own appetite seemed unimpaired by their meeting, judging by the way he was tucking into his sirloin steak.

'Surely you must have been wondering how I've managed to keep myself and the children?'

'I suppose I thought you'd be on benefit, or that you'd got a job . . . but a business of your own . . . and a car . . .'

'I have my own house too,' she said. 'At least, I'm paying for it on a mortgage.'

'A mortgage . . . *you*?' He stopped eating and stared at her.

'That's right. I have an old cottage by the river near Kew Bridge. It's very pretty. I really love it there.'

So much for his idea of rescuing her from poverty and desolation! His wife had apparently become some sort of a tycoon while he'd been away, and this didn't please Mick one bit. Success was strictly his prerogative in the Parker family and he took a dim view of Jane's stealing his thunder.

He felt obliged to ask her what sort of business she was in, though.

She told him all about the shop and when he looked worried, added, 'Don't worry, it's all perfectly above board.'

Which was more than he could say for his own business! But Mick just said, 'I wasn't suggesting otherwise. I just can't get over the fact that you actually have a business of your own.'

'Why?'

'Well . . . you were never interested in even getting a job outside the home, let alone starting your own business.'

'That's quite true. Before you left, I was perfectly content to be a full-time housewife. But I had to do something to earn money to keep the kids decently after you'd gone,' she explained, 'and I wasn't prepared to

279

scrub floors early in the morning and work the late shift in a factory to put food on the table indefinitely. I didn't want to have the children looked after all day while I went out to work, either. Working for myself meant I could be more flexible.'

'Okay, okay, don't rub it in,' he said, aiming for her sympathy because he felt unable to dominate her as he once had. 'I know I hurt you all.' He looked deliberately cast down. 'But I couldn't help having a mental break-down, could I?'

'No, of course you couldn't, Mick,' she said. 'But you're making me feel guilty for having made a decent life for the children and myself, and that really isn't fair.'

'Sorry, I didn't mean to upset you,' he lied, sipping his wine for comfort.

'That's all right.'

'Anyway, you won't have to worry about earning a living any more, will you? Now that I'm back to take charge.'

With sinking heart, she put down her knife and fork and stared at him.

'What exactly do you think is going to happen now, Mick?'

'I'm surprised you even have to ask that,' he told her.

'But I *am* asking.'

'It's obvious, innit?'

'No. Not to me.'

'You've been left to take care of things for far too long,' he said. 'Now I'm back to take my rightful place, looking after you and the children.'

'But, Mick . . .'

'All the worry is going to be taken off your shoulders from now on, babe, I promise you,' he said eagerly. 'You can sell your business and be a lady of leisure again.'

God, what a nightmare this meeting was turning out to be! She felt irritated by his arrogant assumption that he could just come back and take over as though she didn't have a brain in her head or the right to an opinion.

This was immediately followed by compunction because he had been ill.

How could you tell a man who had had some sort of mental breakdown that you didn't want him back in your life, that you couldn't even bear the thought of his touching you, that you were in love with somebody else?

'I'm doing really well again,' continued Mick as she sat looking at him in silent agony. 'I'm making big money now . . . bigger than anything I made before I went away.'

'Really?' said Jane dully.

'Oh, yeah,' he said proudly.

'Good,' she said miserably.

'I can afford to get us all moved into a big luxury house, like we had in Maple Avenue, with all the latest modern fittings,' he enthused. 'You can get rid of your place as soon as you like . . . you said it was only an old cottage?'

'But . . .'

'There's some cracking new properties going up in and around Brighton,' he cut in before she could say another word.

'*Brighton!*'

'Yeah. It's a great place to live,' he said as though he hadn't noticed her distress.

'I don't doubt it but . . .'

'All that lovely sea air and the countryside nearby,' he rattled on.

'But, Mick . . .'

'Just think how thrilled the kids will be to move to the seaside.'

His calm assumption that she would automatically relinquish everything she had worked so hard for, and the casual way he denigrated her beloved cottage, filled Jane with a kind of bewildered rage. She knew that if she didn't stand up to him, he would destroy her.

'So what do you say to that, eh, babe?' he asked proudly.

She remained silent, planning her next words carefully.

'Relieved, I bet?' he said. 'It must have been hard for you this last few years.'

'Yes, it was hard for me at first,' she said. 'But as I've said, I've been managing very well recently.'

'Oh . . . I see,' he said, clearly peeved.

'You've been away a long time, Mick,' she said. 'Things have changed for me.'

'Nothing that can't be altered back to how it was, though, eh?'

'It isn't quite as simple as that, I'm afraid,' she told him.

'Oh . . . and why is that?'

Jane braced herself to answer his question.

Chapter Eighteen

'Well, for one thing, I've got used to supporting myself,' she told him, biting her lip anxiously because, despite his thoughtless disregard for her feelings, she didn't want to hurt him.

' 'Course you have, babe,' he said in a blatantly patronising manner. 'But you can put all that behind you now that I'm back.'

His apparent inability to grasp what should have been obvious to anyone – that a long absence would inevitably bring changes – only emphasised the gulf between them.

'That isn't really the point, Mick,' Jane tried to explain.

'What *are* you going on about?' he asked with seething impatience. 'You're in business for the sole purpose of making money. Now that I'm back, I'll supply that . . . and plenty of it.'

'But I enjoy running my business and don't want to give it up,' she blurted out. 'Neither do I want to move to Brighton.'

'But you're my wife . . . you'll go where I think is best for us.'

The appearance of the waiter to take their dessert order gave Jane an opportunity to gather her wits after that frightening reminder of Mick's domineering personality. How could she tell him that there was no 'us' for them any more? She knew instinctively that her being in love with Giles had nothing to do with her changed feelings for Mick. She had simply grown out of loving him in the way she once had and that would have happened had she never set eyes on Giles. It was all to do with the irreversible process of her having matured and developed as a person.

'The cottage is the best place for the children and me,' she said, having declined dessert and ordered coffee. 'I've built a life for us there and I'm not prepared to uproot the kids. It wouldn't be fair to make them leave their friends and put them through the trauma of starting a new school when it isn't necessary. They're established where we are and we're all very happy there.'

'You've been happy... *without me*?' he said with unconcealed disapproval.

'Well... yes. Surely you didn't think I'd spent the whole of the last seven years being miserable?'

'No, but neither did I imagine you'd be having a whale of a time!'

'And I haven't been,' Jane denied hotly.

'I should damned well hope not!'

'You couldn't possibly imagine the hell I went through after you left. The pain of missing you, the worry of trying to make ends meet. *And* I was pregnant...'

'Another child?' said Mick, his expression brightening.

'I lost it.'

'Oh, I'm sorry.'

'So was I. But I had to get on with life, for the sake of Davey and Pip. After a while I got used to the responsibility and even began to enjoy it. I'm not the same woman you left all those years ago.'

'Well, you'll just have to change back to how you were before I went then, won't you?' he said dogmatically. 'And sharpish.'

She shook her head.

'Surely you must know that isn't possible, Mick? People can't change to order.'

'But I'm your husband... you do as I say because I'm the boss.'

Delaying her reply until the water had finished serving them with coffee, she said, 'Now you listen to me, Mick. You went away and left me in trouble. Okay, so you lost your memory and I'm really sorry about that. But it doesn't alter the fact that I was forced to become independent.'

'Everything I did was for you and the kids,' he said again morosely. 'I only worked hard so that you could have a good life.'

'You might be able to deceive yourself into believing that was the way it was but you won't convince me,' Jane felt forced to point out, because he was being so blatantly untruthful. 'Not any more.'

'I don't know what you're babbling on about, woman . . .'

'You were obsessed with money and success,' she said, 'and you wanted it for your own gratification. I was simply part of the package to show off to the world. The obedient wife living in the big house with two cars on the drive and the children you could afford to indulge whenever you felt like it. But you couldn't afford any of it! You'd been deceiving me for years, leading me to believe we had something behind us when we had nothing. Everything we had was on credit.'

'Us and most other people,' he said. 'This is the age of credit.'

'It was all show, Mick,' she reproached him, spooning sugar into her coffee.

'I didn't hear you complaining at the time.'

'Because I thought we could afford our expensive lifestyle. I'd soon have put a stop to it if I'd known the truth. Those things were never that important to me, anyway.'

'There was no need for you to know the details of my financial affairs,' blustered Mick. 'If it hadn't been for the fire, there wouldn't have been any trouble.'

'Don't kid yourself about that,' Jane told him firmly. 'We were living way beyond our means. The fire just brought things to a head. It would have happened sooner or later anyway. Your bank manager told me that.'

'Bank managers,' he snorted dismissively. 'Destroyers of the entrepreneurial spirit.'

'Hardly . . .'

'Anyway, I saw it as my job to protect you from responsibility,' he cut in.

'And you did it so effectively that after you left, I was so helpless I barely had the courage to go outside the door. I knew nothing about managing money. I'd never even written a cheque. That's what your protection did for me . . . it made me feeble! I soon discovered what a tough world it is out there, and I never want to be that dependent on anyone again.'

'Okay, so I'll let you know what's going on in future,' he said, without any intention of doing so because Jane would have a fit if she knew how he earned his living. 'The sooner we move to Brighton, the better.'

'I can't move to Brighton,' she told him for the second time. 'I just can't do it.'

'All right, I'll move in with you for the time being, then,' he told her.

'But . . .'

'I'll have to spend a lot of time in Brighton, though, especially during the week 'cause my business is there,' he said, ignoring her attempts to speak. 'I'll keep my flat on for the moment and spend weekends with you and the kids.'

'But you can't move in with us, just like that,' she burst out.

'Why not?' He narrowed his eyes at her. 'You haven't got some bloke living there, have you?'

She knew this wasn't the moment to tell him about Giles.

'No.'

'Why can't I move in then?'

'Because I need time.'

'To do what?'

'To think things over.'

'What is there to think about?' demanded Mick. 'You're my wife. You'll bloody well do as I tell you!'

'As I've already said, I've changed while you've been away . . .'

'I hope you're not trying to tell me you don't want me

back?' he said, looking dejected and helpless suddenly. 'Because I just couldn't accept that, Jane. You *have* to let me back into your life. It's no more than your duty.'

He seemed almost manically determined that they should get back together and this attitude worried her. There was something odd about him now . . . something that scared her.

'Try to see this from my point of view,' she pleaded. 'Seven years is a long time. I've got used to being without you.'

'Look, I know I did wrong in going off, even though I didn't know I was doing it,' said Mick, playing the humble card for all he was worth to try and win her over since his natural tendency to bully no longer seemed to work. 'But please give me another chance, babe? I promise you won't regret it. I intend to make up to you for all the suffering I've caused you and the children.'

'But things are so different now, I'm not sure if it'll work for either of us.'

' 'Course it'll work,' he said, dismissing her doubts as though they were of no consequence. 'Okay, so there'll be a few changes, I accept that. But I'm your husband. My place is by your side.'

'Can you give me a little time, please?' she urged him. 'It's been such a shock, your turning up after all this time.'

'I can't see why you need time, but okay, I'll go along with that,' he said. 'I'll stay on here at the hotel for a few days. As I'm back on the scene, I might as well catch up with a few old mates. Go and see my folks.' He paused as though working something out in his mind. 'I'll have to go back to Brighton to see about business an' all. So I'll give you a bell in a couple of days.'

'No, leave it to me to ring you . . . I'll give you a call when I'm ready,' said Jane in a forthright manner that shocked Mick, who could hardly believe the submissive woman he had married could be so definite about anything. First Patsy, now Jane. It was nothing short of anarchy and he blamed the feminists for it, upsetting the status quo by putting ideas into women's heads!

'Cor, it's coming to something when a man can't even move in with his wife and kids without having to wait until she's ready,' he complained. 'But, okay, have it your way. Just don't keep me waiting too long 'cause I need to be with you.' He reached across the table and put his hand on hers. 'We'll make a go of it, babe, you'll see. Once we're together again, everything will fall into place. We're a pair, you and me.'

There was something decidedly unwholesome about Mick's attitude towards her. Jane got the impression he would stop at nothing to force her to do what he wanted.

When she left the hotel later that afternoon, she was relieved to be away from him and very worried indeed about the future.

Jane was in the kitchen cooking fish fingers and baked beans for the children's tea when the sound of squabbling drifted in from the living room.

'You touch the cat again and I'm telling Mum,' threatened Davey.

'I'm not hurting him,' came Pip's retort. 'Anyway, he likes me better than he likes you.'

'You mustn't keep picking him up and carrying him around,' said Davey. 'He doesn't like it.'

'He does!'

'Doesn't!'

'You're stupid.'

'Oh, keep quiet, you pest,' ordered Davey. 'Magpie's coming on in a minute.'

'I wanna watch Animal Magic on the other side,' protested Pip.

'We're watching Magpie . . .'

Neither of them had any after-school activities today which was unusual. When they were bored they were anathema to each other and passed the time trading insults. Usually it went straight over Jane's head but today it made her want to scream.

It was a week since her meeting with Mick and her

nerves were in shreds. She dreaded the telephone's ringing in case it was him. She lay awake at night worrying about what she should do. Her head was throbbing and her eyes were sore with tiredness. The children's voices were grating on her already overstretched nervous system and it was a relief when they finally fell silent.

But not for long. A sudden shriek pierced the air and Pip, red-faced and howling, thudded into the kitchen with Davey behind her.

'He hit me, Mummy!' the girl wailed to her mother who was busy turning fish fingers over on the grill-pan.

'She hit me first,' declared Davey.

'He started it!'

'Liar . . .'

'Tell him, Mum.'

'Tell her, Mum,' said Davey.

Something snapped inside Jane. She rammed the grill-pan back into place, threw the fork she'd been using down on the table and turned on them, marching them both back into the living room.

'What is it with you two?' she demanded, standing before them. 'Why can't you be pleasant to each other for more than five minutes at a time?'

'It was him . . .'

'It was her . . .'

'It was *both* of you,' she screamed, at such volume they both shrank back and stared at her in bewilderment because their mother didn't normally carry on like this.

'You, Davey, are eleven years old, and you, Pip, are ten,' she said. 'And you are both behaving like a couple of three year olds!'

Neither said a word. United now against the enemy adult, they stood close together. Pip slipped her hand into Davey's.

Jane couldn't stop herself. The words poured out as though of their own volition.

'As if I don't have enough on my mind, you two have to give me trouble I can do without.' She put her hand to her aching head. 'I've just about had enough, do you hear . . . *enough!* If you're going to behave like babies, I shall have to treat you like babies and put you to bed . . . *now.*'

They stared at her in silence. The threat of an early bedtime was the ultimate deterrent.

'So if I hear so much as one more cross word pass between you, that is what I'll do,' she roared. '*Is that clear?*'

They stood trembling before her.

'Sorry, Mum,' said Pip, eyes brimming with tears.

'We won't argue again,' said Davey, looking pale and worried.

All Jane's anger drained away, leaving her remorseful and near to tears herself. They had been troublesome but they hadn't deserved quite such an onslaught. She shouldn't take her own wretchedness out on them.

'Okay.' She put her arms around them both. 'Let's all calm down, shall we?'

They nodded warily.

'You've probably missed most of the programmes you were quarrelling about by this time, anyway,' she said. 'But tea will be ready soon.'

Leaving them sitting quietly in front of the television, she departed to the kitchen to rescue the burning fish fingers, her own eyes smarting with tears. This couldn't go on. She had to decide what to do about Mick, one way or the other.

Giles look stricken later that evening after she'd told him of Mick's return.

'I thought you seemed a bit edgy this last few days.'

'I didn't want to say anything to you about it until I'd decided what to do,' said Jane, perching on the edge of the armchair opposite him in his living room. He was sitting on the sofa with a pile of exercise books beside him.

'And now you have decided?'

She nodded.

'You're taking him back, aren't you?' said Giles bleakly.

'I honestly don't know what else I can do, Giles,' she said, sounding distraught. 'I've nearly gone out of my mind this past week, thinking about it. But when all is said and done, he is still my husband and the father of my children and he wants us all to be together again.'

'Do you think you can make it work after everything that's happened?'

'I really don't know,' she said with a sad shake of the head. 'But I do think that I have to try.'

'Well, Jane,' he said dully, 'I can't pretend it isn't a blow.'

He looked utterly desolate but was far too much of a gentleman to make things worse for her by causing a scene, she knew that. Her heart bled for him, especially knowing what agony he had already suffered over the loss of a woman.

'I'm so sorry, Giles.'

'No more than I am. Do you still love him now that you've seen him again?'

She shook her head.

'I still feel a certain affection for him. It could hardly be otherwise as we've been together since we were teenagers. But I'm not in love with him. Not any more.'

'I see.'

'I feel sorry for him, though,' she said. 'He's a pathetic character somehow now, despite the fact that he's doing well.'

'So you're having him back out of duty and pity?'

'And because I care what happens to him.'

'It doesn't sound like a recipe for success to me.'

'I have to try, Giles,' she said, her voice thick with feeling. 'I can't turn him away. I married him for better or worse.'

'Yes, of course.'

'I feel I have a duty to the children as well as to Mick, to try again,' she said. 'He is their father after all.'

'There's nothing I can say to that, is there?' said Giles bitterly. 'The last thing I would ever do is come between man and wife.'

'Oh, Giles, *I'm so sorry*,' she said, going over to him with tears in her eyes and sitting beside him to take his hand. 'You'll have to try to forget me.'

'You know I can't do that.'

'We'll both have to give it our very best shot.'

'Which will be impossible while we're living next-door to each other,' he told her. 'I'll just have to put my cottage up for sale.'

'Oh, Giles, I can't let you do that! It wouldn't be fair to you or Kevin.'

'I won't go far,' he said. 'I'll stay in the area so that the boys can still see each other on a regular basis. But actually living next-door to you will be just too much for me to bear.' He drew in his breath sharply, eyes full of pain. 'Seeing you with him in the garden and knowing you're with him on the other side of the wall . . . I couldn't take that.'

'It would be wretched for us both,' agreed Jane sadly.

'I'll put my place on the market.'

'But I feel so guilty . . . you're having to move house because of me,' she said.

'It isn't because of you, it's because of the circumstances. Just one of those things.'

'I'm the one who should move, not you, since I'm the one who's causing the problem,' she said. 'Mick's keen to get me out of my cottage anyway.'

'But you love the place.'

'I know. I've told him I'm not prepared to give it up. But he wants us to live in a new des. res. on some executive estate in Brighton.'

'Oh, dear.'

'Exactly.'

'And Brighton?'

'His business is there.'

'And yours is here.'

'That's of no importance to Mick,' she said. 'He's finding it difficult to adapt to the idea of my being in business and wants me to give it up. He isn't used to my having any sort of independence.'

'Sounds to me as though you need to hang on to your cottage then. Especially as your kitchen there is kitted out for baking.'

'There is that.'

'Don't worry . . . it'll be easier if I'm the one to move.'

Although Jane felt bad about Giles having to go away, she was relieved to be able to stay put because she was convinced that to give up her cottage would be the first step back to total domination by Mick. She didn't want to burden Giles with her doubts about the success of the reconciliation. Firstly because she didn't want to worry him or give him false hope, and secondly because it seemed disloyal to Mick somehow. She had to do everything in her power to make it work with him and this meant a clean break with Giles.

'I'm so sorry it's come to this,' she told him again.

'Well, I suppose I've always known there was a chance he'd come back. I mean, it isn't as though he was dead.'

'Whereas I always knew that Lena couldn't come back.'

'Yes.'

Their eyes met in an agonising moment of regret. Jane wondered if she might feel less guilty if Giles were to throw his weight about and make a scene. But that wasn't his way. He was far too gentle.

'I've been so happy with you, Giles,' she said. 'I'm going to miss you more than you could possibly imagine.'

'And I you.'

Then she was in his arms for one final bitter-sweet embrace. When she slipped quietly out of his back door and through the gap in the fence, with tears streaming down her cheeks, she knew that nothing would ever be the same again.

Chapter Nineteen

One Saturday in the spring, around noon, Mick came down the narrow, winding staircase of Jane's cottage, muttering a string of expletives.

'One of these days someone is gonna fall and break their neck on those bloody stairs,' he complained, marching into the kitchen where his wife was busy at the table doing some paperwork. 'They're nothing short of primitive . . . like everything else in this dump!'

'The children and I have never had any problem with them at all,' she said through clenched teeth because Mick's constant criticism of her home was becoming tedious.

'I don't know what you've got against moving into a decent-sized house,' he grumbled. 'As well as being a museum piece, this place is far too poky for a family to live in.'

'I don't agree,' she said. 'There's more than enough space for what we need.'

'Don't make me laugh,' he mocked. 'There isn't room to swing a cat in here.'

'It isn't as big as the sort of house you want us to move into, certainly,' she said. 'But it's perfectly adequate . . . and lovely and cosy.' She looked at him. 'Don't you think it has a special kind of feel about it?'

'Yeah, it feels as though it's about to fall down at any minute,' was his facetious reply.

'Oh, very funny,' she countered.

'It's an absolute hole and not our sort of thing at all.'

'Speak for yourself,' Jane objected. 'I really love it here.'

'But you've always liked modern houses,' he said, sounding puzzled. 'Big ones with plenty of luxury fittings.'

'A long time ago I might have,' she corrected him. 'Now I prefer this place and I wish you'd stop finding fault with it.'

Shadow came in through the cat-flap and rubbed himself in circles around Mick's legs, purring loudly in the hope of attention.

'Bloody moggy,' he said, sending the animal flying across the room with his foot. 'God knows why you wanna have a cat.'

'He's one of the family and we love him,' she said, leaping up and rescuing the cat who was cowering in the corner. 'And I won't have you being cruel to him.'

'I was being firm,' said Mick. 'It's the only language cats understand.'

'Rubbish! You be gentler with him in future or you'll have me to answer to.' Jane sat down again at the table with the cat in her lap. 'It's a good job the children didn't see you boot him across the kitchen. They'd never forgive you.'

'Where are they?' he asked.

'Davey is next-door with Kevin and Pip is at a friend's house.'

'They always used to be around the house before I went away,' he said grudgingly.

'They were younger then,' she said, stroking the cat before setting him down to wander off into the other room. 'They have a life of their own outside the home now, and on Saturday mornings they usually go out to see friends. It's perfectly normal for kids of their age.'

'You'd think they'd stay in to see their dad at the weekend, wouldn't you?' he moaned. 'It isn't as though I'm here during the week.'

Glancing up at the kitchen clock, then lowering her gaze meaningfully to the pyjamas and dressing gown in which he was dressed, she said, 'If you were to get up at a reasonable hour, you'd see them before they go out.

You can't expect them to wait in until lunchtime.'

'I'll get up what time I please,' said Mick gruffly.

'That's fine. But don't complain about not seeing the children.'

She turned her attention back to her figures.

'What's for breakfast?' he asked after a while.

In the middle of adding up a column of figures, Jane jotted something down to save having to repeat the entire process.

'The children and I had toast and cereal,' she said, looking up.

'I don't want that rubbish,' he declared. 'I want a proper breakfast . . . a fry up.'

'But it's almost lunchtime.'

'I still want a fry up.'

'Okay, Mick,' she said patiently. 'There are eggs and bacon and stuff in the fridge. Could you be a dear and see to it?'

'You're joking?' he said, horrified. 'I'm not doing that!'

'But you can see how busy I am at the moment,' she said, exasperated by his lack of co-operation. 'Surely you don't mind frying some eggs and bacon for yourself when you get up so late?'

'I do mind and I'm not doing it,' he said. 'It's your job.'

'But I'll be getting the lunch ready in a minute,' she told him.

He looked at her coldly. 'Eggs, bacon, fried bread, tomatoes and sausages . . . that's what I want, *and I want it now*,' he commanded.

'Please, Mick. I have to finish this . . . it's really important.'

'You can finish it when you've cooked my breakfast,' he growled. 'I'm sick and tired of coming second to some tinpot business you've got yourself involved in.'

'Hardly a tinpot business,' she objected. 'It's done well enough to keep the kids and me this last few years.'

'But it doesn't need to keep you now that I'm here, does it?' he said for the umpteenth time since he'd been back. 'It's your own fault if you won't do as I say and get shot of the cake shop . . . your own fault if you don't have time to look after your husband properly.'

'My business benefits us all . . . and our family life doesn't suffer because of it,' she insisted. 'I've always made sure of that.'

'*I* suffer.'

'You don't know the meaning of the word . . .'

'But we don't need you to make any money now,' he continued as though she hadn't spoken. 'And I *do* need my breakfast.'

Realising there was no point in trying to reason with him in this mood, Jane gathered up her papers and put them away in the bureau in the other room. Then she went back into the kitchen and took the frying pan from the cupboard. She was just getting some bacon out of the fridge when the telephone rang in the living room. It was Doris from the shop to say that her assistant had gone home sick and she urgently needed help until the Saturday morning rush was over. Jane told her she'd be right over.

'Sorry, Mick, but I have to go out,' she said, going back into the kitchen where he was sitting at the table, smoking and reading the newspaper.

'Where to?'

'The shop . . . staff problems,' she explained. 'It'll only be for an hour or so.'

'What about my breakfast?'

'I'll have to ask you to help out by getting it yourself after all,' she said. 'I'm sure you won't mind co-operating with me in a crisis?'

'Haven't I made myself clear? I do mind . . . I mind very much!' he boomed.

'In that case you'll have to wait until I get back then, won't you?' she said. 'Pip's having lunch at her friend's and I'll pop next-door on my way out to tell Davey where I'm going.'

'You're not going anywhere.'

'You can always make yourself useful and start preparing lunch,' she said, ignoring his threat. 'There's a selection of cooked meats in the fridge and I've made a salad . . . also in the fridge. Plenty of crusty bread in the bread bin.'

Leaving him scowling after her, she hurried upstairs to get her jacket.

'I won't be long,' she called on her way through the kitchen to the back door.

'I've told you, Jane . . . you're not going anywhere,' he said, voice rising with temper.

'Oh, don't be so daft.' She opened the back door and stepped out into the garden – only to feel his hand on her arm, pulling her back.

'Back inside,' he ordered.

'Don't be so ridiculous, Mick,' she said, struggling to get free, hardly able to believe this was happening. 'I have to go.'

He stared at her in a fury, dark eyes wild and strange, hand clamped to her arm in a bruising grip.

'I've told you, you're not going anywhere. And I meant it.'

'You can't dictate to me as though I'm some nineteenth-century scullery maid,' she said, staring furiously into his eyes, her face screwed up with pain from the pressure of his hold on her. 'I meant it when I said I am not going to give up my business just for the sake of your male pride. I don't think it's fair of you to ask it of me.'

'And I don't think you're being at all fair to me . . .'

'I'm doing my best for all of us,' said Jane, wincing from his grip. 'I warned you that things would be different if you moved in with us. If you can't accept that, you'd better leave.'

'Don't you *dare* tell me to leave, woman. This is my . . .'

'But it isn't, is it, Mick?' she said as his words died on his lips. 'It isn't your house. Now let me go and do my work, please.'

His hand slowly dropped from her arm and he

immediately became the injured victim, looking deeply wounded with the deliberate intention of making her feel guilty.

'Oh, do what you like,' he said and went inside, slamming the door after him.

As she nipped next-door through the gap in the fence to see Davey, she saw Giles in his garden working on the flower beds.

'Everything all right?' he asked, coming over to her, dressed in an old pair of jeans and the navy blue sweater he used for gardening.

'Fine,' she lied. 'I've just popped in to tell Davey that I have to go to the shop for an hour or so. But Mick's in if he wants to come home before I get back.'

'I think Kevin's hoping he'll be staying to lunch with us. I was going to send him in to check with you first.'

'That's fine by me, so long as you don't mind,' said Jane with a sense of relief because Davey resented his father's being back and didn't try to hide it. She felt easier in her mind if he wasn't at home with Mick when she wasn't there to keep the peace between them.

'I'll tell him then.'

'Thanks, Giles.'

'It's a pleasure.'

'See you,' said Jane, and hurried up the path and out of his back gate to her car.

Alerted by the sound of raised voices in the adjacent garden, Giles had watched the incident between Jane and Mick through a crack in the fence. If Mick had got any rougher with Jane, he wouldn't have been able to stop himself intervening. But he'd kept out of it for her sake.

Mick Parker wouldn't take kindly to interference and was the type to take his resentment out on his wife. Jane was making a supreme effort to convince the outside world that all was well within the Parker home which was why Giles had said nothing to her about witnessing the argument.

He'd had his doubts ever since first meeting Mick Parker, who'd seemed very full of his own importance. Now Giles had seen proof that things were going horribly wrong. Davey was a changed boy since his father had been back. He was much more subdued than he used to be and always reluctant to go home though, like his mother, he insisted that everything was fine with the family.

Making a sudden decision, Giles hurried indoors and made a telephone call to the estate agent's office, instructing them to remove his cottage from the market for the time being. He didn't trust Mick Parker. There was something abnormal about his behaviour that made Giles sense danger for Jane and the children.

As painful as it was living next-door to the woman he loved under the current circumstances, he couldn't move away. He'd rather be close at hand in case she needed him.

Jane was trembling with reaction as she drove to the shop, mouth dry, stomach knotted. This past couple of months had been hellish. Thank God Mick chose to stay in Brighton during the week. At least that allowed her to attend to her business and recover from the appalling stress of having him around at the weekend.

It was an impossible situation which would only be resolved, so far as Mick was concerned, when she relinquished her home, her business, her identity, and reverted to being merely an appendage of his. He was determined to wear her down and it was an uphill struggle to stop it happening.

Was it wrong to want to be allowed to have her own interests and opinions? she asked herself. Was she being selfish in wanting to keep a business she had worked hard to build and which would eventually be passed on to her children? To ask her to revert back to the way she'd been before was like asking someone to forget how to walk. Surely no one had the right to demand that of another person?

To make matters worse, there was constant friction between Davey and his father, despite her pleas to her son to make more of an effort. She supposed it was a protective thing with Davey. He had always been closer to Jane than Pip was. She guessed also that he'd found life pleasanter when Giles had been like one of the family, admiring him as the boy did.

Determined to regain authority over his family by any means, Mick exacerbated the situation by picking on Davey at every opportunity. Consequently, if Jane wasn't battling against his attempts to trample her into the ground, she was acting as peacemaker between father and son. It was exhausting as well as dispiriting.

The only person who seemed pleased about Mick's return was Pip. She'd always been a Daddy's girl and had slipped straight back into the role, assisted by the fact that Mick thoroughly spoiled her. This also caused trouble between Jane and Mick because she was opposed to such blatant favouritism.

More personally distressing was the problem of bed. Jane had feigned more headaches recently than she cared to remember. But Mick wasn't easily deterred. He'd always been very demanding in that department.

For all his domination, though, there were times when he seemed so sad and vulnerable. Then he would be overly apologetic to her – after an incident like the one they had just had, for instance. At such times he was so pathetic in his eagerness to please her, she pitied him and reminded herself that he had been through a bad time and it was her duty to try to make their marriage work.

Unfortunately, they had grown so far apart they no longer had any mutual interests on which to rebuild their relationship. This led Jane to feel suffocated by his presence at weekends and to long for Monday mornings when he departed for Brighton.

After Jane had left, Mick went back into the kitchen and slumped into a chair at the table, consumed with melancholy. What was the world coming to when a man couldn't even get his breakfast cooked for him by his wife? This reconciliation with Jane had fallen far short of his expectations. It didn't occur to him to attach any blame for that to himself. Once again he put the responsibility for this miserable state of affairs firmly at the door of the 'women's rights brigade', for unsettling the nation's women so they didn't know their place any more.

Whoever heard of a wife going out on business and leaving her husband at home to cook for himself? It was outrageous! Business was strictly a male preserve with women working in menial positions, not running the show. He'd never had any of this sort of nonsense from Patsy, for all that she'd shown a determined side to her character about moving out. Patsy knew her place in the scheme of things. You never heard her wittering on about her own identity, and she certainly never expected him to cook his own breakfast. Thinking of Patsy gave him an unexpected pang. He missed her a lot.

But it was Jane who drove him crazy with the need to possess and control her; Jane with whom he wanted to share his life. But she'd changed so much, he didn't know how to handle her. In the old days, he'd been at the centre of her world; they had liked the same things and been as one in their expectations of life.

These days she seemed to enjoy the most peculiar pastimes, such as walking without needing to get any-where, and reading – in bed of all places. He'd put his foot down about that. Oh, yes! He'd told her the light was keeping him awake but his objection actually lay in the fact that her absorption in her book excluded him.

She indulged in other useless activities now too; things that were a sheer waste of time, like watching the sunset and observing the birds that came to her precious bird table. And she didn't half go on about the plants and flowers in the garden! As if she didn't have enough to do, she spent time out there working instead of employ-ing a gardener to do it for her.

Then there was her odd taste in accommodation. She seemed to have lost all interest in moving upmarket and claimed actually to like living in this damned shed of a place. But he suspected she was determined to hang on to it for the same reason she wouldn't get rid of her business: to prevent him from resuming his rightful place in the family as sole breadwinner and head of the house, something he wanted desperately.

Frustration reached exploding point inside him. He leaped up, growling, and kicked the wall, swearing loudly at the pain in his toes because he was only wearing bedroom slippers. Hopping about on one foot and beside himself with rage, he punched the door and felt even worse because it hurt his knuckles.

He simply *must* get back to his old footing with Jane. It was driving him mad, the way things were. He'd do whatever it took, he thought, with a surge of determination.

Then suddenly a sense of powerlessness beset him and he began to cry. Sitting down at the table with his head in his hands, he wept with self-pity. What had happened to the wonderful life he'd had before the warehouse fire? Where had it all gone? Why was everything so difficult now?

He felt a sudden longing for Patsy who would soothe away his tears and tell him he was wonderful. Jane used to do that. And she would do it again. He would make her – *somehow*!

'It's just like old times, isn't it?' asked Rita Parker a few weeks later when Jane and Mick and the children were at his parents' place for Sunday tea.

'Not half, Mum,' Mick agreed.

'Lovely to have him back, isn't it, Wilf?' she said to her husband.

'Would have been better if he'd never gone away in the first place,' snorted Wilf, causing an awkward silence.

'Now, now. Don't be like that, Wilf,' said Rita with an

unusual show of boldness. 'We all know he went because he wasn't well.'

'We've only got his word for that,' declared her husband.

'And what exactly do you mean by that?' asked Mick, glaring at his father.

'Exactly what I say, son. We only have your word for it that you lost your memory,' he said. 'Sounds like a story to me.'

Sitting opposite Mick, Jane could see from the pain in his eyes that he was hurt as only his father could hurt him. She felt a stab of empathy. She knew he wouldn't challenge his father as he would anyone else who made such a suggestion.

'You believe what you like,' said Mick in a subdued manner. 'I've no way of proving anything.'

'So long as I believe him, that's all that really matters, isn't it?' said Jane, addressing her remark directly to her father-in-law with an audacity she would never have dared show towards him at one time. 'Since I was the one who was most affected.'

While Wilf threw a fierce glance in her direction, Mick looked at his wife in surprise. He greeted this further show of her newfound confidence with a certain ambivalence. On the one hand her support warmed him and gave him hope, but it also illustrated just how assertive she had become. He didn't need a woman protecting him from his own father.

'It's all in the past anyway. He's back now and that's the important thing,' said Rita in a swift attempt to defuse the rising tension. She looked at Jane. 'I bet you feel as though it's Christmas and your birthday all rolled into one, don't you, having your husband back?'

Jane knew she mustn't cause a scene by telling the truth, so concentrated on passing the bread and butter to Davey and said, 'Naturally.'

'Would you like a bit more ham, Davey?' enquired Rita.

'No, thank you, Gran.'

She gave him a close look, noticing how downcast he was.

'You're very quiet, son,' she said. 'That isn't like you.'

'Take no notice of him, Mum,' said Mick, giving his son a disapproving look. 'He's always in a mood about something.'

Davey said nothing but, looking at him beside her, Jane saw a strawberry blush creep up his neck and over his ears.

'He's all right, aren't you, Davey?' she said, giving him a reassuring pat on the arm.

'I'm fine,' he said, but Jane knew he was feeling wretched.

This wasn't helped by his sister's contribution.

'Davey's always sulking lately,' Pip informed her grandparents with childish thoughtlessness. 'Dad keeps telling him off about it.'

'Not like you, is he, Princess?' said Mick, smiling indulgently at his daughter. 'You've always got a smile on your face.'

Jane could have throttled him. Couldn't he see how wrong it was to use favouritism for Pip as a weapon against Davey? Had he no sensitivity at all towards growing children? If anyone should know about the pain of parental victimisation, Mick should.

'It'll be his age, I expect,' said Rita diplomatically. 'They do start to get moody at this stage.'

'I thought that was when they were teenagers?' said Mick.

'You were a miserable little bugger from birth,' growled Wilf.

Sitting there in the cross-fire of all this animosity, Jane thought how out of place she felt now with her in-laws. She no longer seemed like a member of their family.

That evening when the children were in bed and Jane spoke to Mick about his unfair behaviour towards Davey, she felt even more isolated and as though she was fighting a lone battle.

'The boy is rude and sulky and deserves every telling off I give him,' Mick said. 'And I expect you to take my side, not his.'

'I'm trying not to take sides,' she said. 'But I am asking you to be a bit more patient with him. He obviously feels threatened in some way by your coming back. He needs to get to know you again . . . and learn to trust you.'

'I'm his father and he'll show me some respect,' Mick announced. 'He ought to be grateful I've not landed him one.'

'Hitting him isn't the answer.'

'Okay, so I won't wallop him. But whatever I do it would be wrong in your eyes,' he protested. 'There's no pleasing you these days.'

'Oh, Mick,' she said sadly. 'It just isn't working out, is it?'

'And who's to blame for that?' he said, looking at her accusingly.

'You obviously think I am.'

'You are,' he stated categorically. 'All you have to do is to give up this ridiculous business nonsense and be a proper wife to me again then everything will be just like it used to be.'

'I *am* being a proper wife to you,' she said. 'I look after you when you're here. Just because I do other things as well, doesn't mean I'm failing in my duty as a wife.'

'It feels like that to me.'

'Do you really want me to be unhappy, Mick?' she asked emotionally. 'With no interests of my own outside the home and no challenges in my life?'

'It's my job to make you happy, and I would if only you'd let me.'

'It doesn't work like that . . .'

'It used to.'

'Well, it doesn't now.'

'Most women would kill for what I want to give you,' he informed her. 'A lovely house and a car and plenty of money to live on without having to go out and earn it.

But, oh, no, that's not good enough for you.'

'It isn't that it isn't good enough, Mick,' she said, weary from trying to make him see her point of view.

'Sounds that way to me.'

'It's just that it isn't the way I want to live. Those things aren't important to me any more,' she said. 'Please try to understand.'

'You're beyond understanding,' he mumbled crossly.

'Try, Mick,' she begged him. 'Just try to see this thing from my side.'

He shrugged his shoulders for reply and she knew she was wasting her time.

In despair of ever being able to communicate with him, she left him slouched in the armchair in the living room, smoking, and went to bed feeling utterly dejected.

Jane's father had never been a fan of his son-in-law and disapproved wholeheartedly of Jane's having taken him back. He couldn't forgive Mick for leaving her in financial trouble.

'Lost his memory, my Aunt Fanny!' Joe could be heard to say when Mick wasn't around and Jane was defending him. 'He buggered off and left you 'cause he was skint and not man enough to stay and face up to it. It's as simple as that.'

Mick was equally as lacking in enthusiasm for his father-in-law so there was always a bad atmosphere when Joe came to the cottage. He wouldn't have come at all if Jane hadn't insisted on inviting him, which she did frequently because she was trying to make them all into a normal family again, which meant tolerating each other's relatives.

One wet Sunday evening in June when Joe had been for tea and they were all watching a comedy show on TV called On the Buses, Trudy Hamilton called in to see Jane.

'I've been spending the day with Giles,' she explained. 'I was hoping to catch you in the garden actually, but the rain put paid to that.'

'It's lovely to see you anyway,' Jane was quick to assure her.

The children seconded that and Joe greeted Trudy, albeit in his terse way. Having introduced her to Mick, Jane offered her a cup of tea and asked her to sit down and join them.

'I won't stay, thank you, dear,' she said. 'I don't want to intrude. I haven't seen you for a while and I've missed you, but I've actually called to put a bit of business your way.'

'That's nice of you.'

'A friend of mine wants a wedding cake made and I wondered if you might be interested?'

'I'll say I'm interested,' was Jane's enthusiastic response. 'I'm trying to build up that side of the business.'

'Yes, that's what I thought.'

The next instant Jane burned with embarrassment when Mick showed his bad manners by getting up and turning up the volume on the television set while Trudy was speaking.

'Come into the kitchen and you can tell me more about it,' invited Jane diplomatically.

'All right, dear.'

They were about to depart when Mick sprang up and marched over to Trudy.

'Can't you see that my wife is trying to spend a quiet evening with her family?' he said accusingly. 'And she certainly doesn't want people bothering her about business.'

'Mick, really,' admonished Jane, throwing him an icy look.

Trudy looked at him candidly.

'I think Jane will soon tell me if I'm being a nuisance,' she replied.

' 'Course she won't,' he growled. 'She's far too soft to speak her mind. I'm not, though, and I'm asking you to clear off.'

Humiliated almost beyond bearing, Jane said to Trudy,

'Come on, let's go into the kitchen and talk about it. Don't mind Mick. He has a perverse sense of humour.'

She was ushering her visitor into the kitchen when Mick grabbed his wife by the arm and pulled her back, standing between the two women and staring angrily at Trudy.

'It's people like you who've changed Jane,' he shouted. 'Filling her head with silly ideas and making her think she can play at business and neglect her family!'

'Jane was in business long before I met her,' explained Trudy, who was no shrinking violet herself. 'And she isn't just playing at it.' She paused and met his eyes in a challenge. 'You should be boasting about her instead of putting her down.'

'She's changed, doesn't want to know about her family any more.'

'That isn't true . . .' began Jane, stopping when her normally reserved father made a surprising intervention.

'Don't you dare accuse my daughter of neglecting her family,' he roared at Mick. 'She's making a fine job of raising those children . . . and with no help from you!'

'You keep out of it . . . this is between me and Jane,' protested Mick.

'You've made it my business by insulting my daughter in public,' said Joe. 'As well as Mrs Hamilton who is a guest in her house.'

'It's nothing to do with you!'

'You insult my daughter and you insult me,' said Joe, voice shaking with emotion because he rarely got involved in arguments. 'Well, let me tell you this much, mate – it was Jane who fed the children and looked after them while you were away. She's worked harder than you ever will, starting a business from scratch to keep them. So I'll thank you to apologise to her.' He looked at Trudy. 'And to Mrs Hamilton.'

'Oh, bugger the lot of you!' was Mick's answer to that. 'I'm going down the pub.'

And leaving Joe offering profuse apologies to Trudy for his son-in-law's appalling behaviour, while Jane calmed the children who had retreated to their bedrooms, Mick stormed out of the house.

After a couple of drinks he felt even more morose. Why couldn't Jane see how hurt he was at being excluded from her life so cruelly? Why couldn't the woman just do as he asked and give up her stupid notions of independence so that things could return to normal? How did she think it made him feel with everyone saying how well she'd done while he'd been away? What they *should* be saying was how wonderful it was for her to have him back.

He drew hard on a cigarette, thinking that no one, apart from his mother, sister and daughter, seemed pleased that he was back. In fact, no one else seemed to have much time for him at all. He wondered if perhaps he ought to try to make it work Jane's way, with her continuing with her business and them all staying on in the cottage indefinitely.

But, no. It simply wouldn't do. Apart from all the aggravation of having to live in that relic of a place and occasionally fend for himself, it just didn't feel right. He needed the buzz of hero-worship to keep his adrenaline flowing. As things were now, he was in competition with Jane for the position of head of the family.

Well, he'd tried persuasion and she wouldn't listen. So she'd left him no choice. He would have to apply a little guile to get her to do what he wanted.

Having come to this decision, he ordered another drink, feeling a whole lot more positive as he planned his next move . . .

Chapter Twenty

Jane waited up for Mick to get back from the pub that night. Having had time to calm down after their contretemps, she'd decided it was vital they should have a serious talk.

Yelling at him would solve nothing. They needed to address the cause of his aggression, which was undoubtedly the success she had found in her own right and his inability to alter his perception of their life together. If she could reassure him that her having a mind of her own didn't lessen her commitment to their marriage, he might be able to see things in a new light. As disgusted as she was with his behaviour earlier, she hated to think of him being so unhappy.

When he got home, however, he was mildly squiffy and wanted to go straight to bed.

'But we need to talk, Mick,' she said. 'It's really important that we get things sorted out between us, for all our sakes.'

'Yeah, yeah, but not now . . . another time, eh, babe?' he said, swaying slightly as he stood at the bottom of the stairs.

'It needs to be soon.'

'Will tomorrow do you?'

'But you'll be back in Brighton.'

'I can go a bit later in the morning, if you like?' he suggested amicably. 'And we can have a chat before I go.'

'Okay,' she said, surprised at his unusual offer of co-operation.

'I'll take the kids to school and come back here for an hour or so, yeah?'

'Great.'

She guessed she had the alcohol to thank for this unusual concession but at least he'd agreed to talk. She hoped he hadn't forgotten all about it in the morning.

Mondays were always especially hectic in the cottage kitchen because her assistant didn't come in to work. But Jane would make time for a discussion with Mick. It was imperative they got things on to a more even keel. They couldn't continue to live in such an explosive and unhappy atmosphere. It wasn't good for the children and it was beginning to make her feel ill.

The next morning there was the usual pre-school rush, the last-minute search for misplaced gym shoes and school bags, childish tempers frayed at the prospect of some difficult lesson, and a dental appointment for them both straight after school. But the atmosphere over breakfast was quite pleasant because Mick was in such a good mood.

Since it was his policy never to lift a finger in the house, Jane was amazed when he offered to clear the breakfast things, which he did while waiting for the children to collect their raincoats because it was another wet day.

'I'll go upstairs and make myself decent while you're doing that,' she said.

'Okay,' he agreed amicably. 'I'll see you when I get back from the school.'

Having plonked a farewell kiss on the cheek of each offspring, Jane hurried upstairs and made the children's beds, heartened by Mick's co-operation. Her optimism was increased by the discovery that he'd stripped their bed, a definite indication that he was trying to be helpful. It wasn't actually her day for changing beds but it was the thought that counted. Making a mental note to get clean bedlinen from the airing cupboard and remake the bed, she sat down in front of her dressing-table mirror to put on some lipstick.

Rummaging in her make-up bag, she listened to the

children chattering as they went down the back path to Mick's car. Swamped with affection for them, she went over to the window and looked out into the rainsoaked garden as they hurried through the gate and were ushered by their father into his Jaguar, parked in the alley behind her modest estate car.

Feeling more optimistic than she had in a long time, she went back to her dressing table and applied her lipstick. She was brushing her hair in front of the mirror when she heard footsteps coming up the stairs.

'Who's forgotten what?' she called out, thinking it was one of the children.

There was no reply but she could hear someone outside the door. Whoever it was seemed to be fiddling with the handle.

'Who's there?' she called, going over to the door and turning the handle to find that the door was locked. 'Mick, is that you?'

'Yeah, it's me.'

'What's going on?' she demanded. 'Why is the door locked?'

'To keep you in there.'

'What on earth for?'

'You won't do as I ask and give up your business, so I've no choice but to force you into it,' he replied. 'You won't be baking any cakes today, babe.'

'Oh, don't be so ridiculous,' she said, pummelling on the door with her fists. 'You can't do this.'

'I've already done it,' he said triumphantly. 'For once, this old-fashioned cottage has worked in my favour. It has bedroom doors that lock.'

'Mick . . . this has gone far enough.'

'It hasn't gone nearly far enough.'

'Meaning?'

'Meaning I shall do everything I possibly can to upset the smooth running of your business until either the lack of efficiency closes you down or you agree to sell up.'

'But what about the children?' she asked, far more worried about their welfare than the future of her business. 'If I can't get out, who will collect them from school this afternoon?'

'They can walk . . . it'll do 'em good.'

'But I'm taking them to the dentist for their check-up straight from school. They'll be waiting for me at the school gate.'

'They can miss that. I'll tell 'em you've decided to cancel it and they are to make their own way home.'

'No, Mick . . . this isn't on.'

'I'll leave the front door key under the flower pot on the window sill so they can let themselves in,' he said, ignoring her plea. 'I'll leave the bedroom key here in the door. You can call them when they get in and they'll let you out. I'll tell 'em I locked it by accident when I see 'em at the weekend.'

'You're leaving me here all day?' she said, astounded.

'That's right. I'm off to Brighton when I've dropped the children at school.'

'This is crazy.'

'You've driven me to it,' he said. 'You won't do as I ask voluntarily so I have no choice but to use force.'

'Let me out,' she said, frantically banging her fists on the door.

'No fear. And if you're thinking of getting out of the window, you can forget it because I've taken the sheets off the bed so you'll have nothing to climb down.'

'You scheming bastard,' she gasped. 'You had this all worked out . . . and there was me thinking you were being helpful.'

'You've brought this on yourself.'

'Stop this, Mick,' she said more gently in the hope of persuading him to let her out. 'I thought we were going to have a serious talk?'

'No point in talking,' he said. 'Actions speak louder than words.'

'Locking me up for the day won't put me out of business.'

'It'll make you realise that I intend to have my way, though, won't it? Anyway, this is just the beginning.'

'Now stop this nonsense, Mick, please . . .'

'I'm off,' he said as though she hadn't spoken. 'I'll go straight to Brighton when I've taken the kids to school. See you at the weekend. Ta-ta.'

And she heard his footsteps receding down the stairs.

Tearing across to the window she leaned out, calling to him as he swaggered down the path, wearing a black anorak over his business suit. He turned and waved to her, smiling sweetly to create a picture of domestic bliss – a happily married couple saying a fond farewell for the day. She shouted to the children for help but they were ensconced inside the Jaguar with its windows misted up, oblivious of the drama unfolding around them.

As the car rolled away out of sight, Jane went to the bedroom door and rattled the handle, banging her hands on the solid wood in frustration. Back at the window, she looked gloomily at the sheer drop to the ground with nothing to get a hold on. She began to pace the room in a fury, cursing the fact that there was no telephone extension in the bedroom. Her only hope was to attract the attention of someone outside, someone walking along the back alley. She could always say she'd got locked in accidentally to save Mick's reputation.

But there was not a soul about. People were either out at work or busy indoors with Monday morning chores. She would have stood more chance had this room been at the front of the house overlooking Tug Lane. But the gardens backing on to the alley, mostly secluded behind high walls and fences, were deserted. This wasn't the sort of day to dry washing outside.

An hour crawled past, then another, with agonising slowness. The alley remained empty and the heavy rain turned to a discouraging drizzle, making Jane's bedroom feel damp and chilly. She slipped on a sweater over her tee-shirt but by midday was really uncomfortable, being cold, hungry and in need of the bathroom.

She lay on the bare mattress, staring at the ceiling and thinking that Mick must be sick to do a thing like this. He'd always been obsessive, she could see that now. His craving for money and success had gone beyond normal ambition. But now he seemed to have become paranoid about her as well.

Her heart beat faster at a familiar noise outside. It sounded like Giles's car pulling up in the alley. But he didn't usually come home for lunch. Leaping up and rushing to the window, she saw that it *was* him. Tears of relief gushed down her cheeks as she opened the window and shouted to him.

'Please don't get involved, Giles,' Jane said over sandwiches and coffee at her kitchen table after he'd let himself into the house with the key Mick had left under the flower pot, and had released her. Luckily for Jane, Giles had come home at lunchtime to collect a book he needed for a lesson that afternoon. 'I have to deal with Mick in my own way.'

She had found it impossible to lie to Giles about the reason for her captivity, and he'd been horrified by the story. He'd already been worried about her, having heard about the incident last night from his mother.

'But the man must be unhinged to do a thing like that! Who knows what he'll do next? You're not safe with him about.'

'Mick would never actually harm me.'

'Locking you up in the bedroom isn't causing you harm?'

'I mean, he wouldn't beat me up or anything.'

'I'm not so sure . . .'

'He's having a hard time accepting me as I am now and not as I was before he went away, that's what all this is about.'

'He obviously isn't in a stable frame of mind, though,' insisted Giles. 'I'm really worried about you.'

'It's nice of you to care and I appreciate it, Giles,' she said, reaching across and taking his hand. 'But it'll only make things worse if you enter into it. The last thing I need is for Mick to find out about us . . . and he's bound to suspect something if you try to help me. So far as he is concerned you are just a neighbour and the father of Davey's best friend.'

'It's a wonder his sister hasn't spilled the beans to him about us.'

'I had a feeling she wouldn't,' said Jane. 'It'll be for his sake, though, not ours. Marie wouldn't do anything to hurt her brother, or that might stop him and me making a go of it. That's why she's kept quiet. Only our parents know what happened between us and they have the sense not to say anything. I think Mick really would go berserk if he found out I'm in love with you.'

'He was away for a long time, Jane, what did he expect?'

'Mick isn't rational when it comes to me, not now anyway.'

'Thank God I decided to stay around. At least I'm at hand.'

She narrowed her eyes at him.

'You didn't take your cottage off the market because you weren't getting any decent offers, did you?' she said, referring to the reason he had given her.

'No, I took it off the market after seeing Mick getting rough with you one day,' he admitted. 'I decided that my place was here, near you and the children . . . just in case you needed me. Today's incident has proved I did the right thing.'

'Oh, Giles, you're such a good man.'

'You wouldn't say that if you could read my thoughts about Mick when I see the two of you together!'

'It's been awful for me too, being just a neighbour to you.' She squeezed his hand, looking into his warm brown eyes. 'But I really do have to try to make a go of my marriage.'

'Mick isn't making it easy for you, though, is he?'

'I'll say he isn't. But I have to keep trying.'

'Don't let him grind you down with bullying tactics like he used today.'

'It would be all too easy to give in and let him have

his way,' she said. 'But it isn't in my nature to give in to something I think is unfair.'

'That's the stuff,' Giles replied, smiling at her in a way that, while making her sad she couldn't stay with him, also gave her the courage to do what she had to with Mick.

'You won't break my spirit by locking me up, you know,' Jane said to him the following Friday night after the children were in bed.

He hadn't been in touch all week and had arrived home earlier than usual this evening, behaving as though nothing had happened. Jane had played along with him in front of the children but now that they were alone she was speaking her mind.

'All I want is for us to be together like we used to be,' he said, dark eyes appealing to her as he sat at the other side of the hearth, which was filled with a large vase of flowers on this warm July evening, the rain in the early part of the week having cleared up.

'Can't you see that that isn't possible?' said Jane patiently. 'Everyone changes with time. Nothing stays the same indefinitely.'

'I haven't changed.'

She thought he had probably changed less than anyone else she knew which was part of the trouble: the fact that he hadn't matured or broadened his outlook as she had.

'You must have to a certain extent, at least. We all do.'

'Nah, not me,' said Mick proudly.

'Well, if you want our marriage to work, you're going to have to have a more mature attitude towards it.'

'Oh?' he said, scowling. 'And what do you mean by that?'

'I don't want to share my life with someone who plays infantile pranks like the one you played on me last Monday,' Jane told him. 'All that does is make me think the whole thing is hopeless . . . that we've drifted too far apart.'

'Okay, maybe I did go a bit too far,' Mick conceded, voice clipped with tension. 'But can't you see what it's like for me, having my status in the family taken away?'

'You haven't lost your status, Mick. You're still the children's father and my husband.'

'You're not reliant on me any more, though, are you?'

'Not totally, no,' she said. 'But that should be a help to you rather than a burden. At least it takes some of the worry off your shoulders.'

'I don't need help . . . all that does is belittle me,' he said. 'If you care about my feelings, you'll do as I ask.'

'That's emotional blackmail.'

'All I'm asking is for you to go back to being a full-time wife.'

She gave an eloquent sigh.

'Look, Mick, I didn't want the responsibility of earning a living. I had it forced on me when you went missing. But fending for myself comes naturally to me now. I can't go back to being dependent on you for company, for money, for every single thing, as I used to be. I need something else, especially now that the children are growing up. I'd be only half alive if I did what you're asking of me . . . surely that isn't what you want?'

'You'd enjoy it once you got used to it again,' was his stubborn response.

'Many marriages work very well with both parties having a career,' she pointed out. 'I can't see why you're so dead set against it. It isn't even as though I'm away from the house much. Most of the time I'm at home working in the kitchen. My profits aren't for me, they're for us – all of us, the family. Why can't you be pleased that I'm doing well and enjoy it with me?'

'I'm afraid of losing you.'

'Well, you will lose me if you carry on as you are,' she told him gravely. 'Because I can't stand much more of the way things are.'

'Oh, God, Jane, don't say that!' he said, looking stricken.

'There has to be give and take in any relationship,'

she said. 'I'm doing my best to adjust to your being back. Why can't you do your part and try to accept me as I am now? I'm sure you'll find it's easier than you think once you start to make an effort.'

'I could try, I suppose,' he said, smiling, his mood seeming to change.

'Oh, Mick, do you really mean that?' said Jane uncertainly.

'Yeah. I'll give it a try.'

'Oh that's wonderful,' she said, her hopes renewed.

But it was all just words to Mick. He had no intention whatsoever of losing this battle. For the moment his main concern was to end this discussion to Jane's satisfaction so he could get her into bed feeling well-disposed towards him.

One autumn evening Wilf Parker was in the King's Arms with his cronies, setting the world to rights. The subject under discussion was the latest fashion craze with youngsters: platform-soled shoes.

'They should ban 'em,' declared Wilf. 'It's a recognised fact they're dangerous. Lethal, in fact. There was something in the paper about it a couple of months ago.'

'Women falling over in 'em, you mean?' said a man called Ginger.

'Well, yeah, but mostly women driving cars in them,' said Wilf. 'I mean, how can they feel the pedals through thick soles like that? Might as well have bricks strapped to their feet.'

'It isn't only women,' said Ginger. 'I've seen men wearing them too.'

'Only on the telly,' said Wilf. 'Pop stars and that.'

'I've seen 'em in the street an' all,' said Ginger.

'You'd have to be a right . . .' Wilf stopped in mid-sentence because of a sharp pain in his chest. He felt suddenly very hot and peculiar.

'What's the matter, Wilf?' he heard someone ask as though from a distance.

He stood there in terror, bathed in sweat . . .

'You all right, mate?' asked Ginger.

The pain subsided and Wilf calmed down and rejoined the conversation.

'Yeah, I'm all right,' he said, feeling better. 'I was just saying, you'd have to be a right ponce to go out in shoes like that.'

'Anything goes with young people today,' said Ginger.

'Not half,' agreed Wilf. 'What with kids and women, I don't know what the world's coming to. The government's talking about setting up some sort of Equal Opportunities Commission now, to give women more equality with men. God knows where it'll all end.'

'With women ruling the world, if they have their way.'

Wilf winced at another twinge.

'Yeah . . . anyway, I'm off now, lads,' he said and proceeded to do the unthinkable – he left without finishing his drink.

When he got home, Rita was surprised to see him.

'You're back early,' she said.

'Mmm.'

'Anything wrong,' she asked looking at him closely. 'You look a bit pale.'

'I came over queer in the pub,' he said, sinking gratefully into an armchair, very shaken by the incident though no longer in pain. 'But I'm perfectly all right now.'

'What sort of queer?'

'I had a pain in my chest,' he said. 'Must have been a touch of indigestion.'

'Are you sure that's what it was?'

' 'Course I'm sure, you silly cow,' he said impatiently.

'You must have been feeling rotten to come home this early . . .'

'I'm all right. Don't fuss.'

'Perhaps you ought to pop down the doctor's in the morning?'

'There's no need for that,' he said. 'You know me, I haven't the time to waste sitting about in a doctor's waiting room.'

'I think you should.'

'Well, I'm not going, so you can shut up about it.'

'I'll go and make a cuppa tea,' said Rita worriedly.

'How are things in London, Mick?' asked Patsy across the bar of the Drake's Arms as she served him with a scotch one evening in the autumn.

To anyone else he would have lied and said everything was wonderful. But to Patsy he said, 'Not brilliant, Pats.'

'Still finding it hard to adjust?' she said, handing him his change.

'Very.'

'Give it time.'

'Jane and I have been back together for over six months now,' he said gloomily. 'How much more time do we need?'

'Dunno . . . I'm no expert on marriage.'

She went to serve another customer. Mick sipped his drink and lit a cigarette, drawing on it with pleasure. After the tension of weekends at the cottage with Jane and the children, it was a blessed relief to return to his bachelor life in Brighton. He felt much more at home here than he did in London. He'd be even happier if he could persuade Patsy to move back in with him, but she wouldn't entertain the idea now that he was back with Jane. It was probably for the best. Keeping two women happy might be a bit too demanding.

The Drake's Arms was practically his second home during the week and felt much more like his local than the pubs near Jane's cottage which were full of arty types and office workers. He wouldn't even consider the idea of moving back to London full-time. Jane would have to concede to his wishes and move to Brighton eventually. Jane . . . just the thought of her depressed him because things weren't going at all as he'd planned.

'Hey, watch what you're doing with that fag, Mick,' said Patsy, returning to finish their chat and hastily extinguishing a mini bonfire in the ashtray, caused by the match he hadn't put out setting light to the cellophane paper from his cigarette packet. 'Are you trying to put us out of business by burning the pub down or something?'

The idea came to him in a flash. His next move was obvious. Fire had worked against him once. Now it could be made to work in his favour . . .

'Mick, what are you grinning at?' Patsy was saying. 'Have you come into money?'

'No, but I have found the answer to my problems,' he said gleefully. 'Ooh, Pats, I could kiss you!'

'Oh, no, you don't,' she said, lightly but firmly. 'I'm strictly off limits to you now that you're a properly married man again.'

The fire at Cottage Cakes was the talk of Chiswick High Road that November. The other traders were shocked by the rumours of its being arson, fearing they might become the next victims. The general feeling was that it must have been vandals, high on drugs, who had broken into Cottage Cakes in the middle of the night and torched the shop just for kicks, having gained access by breaking a window at the back. What other explanation could there be for the fire?

Unbeknown to anyone, Jane knew the rumours weren't true. She knew who had been responsible for destroying her business premises in the early hours of that Wednesday morning. But she could never prove it and wouldn't shop him to the police even if she could.

'You won't break me down this way,' she said to her husband when he came home the Friday after the fire. He was late arriving and the children had already gone to bed. Mick settled in an armchair in the living room with a cigarette and a glass of whisky. 'You can lock me in and set fire to my shop but I still won't give up everything I've worked hard for when it isn't necessary.'

'I don't know what you're going on about,' he said.

'You know *exactly* what I'm talking about,' she told him. 'You came up from Brighton on Tuesday night after dark, set fire to my shop and went straight back to

Brighton without anyone knowing you'd been in the area. You're the last person anyone would suspect. Apart from the fact that a husband usually has his wife's best interests at heart, everyone knows you're away during the week.'

'You're mental!' he bellowed.

'Shush! Keep your voice down,' she warned him. 'I don't want the children to hear us quarrelling again. Nor do I want them to know that their father is an arsonist.'

'You're crazy.'

'Oh, no, you're the one who's crazy – crazy with determination to get your own way,' she corrected him firmly.

His reply was a mocking look.

'It won't work, Mick,' she continued through gritted teeth. 'This latest dirty trick has made me even more determined not to give in to you. I'll be back in business again before you can say Swan Vestas. Fortunately, I'm insured against fire.'

'I suppose that's a dig at me?'

'Not really,' she said, voice rising with anger and frustration. 'I just want to make sure you know that your latest piece of malice failed completely.'

'What makes you so sure it was me?'

'Because you are so paranoid about my being in business, you'll do anything to ruin me,' she said. 'Locking me in didn't make any difference so you thought you'd make a real job of it this time. You're damned lucky I'm not going to say anything to the police!'

'They wouldn't listen . . . you've no proof.'

'You're right, I haven't. But I don't need proof to know it was you,' she said. 'I've been waiting for you to make another move ever since the locking in incident. I didn't think even you would sink this low.'

'Honestly, babe, I think you ought to go and see a doctor and get something to calm your nerves,' he sneered. 'All this work you're doing is turning your brain.'

'No matter how many times you knock me down, I'll

pick myself up and start again,' Jane vowed. 'And even if I didn't have a business or this cottage, I would never be like I was before because I have grown up and moved on. It's a natural progression and you can't change that.'

'Don't underestimate me, Jane,' said Mick, tight-lipped with anger. 'You're stubborn but I'm even more so.'

Their eyes met.

'You did do it, didn't you?' she said.

His half smile was all the reply she needed but he just said, 'That's a very serious allegation, especially when you've no proof. You wanna be careful . . .'

The door opened and Davey burst in, marching straight over to his father.

'Why don't you go away and leave us alone?' he said, voice trembling.

'Davey, love . . .' Jane was up in an instant and at her son's side. 'Back to bed, this minute. This is grown-up talk.'

'He set fire to your shop!' said Davey, who had obviously heard it all. 'He's spoiling everything!'

'Back to bed now,' she urged.

But the boy didn't seem to hear and turned angry eyes on his father.

'You've done nothing but cause trouble since you've been back . . . bullying my mother and making her miserable. You're upsetting us all. So why don't you stay in Brighton and leave us in peace?'

Mick looked grim. His face was flushed from the whisky but his eyes were ice-cold.

'If you aren't out of my sight in two seconds, boy, you'll really know that your father's home,' he barked. 'Because you'll feel my fist in your face and my boot in your arse – something I should have done when I first got back, instead of letting you sulk around the place like a spoiled brat!'

'I hate you,' said Davey vehemently, his eyes full of tears. 'You've ruined everything by coming back. Things were good when Uncle Giles was here. We were all happy then.'

There was an echoing silence as Mick looked at Jane questioningly.

'He means our neighbour, Kevin's dad,' she explained, trembling with fear at this alarming development.

'I know who Giles is,' Mick said gruffly. 'But what's all this about him being here?'

'He used to pop in quite often before you came back,' she said, mouth dry with dread. 'Just in case we needed anything. You know, with us not having a man about the house.'

'He was Mum's boyfriend,' said Davey, glaring at his father in triumph. 'And she would have married him if you hadn't come back. And then *he'd* have been our father and I've have been glad 'cause he's a lot of fun and really cares about people.'

Mick stood up and stared at Jane accusingly.

'You and the bloke next-door?'

Since there was no longer any point in denying it, she nodded.

'You bitch!' he exploded, grabbing her roughly by the arms and shaking her. 'You dirty, filthy whore!'

'Mick, calm down . . .'

'So while I'm away in Brighton, you and him are at it . . .'

'No, Mick, no,' she gasped, face twisted with pain from the iron grip he had on her arms. 'It's over. I ended it when you came back.'

A guttural cry rose from the back of his throat and he hit her across the face so hard it stunned her. While she was still reeling from the blow, he hit her again and again across the face and body.

'Leave her alone! Leave her alone, will you?' Davey screamed, desperately trying to pull his father away from her.

With a mad look in his eyes, Mick turned on his son and punched him in the face so hard he staggered back and fell to the floor.

The noise had woken Pip, who stood in the doorway screaming.

'Daddy, Daddy, stop it!' she wailed. 'Leave them alone!'

Mick was too lost in his own feelings to pay her any attention. Leaving Jane in a state of near collapse on the sofa and Davey lying on the floor, he stormed from the house.

Giles was listening to some jazz on his record player when there was a loud knocking on the front door. Puzzled, he went to answer it and found himself being pushed inside on the receiving end of a brutal attack.

'You bastard!' Mick fumed, pinning him against the wall. 'I'll teach you to mess about with another man's wife . . .'

'Oh, for God's sake,' said Giles, the surprise element having put him in the weaker position.

'You ought to be ashamed of yourself,' growled Mick, banging Giles's head against the wall. 'You're supposed to be setting an example to youngsters, not screwing around and turning another man's wife and son against him. Men like you didn't ought to be allowed to work with children!'

Although normally opposed to violence, Giles was so enraged he found the strength at last to defend himself. He brought his knee up into Mick's groin, and while he was creased over, held him fast.

'*You're* the one who should be ashamed,' Giles told him. 'Treating your wife like a possession and making her life a misery just because she had the guts to make a decent life for herself and the children while you were away.' He paused to get his breath. 'And, yes, I admit it, I am in love with her. But there was nothing immoral in our love affair.'

'Not immoral?' said Mick cynically. 'She was married to me and sleeping with you. You can't get much more immoral than that, mate.'

'The fact that she was married to you was only a technicality at that time,' Giles solemnly pointed out. 'You'd been gone for years, she wasn't to know you'd ever come back. You could have been dead for all she knew.'

'The bitch . . . the cheating bitch!' said Mick, ignoring the other man's comments. 'She was lucky I didn't kill her.'

'Jane . . . oh my God!' gasped Giles as the implication registered. 'What have you done to her?'

Without waiting for a reply, and leaving Mick slumped against the wall, he rushed next-door.

Jane had locked the doors to keep Mick out while he was in such a violent mood. Feeling bruised and sore, she was in the kitchen bathing Davey's cut lip when Giles knocked on the door, announcing himself at the same time.

'He paid you a visit then?' she said, noticing his dishevelled appearance. 'Are you all right?'

'I'm fine,' he assured her. 'It's you I'm worried about . . . and Davey.'

'We're okay,' she said. 'A bit shaken up but we'll live.'

'You're more than just shaken up, both of you,' he said, looking at the angry red marks on her face and Davey's bleeding lip.

'I'm sorry, Uncle Giles,' he said. 'It's all my fault. I told Dad about you being Mum's boyfriend. I didn't mean to say anything. It just sort of came out. I'm sick of all the arguments . . . and seeing Mum so miserable. I just wanted everything to be nice like it used to be before he came back.'

'Don't worry about it, Davey,' Giles reassured him.

'It's best out in the open anyway,' said Jane. 'I should have told your father when he first came back.'

'How about you, Pip?' asked Giles, looking at the girl who was sitting at the kitchen table looking very pale and sad. 'Did he hit you too?'

'Daddy would *never* hit me,' she said emphatically, tears streaming down her cheeks. 'He wouldn't have hit Davey either if he hadn't been so horrible to him.'

'Come on now, Pip,' said Jane, leaving Giles to finish

seeing to Davey while she went to her daughter and put a comforting arm around the sobbing girl's shoulders.

'Leave me alone,' she said, scrambling off her chair and staring at her mother with undisguised hatred.

'Pip, calm down,' said Jane gently.

'This is all your fault.' She stared at her mother and then at Giles. 'And yours. You've hurt my dad and put him in a bad temper. That's why he got rough. He wouldn't have done it otherwise.'

And with that she stormed from the room and thundered upstairs.

'God, what a mess,' said Jane with a helpless shake of her head before she left the room to console Pip.

When she was halfway up the stairs, there was a knock at the front door. Had it not been for the fact that she had pulled the bolts across, Mick would have used his key.

She was tempted to ignore him and leave him outside. But the subdued way he had knocked indicated that his mood had become conciliatory. Anyway, there had to be a showdown some time. Things couldn't go on as they had been. Not after what had happened here tonight.

There's no time like the present, she thought, going down the stairs to open the door to her husband, full of trepidation.

Chapter Twenty One

'But I'm not happy about leaving you here on your own with him,' protested Giles a short time later as Jane ushered him firmly out of the back door.

'I'll be perfectly all right . . . don't worry.' The children were now in bed and Mick was sitting quietly in the living room, full of contrition. For all his faults, he'd never before been violent towards Jane. 'He's a lot calmer now.'

'I think I should be here, even so.'

'Thank you for being so caring, Giles,' she said in a warm but firm manner. 'But I'd rather you didn't stay. Mick and I need to be on our own . . . to talk this thing through.'

'It's the police you should be talking to,' he said, his gaze lingering on the strawberry-coloured marks and swellings Mick had left on her face. 'About a charge of assault.'

'Look . . . I know he probably deserves it but that isn't the way to deal with this.' She was adamant. 'I'm not trying to make a martyr of myself, I just happen to believe that this is something Mick and I have to sort out between ourselves. Trust me, Giles . . . I know what I'm doing.'

'But, Jane . . .'

'Just go home and leave this to me, Giles . . . please.'

'Oh, all right, if that's what you really want,' he agreed reluctantly. 'But promise you'll call me if he gets stroppy again? Just knock on the wall.'

' 'Course I will . . . and thanks for everything. You've been wonderful.'

'There's no need to thank me,' he said, looking pale

and strained. 'Just make sure you call me if he starts to get nasty again.'

Having seen him off the premises, she hurried upstairs to make sure the children were asleep. Then she went into the living room, closed the door firmly behind her and settled down in a chair opposite Mick.

'You'll never know how much I wish I could turn the clock back, babe,' he said, putting his head into his hands in despair. 'I didn't know what I was doing.' He looked up at her bruised face with a sharp intake of breath. 'I can't believe I did that to you. I've never hit a woman before in my life.'

'I know.'

'What a mess.'

'I'm glad to hear you admit it at last,' she said. 'Because our marriage is a mess and it isn't going to get any better.'

'You can't be sure . . .'

'Enough is enough, Mick,' she cut in. 'You and me staying together is destroying us all. It's making you violent, and that isn't the Mick I used to know.'

'You want to be with him, don't you?' he said miserably.

'Giles has nothing to do with this,' she said. 'Our marriage is over because we've grown apart. You must know that as well as I do, in your heart. You can't honestly say you feel happy when you're with me, can you?'

'That's only because you've changed so much,' he muttered.

'I can't stop nature taking its course,' she told him.

His face was grey and haggard, his eyes dull with pain.

'I just can't bear to think of you with another man,' he said. 'It was always us two. Neither of us ever wanted anyone else.'

'Before you went away that was true.' This was very painful for Jane because she still cared for him, despite everything. 'But can you tell me truthfully that in the years you were away, there hasn't been another woman in your life?'

His hesitation confirmed her suspicion.

'I thought so,' she said.

'Patsy and I were never serious.'

'Just a casual affair?'

He remained silent, avoiding her eyes.

'It was more than that, wasn't it?'

'I suppose so.'

'Did you live together?'

'For a while, yeah.'

'Oh, Mick,' she admonished, shaking her head. 'You're making all this fuss about my finding someone else when you've been living with another woman. Honestly! Talk about double standards.'

'You're in love with him, though,' he said. 'I never was with Patsy.'

'You were fond of her, though?'

'Yeah, she's a good sort,' he said, looking utterly dejected. 'But she could never mean the same to me as you do.'

It was incredible how this man could fill her with fury and pity almost simultaneously, she thought. Even more distressing than the frustration of not being able to make him recognise the truth about their relationship, was the knowledge that what had changed between them was beyond her control.

'You'll always be very special to me, Mick,' she said. 'You were my first love and nothing can ever match that.'

'Surely that in itself is something for us to build on?' he suggested hopefully.

'It isn't enough,' she said. 'We've grown too far apart.'

'We could give it one more try . . .'

'I'll always love you, Mick.' Jane hesitated, knowing she must be brutally frank. 'But I'm not *in love* with you any more.' She saw him wince but knew she must continue. 'I had stopped being in love with you a long time before I met Giles. It happened gradually over the years you were away and when I saw you again I knew for certain that it was over. I'm sorry to hurt you but I want to be honest with you.'

He heaved a sigh of resignation. 'Yeah, I know, babe.'

'I hope we can part good friends,' she said truthfully. 'Obviously you can see the children whenever you like.'

'Pip maybe. I've given up on Davey,' he said. 'He hates my guts.'

'I don't think he does . . . not really. He's upset by everything that's happened, that's all. And you haven't really made much of an effort to get along with him since you've been back, have you?'

'He was so hostile to me, I didn't know how to handle it.'

'I thought that was probably what it was.'

'He obviously thinks more of your boyfriend than he does of me.'

'At this moment in time, that's probably true,' she said frankly. 'He's seen a lot of Giles over the last few years. After his wife died he spent time with us because he was lonely. As Kevin was usually in here with Davey anyway, it seemed sensible for us all to be together. I was glad of the company.'

Mick lit a cigarette, looking at her through a cloud of smoke.

'Giles was there for Davey, you weren't, so it's only natural Davey began to see him as a father figure,' she continued. 'You must also take into account the fact that a man like Giles is a hero to an impressionable lad of Davey's age, being games master at school and founder manager of our local youth football team. Now that Davey goes to the school where Giles teaches, he's become even more important to the boy. You know what children are like about their teachers – they either hate them or put them on a pedestal. The ones who teach PE and games usually get into the second category with the kids who are keen on sport.'

'I don't stand a chance with Davey against that kind of competition,' said Mick gloomily.

'That isn't true. You are his father, Giles isn't,' she pointed out. 'But I think you need to start from scratch and build a new relationship with him rather than trying to breathe life into the old one. Davey was only four years old when you went away so you were a stranger to him when you came back. Once you've moved out of here, you might find it easier to communicate with him because there won't be any arguments between you and me to complicate matters.' She gave him a hard look. 'It might also help if you were to stop showing quite so much favouritism towards Pip.'

'She has time for me, Davey hasn't, that's the reason for it.'

'You always favoured her, though, even before you went away.'

'That's fathers and daughters, isn't it?'

'Maybe. But if you want to make headway with Davey, don't make it quite so obvious.'

'I'll try not to.' Mick drew on his cigarette and stood up, looking defeated. 'Well, I'd better be making a move.'

'There's no need for you to leave tonight, Mick,' she said. 'It's very late.'

'I think I should.' He looked at her bruised face. 'Before I do any more damage.'

'As you wish,' she said. 'Shall I tell the children you'll be in touch about seeing them?'

'Yeah.'

'Okay.'

It was as though all the fight had gone out of him as he packed his suitcase. Seeing him off the premises was so formal it was almost like saying goodbye to the man who'd come to read the gas meter.

But at the door he asserted himself by saying, 'I'm not going to agree to a divorce. And I'll make things as difficult as I possibly can if you start proceedings.'

Bitterly disappointed but knowing this wasn't the moment to pursue it, Jane said, 'Okay, Mick.'

'Just so long as you know where I stand on that one.'

Avoiding too much physical contact, she kissed him lightly on the cheek.

'Let me know when you want to see the children.'

'Yeah, I'll give you a bell,' he said, and went striding

down the garden path to his car, carrying his suitcase.

Jane went into the living room and sat down, weeping silently. In hurting Mick she'd inflicted pain on herself because he'd been a part of her life for so long. She remembered how proud she'd been to marry him and how happy they'd been together for so many years. Part of her was as regretful as Mick that those days had gone forever, as she knew they had. Even if they stayed together, they couldn't recreate the past because their love was dead and they both knew it. Even though Mick refused to admit it.

Mick had to pull off the road into a lay-by on the way to Brighton because his vision was blurred by tears. He leaned his head on the steering wheel and sobbed. So it had all come to nothing. He had lost the only woman he could ever really love. His powerlessness over the situation frightened him, as did the violence he had used on Jane and Davey tonight.

In a way he was glad to be out of the marriage; the anger and misery of the whole damned situation, the constant rows, the frustration of not getting his own way. Fitting into the strictures of family life had been difficult for him after the easygoing lifestyle he had in Brighton. Although he could barely admit it to himself, being a weekend husband and father had been more than enough for him.

But a recalcitrant streak in his nature made him cling to the desire to be a family man, admired and in control. He could go ahead and buy a posh house, of course, but without Jane there was no point. She had become synonymous with the lifestyle of his dreams.

He tried to substitute Patsy in the picture and found himself smiling through his tears. She wouldn't thank him for any of it. He'd had enough trouble getting her to accept her position in a decent block of flats.

Dear old Pats. A longing to see her bore down on him. He needed the comfort of her accommodating body and the reassurance of her unconditional love. He dried his tears and continued on his journey.

'A boring schoolteacher,' he muttered to himself, still unable to accept the real reason his marriage had failed. 'How could I have lost Jane to a schoolteacher who can never give her the sort of life I can offer?'

The word 'schoolteacher' lingered in his mind, inspiring him with an idea. Mick was feeling wounded and wanted to hit back. Suddenly he knew how to do it without any physical violence to anyone. He'd teach that bugger to steal another man's wife!

Revitalised by a new sense of purpose, he increased his speed, eager to get back to Brighton. Oh, yes, the time had come for that teacher to learn a lesson!

The fire at the shop and subsequent events with Mick, then having to tell the children that their parents were splitting up, left Jane in a state of nervous exhaustion.

Pip didn't help matters by blaming her mother for Mick's departure, which she saw as the end of their family. In the same way as Mick's first departure had traumatised his family, so did the second. Jane was patient with her daughter because she knew how fond she was of her father, but having constantly to deal with tantrums and hurtful accusations was very taxing.

'She'll probably feel better once she starts seeing her father on a regular basis,' Giles suggested. 'Children never cease to amaze me with their ability to adjust.'

'Mick certainly knows how to create emotional havoc,' she said.

'Once Pip gets some stability back in her life, she'll be all right,' he replied. 'And also . . . once she gets used to the idea of us.'

Jane frowned, chewing her lip.

'Actually, I've been meaning to talk to you about that.'

'Oh?'

'I think we ought to keep things casual for the moment.'

'Because of Pip?'

'Not just because of her,' Jane explained. 'This whole

business with Mick has left me feeling drained and I just don't feel able to take up where we left off, not at the moment. I still love you, Giles, but I need time to recover . . . without being committed to anything too heavy. Also, Mick doesn't want a divorce so he'll make trouble if I start proceedings, and that will block our plans anyway. If we keep things cool for the moment, there'll be nothing to incite him to revenge against you. I still don't trust him as regards that.'

'I thought you said you'd parted in a civilised manner, with him being sorry for the violence and accepting the fact that your marriage is over?'

'He seemed to accept that it's over but I'm not sure if he's really accepted the reason,' she said. 'I think he still blames you and will make trouble for you if he can. Best he isn't provoked. He'll make it his business to find out what's going on between us from the kids.'

'Mick doesn't frighten me.'

'No, but I think we ought to keep things on a friendly basis for now,' she said. 'After all, there's still your position as a teacher to consider, with my being married and not able to make our relationship legal.'

'I'm prepared for that.'

'I'd rather keep things light for the moment,' she insisted.

'All right, Jane,' he sighed, looking disappointed.

'Thanks for being so understanding.'

'There's no need to thank me,' said Giles, putting a brave face on it. 'I love you and want what's best for you. I know all about emotional exhaustion, having had my fair share of it after Lena died.'

'It won't be for long,' she said. 'Just until the dust settles. And we'll see each other around all the time anyway.'

Jane reopened for business again at the end of November, after laborious days spent scrubbing the soot off the walls and painting them. Fortunately there wasn't too much structural damage but the shop fittings had to be renewed.

340

Work was the perfect antidote to the stress she was under, and she was glad to have a structure to her life again. She liked routine. It comforted her somehow.

Perhaps now we can put the events of the last few months behind us and rebuild our family life at the cottage, she thought.

But when Trudy Hamilton called in to see her one frosty morning in December, it was obvious that this wasn't going to be possible.

'I don't suppose Giles has said anything to you about his latest spot of bother, has he?' she asked, drinking coffee in the kitchen while Jane spooned creamy mixture into cake-tins ready for the oven. Her assistant was out delivering to the cafes they regularly supplied, so the two women were able to speak freely.

'I've heard nothing about any trouble,' she said, looking worried.

Trudy looked concerned too. Jane and Giles had taken her into their confidence about Mick so she knew what he was capable of.

'I don't suppose he will tell you,' she said darkly.

Jane paused in her work, giving her visitor a shrewd look.

'What's happened?'

'Giles doesn't want to worry you with it but I think you ought to know,' said Trudy, reluctant to be the bearer of such bad news. 'Just in case it's the forerunner to other things.'

'Mick's done something to Giles, hasn't he?' asked Jane.

'An anonymous letter was sent to his headmaster,' explained Trudy.

'Oh, no . . . what was in it?'

'Words to the effect that Giles isn't fit to be working with children, that he's a bad example because he's morally degenerate . . . that he's been having an affair with the mother of a pupil at the school.'

'My God!'

341

'At least you weren't named . . . that's something to be thankful for, I suppose.'

'That's terrible,' gasped Jane, dropping her spoon into the bowl and sinking weakly on to a chair. 'How did the headmaster take it? Will Giles lose his job?'

'No. He was given a dressing down by the headmaster, who reminded him of the need for a teacher to be above reproach and of the stupidity of allowing himself to become vulnerable to this type of mischief maker. But his job's safe. I hope there'll be no more letters, though.'

'So do I.'

'There's no proof that your husband was responsible, of course . . .'

'But we all know it was him,' sighed Jane.

'Could it have been a neighbour wanting to make trouble?' suggested Trudy.

'I don't think so. Mrs Robinson is a nosy old gossip but she'd make her feelings obvious to us rather than make trouble for Giles at school,' said Jane. 'No, this has Mick's hallmark written all over it. I suspected he hadn't finished with us when he left. Despite all that contrition, there was something about him that made me suspect he *still* hadn't accepted our marriage was over. Honestly, Trudy, I just don't know him any more. He never used to be so malicious.'

'The letter had a London postmark, apparently,' she pointed out. 'Not Sussex.'

'That's easily explained . . . either he gave it to some-one who was coming up to town to post or he took a trip up himself.' Jane looked at Trudy in despair. 'How could he stoop so low? He was once the light of my life. Now he brings me nothing but trouble. I just don't know what he's going to do next.'

'Yes, I'm worried about what else he might do too,' agreed Trudy. 'I don't know if Giles's headmaster will be quite so understanding if there's any more trouble. He does have the reputation of the school to consider.'

'I'll have to go and see Mick and put a stop to this, once and for all,' said Jane.

'Go to Brighton?'

'Yes. It's no good phoning or writing,' she said. 'I need to see him face to face. I've got his address somewhere.'

'Confronting him in person would probably be the best thing.'

Jane looked at the clock, frowning. 'But I can't leave here until my assistant gets back, which means I won't be back from Brighton when the children get home from school.'

'Don't worry,' said Trudy. 'I'll pick them up from school and bring them home and give them their tea.'

'That would be a tremendous help,' said Jane, rising purposefully and getting back to work. 'I'll be on my way as soon as I can.'

It was late-afternoon when she arrived at Mick's flat. Relying on the element of surprise to wring the truth from him, she didn't telephone to let him know she was coming and had to take a chance on finding him in. She planned to wait outside until he did come home if he wasn't there but that proved to be unnecessary.

'Jane,' he said, opening the door and beaming at her. 'What a lovely surprise.'

'Cut the flattery,' she said, marching into his hallway. 'You know why I'm here.'

'Could it be that you've brought me a Christmas present?' he suggested lightly.

'Leave Giles alone,' she said as Mick ushered her into his luxurious living room.

He invited her to sit down.

'No, thanks, I'm not staying,' she said, standing stiffly in the middle of the room, her feet sinking into the thick-pile carpet. 'I've just come to tell you to stop making trouble for Giles.'

'I haven't touched the bloke.'

'No, but you sent an anonymous letter to his school, didn't you?'

'There you go again . . . blaming me when you've no proof.'

'I know no one else who would want to make trouble for Giles.'

'Don't kid yourself, Jane. A man who plays around with other men's wives won't be short of enemies.'

She slapped him so hard across the face, it hurt her hand.

'Now see what your poison has driven me to!'

'Why doesn't lover boy come and see me himself if he's an accusation to make?' asked Mick, looking aggrieved, hand to his face.

'He doesn't even know I'm here.'

'The bugger deserves everything he gets. I hope he loses his job and rots in hell.'

'So you admit to sending the letter?'

'Yeah, I admit it, and there was nothing in it that isn't true.'

'You're sick!'

'Sick at heart because of what that bastard's done to me.'

'He hasn't done anything to you,' said Jane with rising impatience. 'You are the architect of your own misfortune.'

'He took you away from me.'

'*He did not*. How many more times must I tell you?' she said with a weary sigh. 'Anything that happened between Giles and me, I entered into of my own free will. But it's all over between us now anyway. You've seen to that.'

'I bet you were back in his bed as soon as I'd gone?'

'It may come as a surprise to you to hear that sex isn't the main priority in my life,' said Jane scathingly. 'At the moment I'm concentrating on trying to bring back some sort of stability to my children's lives after the upheaval you've caused. Giles and I aren't seeing each other in that way.'

'Oh, do me a favour, Jane,' he said cynically. 'When you're living next-door to each other? Don't insult my intelligence.'

'I'll move out of the cottage if it'll stop you making trouble for him.'

'Huh! You'd move out to protect him but you wouldn't move out of there when *I* wanted you to.'

'And I don't want to move out now,' she said. 'But if Giles and I aren't neighbours, maybe your nasty little mind will stop jumping to the wrong conclusions and you'll leave him alone.'

'Don't move out on my account,' said Mick, but it was only a token protest. The sooner she moved away from the hero of the playing field, the better he would like it.

'I'll have to. You've made it impossible for me to stay there.'

'Well, it's time you were out of that dungeon of a place anyway.'

'It isn't a dungeon,' she said, glancing around this room which had more show than David Bowie but remained dull and uninteresting despite its cream leather sofas and marble-topped tables. 'I like living there, as you very well know.'

'Time you were moving on, though.'

'Seems I have no choice.'

'Where will you go?'

'I can't leave the area because of the children's school and the shop,' she said, adding with a sigh, 'See what difficulties you've made for me?'

'No one's forcing you to move from that dismal dump.'

'I can't stay there now, being terrified to speak to my next-door neighbour for fear you'll hear about it and make more trouble for him. It was a wicked thing you did.'

'I was *feeling* wicked.'

'Anyway, it'll probably be just as well if I'm not living next-door to Giles. At least it will prevent any gossip since you won't agree to a divorce so we can be together legally.'

'I'm surprised you're not gonna shack up together anyway.'

'And give you an excuse to complain again about Giles

setting a bad example to his pupils?' she rasped. 'Not likely!'

'Well, now that you've got all that off your chest, can I offer you anything? A drink . . . something to eat, perhaps?'

'No, thanks,' she said coldly. 'I have to get back to London.'

Mick didn't try to persuade her to stay but led the way to the door. She got the distinct impression that he wasn't sorry to see the back of her.

'I can't forgive you for what you did to Giles,' she said at the door. 'Hurt me if you must but not him . . . leave him alone.'

'If you keep away from him, I will.'

'I could have you done for threatening behaviour.'

'You won't though, will you?'

Jane stared hard at him.

'I don't know what I ever saw in you,' she said in reply.

And on that parting note, she went out into the cold night air and hurried down the steps to her car parked outside.

Driving along the London Road, she was shivering violently despite having the heater on full. She kept her speed down and drove with extra care because the roads were slippery. Her head ached and she felt sick. She thought this was probably a physical reaction to the misery of losing the cottage she adored and the man she loved, both victims of Mick's selfish refusal to face the truth about the failure of their marriage.

What upset her most of all, though, was the loss of something good and special such as she had once had with Mick, and how this loss had changed him from a person of charm and vitality into a vicious and evil man. She knew in her heart, though, that he had never shown his true colours in those halcyon days because she had always let him have his own way about everything. She had a nasty suspicion that the darker side of his nature would have come to the fore rather sooner had she been more assertive then.

Soon after Jane had left, Mick went to the Drake's Arms to see a man about some leather handbags, the spoils of a robbery on a leather goods merchant in North London. With Christmas approaching, he could shift any number.

Having completed the deal to his satisfaction and seen his business contact off the premises, he went over to the bar and spoke to Patsy.

'Well . . . have you got an answer for me?' he asked, leaning on the counter and giving her one of his most winning smiles.

'That depends,' she said with a half smile, teasing him a little.

'Now don't mess me about, Pats.'

Her expression became more serious.

'It depends on whether or not it's definitely all over between you and your wife?'

'It is,' he assured her. 'How many more times must I tell you?'

'I have to be really sure of that before I make my decision.'

'You can be.'

She still looked doubtful.

'I need to know for certain that you're being straight with me?'

'I am, I am. Honest, Pats,' he said, his dark eyes meeting hers persuasively. 'I've told you, my marriage didn't work out so I'm as free as a bird again.'

Treating him to one of the wide and warm smiles that Mick found so endearing, Patsy said, 'Okay, Mick, you win. I'll move back in with you as soon as you like.'

'That's brilliant,' said Mick, who had been working really hard to persuade her to move back in with him ever since Jane had given him his marching orders. As heartsick as he was for his wife, he saw no point in denying himself the comforts that *were* available to him.

Chapter Twenty Two

The improvements Jane had made to the cottage meant she had no trouble in securing a buyer for it. Finding something she liked as much, however, proved to be impossible so she settled for a traditional semi in Wilber Road near to Chiswick High Road and they moved in March.

Leaving the cottage was a painful wrench but there were certain advantages to the new house; Jane's shop and the school were within walking distance and the house was larger than the cottage and had a spacious kitchen which adapted easily for commercial use.

After the usual trials and tribulations of moving house, including general hysteria when Shadow went missing for a few days, presumably to explore his new territory, life settled into a new pattern for Jane. As spring turned to summer she committed herself to making the house into a comfortable home and creating a secure atmosphere for Davey and Pip after the disruption caused by Mick.

She saw him about once a month when he came to collect the children for a weekend outing. Although she went to pains to persuade Davey to make an effort with his father, she herself kept her distance.

Because Davey and Kevin continued to be close friends despite the move, she saw Giles fairly often. But they didn't resume their affair. Not from any lack of interest on either side but because of Jane's determination to protect both his reputation and his health, while living in hope that Mick would eventually agree to a divorce. Until then, it was safer this way.

Cottage Cakes continued to thrive and the celebration cakes side of the business grew. Jane's biggest problem was finding a reliable assistant to work with her in the kitchen. There had been several since Marie but none with the same commitment to the job as she'd had. They never stayed long, despite the excellent pay and conditions. Jane supposed that working in someone else's kitchen just wasn't glamorous enough for a lot of people. Marie had been more like a business partner than an employee, and Jane still missed her, even now.

That autumn Pip joined her brother as a pupil at the Grammar School which was soon to become a comprehensive, in accordance with government policy. In September also Jane's father astonished them all by enrolling for evening classes at the Technical College.

'Dad's woodwork classes certainly seem to have given him a new lease of life,' Jane remarked to Trudy one day when she'd called at the new house.

'Do they really?' asked Trudy, choking back a giggle.

'What's so funny about him joining a woodwork class?'

'Nothing . . . nothing at all.'

'Personally, I think it's great,' enthused Jane, surprised by Trudy's obvious amusement. 'I've been nagging him for years to take up a new hobby.'

Trudy snorted into her handkerchief.

Jane was puzzled by her friend's attitude.

'Is it the thought of some hideous coffee table or wobbly stool he might present me with that you're finding so hilarious?' she asked, smiling. 'I'm quite looking forward to seeing the end result of his work, actually.'

Managing to compose herself, Trudy said rather lamely, 'Sorry, Jane. I'm not laughing about your father's classes. Something amused me at a showgroup rehearsal the other day and it came back to mind. You know how it is when something makes you laugh and you can't forget about it?'

Jane knew exactly how it was. So why didn't she believe Trudy? Why did she get the distinct impression that she was hiding something? What could she possibly want to conceal from Jane about her own father? Nothing at all and you're imagining things, she told herself, and put it out of her mind as the conversation moved on to other things.

Joe Harris gave his shoes a last polish before inspecting himself in front of the wardrobe mirror. His tie was straight, his hair, what was left of it, neatly combed into place, blazer brushed, the crease in his trousers razor sharp. You'll do, he told himself, eyes bright with excitement. His new hobby had taken years off him. He was having a wonderful time.

His conscience troubled him slightly for being dishonest about it. But he just couldn't face the ribbing he'd have to take if people knew where he *really* went twice a week when he was supposed to be at the tech learning how to be creative with wood. He could hardly believe he was having such fun. It was the last thing on earth he'd expected to enjoy.

But he found it so exhilarating having something to look forward to outside the family and work. And he was getting better at it all the time, learning something new at every session. He was bursting to tell Jane the truth, but even his warm-hearted daughter wouldn't be able to keep a straight face then. Heaven only knew how he was eventually going to explain the absence of any evidence of his supposed handiwork.

Time enough to worry about that later on. Right now he was going out to enjoy himself. The sound of a car's horn outside in the street informed him that his companion had arrived. He hurried out of his flat with a spring in his step.

'Why don't we have the children here sometimes, Mick?' suggested Patsy one Sunday afternoon in February of the following year as they lounged around the flat drinking tea, smoking and browsing through the Sunday papers. 'Instead of you always going to London to see them.'

'Here?' he said, peering at her over the top of the *News of the World* in a manner that questioned her sanity.

'Yeah,' she said with rising enthusiasm. 'They could come for the weekend. If you don't fancy driving up to fetch them, Jane could put them on the train at Victoria and we could meet them at the station here.'

'No . . . it isn't a good idea.'

'Why not?'

'I don't know,' he said impatiently. 'I just wouldn't feel right about it.'

'Because I'm here?'

'Partly that, yes.'

'You're ashamed of me?'

'No, o' course not,' he said, though he wasn't sure if he was speaking the truth about that because Patsy wasn't the sort of woman his children were used to. 'I'd feel awkward having them here, that's all. I am married to their mother, after all.'

'That is only a technicality now, though, isn't it?'

'Even so . . .'

'I've never had much to do with children but I'd make them very welcome,' she persisted.

'We only have one spare bedroom.'

'There are twin beds in there, though,' she reminded him. 'They wouldn't mind sharing a room, just for a night or two.'

'I don't suppose Davey would want to come anyway,' said Mick gloomily. 'We can only just about manage to tolerate each other for an afternoon at a time.'

'Let Pip come without him then,' she suggested excitedly. 'You can go and collect her in the car if you don't like the idea of her travelling by train on her own.'

Mick liked that idea despite himself. He had kept his children at a safe distance from Brighton because his life with Patsy was so different from that of Pip and Davey. He and Patsy weren't traditional family people. They led a bohemian life, sleeping a lot in the day and coming to life at night. They ate what they liked, when they liked, most of their meals eaten in pubs or cafes, or collected from takeaway places. Patsy was as untidy about the flat as he was, so the place was usually a tip. It didn't bother either of them but would probably horrify Pip who was used to everything being pin-neat and spotless. But for all that, he would like to see his daughter for longer than an afternoon at a time. And it wouldn't hurt him and Patsy to change their ways just for a weekend now and again.

'I could take a weekend off from the pub, if you like?' she suggested, her eagerness growing. 'We could take her out and show her around.'

'Mmm, maybe we'll do it sometime,' he said, still doubtful as to the success of such a project. 'But let's leave it 'til the summer when there's more going on around here.'

'We don't need to wait until then,' she said. 'You can always find things to do in Brighton.'

'What's the hurry?'

'I'd like to get to know your children.'

'Why?'

' 'Cause they're part of you and we're a couple now,' she said.

Despite what she'd said, Patsy knew that she and Mick could never truly be a couple until he finally let go of the past. He still hankered after Jane which was why he was being so difficult about a divorce. Patsy was quite happy to settle for being second best and wanted him to do the same. Theirs might not be the love affair of the century but they were very well suited. She had the idea that if she got to know his children, it would make their relationship official somehow and bring them closer together.

'Yeah, all right,' he said. 'We'll get something arranged sometime soon.'

Well, at least he hadn't rejected the idea altogether and that was progress so far as Patsy was concerned.

One thing Jane had learned as the proprietor of a business was the need for flexibility. She had to be able to switch from one role to the other at a moment's notice. This happened one February morning when she found herself serving at the counter, having arrived at the shop with a fresh batch of cakes to find a queue of people trailing out on to the pavement, and one of the assistants needing to go home to bed because she was in the early stages of 'flu.

Working in the shop made a pleasant change. She enjoyed meeting the people who actually bought her cakes, some of whom she had known all her life.

'You've come out of the kitchen, then?' said a woman whom Jane didn't recognise as she served her with an apple cake and a jam sponge. She guessed the woman had assumed who Jane was from the comments being made by other customers. She was a bright-eyed, elderly woman wearing a red woolly hat and muffler.

'Not for long, though,' said Jane. 'Or I'll have nothing to sell tomorrow.'

'And that would never do,' said the woman. 'I can't bear mass-produced cakes now that I've got used to your lovely home-baked ones.'

'Glad you like them,' said Jane, putting her cakes into light cardboard cartons and setting them down on the counter.

'How's your dad?' asked the customer.

'He's fine.' She threw the woman a querying look. 'You know him then?'

'Yeah. It was Joe who told me about your cakes, as a matter of fact,' she explained, handing Jane some money. 'And I'm very glad he did.' She grinned. 'You've got a very good publicity agent in your father.'

'Don't tell him that or he'll want commission,' she joked.

'Is he still going?' asked the woman as Jane gave her her change.

'Going where?'

'To the dance club.'

Jane stared at her.

'I haven't been for quite a while,' the woman

continued, putting her change into her purse. 'Once the cold weather sets in, I'm too lazy to go out of an evening. I don't suppose the weather would put Joe off, though.'

'Dance club!' said Jane, stunned.

'That's right, dear,' the woman replied chirpily. 'Ballroom dancing.'

Ballroom dancing? Her father? Jane couldn't believe it.

'Oh,' she muttered, dumbstruck.

'Hasn't he told you?'

'No.'

'Oh, well, I suppose he just hasn't got around to it,' she said, putting her cakes into her shopping bag. 'He's very keen, though, him and that partner of his.'

'Partner?'

'That's right, the woman who brought him along in the first place. Ooh . . . what's her name, now? It's on the tip of my tongue. Good-looking woman, very striking.'

'Trudy Hamilton,' Jane muttered almost to herself as the pieces of the jigsaw fell into place. Trudy's amusement, the lack of any finished woodwork . . .

'That's the one,' said the woman, putting her change in her purse. 'Nice woman.'

'Indeed.'

'Anyway, I mustn't hold you up,' said the customer as people behind her in the queue began to get restless. 'Give your dad my regards. Tell him Betty was asking after him.'

'I'll certainly tell him,' said Jane, adding to herself, In fact, I can't wait to pass on your message to the lying old devil!

'I thought you'd laugh at me, that's why I didn't tell you the truth,' said Joe when she confronted him about it that evening.

'Why on earth would I do that?' asked Jane. 'When I've been trying to persuade you to take something up for years?'

'But ballroom dancing . . . I mean, it isn't exactly the

sort of thing the men on the Berrywood Estate go in for, is it?'

'That's their problem,' she said. 'If you enjoy it, that's all that matters.'

'They'll think I'm a right pansy when they find out about it around here.'

'Only because they're ignorant,' she said. 'Take no notice.'

'You're not cross with me for telling you fibs then?'

'I'll forgive you. But wait 'til I see Trudy,' she said teasingly. 'No wonder she went into fits every time I mentioned your woodwork classes.'

'My fault, not hers,' said Joe with a sheepish grin. 'I asked her not to say anything. Even Giles doesn't know.'

'I hope you're not going to keep it a secret any longer?' said Jane.

'I don't suppose it matters who knows really. I felt embarrassed about it when I first started because I've never done anything like that before. I'd always thought it was rather an effeminate thing for a man to do – until Trudy persuaded me to go along to the beginners' class and I realised that the men were all just ordinary chaps like myself.'

'And that surprises me even more than the dancing,' said his daughter emphatically. 'The fact that Trudy managed to talk you into it, since you've been fending her off for years.'

'Well, I suppose she just wore me down in the end. And I'm very glad she did.'

'She can be very persuasive.'

'Phew, not half!' he readily agreed. 'But she's good company once you get to know her.'

'So is there anything else I should know . . . about you and Trudy?'

'No, we're just good friends and dancing partners,' he said, and Jane would have been astounded had it been otherwise. 'Trudy has lots of friends and is involved in many other things, especially her showgroup. But I enjoy her company and I'm very grateful to her for getting me out and doing something. Anyone else would have given up on me years ago.'

'I'm very glad she didn't,' said Jane.

'So am I,' Joe agreed. 'I used to dread retirement. Now I'm really looking forward to it. There are dance clubs you can go to in the daytime.'

'Oh, Dad, I'm so pleased that you're happy,' she said, hugging him.

Because Jane wanted Pip and Davey to retain a relationship with their paternal grandparents, she continued to take them to see Rita and Wilf even though she herself no longer felt bonded to them. The children went along very much under protest, however . . .

'Gran Parker is okay,' said Davey. 'But Granddad's a pain.'

Although she admonished her son for being disrespectful about his grandfather, Jane secretly shared his opinion. Wilf had aged dramatically this last couple of years, more in the way he behaved than in appearance. His hair was completely white now but still fairly thick and he remained handsome in a gypsyish sort of way. But he'd become very lugubrious. Instead of spending all his spare time in the pub, he stayed home of an evening and went to bed early. When he did speak it usually took the form of a complaint.

It was no wonder the children didn't want to visit. He ticked them off if they giggled, which sent them into paroxysms of nervous laughter and angered him even more. And as for his poor wife, he was even more demanding of her, making her wait on him hand and foot with never a word of appreciation.

Because he didn't go out in the evenings, Rita had more of his company to endure. Jane didn't know how she put up with him. But Rita being Rita, she remained loyal to her ungrateful husband and never once admitted that he was a real trial to her. Apparently he'd had several funny turns while he'd been out drinking and that had put him off going out again after he got in from work.

'I don't think he's feeling too well,' she would whisper when he was out of earshot. 'But he'll never admit it, not in a million years.'

One particular Saturday in the spring of 1975, when Jane and the children went to the Parkers' flat for tea, Wilf seemed a lot more cheerful and made quite a fuss of his grandchildren.

'So how's your soccer coming on, young Davey?' he asked.

'I play rugby now that I'm at the big school,' the boy explained, buttering a toasted tea cake. 'I'm hoping to be picked for the junior team.'

Wilf sucked in his breath. 'Rugby always seems a very rough game to me . . . you mind how you go, son.'

'It's okay if you know what you're doing,' Davey assured him.

'What about the other football team you were in?' asked Wilf, taking a sip of tea.

'I'm too old for the Riverside Juniors now that I'm turned eleven.'

'Fancy being too old for anything at your age,' Wilf turned his attention to Pip. 'And what about you, young lady? What do you do with yourself outside of school?'

'Girl Guides, gym club, playing music.'

'Playing music, eh?' He sounded impressed. 'On the piano . . . Beethoven, Bach, all that sort o' stuff?'

'On the record player. The Bay City Rollers . . . the Osmonds,' corrected Jane, grinning.

'Oh, pop music,' said Wilf, smiling. 'I should have known . . .'

'You know who they are, Granddad?' asked Pip, looking astounded.

'You cheeky young miss!' he said, smiling. 'I'm not that much past it.'

Everyone laughed. Wilf was like a different man and this was one of the most companionable interludes Jane had had with her in-laws for a very long time. She said as much to Rita when she was helping her wash the dishes in the kitchen while the children stayed in the other room with their grandfather.

'Has Wilf won the pools or something?' she asked. 'He's in a very good mood.'

'I dunno what's causing it,' said Rita. 'But it certainly isn't the pools.'

They chatted about this and that, Rita washing, Jane drying. They had almost finished when there was a loud scream from the other room and Davey came tearing into the kitchen, followed by his sister.

'Come quick,' he said in a shaky voice. 'It's Granddad.'

Wilf was lying on the floor with his eyes closed, making rattling sounds as he gasped for breath. Rita fell on her knees beside him while Jane rushed to the phone in the hall and called an ambulance.

When she went back into the living room, Rita was leaning over him, saying, 'Oh, Wilf, Wilf love . . . come on now. It's Rita . . . calm down. You're having a funny turn, that's all. The doctor will soon put you right.'

Jane wasn't at all sure about that but she just said, 'The ambulance is on its way. It'll be here in a few minutes.'

Jane was waiting at the hospital entrance for Mick to arrive, needing to speak to him before he went inside. Having stopped only long enough to take the children to her father's, she'd come to the hospital in her car behind the ambulance. Rita wouldn't leave Wilf's bedside so it had fallen to Jane to telephone Mick to tell him that his father had been taken ill. That had been more than two hours ago.

Now he came rushing into the building, grey with worry.

'Hello, Mick,' she said.

'Hi, Jane. I got here as soon as I could. Bloody traffic on the way up from Brighton! I've been doin' my nut.'

'Mick . . .'

'Where is he . . . which ward is he in?'

'Mick,' she said again.

'Come on, Jane, don't hang about. Show me the way to his ward.'

'Mick, your father's . . .'

'What's the matter with you?' he said impatiently. 'Don't stand there as though tomorrow will do.'

She grabbed his arm firmly and looked up into his face, forcing him to listen.

'I'm afraid your father died half an hour ago,' she blurted out.

He stared blankly, as though turned to stone.

'I'm so sorry.'

'You're having me on?'

'He never regained consciousness after he collapsed at home,' she told him gently, still holding his arm. 'They think it was a heart attack but they won't know for sure until after the post-mortem.'

'Mum?'

'In the relatives' room. One of the nurses is with her,' she said through parched lips. 'They're very kind.'

'I must go to her,' he said, but didn't move. It was as though he couldn't.

'Marie doesn't know yet,' said Jane. 'I tried to get hold of her earlier to tell her that he'd been taken ill but they weren't answering their phone. I didn't think it was my place to tell her that he'd . . .'

'No, of course not. I'll do it.'

'Okay. I'll go now and leave you and your mother together,' she said. 'I have to collect the children from Dad's. Anything I can do, just let me know.'

'Thanks, Jane,' he said bleakly. 'Thanks for everything.'

'Oh, Mick.' She reached out to him with compassion, putting her arms around him and holding him while he sobbed brokenly.

'I really loved that man.'

'I know you did, Mick . . . I know.'

'God knows why 'cause he never had any time for me.'

'I expect he did in his heart,' she said kindly.

'That's something we'll never know.'

'He was really nice to the kids today,' she said with tears in her eyes. 'Almost as though he was making one last effort. They'll remember that and think kindly of him.'

'I know he was often a nasty bugger but he was still my hero,' said Mick, his voice barely audible.

'He was just a man,' she said. 'Just a man like you.'

Quite suddenly he straightened up and composed himself.

'I must go to Mum.'

'Yes, she'll be needing you.'

And he was gone, striding through the swing doors with his customary swagger.

Jane drove home full of sorrow for Mick. She knew how deeply affected he would be by his father's death, and she felt it too. Her empathy with him was still very strong. She supposed it always would be, just as a small part of her would always be his.

The next day Mick went back to the flat in Brighton to collect some clothes. Being a Sunday afternoon, Patsy was at home.

'I'll be staying with my mother until after the funeral,' he told her. 'Obviously it's down to me to make all the arrangements.'

'How is she?' asked Patsy, who'd been told of the death last night on the phone.

'She's coping.'

'Would you like me to come with you to London?' she offered.

He looked surprised.

'No, of course not,' he said adamantly, because such a thing had never even occurred to him. The last thing he would ever do was include Patsy in family matters.

'Why not?'

'Well . . . you've got your job at the pub, haven't you?' he said evasively, because he didn't want to hurt her feelings.

'I could easily take some time off, if you need me?'

'No. Thanks for offerin', but it won't be necessary,' he said. 'I'll be all right.'

'Would you like me to come to the funeral then?' she suggested.

'No.'

'Why not?'

'Well . . . you didn't know Dad and you wouldn't know anyone there.'

'I just thought you might like a bit of moral support.'

'It's a kind thought, but it'll be better if you don't,' he said. 'I'll be busy looking after my mother and you might feel left out of things. I'll be back in a week or so.'

'Just as you like then,' said Patsy, deeply hurt that he didn't want her with him at this time of personal sadness. He preferred to exclude her from a family gathering, presumably because he didn't consider her to be close enough to him. She wondered if he still thought of her just as a temporary girlfriend rather than a permanent part of his life. But this was a very delicate matter. Any change in their relationship had to come from him for it to mean anything. There was no point in her nagging him about it. 'You know where I am if you need me.'

'Yes, I do know that,' he said, and felt unexpectedly comforted in the knowledge that she would be here waiting for him when the ordeal of the funeral was over.

Crowds of people from the Berrywood Estate turned out on to the streets to give Wilf a send off, for he'd been well-known and popular on the manor. It was the wrong sort of day for a funeral, somehow; a glorious May day, more suitable for wearing bright summer clothes than the dark sober apparel worn by the mourners at the cemetery.

Jane and the children stood with the family to pay their final respects. Mick looked strong and upright by his mother's side, with a steadying hand on her arm. Marie and Eddie were standing close together with their children. Jane thought only of Mick. Having lost her own mother, she knew exactly what he was going through. She was afraid he might go to pieces, but he remained strong for his mother and hosted the funeral gathering at the flat with dignity.

Rita, who seemed surprisingly confident, provided a substantial buffet. There was also plenty of booze around. Jane guessed that this sad assembly would turn into a party later on with everyone ending up at the pub. It was their way of coping and was what Wilf would have wanted. Jane planned to leave soon, though. She needed to get back to the kitchen to see how her assistant was coping without her.

She was doing a farewell round of the guests when Marie approached her, the two women having exchanged just the briefest of formal greetings earlier.

'You leaving so soon?'

'Yeah . . . I have to get back, duty calls and all that,' said Jane. 'I'm really sorry about your dad, though.'

'Thanks.' Marie was very subdued. 'He could be a bit of a swine but he'll be missed.' Her eyes filled with tears. 'It's the end of an era, losing a parent. I feel so old suddenly.'

Jane nodded and touched her arm sympathetically.

'I know exactly what you mean.'

Marie dabbed her eyes with a handkerchief and changed the subject.

'Your business is still going strong, I gather,' she said. 'The shop always seems to be packed out when I go past.'

'Yes, it's doing very well,' confirmed Jane. 'I hope I'm not going back to find chaos in the kitchen, though.'

'Might you?'

'Put it this way,' she said with a wry grin, 'my current assistant isn't exactly overloaded with initiative.'

'Current . . . does that mean you've had more than one since I left?'

'I'll say I have! They never seem to stay long enough to settle in,' explained Jane. 'Either they don't suit me or I don't suit them. I haven't found anyone with a real interest in the job yet. I suppose I've just been unlucky.'

'Yeah.'

'What are you doing these days?'

'I'm working on the checkout in a supermarket in Hammersmith.'

'That's right,' said Jane. 'I remember your mum mentioning it. Do you like it?'

'It's okay.'

There was an awkward silence which neither seemed able to fill.

'I'm sorry it didn't work out for you and Mick,' said Marie.

'It's just one of those things,' replied Jane, tensing as they drifted into dangerous territory. 'We'd grown apart while he was away.'

'From what I've heard, you're not with Giles either?'

'No,' she said with undisguised regret. 'There are too many complications.'

Marie cleared her throat.

'I'm really sorry I came on to you so strong about your relationship with him,' she said through dry lips. 'I realise now I had no right . . . that it was none of my business.'

'Oh.' Jane was heartened to hear this. 'I was upset for ages after that row.'

'I've always had a blind spot when it comes to Mick.'

'Yes . . .'

'But I know now that I have to let go and stand back from my brother's personal affairs,' Marie continued. 'Will you forgive me?'

'Of course I will.'

'I've wanted to say all this to you for a long time but I couldn't bring myself to contact you,' she said. 'I just didn't have the bottle.'

'I wish you had.'

'Me too. But the longer it went on, the harder it was.'

'Well, it's all over now,' said Jane, smiling mistily. 'And I'm really pleased. I can't tell you how much I've missed you.'

'Likewise . . . it's been awful.'

'If you fancy coming back and working for me at any time, there'll always be a job for you,' said Jane, swallowing a lump in her throat. 'I've a feeling my latest assistant is about to hand in her notice.'

'Oh, Jane, I'd love that!'

'Let's get together and talk about it soon then, shall we?'

'The sooner the better.'

They hugged each other, laughing emotionally, both close to tears.

Driving the children home a while later, Jane said to herself, Well, Wilf, you were never my favourite person but you've given me a gift from beyond the grave that makes me want to forgive you anything. You brought Marie and me together again and I thank you for that with all my heart!

Chapter Twenty Three

'Shall we go to the place with red tables for tea?' suggested Pip as she walked arm-in-arm with her father and Patsy along the seafront at Brighton.

'You mean the one where they do those enormous ice-cream sundaes?' said Patsy.

'That's the one,' giggled Pip.

' 'Course we can,' Patsy agreed.

'I suppose you'll be wanting one of those sickly concoctions and a milk shake instead of a proper tea?' said Mick teasingly.

'I'll have both if you're in a good mood!' Pip laughed, eyes shining, cheeks glowing against the blue and white woolly hat she wore with a matching muffler.

She enjoyed staying for weekends in Brighton with her father and Patsy. They'd assumed she wouldn't want to come at the end of the season when things closed for the winter, but she liked it even better now when the day-trippers had gone and she felt like one of the residents. This afternoon in early-December it was cold and wild, the salty wind stinging their cheeks, the dark sea rolling against the shore and setting the pebbles shifting.

Pip came down about once a month; she had started doing so just after Granddad Parker died. She'd been surprised when her father had invited her and Davey out of the blue. Because Davey didn't get on with Dad, he preferred to spend the weekends at home in Chiswick, hanging out with his mates.

Sometimes Pip shared the spare bedroom with her grandmother who often stayed with Dad and Patsy, though she wasn't here this weekend. Gran was great. Everyone said she'd changed a lot since Granddad died. She was full of life and always interested in what you had to say. She'd always seemed distant and timid before. Now Pip felt as though she could talk to her about anything.

Dad was different here in Brighton with Patsy, too, she'd noticed. He wasn't grumpy like he'd been at the cottage. You could bring a friend to the flat without being scared he'd embarrass you by losing his temper and using bad language. He didn't quarrel with Patsy as he did with Mum either. He laughed a lot and was really good fun. He and Patsy were always joshing with each other about something. Pip couldn't remember her parents ever doing that.

She liked Patsy now though she hadn't been sure about her at first. She'd seemed so rough and common with her dyed hair, thick make-up and loud raucous laugh. But her all-embracing warmth had been such that Pip had soon stopped noticing the outer packaging and now just enjoyed her company. Patsy usually managed to get the Saturday off from the pub when Pip was coming to stay, and going out for tea had become something of a ritual.

On warm summer evenings they would stroll along the front and stay awhile in the amusements on the pier. But now that the weather was more suited to indoor entertainment, they would either go to the cinema or watch television at the flat, and Dad would go out to get Chinese takeaway or fish and chips for supper.

Dad and Patsy drank beer and whisky; Pip had Coca-Cola. No one bothered to clear up until the next morning. Staying with them was excitingly casual and completely different from home where Mum was scrupulous about making sure Pip and Davey had regular, nourishing meals.

'I'm always in a good mood for you, Princess,' her father was saying in reply as they approached the ice-cream parlour which also served teas and lunches, was open all year round and was a favourite with the locals.

How true that was, thought Patsy, watching father and daughter together. He really did adore her and Pip seemed to be genuinely fond of him. Patsy liked her. Her youthful exuberance was like a breath of spring about the place.

Having Mick's daughter around made Patsy feel like family, as did having his mother to stay. She was glad she'd persevered in persuading him to invite his relatives to the flat. As well as making her feel as though she'd been accepted as his partner, it had helped him to cope with his father's death which she knew had affected him deeply. It seemed strange to see Mick being the devoted father, though. He even missed his regular Saturday night binge at the pub when his daughter came to stay.

Inside the cafe, they settled at a table by the window looking across the road to the promenade, the street lights beaming into the greyness of the gathering dusk. There were quite a few people about despite the weather.

Having given the waitress their order, Patsy said, 'So what do we all fancy doing this evening? Is it to be the cinema, the telly or a game of Monopoly?'

'Some of each of the last two,' said Pip. 'If that's all right with you two?'

'Suits me,' said Mick.

Patsy laughed.

'I'll bet it does,' she said. 'I could never get him to go to the pictures until you started coming to stay.'

'I'm a good influence then.'

'Not half.' Patsy smiled. 'Because I like the cinema. I wish you'd started coming to see us long ago.'

'That goes for me too.' Mick sighed. 'You'll be thirteen soon. I missed so many of those years.'

'You should have asked me to come sooner,' said Pip lightly.

'I thought you'd be bored with us two oldies,' he said. 'It was Patsy who talked me into suggesting it.'

'Should have done it ages ago,' said Patsy, looking at him.

'Definitely,' agreed Mick, feeling at ease and happy.

'It takes you so long to get round to doing anything like that, Mick,' said Patsy casually. 'God knows, it took me long enough to get you to go home to your family. I'd been on at you about that for years.'

'You're not kidding,' he said. 'You nearly drove me mad.'

Both Patsy and Mick were too far relaxed and off their guard to hear the squeal of the cat being let out of the bag or to notice the perplexed look on Pip's face.

'How could Patsy have been telling you for years to go home if you didn't know where your home was?' she asked.

They both stared at her.

'I thought you lost your memory?' she said, looking at her father.

Completely taken aback, he struggled for a way out.

'I did lose my memory . . . 'course I did,' he stammered. 'What Patsy means is that she tried to get me to go home as soon as it came back.'

'But I thought you came home more or less as soon as you remembered about us . . . in a matter of months, anyway?'

'That's right, I did.'

'Then why was Patsy trying to persuade you to come for years . . . if you didn't know anything about us?' she persisted.

'Because . . .'

'You didn't lose your memory at all, did you?' she cut in as he struggled for words, her eyes hot with accusation. 'Granddad Joe was right. It was all just a story.'

'No, it wasn't,' denied Mick. 'I did lose my memory.'

'He did, Pip,' confirmed Patsy.

'But you got it back sooner than you led Mum to believe, didn't you?'

Mick glared at Patsy. 'Nice one, Pats. You and your big mouth.'

'How was I to know you'd not been straight with Jane about that?'

There was a painful silence as the waitress brought their order.

'How much sooner, Daddy?' demanded Pip.

'Oh, not long . . .'

'Tell her the truth, for goodness' sake, Mick,' interrupted Patsy. 'These lies have gone on for long enough. It's about time you were honest.'

'Daddy . . .' urged Pip, voice quivering on the verge of tears.

'Oh, I suppose it must have been about . . . well, I'm not sure exactly.'

'It must have been more than four years, Mick, because you'd been with me for three years before you went back and you'd known who you were for about a year when we first met, I remember you telling me,' Patsy supplied, then meeting Mick's furious glare, added, 'and it's no good you looking at me like that, mate. This is where the pretence ends, once and for all. Your family deserves the truth.'

'Daddy, how could you?' accused Pip, her eyes brimming with tears. 'Mummy struggled to keep us . . . we all needed you. And all the time you were in Brighton with Patsy!'

'Not all of the time, love,' she put in. 'Your dad did lose his memory for a couple of years.'

'But even so . . . for more than four years you knew who you were and you didn't come back to us,' said Pip, her brown eyes heavy with pain, her voice high and bitter. 'You didn't care about us.'

'That isn't true,' said Mick quickly and with strong emphasis. 'I did care . . . very much. It's because I cared so much that I didn't come back.'

'I don't understand?'

'I didn't have anything to offer you, no means of support. I'd lost everything. I had no money, no business, and I was very ashamed,' he explained, ashen-faced and tense. 'I had to wait until I'd got back on my feet before I could come home and face you all. I couldn't come back to my family a failure.'

'It wouldn't have mattered to us, just so long as you were there,' she said.

'I think it would, you know.'

'I was too little when you went away to remember much about it,' she said, sounding very grown-up suddenly and speaking almost as though she was talking to herself. 'But I do know how hard Mum worked and struggled to keep us for all those years. I do know that she was sad and lonely. Have you any idea how terrible it must have been for her?'

'I know, I know,' said Mick, feeling his beloved daughter slipping away from him just when he was beginning to grow really close to her. 'Don't you think I'm ashamed to have let you all down?'

'Even though I didn't remember much about you, I always had dreamed of my father returning to us one day,' she continued. 'And you didn't even care enough about us to come back as soon as you could!'

'Pip, it wasn't like that.'

'All you could think of was your pride . . . people thinking you'd failed,' she went on, tears streaming down her cheeks. 'And when you did finally put in an appearance, you lied to Mum – told her that you'd only recently got your memory back. And as if all that wasn't enough, you tried to force her to give up the business she'd worked so hard to build up so she could give Davey and me a decent life.'

'Only because I wanted to look after her . . . to support you all.'

'I defended you,' his daughter went on, becoming even more distraught. 'I quarrelled with Davey for being mean to you and blamed Mum because you went away again. And all the time you'd lied to us . . .'

'I'm sorry, Pip.'

'You should have come back, Dad,' she said, wiping her eyes with a handkerchief. 'We are your family. But you didn't care about us – didn't care how hard it was for Mum bringing us up on her own.'

'But I've told you, I did care, Pip,' he said, his voice

thick with emotion. 'That's why I wanted to provide for you all when I got back. You have to believe me.'

'I'll never believe anything you say again . . . because you're a *liar*!'

'Your father really did care for you all, Pip, in his own strange way,' said Patsy gently. 'I've lived with him for a long time and I can vouch for that.'

'I want to go home,' said the girl.

'Okay, we'll get the bill and go back to the flat and talk this thing through,' said Mick.

'Your flat isn't my home,' she said through tight lips. 'Back to London, I mean.'

'But, Pip, please listen . . .'

'I'll get a train tonight.'

'Don't be ridiculous,' said Mick. 'You can't travel on your own at night.'

'You'd better drive her back to London, Mick,' said Patsy. 'If she really wants to go.'

He glanced at her in surprise and her warning look told him to do as she suggested.

'Okay, Pip,' he said. 'I'll take you back as soon as you like.'

Back at the flat, while Pip was packing her things, Mick asked Patsy why she'd not tried to persuade the girl to stay so that he could try to put things right.

'Because you'll only drive her further away if you try to win her over by making excuses for what you've done.'

'What else can I do?'

'She's going to have to accept you as you are and not how she thinks you ought to be, and she needs time to do that.'

'There must be some other way . . .'

'No, Mick. There isn't.' Patsy was adamant. 'This is one situation you can't talk your way out of. You didn't go back to your family when you should have and you lied about it to Jane. That was wrong and it's time you admitted it to yourself.'

'But surely you can understand why I didn't go back?'

'Yes, I understand why, but that doesn't make it right,' she said. 'You can't expect a twelve-year-old girl to understand the complexities in your nature that made you behave in such a way. She needs to be with her mother and you have to let her go . . . for the time being anyway.'

'Okay, Pats,' he said sadly. 'Okay.'

Jane was far more angry with Mick for hurting Pip than she was personally aggrieved when she heard her daughter's story. Knowing Mick as she did now, she wasn't really surprised.

'Your father does care about us in his way, but he has a very peculiar view of life,' she explained to Pip, hoping to ease her pain but at the same time wanting to discuss the subject with her honestly because she was an intelligent girl and advanced for her age. 'Since he considers money and success to be the most important things in life, he thinks everyone else does too. It never occurs to him that some of us aren't particularly impressed by these things and take people as they are.'

'But to leave you struggling to bring us up on your own when he could have been there for you, and then to try to make you give up the business you'd worked so hard to build when he did come back!' she said. 'That isn't a kind of caring that I can understand.'

'It does take a bit of working out,' said Jane. 'Shame, guilt, a deep sense of inadequacy . . . all of them played their part. When you're older you'll be more able to understand. It's all a bit sad really. Because your father was so serious about wanting to provide for us, he ended up not providing for us at all. He wanted too much and ended up with nothing.'

'Oh.'

'Then, when he was back in the money, he wanted to make up for letting us down because he was riddled with guilt. But by that time, I didn't need anyone to provide for me and he found that impossible to come to terms with. I'd deprived him of his means of making amends and that's what made him so angry.'

'All he cares about is himself and being able to flash his money about!'

'No. It's much more complicated than that,' said Jane. 'Because deep down your father has such low self-esteem, he is an egoist.'

'Why is he like that?'

'I think a lot of it is due to the fact that his own father never took much notice of him,' said Jane. 'Your dad isn't a bad man, he's just misguided and has difficulty facing up to things. I know you're upset, love, but later on you'll see all this in a different light.'

'I certainly don't understand it now.'

'One thing I do know for certain, though, Pip,' said Jane with emphasis, 'your father really does love you – very much. You were always the apple of his eye.'

'I don't want to have anything more to do with him.'

'That's a bit hard, love.'

'What he did to you was hard.'

'You mustn't take that on board,' advised her mother. 'That's between your father and me. Anyway, it's all in the past and I think he's probably suffered for it. Besides, you've enjoyed going to stay with him in Brighton.'

'That's true.' She paused thoughtfully. 'Dad's different when he's with Patsy. He doesn't show off or get angry all the time. He's just . . . sort of ordinary.'

'Perhaps he's found someone he doesn't feel the need to impress?'

'Yes, that's probably it,' Pip agreed. 'Patsy doesn't care about money.'

'Why not accept his faults and give him another chance?' suggested Jane, because she thought Pip would lose so much if she ended her association with her father.

'I don't trust him any more,' she said. 'He's proved that he's a liar and a coward.'

'What he did was wrong but if I can forgive him, so can you.'

'I don't feel as though I can, Mum,' she said miserably.

'He *is* your father, whatever he's done,' Jane reminded her.

'At the moment, I wish he wasn't,' said Pip sadly.

Mick was devastated to have his relationship with Pip cut short. He telephoned and wrote to her in the hope of persuading her to see him but she didn't even want to for five minutes, let alone spend the weekend with him and Patsy in Brighton.

'Surely there must be something I can do to make her give me another chance?' he said.

'I think you should leave her alone and she'll probably come round in her own time,' said Patsy, with the clarity of an outsider's view of the argument. She could understand why Pip had reacted as she had on learning the truth about her father. Mick had done wrong, there was no doubt in Patsy's mind about that. But if you loved him you had to take him as he was – a man of many faults. That couldn't be easy for a young girl like Pip.

Patsy was no expert on children but she did know that Pip loved her father very much. She hoped that that one redeeming fact would eventually override all other considerations.

'Let's hope you're right,' said Mick with an unhappy sigh.

The ending of his relationship with Pip made Mick feel as though the last link with his family had gone, and he couldn't bring himself to call at Jane's place when he was in London on business or to visit relatives.

Losing Jane and Davey was bad enough but Pip too . . . that really was the final twist of the knife.

But something happened in the spring of the following year, something so terrifying that everything else was pushed to the back of his mind.

Chapter Twenty Four

Mick was standing at the bar in the Drake's Arms one afternoon in spring, idly drinking whisky while he waited for Patsy to finish her shift, when Podge appeared beside him.

'I guessed I'd find you in here at this time o' day,' he said, looking unusually grave, his big round eyes brimming with worry.

'You know me, Podge, I always shut up shop for a couple of hours at lunchtime,' said Mick, and went on to offer the other man a drink.

'That's very civil of you, mate . . . I'll have a scotch.'

'So, what nice little earners have you got for me today?' enquired Mick as they waited for Podge's drink to be served.

'None, mate,' he said, looking doom-laden. 'Nothing at all.'

'Nothing?' Mick paid Patsy for the drink and led the way to a table where the two men sat down. 'Don't tell me a hard-working burglar like yourself has been taking time off?'

'I've had to, mate . . . had to. I'm gonna lie low for a while an' all,' explained Podge. 'And so will you if you've any sense.'

'Oh?'

'That's why I've come looking for you . . . to warn you.'

Mick looked at him, waiting.

'Bristle Sharp has been arrested.'

'Blimey!'

'And even more worrying . . . the Old Bill have taken

Charlie Budd in as well,' announced Podge, referring to a fence who dealt regularly with Bristle.

'You reckon Bristle grassed on him?'

'It's obvious, innit?' said Podge. 'The cops have offered him a deal to help his own case and he's singing like a bird.'

'Mmm . . . it does look that way.'

'They'll be coming after us if he decides to give 'em more names,' Podge went on. 'So I should get shot of anything hot you've got stashed at the warehouse, sharpish.'

Mick's heart raced and his skin turned cold with nervous sweat as he thought of the underground store beneath the floorboards in his office at the warehouse. It was full of stolen goods: stereo units, handbags, men's leather shoes, jewellery. He tried to calm himself with the fact that it was well hidden under the lino. Surely the fuzz wouldn't find it?

As though reading his thoughts, the other man said, 'If they turn your warehouse over and you've got anything hidden, they'll find it, mate. It doesn't matter where it is . . . under the floorboards, up the chimney, in the roof. They know all the dodges . . . they'll soon root it out.'

'Oh, Gawd,' said Mick, finishing his drink in one swallow. 'I'd better get over there right away then.'

'Wise man,' said Podge. 'The last thing any of us want is you banged up. You're too useful to us on the outside.'

'See you,' said Mick.

'Cheers,' said Podge, but Mick was already on his way to the door.

Mick's warehouse was situated in an industrial area just outside the town, between a small printing firm and a clothes factory.

So far as all but a select few knew, he ran a legitimate operation supplying small shops and market traders with stock. Some of these same customers also bought his illegal lines which they could buy cheap and sell at a

378

high mark up because of the quality, but for which there was no receipt. Other takers for the stolen goods were street traders and those who pedalled their wares in pubs. Mick had gathered a lot of contacts since he'd been in Brighton and never had any trouble shifting stock. The bent gear currently in his underground store would all be sold within a week or two.

But where to store it until the heat was off? That was the problem filling his mind as he drove to the warehouse at high speed. His flat wasn't an option because that would be the second place the police would look if they were on to him. He wondered if the landlord of the Drake's Arms might oblige but didn't think he'd be prepared to take the chance.

Turning the corner so that the warehouse came into view, his heart lurched at the sight of a police car parked outside. He was too late to move the gear; the fuzz were already inside. He could see from here that the door was swinging open. The buggers must have forced an entry.

He was trembling so much he had difficulty controlling the car as he made a hasty retreat, almost hitting another vehicle and causing other drivers to blast their horns angrily. He felt panic-stricken and alone, like a child lost in a crowd. Where could he go? His flat would be their next port of call so he daren't go there. His first thought was Patsy. She would know what he should do. He was almost at the Drake's Arms when he realised that that wouldn't be safe either. Bristle was sure to have told the coppers where Mick did his drinking.

There was only one solution: he would have to leave the area. He thought briefly of going back to the flat to collect some clothes and leave a note for Patsy. But he daren't risk it. If the cops came while he was there, he'd be trapped.

As the answer to his problems came to him, he headed for the London Road.

That evening, Jane and Pip were having a light supper

together in the kitchen. Davey had gone to watch a football match with Kevin and his father and would be eating at their place afterwards. Giles had offered to bring him home in the car later on.

There was a loud and insistent ringing at the door-bell.

'Mick,' said Jane in surprise when she opened the door. 'I wasn't expecting you . . .'

Before she could finish the sentence, he pushed past her into the hall, body quivering, face ashen and suffused with sweat.

'What on earth's the matter?' she asked.

'Where are the kids?'

'Davey's out, Pip's in the kitchen having something to eat . . . why?'

'I need to talk to you . . . *in private.*'

'All right, there's no need to be so aggressive about it.' She went to the kitchen, put her head round the door and, forcing a calm tone, said, 'Carry on without me, love. Daddy's here. We'll be in the living room if you need us.'

'Okay.'

Jane turned to Mick and ushered him hurriedly into the living room at the front of the house.

'So what's all this about?' she wanted to know, closing the door firmly behind her. 'Why have you come bursting in here as though all the demons in hell are after you?'

'Oh, Mick, you damned fool!' she said later, shocked by his story which he'd only told her because he needed her help. 'You've done some pretty silly things in your time but I never thought you'd be so stupid as to break the law.'

'Okay, you can cut the lecture,' he said, pacing up and down the elegant room, smoking feverishly. 'And help me to find a way out of this.'

'There's only one way out of this so far as I can see,' said Jane, standing stiffly with her back to the window, across which the burnt orange velvet curtains were already drawn.

'And that is?'

'Give yourself up.'

'Are you mad?' he said, voice ragged with tension. 'You know what will happen if I do that, don't you?'

'Yes, you'll go to prison.'

He was astonished by her attitude.

'How can you stand there calmly telling me I'll have to go to prison, as though it's not much different from going down the pub?'

'What else can you do but give yourself up, eh, Mick?'

'I dunno yet but I'm not going to prison, it would kill me.'

'Of course it wouldn't,' she said assertively. 'You're tough enough to get through something like that.'

'You know I can't bear to be locked up.'

'You should have thought of that when you embarked upon a life of crime.'

'You nasty, unfeeling bitch!' he accused her venomously.

'That's right, Mick, do what you always do when you're in trouble,' she rebuked. 'Hit out at someone else!'

'Well, the least you could do is be a bit more sympathetic.'

'You don't deserve sympathy,' was her sharp retort to that.

'Rub it in, why don't you?'

'I'm not trying to rub anything in,' Jane denied. 'I just don't see what else you can do but give yourself up. Not unless you want to live the rest of your life in fear of the police.'

'It'll all blow over in a few days,' he told her dismissively, perching on the edge of the sofa and extinguishing his dogend in an ashtray. 'Finding me won't be a priority for very long. The police have too many other things to do with their time, I should think. Anyway, if they don't find the stuff at the warehouse, they'll have nothing on me.'

'Even if they don't find it, they'll nail you eventually,'

she said. 'Now that they've been tipped off about your activities.'

'You really know how to cheer a bloke up, don't you?' he said grimly.

'I'm just trying to get you to face the facts. You must have known you couldn't get away with it forever.'

'Plenty of people do.'

'More get caught, I should think,' she said. 'Frankly, Mick, I don't know how you've slept at nights.'

'When I first started dealing in hooky gear, I used to be scared, I admit it. But when I got away with it, time after time, it just became a way of life and I hardly ever thought about the cops,' he said. 'It was all so easy. I suppose I did think it would go on indefinitely.'

'And now you're planning on hiding out here, I suppose?'

'Yeah.'

'You can't.'

'Oh, Jane,' he said, sounding hurt. 'I can't believe you would turn me away at a time like this?'

'And I can't believe you would come here asking me to break the law,' she countered. 'Harbouring a criminal is an offence.'

He didn't feel good about that, but any compunction was soon overruled by his strong sense of self-preservation.

'But I don't know where else to go,' he said. 'Help me, Jane, please?'

She sat down and ran a hand across her brow, biting back the tears.

'The only way I can help you is to persuade you to go to the police,' she said. 'Perhaps it will act in your favour if you go to them before they get to you?'

'I'll still go down for a stretch.'

'But you've had a good run, haven't you?' she said. 'You've been breaking the law for years and getting away with it. You've done the crime, now you have to do the time, as they say. Start with a clean slate when you come out.'

'Surely you wouldn't really turn me away?'

'I don't know what else I can do,' said Jane through trembling lips. 'Giving yourself up will be the best thing for you in the long run. Anyway, when the police can't find you in Brighton, they're bound to come looking here.'

'No one in Brighton knows this address,' he said. 'Not even Patsy. There was never any need for her to know it.'

'They have ways of finding these things out,' said Jane. 'You don't want your children to see you hounded by the police, surely?'

' 'Course I don't.'

'Then go to the nearest police station and give yourself up . . . *now*.'

'No, I can't do that.'

'Oh, well, that's up to you. You'll have to leave here, though,' Jane pronounced. 'I'm not having the children involved in something like this. And if you care for them, you won't want that either.'

'Where else can I go?' he asked feebly.

'You must have a mate who'll put you up? You must *not* go to your mother . . .'

'She'd take me in.'

'I know she would but you mustn't put her in that position, Mick. It wouldn't be fair.' Jane felt very strongly about this. 'She had a miserable time with your father for all those years. Now he's gone, she's managed to make a decent life for herself. Don't spoil it for her. Do the decent thing and leave her out of this.'

'But . . .'

'Don't sink so low as to put your own mother in a position where she could get into trouble with the police . . . *for goodness' sake*.'

'Jane . . . please let me stay here.'

'I want you to leave, Mick.'

He didn't move. Just stared at her in a bemused state.

'Right. I'm going to join Pip in the kitchen,' she said. 'And I shall expect you to have gone by the time I come back into this room. Leave by the front door so as not to upset your daughter . . . please.' She reached up and kissed him on the cheek. 'I really believe that the best thing you can do is to go to the nearest police station. But whatever you do, good luck.'

She left the room and went into the kitchen. She was about to sit down and join Pip at the table when Mick burst in and charged over to the back door.

'Where's the key?'

'Mick, what the devil . . .'

'The key.'

She pointed to a row of keys hanging on hooks on the wall.

'The one with the yellow tag,' she said.

He grabbed the key, locked the door and put the key in the pocket of his leather jacket. Shadow, who had been curled up on a chair, sensed danger and shot out through the cat-flap at such speed there was a loud metallic clatter.

'I'm sorry to have to be like this,' said Mick breathlessly, looking from one of them to the other, 'but I really do need to stay here.'

Pip stood up, horrified as she looked at her father who was shaking all over, his eyes wild and peculiar.

'Daddy . . . what's going on?' she asked, trembling. 'Why have you locked us in?'

'To keep visitors out, Princess.'

Jane was imbued with a feeling of dull rage at his selfishness in coming here, followed by a surge of pity for the desperation that allowed him to let his beloved daughter see him stripped of all dignity. She reminded herself that all his problems stemmed from greed, and she herself was tired of making excuses for him.

'He's in trouble with the police and wants to stay here,' she told Pip calmly.

'The police?' said the girl, turning pale with fright. 'Oh, Daddy.'

'Oh, I've had enough of this, I'm going to get help,' said Jane, running towards the door to the hall in the hope of getting to the front door. But Mick was there first and blocked her way.

'You're not going anywhere,' he said.

'Oh, for heaven's sake, Mick! Enough's enough. Give us all a break and grow up.'

Holding her by the arm, he dragged her over to the worktop and took a carving knife from the drawer.

'If you don't do as I say, I'll have no option but to use this,' he threatened.

Pip screamed.

'Daddy, stop it, stop it!' she yelled, on the verge of hysteria.

But Mick had lost his head completely and could think of nothing but saving himself from prison and doing whatever he had to. He was twitching so much, he reminded Jane of someone in the early stages of a fit.

'It's all right, Pip,' she said, managing to get free from Mick to go to her daughter and put an arm around her. 'Your father won't hurt us.' She looked at him. 'Will you?'

Standing with the knife pointing towards her, he said, 'Not so long as you do as I tell you.' He was shivering, his face wet with tears. 'Look . . . I don't want to hurt you . . . I love you both more than you could possibly know. But you've gotta let me stay here and not shop me to the police if they come looking for me.'

'You need help, Mick,' said Jane.

'Huh, tell me something I don't already know!'

'Medical help, I mean,' she said. 'You need to get your head sorted out.'

'If you mean in a prison cell, you can think again.'

'They have doctors who specialise in problems of the mind . . .'

'You think I'm a nutcase?'

'No. But I do think you are very confused and obsessional about things. You are also very frightened,' she said. 'Look at you, you're terrified out of your wits.'

'Who wouldn't be in my situation?'

'This is what it will be like for you for the rest of your life, if you don't give yourself up,' she told him. 'You'll always be afraid. Always be waiting for someone to tap you on the shoulder . . .'

'Sooner that than prison.'

'Oh, Daddy,' said Pip sadly. 'How have you got into such a mess?'

'I'll be all right, Princess,' he said. 'Once I get out of this bit o' bother, everything will be fine.' His face hardened. 'But no one is leaving here or coming in.'

'Davey will be home from a football match soon,' said Jane.

'He'll come in, o' course. And once he's in, we'll be one big happy family together.' Mick glared at Jane, brandishing the knife. 'Apart from that, no one comes and no one goes. Right?'

Jane put her arm more tightly around Pip. She had a terrifying suspicion that Mick was no longer in control; that he had now crossed the fine line into insanity.

Giles was driving Davey home, idly listening to the two boys chattering in the back of the car, sounding so grown-up now that their voices had broken. How fleeting childhood was, he thought. He was glad they hadn't drifted apart when Davey moved away because they were such good pals.

As gales of youthful laughter filled the car, he found himself wishing again that he and Jane and their children could become one family. But despite his very best endeavours, she remained staunchly opposed to the idea of resuming their love affair, still convinced that such an arrangement would mean trouble for Giles. He'd told her that didn't worry him. He'd even suggested that she start divorce proceedings. But Jane said to do that while Mick still wasn't in agreement was just inviting trouble.

It was painful to see her on a regular basis, the way things were. He missed her at home too. It wasn't the same at the cottage now that the Parkers didn't live next-door. There wasn't the fun and the warmth and the sociable atmosphere. An elderly couple lived in Jane's cottage now. They were nice people but liked to keep to themselves.

The truth was, his life was lacking a vital element without Jane. Because of this, he had decided that when Kevin left home, he himself would leave the area and make a new start somewhere else.

But now he pulled up outside Jane's house and Davey clambered out, thanking him for the lift and laughing with Kevin over some private adolescent joke. Giles waited, watching the boy, his dark hair shining in the street lights as he sauntered down the front path and disappeared through the side gate on his way to the back door which was the one the family always used. Then Giles drove to the end of the street to find a suitable spot to turn the car around.

Passing Jane's house on the way back, he was surprised to see Davey standing at the front, looking bewildered.

'What's the matter?' he asked, poking his head out of the car window.

'The back door's locked and I can't get any answer from the front.'

'That's odd,' muttered Giles, getting out of the car and walking towards the house, noticing that the lights were on behind closed curtains, indicating that Jane was at home.

'I can't understand why Mum has locked the back door 'cause we all come in and out that way.'

'Perhaps she's had to go out unexpectedly and left the lights on to deter intruders?' suggested Giles, who knew Jane would never allow either of her children to come home to an empty house unless something out of the ordinary had happened.

Davey shook his head. 'I know she's in because I can hear her and Pip moving about in the kitchen. They must have the portable telly on in there because I can hear a man's voice. They've probably got it on so loud, they didn't hear me banging on the door.'

They would hear that, surely? Giles thought, but said,

'Let's give the front doorbell another try, shall we?'

'Yeah, okay.'

Davey was reaching up to press the bell when his mother opened the door.

'Ah, there you are Jane. We were beginning to think you'd gone out,' said Giles with a friendly grin. 'Davey couldn't get you to hear him.'

'Sorry. I did hear, I was . . . er, busy doing something,' she said quickly and breathlessly, looking very preoccupied.

There was something disturbing in her eyes when she looked at Giles for a second before ushering Davey inside with unusual haste and closing the door after only the briefest of thanks for bringing him home. Had it been fear he had seen there? Or was he overreacting to the signs of some mild domestic anxiety? He wasn't sure. But Jane certainly hadn't been her usual cheerful self. An uneasy feeling lingered as he drove away. It wasn't like her to be so abrupt.

In one of the neighbouring streets, something he saw in his rear-view mirror caused him to pull up suddenly.

'Hey, Dad,' rebuked Kevin as he was jolted forward. 'What are you trying to do, send us both through the windscreen?'

'Sorry, Kevin.'

'What's the matter? Why are we going back?' he asked as his father turned the car round and headed back to Jane's.

'Nothing for you to worry about,' said Giles, not wishing to cause alarm. 'I need to speak to Davey's mother about something, that's all.'

What he had seen in his mirror had been Mick Parker's Jaguar. Giles would know that metallic blue car anywhere. Even in the pale glow of the street lights, he knew it was Mick's. But why was it in the next street if he was visiting Jane? It could only be because he didn't want his presence there to be known. Parking problems certainly weren't the reason because he could have parked his car on Jane's drive. And why hadn't Davey been able to get in the back door as he normally could? Mick Parker was up to no good in that house, Giles was sure of it.

'Wait here, Kevin, I won't be long,' he said, getting out of the car.

'Okay,' said the boy, leaning forward and tuning the radio to pop music.

Giles hurried straight round to the back of Jane's house, his rubber-soled sports shoes silent on the concrete path. The curtains were drawn across the kitchen and dining-room windows so he couldn't see in but he knew Mick was in there.

He rapped his knuckles on the back door.

No reply.

He knocked again, harder.

'Who is it?' came Jane's muffled tones.

'Giles.'

'I'm busy right now, Giles, I'll see you tomorrow.'

'I'm not leaving until you let me in,' he said. 'I know Mick is in there with you.'

There was silence then the door opened a fraction.

'Go away, Giles,' said a whey-faced Jane, peering out at him.

'Not until I've spoken to Mick.'

The door was opened wide, Jane was pushed inside and Mick, brandishing a knife with one hand, grabbed Giles with the other and dragged him inside, closing the door behind them.

'If you interfere in something that's none of your business, you're likely to get hurt,' he threatened.

'For goodness' sake, stop playing gangsters and put that thing down,' said Giles impulsively.

'He isn't playing,' warned Jane, looking at Giles gravely.

There was a brief hiatus while he assessed the situation.

'Come on now,' he said, moderating his manner as the danger of Mick's state of mind registered fully. Giles was a very fit man. He could easily overpower an unarmed Mick. But in his current mental state any move on him might push him over the edge and send him berserk with the knife. 'Whatever the problem is, I'm sure it can be sorted out without the knife. That thing is lethal. Someone is going to get hurt if you don't put it down. You don't want that for your wife and children, do you?'

' 'Course I don't. What do you take me for?'

'What's all this about anyway?' enquired Giles firmly.

'Mick's in trouble with the police and wants to hide here,' Jane informed him.

'You know that isn't fair to Jane, don't you, Mick?' said Giles.

'Oh, for God's sake! All I want is somewhere to lie low for a few days,' he said. 'I'm not asking her to go out and rob a bank.'

Giles suggested that the police would trace him to this address and was told the reason this wouldn't happen.

'They'll soon find Jane's address,' he argued. 'They'll go through your place in Brighton with a fine tooth-comb.'

'They won't find it because it isn't there,' insisted Mick. 'I don't keep a personal address book.'

'But I've written to you there, Daddy,' said Pip. 'They'll see this address on the letters. Unless you've thrown them away.'

It was obvious from the look on Mick's face that he hadn't.

'You'll make it a lot easier on yourself if you give yourself up,' said Jane.

'She's right,' added Giles.

'Shut up!'

'My son's outside,' said Giles. 'He'll come looking for me soon.'

'We won't let him in.'

'Let Jane and the children go and keep me here as a hostage, if it will make you feel safer?'

'So that they can call the police . . . don't take me for a mug,' said Mick in a mocking tone. 'Now, all of you, go into the living room where I can see what you're doing.'

They all trooped into the room at the front of the house and he stood inside the closed door, the knife pointed towards them.

'You might as well make yourselves comfortable 'cause you're not going anywhere.'

'How long do you plan on keeping this up?' asked Giles.

Mick didn't answer. He was listening to the rumbling sound of a car drawing up outside. He went over to the window and drew back the edge of the curtain, just enough to see out.

'Bloody hell, it's the police!' He glared at Giles. 'You bastard . . . you sent for them before you knocked on the door!'

'Mick, calm down,' said Jane.

'Nothing to do with me,' Giles was quick to assure him. 'They must have traced you through Pip's letters or something.'

There was a loud knocking at the front door.

'Nobody move,' ordered Mick.

'Someone will have to answer it,' Giles pointed out. 'They won't just go away.'

The doorbell rang simultaneously with an imperious rat-a-tat-tat.

'Are you in there, Mrs Parker? It's the police. We want to talk to you.'

Mick's eyes darted fearfully around the room as the trap closed around him. They came to rest on Jane.

'You and the kids go out there,' he said nervously. 'Tell 'em that I'm not leaving this house until they've gone. If anyone tries to come in, I'll kill Giles and turn the knife on myself.'

'Oh, Mick, for pity's sake . . .'

'Daddy, please don't do that, please!' screamed Pip, tears streaming down her cheeks, her pony tail swinging as she shook her head. 'Please . . .'

'Don't, Dad,' said Davey, his dark eyes almost black in his pale, terrified face. 'It isn't worth it. You might not have to go to prison for very long.'

'Better still, I'll tell 'em myself to make sure they know the position.'

Walking out of the room backwards with the knife pointing in front of him, Mick went to the door and shouted his terms to those outside.

'I'm sending the wife and kids out,' he said. 'I want to be free to leave here without being arrested. I won't come out until you've gone. If anyone tries to come in . . . the wife's boyfriend gets it with the knife, and then I'll top myself.'

There was a highly charged silence as Mick came back into the other room and indicated to Jane she should leave. Ice-cold with fear for both men, and assuring Giles she would look after Kevin, she ushered the children along the hall to the front door, pushed them into the arms of the waiting policemen then quickly followed, slamming the door behind her.

Now in full possession of the facts, the police tried to negotiate with Mick through a megaphone. But he wouldn't believe that they wouldn't be lying in wait for him if he tried to leave. This was a tricky situation for the police. Storming the property could prove fatal for one or both men.

Jane and her children, and Kevin, were sitting in a police car outside the house with one of the policemen. There were now several police cars at the scene and a crowd of onlookers had gathered.

'He's completely flipped,' Jane told the police officer. 'I couldn't get through to him at all. And I thought I would be the one person he would take notice of.'

'You never know what someone will do when they're in a blind panic,' said the policeman.

'I honestly don't believe he would actually kill anyone, though,' she said. 'Not even while he's in this state.'

'My guvnors are obviously not willing to take a chance on that at the moment.'

Pip made a sudden announcement.

'I know someone I think might be able to talk Daddy

out of this without anyone getting hurt,' she said.

'You'd better tell us who it is then, hadn't you, young lady?' said the policeman.

Although each second passed at an agonisingly slow pace as they waited for Patsy to arrive, Jane had to admire the efficiency of the police force in getting her to the scene so speedily.

She arrived dressed in a short black skirt and simulated leather jacket. She hugged Pip, said hello to Davey and was introduced to Jane. She then made it clear to the police that she was not prepared to co-operate with them unless she had their promise that they would not send anyone into the house until she gave them the word. Eager to bring this matter to a conclusion, they agreed.

'Let's get on with it then,' she said to the detective in charge, who told Mick through the megaphone that Patsy was here and wanted to see him. There was no response.

The megaphone was handed to her.

'I'm coming up to the front door, Mick,' she said. 'All I want you to do is open it so I can get in. I just want to talk to you, that is all. Please don't do anything until we've talked. I'm coming to the front door now . . .'

Standing beside the police car with the three children, all Jane could hear was the sharp click of Patsy's high heels in the silent street as the crowd held their breath.

'Mick, it's Patsy,' she said, pushing the door open and closing it behind her.

'In here, Pats.'

She went into the living room where he was standing just inside the door with the knife in his hand. His hostage was sitting in an armchair.

'Oh, Mick,' she said, with a mixture of reproach and compassion. 'You've got yourself into a right mess this time, haven't you?'

393

'Don't go on at me, Pats,' he said, waving the knife.

'Put that thing down,' she said. 'This is me, Patsy. You don't have to impress me.'

He stared at her blankly and kept hold of the knife.

'I want to talk to you in private.' She looked at Giles. 'No offence.'

'None taken.'

'Let him go, Mick, so we can talk on our own,' she urged.

'I'm not falling for that one,' he said. 'As soon as he's out, the coppers'll be in.'

'They won't come in here until I tell them to,' she said. 'They've given me their word.'

'And you believe 'em?'

'Yes, I do. They're only doing their job,' she said.

'I'd sooner die than go to prison,' he told her fiercely.

'No, you wouldn't, not really,' she said. 'Anyway, what am I gonna do if you die?'

'You'd get over it,' he said. 'You'd soon find someone else.'

'I wouldn't want anyone else,' she protested, perching on the edge of the sofa and trying to look relaxed in the hope of reducing the explosiveness of the situation.

' 'Course you would . . . a woman like you.'

'You're wrong,' she said. 'I know you can never love me in the same way as you love Jane, but we make a good team, you and me. We're two of a kind . . . a couple of slobs if the truth be told. I've been round the block a good few times but I've never loved anyone like I love you. God only knows why 'cause you're nothing but a worry to me. But that's the way it goes. If you love someone, you have to take the rough with the smooth.' She turned to Giles. 'I'm sorry you're having to hear all this private stuff, Mister, but it can't be helped as this fool is being so damned awkward and making you stay.'

'Carry on as though I'm not here,' he said, moved by the courage and sincerity of this woman who had the looks of a hooker and the heart of an angel.

'I'll lose everything again if I get sent down,' said Mick.

'Not everything,' she pointed out. 'You'll still have me and I'll be waiting for you when you come out.'

'But I'll have no business . . . no home.'

'We'll manage,' she said. 'Like I said, we're a team. We can make a new start. Only you'll stay the right side of the law in future. I'll make damned sure of that!'

Mick looked at her: her permed red hair frizzy and dishevelled, her clothes looking like last year's sale bargains from a market stall. He'd given her no end of money to kit herself out but she'd never bought any decent gear. If she were to become a millionaire, she probably wouldn't change. Suddenly he didn't want her to.

'You wouldn't want a gaolbird?'

'Not any gaolbird . . . just you.'

'Oh, Pats, you're a daft cow,' he said affectionately.

'I might not be much of a catch but I'm right for you, mate, and I think you know that if only you'd let yourself believe it.'

'My life's such a mess.'

'Nothing that can't be sorted,' she said in a positive manner. 'Okay, so you're gonna have to do time and when you come out there'll be no posh flat or flashy car. But only when you truly accept that and settle for less will you have any peace of mind. Breaking the law to get those things doesn't count as success anyway.'

'If you say so,' he said dully.

'We must make the most of what we have, Mick . . . each other. When you've done your porridge, we'll get by. Like I've always said, we only need one roof and enough dough to live on. My wages will come in handy until you get back on your feet.'

'You're quite a woman . . . do you know that?'

'And I'm all yours if you'll have me,' she said. 'But for us to have a happy future together you must *really* accept the fact that your marriage is over. You have to let Jane go. Give her a divorce so you can both start again.'

It took only a second for a lifetime of self-delusion to be stripped away. Mick finally admitted to himself that he was never going to make the big time because he just didn't have the ability. His first business had existed only because of credit, his second had been built on villainy. With the realisation came pain, but resignation also brought peace. He felt calmer now than he had in a very long time, despite the daunting prospect of prison.

He was ashamed of what he'd done here today: threatening his wife with a knife, frightening his children. He thought of the anguish he'd caused them all at the cottage because of his determination to have something he could now admit he didn't even want. Family life with Jane and the children wasn't for him. Not any more.

Putting the knife on the mantelpiece, he sank down on the sofa beside Patsy, sobbing.

'Oh, Pats, what have I done to you all?' he said, voice muffled with weeping. 'I'm so ashamed.'

'Shush,' she said, arms around him. 'It's over now.'

'I've made Jane's life a misery by trying to hang on to her,' he said. 'And all these years you've been there for me, I didn't appreciate you. I just used you, Pats . . . used you.'

'Maybe you did. But you've been good to me as well,' she said softly. 'We've had a lot of fun together. And I've enjoyed every minute.'

With a lump in his throat, Giles slipped unnoticed from the room. When he emerged from the house, the police went to move in but he gave them a reminder.

'You made her a promise that you wouldn't go in there until she gave you the word,' he told them. 'There'll be no trouble, I can promise you that. Just give them a few more minutes together.'

A short time later Mick was taken away in a police car. Patsy blew him a kiss before getting into the police car that was waiting to take her back to Brighton, giving Jane and company a friendly wave as she passed.

One day she might feel able to have a chat with Jane;

in time they might even become friends. But right now Patsy needed to go home to Brighton, to be alone to shed her own tears. It really had been one hell of a day!

Chapter Twenty Five

The long heatwave of 1976 was finally over. On the last day of August, rain stopped play at Lords for fifteen minutes, drawing cheers from the crowds and heralding a change in the weather. The rains came, bringing new life to scorched suburban lawns and dispirited vegetation in parks and public gardens.

Life returned to normal so quickly, it was almost as though the continental atmosphere that had prevailed during the summer had never happened. Sunny days were soon forgotten and complaints about the awful British climate once more became the norm.

But on this October Saturday the afternoon was fine and dry as a young girl walked along Brighton pier with an older woman.

'Your mother doesn't mind your coming to stay with me for the weekend now and again, then?' said Patsy.

'Of course she doesn't,' replied Pip. 'There's no reason why she should.'

'I thought perhaps she might consider me to be a bad influence?'

'Oh, Patsy,' said Pip, turning to look at her with a look of friendly reproof. 'Why on earth would she think that?'

'With my being a barmaid and living the way I do . . . sort of casual like, especially now I'm in a poky little flat.'

'Mum isn't the sort of person to think badly of you because of that.'

'You don't get any family life or much in the way of home cooking when you come to stay with me, though, do you?'

'It's all part of the fun because it's so different from home.' Pip linked arms with her in a companionable manner.

'Oh, well, so long as you enjoy it.'

'I do. And Mum thinks it's a very good idea for us two to see each other while Dad's in prison,' she said. 'As well as the fact that I enjoy our weekends together, she thinks it might help to cheer him up. I know he's pleased that we're friends. He mentioned it in one of his letters.'

'I'm glad of your company,' said Patsy. 'It gets awful lonely sometimes, with him being away.'

'Gran enjoys coming down to Brighton to stay with you too,' said Pip. 'She was telling me about it the other day.'

'Your gran and I get on like a house on fire,' said Patsy. 'She's so full of life! Loves to get out and about, especially to the amusements. If I'm working at the Drake's, she sits at the bar chatting to people. All the regulars know her.'

'It's amazing how much she's changed,' said Pip. 'She never used to go anywhere when Granddad was alive. He was very bossy towards her. Davey and I were scared stiff of him, too.' She paused thoughtfully. 'He was really nice to us, though, on the day he died . . . it's funny that!'

'He left your gran well provided for, anyway, so at least she can afford a few outings.'

At the end of the pier, they leaned on the rail, looking at the sea. Autumn sunlight shimmered on the water and bathed the distant shoreline with a golden light.

'Does it upset you when you go to visit my dad?' asked Pip, staring into the undulating waters. 'You know . . . seeing him in that awful place?'

'No, not really,' said Patsy in a positive tone. 'It's all we have for the moment so I look forward to it . . . and I know he does.'

'I wish he would agree to let me go and visit him.'

'He feels bad enough about letting you all down by being in prison,' Patsy replied. 'Having you see him there would be just too much for Mick to bear. Now that he's beginning to accept himself as the ordinary bloke he is, he's really ashamed of the way he's behaved in the past.'

'I know . . .'

'He's ever so pleased that you write to him, dear,' said Patsy. 'He looks forward to your letters. I think he thought he'd lost you forever when you found out he'd not come home as soon as he should have after regaining his memory.'

'That still hurts but I've managed to forgive him,' said Pip.

'That's good.'

'No point in bearing a grudge.'

'How about Davey? Do you think he might eventually learn to get along with your dad?'

'I'm not sure,' Pip said. 'He's always been closer to Mum than to Dad anyway. I think he'll probably be willing to give Dad a chance when he comes out of prison if he seems determined to go straight. Dad scored some points with Davey for agreeing to a divorce and making Mum happy that way. Now that they're getting divorced, things will be much easier for us all.'

'Including me,' laughed Patsy.

'Yes, of course,' agreed Pip. 'Mum and Uncle Giles are planning to get married as soon as they can,' she said. 'They're really happy together.'

'And so are your dad and me, so that means everyone is settled.'

Pip's expression became serious.

'You don't have any doubts about taking on someone as complicated as my dad, then?'

'Not on your life! I'm a match for him any day. I shall make sure he doesn't stray from the straight and narrow, don't worry.'

'Does he have any idea what he's going to do when he comes out of prison?'

'Yeah, as a matter of fact we do have a plan,' said Patsy.

'Oh?'

'I've suggested that he does some bar work, with the

idea of us running a pub together later on,' Patsy explained. 'The breweries are always looking for couples to manage their houses.'

'What a good idea.'

'It would be perfect for us if we can get it organised. We both have the gift of the gab and I have the experience. I know the pub trade inside out.'

'Might there be a problem, though . . . you know, with Dad having a criminal record?'

'That's possible. But I've spoken to my boss at the Drake's about it and he thinks we'll be able to swing it so long as it's all done in my name. I'd have to take the responsibility.'

'I hope it works out.'

'Me too.' Patsy shivered as the chilly sea-breeze blew straight through her clothes to her skin. 'In the meantime, shall we go and have some tea?'

'Yes, let's. I'm famished.' Pip paused, a shadow passing across her face. 'But I'd rather not go to the place with the red tables . . . if you don't mind?'

A silence fell as they remembered that other tea-time that had ended so unhappily.

'Too many memories, eh?' said Patsy.

'Yes.'

'There's plenty of other places, dear,' said the older woman kindly. 'Places that do equally good ice-cream sundaes.'

'Thanks, Patsy,' said Pip, her voice tinged with sadness as she thought of where her father was at this moment.

'Your dad will be all right,' said Patsy, sensing what was on the girl's mind.

'Will he?'

' 'Course he will,' she said cheerfully. 'And the time will soon pass. He's done nearly six months of his sentence already. Only another eighteen months to go.'

'It seems like forever,' said Pip.

'Yeah, it seems a long time to me too,' said Patsy. 'But as much as we love him, he's done wrong and has to be punished.'

'Of course.'

'Anyway, dear, his being away gives the two of us the opportunity to really get to know each other.'

'There is that,' Pip agreed, and they walked companionably along the pier towards the shore, chatting about other things.

Jane and Giles were both in good spirits that same afternoon as they walked arm-in-arm along the riverside towards Giles's cottage. With Davey and Kevin on a trip to the Victoria and Albert Museum with the youth club, and Pip in Brighton with Patsy for the weekend, they were making the most of the time alone together. They had been for a quiet lunch at a riverside pub and then for a leisurely stroll by the river in the glorious autumn weather.

'As much as I adore the children and having them around, it is rather nice to have some time on our own, isn't it?' Jane remarked.

'I'll say it is,' Giles agreed heartily. 'And to take full advantage of the situation, I think I shall make mad passionate love to you when we get back to the cottage.'

'Love in the afternoon?' she said with mock disapproval. 'What *would* the children say?'

'Something deeply scathing, I should imagine.' He grinned.

She untucked her arm and held his hand, looking at him.

'Seriously, though, Giles, I'm having such a lovely day.'

'Me too.'

'It's so good actually to be together at long last.'

'Well, almost . . .'

'It's only a matter of time now before we make it legal.'

'Yes, I know.'

They came to the maze of narrow lanes and alleyways surrounding Vine Cottages. Approaching Giles's place from the front as they were on foot, they turned into Tug Lane and stopped in their tracks, staring at a new addition to the landscape: a 'For Sale' board outside the cottage that had once belonged to Jane.

'Oh, Giles!' she said. 'Are you thinking what I'm thinking?'

'I'm sure I must be.'

'We could knock through and make the two cottages into one big house, couldn't we?' she said, breathless with excitement.

'My thoughts exactly,' he replied eagerly.

'You'd be able to have a study,' she said, her thoughts racing.

'And you'd be able to have a bigger kitchen for your baking,' he said. 'You could even have two kitchens if you fancied it. One for business and one for domestic use.'

'The kids would have more space to entertain their friends . . .'

'It would also solve the problem of where we are going to live, once and for all.'

Even though they were lovers again, they hadn't moved in together or decided where their home was to be. Jane thought it might be a bit cramped for them all in Giles's cottage, especially as she baked on a commercial scale at home. Neither of them fancied setting up home permanently in her rather characterless house in Wilber Road. Matters were further complicated by the fact that they couldn't bear the idea of Giles giving up his cottage.

Their future home had been the subject of much discussion ever since Mick had agreed to a divorce and Jane and Giles had been gloriously reunited. Having been unable to reach a decision, this estate agent's board seemed like the answer to a prayer.

'Shall we go into your place and phone the agent?' she said, excitedly.

'Yes, let's do that.'

An hour later, Jane had made an offer for the cottage, had it accepted and put her own house in Wilber Road on the market.

'Oh, Giles, isn't it exciting?' she said, hugging him.

'Very.'

'I just can't wait to move back in and get the alterations under way,' she told him, eyes shining. 'All of us together here at Vine Cottages. Won't it be great?'

'Wonderful! The children will be thrilled too.'

'Won't they just? I shall really feel as though I'm coming home when we move back to Tug Lane,' she said.

'I know.'

'What perfect timing!' Jane enthused. 'My old cottage coming on to the market. It's a sign of good things for the future.'

'It'll be good anyway, we don't need signs to tell us that.' Giles smiled at her meaningfully. 'But in the meantime, don't you and I have some unfinished business?'

'We certainly do.'

They were halfway upstairs when someone called from the back door.

'Cooee, dears,' came Trudy's dulcet tones. 'It's only us. Joe and me.'

Cursing good-humouredly at their thwarted plans, Jane and Giles went downstairs to greet the visitors.

'Our tea dance finished earlier than we expected so we thought we'd call in to keep you company,' explained Trudy.

'We know the children have all gone out,' added Joe, smiling.

'And we thought you might be feeling a bit lonely,' Trudy finished for him.

'It's very kind of you both,' said Jane, struggling to keep a straight face. 'Isn't it, Giles.'

'Very,' he said with a dutiful smile.

Escaping to the kitchen to make some tea, they were both helpless with laughter.

'There'll be other times,' promised Jane.

'There'd better be!'

'The rest of our lives, in fact.'

'If we're ever left alone long enough . . .'

They were both still giggling when they went into the other room with the tea for their guests.

Pamela Evans

A Fashionable Address

The Potters of elegant Sycamore Square in Kensington take for granted all the comforts of their position in life, maintained by the large family drapery store. Then, one day, everything changes; Cyril Potter is a secret gambler whose debts have become so crippling that he resorts to suicide. Shocked, disgraced and left to clear the debts, his wife and daughters are forced to sell everything.

Young Kate Potter shoulders the responsibility for her pampered mother, Gertie, and frivolous sister, Esme, finding accommodation in the two dingy rooms of a dilapidated Hammersmith tenement house. Despite the dirt and poverty of their new lives, Kate is ever cheerful as she tries to rally her family to make the best of the situation, and she promises them she will move heaven and earth to make it possible for them to return to Sycamore Square.

As she labours long hours for low pay in Dexter's hat-making factory, Kate's dreams seem far away. The more so when she catches the lascivious eye of the factory owner Reggie Dexter and is left pregnant by him. Close to despair she is persuaded to have her son adopted so that he can enjoy a better life than she is able to offer. As she tries to come to terms with her guilt, Kate struggles to set up her own millinery business – and start on the slow road to achieve prosperity and a fashionable address.

FICTION / SAGA 0 7472 4313 1

More Enchanting Fiction from Headline

PAMELA EVANS
TEA-BLENDER'S DAUGHTER

As a provider, Henry Slater can't be faulted; he is the
owner of a successful tea-trading company, and his
family enjoy a comfortable lifestyle near
Ravenscourt Park. But love has never been on offer
to his children, Dolly and Ken – Henry is above such
things.

For all Dolly's intelligence, her father refused to let
her stay at school beyond the official leaving age, and
she now works at Slaters and is expected to
marry Frank Mitchell, her father's deputy. But
during the General Strike, Dolly is rescued from a
riot by Bill Drake, a factory labourer, and embarks
on an illicit affair with him. Just as they agree to
elope, Henry discovers their relationship and devises
a plan to part them forever.

Stunned by what they both believe is rejection, Dolly
marries Frank, and Bill joins a rival firm, coldly
setting out to marry the boss's daughter, whilst
determining revenge against the Slaters. As the years
progress, they accept that the past is behind them.
Until the end of the Second World War's rationing
heralds new opportunities – and a merger between
the rival tea companies . . .

FICTION / SAGA 0 7472 4491 X

Now you can buy any of these other bestselling books from your bookshop or *direct from the publisher*.

FREE P&P AND UK DELIVERY
(Overseas and Ireland £3.50 per book)

My Sister's Child	Lyn Andrews	£5.99
Liverpool Lies	Anne Baker	£5.99
The Whispering Years	Harry Bowling	£5.99
Ragamuffin Angel	Rita Bradshaw	£5.99
The Stationmaster's Daughter	Maggie Craig	£5.99
Our Kid	Billy Hopkins	£6.99
Dream a Little Dream	Joan Jonker	£5.99
For Love and Glory	Janet MacLeod Trotter	£5.99
In for a Penny	Lynda Page	£5.99
Goodnight Amy	Victor Pemberton	£5.99
My Dark-Eyed Girl	Wendy Robertson	£5.99
For the Love of a Soldier	June Tate	£5.99
Sorrows and Smiles	Dee Williams	£5.99

TO ORDER SIMPLY CALL THIS NUMBER

01235 400 414

or e-mail orders@bookpoint.co.uk

Prices and availability subject to change without notice.